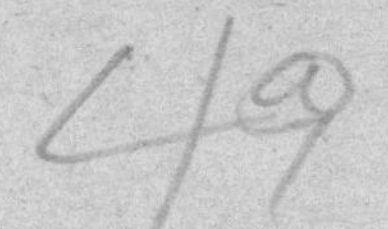

Dear Mystery Reader:

My question to you is: Given the result—a corpse, say—is poison really more civilized than a blunt instrument or revolver?

The British, who have perfected the craft of murder, would answer a resounding yes. Bludgeoning someone or shooting a hole through them leaves a mess, potentially destroying the carpet.

We Americans are cruder; we let our emotions get away from us. This can cause all kinds of disorder, which no one likes.

I recommend you read *Murder Most British,* a collection of excellent stories, plucked from the pages of *Ellery Queen's Mystery Magazine* by the clever Janet Hutchings. You might learn something about the proper way to get unpleasant things done, and possibly even save some quarters in laundry money. Remember: these things add up. Enough quarters saved and one could have a pleasant tea at the Plaza.

Yours in Mystery,

Dana Edwin Isaacson
Senior Editor
St. Martin's DEAD LETTER Paper[illegible]ysteries

Other titles from St. Martin's Dead Letter Mysteries

MURDER MOST BRITISH

STORIES FROM
Ellery Queen's Mystery Magazine

Edited by Janet Hutchings

St. Martin's Paperbacks

MURDER MOST BRITISH

Library of Congress Catalog Number 95-41838

ISBN 0-312-96182-0

Printed in the United States of America.

St. Martin's Press hardcover edition/ February 1996
St. Martin's Press Paperbacks edition/ May 1997

10 9 8 7 6 5 4 3 2 1

We are grateful to the following for permission to reprint their copyrighted material: THE GENTLEMAN IN THE LAKE by Robert Barnard, copyright © 1994 by Robert Barnard, reprinted by permission of Gregory & Radice Authors' Agents; A GOOD THING by Simon Brett, copyright © 1995 by Simon Brett, reprinted by permission of JCA Literary Agency, Inc.; THE NEW HAT by Thomas Burke, copyright © 1926 by Thomas Burke, reprinted by permission of John Hawkins & Associates, Inc.; THE MYSTERY OF THE BAGDAD CHEST by Agatha Christie, copyright © 1932 by Agatha Christie, copyright renewed © 1959 by Agatha Christie Mallowan, reprinted by permission of Harold Ober Associates; YOU CAN'T HANG TWICE by Anthony Gilbert, copyright © 1946 by Davis Publications, Inc., reprinted by permission of Curtis Brown, Ltd.; FEAR AND TREMBLING's by Michael Gilbert, copyright © 1962 by Michael Gilbert, reprinted by permission of Curtis Brown, Ltd.; MY FIRST MURDER by H.R.F. Keating, copyright © 1995 by H.R.F. Keating, reprinted by permission of Sterling Lord Literistic; DEATH OF A DEAD MAN by Gillian Linscott, copyright © 1994 by Gillian Linscott, reprinted by permission of Harold Ober Associates; THE PUSHOVER by Peter Lovesey, copyright © 1995 by Peter Lovesey, reprinted by permission of Gelfman Schneider Literary Agents; THE RAPE OF THE SHERLOCK by A. A. Milne, copyright © 1903 by A. A. Milne, reprinted by permission of Curtis Brown, Ltd.; THE MYSTERIOUS DEATH IN PERCY STREET by Baroness Orczy, copyright © 1909, 1937 by Baroness Orczy, reprinted by permission of A.P. Watt Ltd. on behalf of Sara Orczy-Barstow Brown; BURNING END by Ruth Rendell, copyright © 1995 by Ruth Rendell, reprinted by permission of Sterling Lord Literistic; STRIDING FOLLY by Dorothy L. Sayers, copyright © 1940 by Dodd, Mead & Company, Inc., reprinted by permission of David Higham Associates; THE PASSING OF MR. TOAD by Jeffry Scott, copyright © 1994 by Jeffry Scott, reprinted by permission of the author; A POSTERIORI by Helen Simpson, copyright © 1954 by Davis Publications, Inc.; THE MAN WHO HATED TELEVISION by Julian Symons, copyright © 1994 by Julian Symons, reprinted by permission of Curtis Brown, Ltd.; A LITTLE DOSE OF FRIENDSHIP by Margaret Yorke, copyright © 1994 by Margaret Yorke, reprinted by permission of Curtis Brown, Ltd.; all stories were previously published in *Ellery Queen's Mystery Magazine,* published by Dell Magazines, Inc.

CONTENTS

ACKNOWLEDGMENTS

Special thanks to Keith Kahla of St. Martin's Press for making this project possible, to Marvin Lachman and Edward D. Hoch for information on where to look for some of the stories contained herein, and to Dorothy Cummings of *Ellery Queen's Mystery Magazine* for help in preparing the manuscript.

INTRODUCTION

The first detective stories were written by an American, Edgar Allan Poe, but it was the British who laid most of the early foundations of the genre. In a volume of this size we cannot hope to do justice from either a historical or contemporary perspective to all the ways in which British writers have shaped, and are continuing to shape, the mystery short story. But we do have in the archives of *Ellery Queen's Mystery Magazine* a plentiful source of material from which to create a sampling of their diverse contributions.

British mysteries have always traveled well, especially to America. So familiar is the world the earliest British detective writers created that most American readers have only to see the accoutrements of a Victorian drawing room or picture fog-covered streets in London to think "mystery." Even the homely teapot has become a mystery icon.

It was a secure world those early writers created in their fiction, one of certainties and order, idyllically peaceful but for the occasional disruption of murder—a world which could be understood by reason, and therefore contemplated from the comfort of an armchair. The first true "armchair detective," the Old Man in the Corner—a sleuth who solved his cases without leaving his table in a London tea shop—was the creation of a naturalized Englishwoman, Baroness Orczy. A Hungarian by birth, the baroness came to England in her teens and wrote all of her major works in English.

From the turn of the century through the years before World War I, many other English writers besides Baroness Orczy were making advances in the detective genre. The so-called inverted detective story, in which the culprit is known and suspense turns on how the detective will prove his guilt (as in TV's *Columbo* series, for instance), was born with a novel by Londoner R. Austin Freeman in 1912. Freeman also introduced the notion of scientific evidence to the detective story, paving the way for the use of forensics in later mystery fiction.

Better known, of course, are the contributions of G. K. Chesterton and the immortal Sir Arthur Conan Doyle, the former providing posterity with not only the first clerical sleuth, Father Brown, but the first mysteries whose solutions turn on an understanding of psychology. Doyle's contributions speak for themselves. No one will need to be reminded that the Holmes stories provide the very prototype for the detective story's use of deductive reasoning or that hundreds of Holmeses and Watsons have been created in the mold of the originals. In a brief space of time, the British writers of the age enlarged and transformed all notions of what a detective story could be. But it was only after World War I that the Golden Age of British mystery fiction arrived.

New themes appeared in British mystery writing after World War I, when writers such as Dorothy L. Sayers began to produce novels and stories which were at least as much concerned with characterization as with a well-plotted mystery. In her testing of how closely the mystery story could approach serious fiction, Sayers was joined by Chesterton, who, not only in his stories, but in his critical writings, helped to give the mystery respectability as a literary form. At the same time that some of Britain's finest writers were exploring how far the boundaries of the genre could be pushed, however, others were codifying rules for how the puzzle at the mystery's heart should be constructed. So successful was the articulation of these rules that even today, for many American readers, the "true" British mystery is a formalized construction in which certain conventions for planting clues and revealing evidence must be upheld. It was in this period that the notion of fair play to the reader—of presenting the puzzle in such a way that the reader should have a chance, along with the fictional sleuth, of solving it—was most explicitly outlined. And of course, the era produced that great master of the art of deception and fair-play detection, Agatha Christie, whose cleverness in plotting remains unsurpassed and who demonstrated so remarkable an ability to supply her readers with solutions involving the least likely suspects.

By the thirties, the baton for experimentation in the form had passed to American writers of hard-boiled mysteries, but British writers were quick to adapt American innovations, and in recent years they've created a private-eye literature of their own, with highly eccentric characters and sharply pointed humor. The first humorous mystery stories, incidentally (not, as it happens, in the P.I. vein), were also written by a Briton, A. A. Milne, during the 1920s. During the thirties the spy story, a form the British were principally responsible for developing (even if the first spy novel was written by an Irishman), also came into its own. Current writers such as Michael Gilbert have added new twists to this subgenre of the mystery, developing an art in which their countrymen are universally acknowledged to lead the world.

After World War II, on both sides of the Atlantic, mystery writing began to include more and more realistic material and subjects of a more controversial political and sociological nature. The British poet and critic Julian Symons, describing the development of the mystery from the detective story to the crime novel in his book *Bloody Murder,* concludes that the mystery, while it has limitations that prevent it from being a perfect vehicle for serious literature, can nevertheless have something significant to say. Symons himself expanded the genre with novels and stories that are perhaps as much read by those interested in the author's insights about character and society as by those in search of an evening's entertainment.

Changes in the institutions associated with the classical detective story have also played a part in the evolution of the British mystery. The English village, once home to a genuinely local population, has become a weekend haven for well-to-do urbanites; many English country houses have been sold or opened to the public; and the sort of tea room where the Old Man in the Corner might have lingered is nowadays a place for a fast bite to eat and tea made not with the traditional loose leaves but with a disposable tea bag. Though some of the best of today's British writers, such as Robert Barnard and Simon Brett, self-consciously employ Golden Age conventions, their observations of contemporary society are frequently acerbic, a trait that sets them apart from their Golden Age predecessors, who tended to idealize the society of which they wrote.

The contemporary stories in this collection contain many echoes of the achievements of the past. But as you make your way through these pages, we hope you'll be struck, just as we have been, with how lively and vigorous the mystery fiction coming out of Britain is, was, and promises in the future to be.

—Janet Hutchings

THE ADVENTURE OF THE BLUE CARBUNCLE

A. Conan Doyle

Sherlock Holmes is not the earliest of the great English fictional detectives, but he predates the other sleuths contained in our collection. The first Sherlock Holmes story appeared in 1887, and the series might not have been continued but for a request by an American magazine for a sequel, for Holmes was not received as warmly on his side of the Atlantic. That was, of course, to change with the publication of his second case, so much so that the demand for further adventures soon became a burden to his creator, Sir Arthur Conan Doyle. Though Doyle once tried to do away with Holmes in a famous death scene at Reichenbach Falls, he lives on even today—a true crime-fiction immortal.

My friend Sherlock Holmes was deeply engrossed with perplexing problems when I called upon him that second morning after Christmas, with the intention of wishing him the compliments of the season. He was lounging upon the sofa in a purple dressing gown, a pipe rack within his reach upon the right, and a pile of crumpled morning papers, evidently newly studied, near at hand. Beside the couch was a wooden chair, and on the angle of the back hung a very seedy and disreputable hard-felt hat, much the worse for wear, and cracked in several places. A lens and a forceps lying upon the seat of the chair suggested that the hat had been suspended in this manner for the purpose of examination.

"You are engaged," said I; "perhaps I interrupt you."

"Not at all. I am glad to have a friend with whom I can discuss my results. The matter is a perfectly trivial one"—he jerked his thumb in the direction of the old hat—"but there are points in connection with it which are not entirely devoid of interest and even of instruction."

I seated myself in his armchair and warmed my hands before his crackling fire, for a sharp frost had set in, and the windows were thick with the ice crystals. "I suppose," I remarked, "that, homely as it looks, this thing has some deadly story linked on to it—that it is the clue which will guide you in the solution of some mystery and the punishment of some crime."

"No, no. No crime," said Sherlock Holmes, laughing. "Only one of those whimsical little incidents which will happen when you have four million human beings all jostling each other within the space of a few square miles. Amid the action and reaction of so dense a swarm of humanity, every possible combination of events may be expected to take place, and many a little problem will be presented which may be striking and bizarre without being criminal. We have already had experience of such."

"So much so," I remarked, "that of the last six cases which I have added to my notes, three have been entirely free of any legal crime."

"Precisely. You allude to my attempt to recover the Irene Adler papers, to the singular case of Miss Mary Sutherland, and to the adventure of the man with the twisted lip. Well, I have no doubt that this small matter will fall into the same innocent category. You know Peterson, the commissionaire?"

"Yes."

"It is to him that this trophy belongs."

"It is his hat?"

"No, no; he found it. Its owner is unknown. I beg that you will look upon it not as a battered billycock but as an intellectual problem. And, first, as to how it came here. It arrived upon Christmas morning, in company with a good fat goose, which is, I have no doubt, roasting at this moment in front of Peterson's fire. The facts are these: bout four o'clock on Christmas morning, Peterson, who, as you know, is a very honest fellow, was returning from some small jollification and was making his way homeward down Tottenham Court Road. In front of him he saw, in the gaslight, a tallish man, walking with a slight stagger, and carrying a white goose slung over his shoulder. As he reached the corner of Goodge Street, a row broke out between this stranger and a little knot of roughs. One of the latter knocked off the man's hat, on which he raised his stick to defend himself and, swinging it over his head, smashed the shop window behind him. Peterson had rushed forward to protect the stranger from his assailants; but the man, shocked at having broken the window, and seeing an official-looking person in uniform rushing towards him, dropped his goose, took to his heels, and vanished amid the labyrinth of small streets which lie at the back of Tottenham Court Road. The roughs had also fled at the appearance of Peterson, so that he was left in possession of the field of battle, and also of the spoils of victory in the shape of this battered hat and a most unimpeachable Christmas goose."

"Which he restored to their owner?"

"My dear fellow, there lies the problem. It is true that 'For Mrs. Henry Baker' was printed upon a small card which was tied to the bird's left leg, and it is also true that the initials 'H. B.' are legible upon the lining of this hat; but as there are some thousands of Bakers, and some hundreds of Henry Bakers in this city of ours, it is not easy to restore lost property to any one of them."

"What, then, did Peterson do?"

"He brought round both hat and goose to me on Christmas morning, knowing that even the smallest problems are of interest to me. The goose we retained until this morning, when there were signs that, in spite of the slight frost, it would be well that it should be eaten without unnecessary delay. Its finder has carried it off, therefore, to fulfill the ultimate destiny of a goose, while I continue to retain the hat of the unknown gentleman who lost his Christmas dinner."

"Did he not advertise?"

"No."

"Then, what clue could you have as to his identity?"

"Only as much as we can deduce."

"From his hat?"

"Precisely."

"But you are joking. What can you gather from this old battered felt?"

"Here is my lens. You know my methods. What can you gather yourself as to the individuality of the man who has worn this article?"

I took the tattered object in my hands and turned it over rather ruefully. It was a very ordinary black hat of the usual round shape, hard and much the worse for wear. The lining had been of red silk, but was a good deal discoloured. There was no maker's name; but, as Holmes had remarked, the initials "H. B." were scrawled upon one side. It was pierced in the brim for a hat-securer, but the elastic was missing. For the rest, it was cracked, exceedingly dusty, and spotted in several places, although there seemed to have been some attempt to hide the discoloured patches by smearing them with ink.

"I can see nothing," said I, handing it back to my friend.

"On the contrary, Watson, you can see everything. You fail, however, to reason from what you see. You are too timid in drawing your inferences."

"Then, pray tell me what it is that you can infer from this hat?"

He picked it up and gazed at it in the peculiar introspective fashion which was characteristic of him. "It is perhaps less suggestive than it might have been," he remarked, "and yet there are a few inferences which are very distinct, and a few others which represent at least a strong balance of probability. That the man was highly intellectual is of course obvious upon the face of it, and also that he was fairly well-to-do within the last three years, although he has now fallen upon evil days. He had foresight, but has less now than formerly, pointing to a moral retrogression, which, when taken with the decline of his fortunes, seems to indicate some evil influence, probably drink, at work upon him. This may account also for the obvious fact that his wife has ceased to love him."

"My dear Holmes!"

"He has, however, retained some degree of self-respect," he continued, disregarding my remonstrance. "He is a man who leads a sedentary life, goes out little, is out of training entirely, is middle-aged, has grizzled hair which he has had cut within the last few days, and which he anoints with lime-cream. These are the more patent facts which are to be deduced from his hat. Also, by the way, that it is extremely improbable that he has gas laid on in his house."

"You are certainly joking, Holmes."

"Not in the least. Is it possible that even now, when I give you these results, you are unable to see how they are attained?"

"I have no doubt that I am very stupid, but I must confess that I am unable to follow you. For example, how did you deduce that this man was intellectual?"

For answer Holmes clapped the hat upon his head. It came right over the forehead and settled upon the bridge of his nose. "It is a question of cubic capacity," said he; "a man with so large a brain must have something in it."

"The decline of his fortunes, then?"

"This hat is three years old. These flat brims curled at the edge came in then. It is a hat of the very best quality. Look at the band of ribbed silk and the excellent lining. If this man could afford to buy so expensive a hat three years ago, and has had no hat since, then he has assuredly gone down in the world."

"Well, that is clear enough, certainly. But how about the foresight and the moral retrogression?"

Sherlock Holmes laughed. "Here is the foresight," said he, putting his finger upon the little disc and loop of the hat-securer. "They are never sold upon hats. If this man ordered one, it is a sign of a certain amount of foresight, since he went out of his way to take this precaution against the wind. But since we see that he has broken the elastic and has not troubled to replace it, it is obvious that he has less foresight now than formerly, which is a distinct proof of a weakening nature. On the other hand, he has endeavoured to conceal some of these stains upon the felt by daubing them with ink, which is a sign that he has not entirely lost his self-respect."

"Your reasoning is plausible."

"The further points, that he is middle-aged, that his hair is grizzled, that it has been recently cut, and that he uses lime-cream, are all to be gathered from a close examination of the lower part of the lining. The lens discloses a large number of hair ends, clean cut by the scissors of the barber. They all appear to be adhesive, and there is a distinct odour of lime-cream. This dust, you will observe, is not the gritty, gray dust of the street but the fluffy brown dust of the house, showing that it has been hung up indoors most of the time; while the marks of moisture upon the inside are proof positive that the wearer perspired very freely, and could, therefore, hardly be in the best of training."

"But his wife—you said that she had ceased to love him."

"This hat has not been brushed for weeks. When I see you, my dear Watson, with a week's accumulation of dust upon your hat, and when your wife allows you to go out in such a state, I shall fear that you also have been unfortunate enough to lose your wife's affection."

"But he might be a bachelor."

"Nay, he was bringing home the goose as a peace offering to his wife. Remember the card upon the bird's leg."

"You have an answer to everything. But how on earth do you deduce that the gas is not laid on in his house?"

"One tallow stain, or even two, might come by chance; but when I see no less than five, I think that there can be little doubt that the individual must be brought into frequent contact with burning tallow—walks upstairs at night probably with his hat in one hand and a guttering candle in the other. Anyhow, he never got tallow stains from a gas jet. Are you satisfied?"

"Well, it is very ingenious," said I, laughing; "but since, as you said just now, there has been no crime committed, and no harm done save the loss of a goose, all this seems to be rather a waste of energy."

Sherlock Holmes had opened his mouth to reply, when the door flew open, and Peterson, the commissionaire, rushed into the apartment with flushed cheeks and the face of a man who is dazed with astonishment.

"The goose, Mr. Holmes! The goose, sir!" he gasped.

"Eh? What of it, then? Has it returned to life and flapped off through the kitchen window?" Holmes twisted himself round upon the sofa to get a fairer view of the man's excited face.

"See here, sir! See what my wife found in its crop!" He held out his hand and displayed upon the centre of the palm a brilliantly scintillating blue stone, rather smaller than a bean in size, but of such purity and radiance that it twinkled like an electric point in the dark hollow of his hand.

Sherlock Holmes sat up with a whistle. "By Jove, Peterson!" said he, "this is treasure trove indeed. I suppose you know what you have got?"

"A diamond, sir? A precious stone? It cuts into glass as though it were putty."

"It's more than a precious stone. It is *the* precious stone."

"Not the Countess of Morcar's blue carbuncle!" I ejaculated.

"Precisely so. I ought to know its size and shape, seeing that I have read the advertisement about it in the *Times* every day lately. It is absolutely unique, and its value can only be conjectured, but the reward offered of one thousand pounds is certainly not within a twentieth part of the market price."

"A thousand pounds! Great Lord of mercy!" The commissionaire plumped down into a chair and stared from one to the other of us.

"That is the reward, and I have reason to know that there are sentimental considerations in the background which would induce the countess to part with half her fortune if she could but recover the gem."

"It was lost, if I remember aright, at the Hotel Cosmopolitan," I remarked.

"Precisely so, on December 22nd, just five days ago. John Horner, a plumber, was accused of having abstracted it from the lady's jewel case. The evidence against him was so strong that the case has been referred to the Assizes. I have some account of the matter here, I believe." He rummaged amid his newspapers, glancing over the dates, until at last he smoothed one out, doubled it over, and read the following paragraph:

> Hotel Cosmopolitan Jewel Robbery. John Horner, 26, plumber, was brought up upon the charge of having, upon the 22nd inst., abstracted from the jewel case of the Countess of Morcar the valuable gem known as the blue carbuncle. James Ryder, upper-attendant at the hotel, gave his evidence to the effect that he had shown Horner up to the dressing room of the Countess of Morcar upon the day of the robbery in order that he might solder the second bar of the grate, which was loose. He had remained with Horner some little time, but had finally been called away. On returning, he found that Horner had disappeared, that the bureau had been forced open, and that the small morocco casket in which, as it afterwards transpired, the countess was accustomed to keep her jewel, was lying empty upon the dressing table. Ryder instantly gave the alarm, and Horner was arrested the same evening; but the stone could not be found either upon his person or in his rooms. Catherine Cusack, maid to the countess, deposed to having heard Ryder's cry of dismay on discovering the robbery, and to having rushed into the room, where she found matters as described by the last witness. Inspector Bradstreet, B division, gave evidence as to the arrest of Horner, who struggled frantically, and protested his innocence in the strongest terms. Evidence of a previous conviction for robbery having been given against the prisoner, the magistrate refused to deal summarily with the offense, but referred it to the Assizes. Horner, who had shown signs of intense emotion during the proceedings, fainted away at the conclusion and was carried out of court.

"Hum! So much for the police court," said Holmes thoughtfully, tossing aside the paper. "The question for us now to solve is the sequence of events leading from a rifled jewel case at one end to the crop of a goose in Tottenham Court Road at the other. You see, Watson, our little deductions have suddenly assumed a much more important and less innocent aspect. Here is the stone; the stone came from the goose, and the goose came from Mr. Henry Baker, the gentleman with the bad hat and all the other characteristics with which I have bored you. So now we must set ourselves very seriously to finding this gentleman and ascertaining what part he has played in this little mystery. To do this, we must try the simplest means first, and these lie undoubtedly in an advertisement in all the evening papers. If this fails, I shall have recourse to other methods."

"What will you say?"

"Give me a pencil and that slip of paper. Now, then:

> Found at the corner of Goodge Street, a goose and a black felt hat. Mr. Henry Baker can have the same by applying at 6:30 this evening at 221B Baker Street.

That is clear and concise."

"Very. But will he see it?"

"Well, he is sure to keep an eye on the papers, since, to a poor man, the loss was a heavy one. He was clearly so scared by his mischance in breaking the window and by the approach of Peterson that he thought of nothing but flight, but since then he must have bitterly regretted the impulse which caused him to drop his bird. Then, again, the introduction of his name will cause him to see it, for everyone who knows him will direct his attention to it. Here you are, Peterson, run down to the advertising agency and have this put in the evening papers."

"In which, sir?"

"Oh, in the *Globe, Star, Pall Mall, St. James's, Evening News Standard, Echo,* and any others that occur to you."

"Very well, sir. And this stone?"

"Ah, yes, I shall keep the stone. Thank you. And, I say, Peterson, just buy a goose on your way back and leave it here with me, for we must have one to give to this gentleman in place of the one which your family is now devouring."

When the commissionaire had gone, Holmes took up the stone and held it against the light. "It's a bonny thing," said he. "Just see how it glints and sparkles. Of course it is a nucleus and focus of crime. Every good stone is. They are the devil's pet baits. In the larger and older jewels every facet may stand for a bloody deed. This stone is not yet twenty years old. It was found in the banks of the Amoy River in southern China and is remarkable in having every characteristic of the carbuncle, save that it is blue in shade instead of ruby red. In spite of its youth, it has already a sinister history. There have been two murders, a vitriol-throwing, a suicide, and several robberies brought about for the sake of this forty-grain weight of crystallized charcoal. Who would think that so pretty a toy would be a purveyor to the gallows and the prison? I'll lock it up in my strongbox now and drop a line to the countess to say that we have it."

"Do you think that this man Horner is innocent?"

"I cannot tell."

"Well, then, do you imagine that this other one, Henry Baker, had anything to do with the matter?"

"It is, I think, much more likely that Henry Baker is an absolutely innocent man, who had no idea that the bird which he was carrying was of considerably more value than if it were made of solid gold. That, however, I shall determine by a very simple test if we have an answer to our advertisement."

"And you can do nothing until then?"

"Nothing."

"In that case I shall continue my professional round. But I shall come back in the evening at the hour you have mentioned, for I should like to see the solution of so tangled a business."

"Very glad to see you. I dine at seven. There is a woodcock, I believe. By the way, in view of recent occurrences, perhaps I ought to ask Mrs. Hudson to examine its crop."

I had been delayed at a case, and it was a little after half-past six when I found myself in Baker Street once more. As I approached the house I saw a tall man in a Scotch bonnet with a coat which was buttoned up to his chin waiting outside in the bright semicircle which was thrown from the fanlight. Just as I arrived the door was opened, and we were shown up together to Holmes's room.

"Mr. Henry Baker, I believe," said he, rising from his armchair and greeting his visitor with the easy air of geniality which he could so readily assume. "Pray take this chair by the fire, Mr. Baker. It is a cold night, and I observe that your circulation is more adapted for summer than for winter. Ah, Watson, you have just come at the right time. Is that your hat, Mr. Baker?"

"Yes, sir, that is undoubtedly my hat."

He was a large man with rounded shoulders, a massive head, and a broad, intelligent face, sloping down to a pointed beard of grizzled brown. A touch of red in nose and cheeks, with a slight tremor of his extended hand, recalled Holmes's surmise as to his habits. His rusty black frock coat was buttoned right up in front, with the collar turned up, and his lank wrists protruded from his sleeves without a sign of cuff or shirt. He spoke in a slow staccato fashion, choosing his words with care, and gave the impression generally of a man of learning and letters who had had ill-usage at the hands of fortune.

"We have retained these things for some days," said Holmes, "because we expected to see an advertisement from you giving your address. I am at a loss to know now why you did not advertise."

Our visitor gave a rather shamefaced laugh. "Shillings have not been so plentiful with me as they once were," he remarked. "I had no doubt that the gang of roughs who assaulted me had carried off both my hat and the bird. I did not care to spend more money in a hopeless attempt at recovering them."

"Very naturally. By the way, about the bird, we were compelled to eat it."

"To eat it!" Our visitor half-rose from his chair in his excitement.

"Yes, it would have been of no use to anyone had we not done so. But I presume that this other goose upon the sideboard, which is about the same weight and perfectly fresh, will answer your purpose equally well?"

"Oh, certainly, certainly," answered Mr. Baker with a sigh of relief.

"Of course, we still have the feathers, legs, crop, and so on of your own bird, so if you wish—"

The man burst into a hearty laugh. "They might be useful to me as relics of my adventure," said he, "but beyond that I can hardly see what use the *disjecta membra* of my late acquaintance are going to be to me. No, sir, I think that, with your permission, I will confine my attentions to the excellent bird which I perceive upon the sideboard."

Sherlock Holmes glanced sharply across at me with a slight shrug of his shoulders.

"There is your hat, then, and there your bird," said he. "By the way, would it bore you to tell me where you got the other one from? I am somewhat of a fowl fancier, and I have seldom seen a better grown goose."

"Certainly, sir," said Baker, who had risen and tucked his newly gained property under his arm. "There are a few of us who frequent the Alpha Inn, near the Museum—we are to be found in the Museum itself during the day, you understand. This year our good host, Windigate by name, instituted a goose club, by which, on consideration of some few pence every week, we were each to receive a bird at Christmas. My pence were duly paid, and the rest is familiar to you. I am much indebted to you, sir, for a Scotch bonnet is fitted neither to my years nor my gravity." With a comical pomposity of manner he bowed solemnly to both of us and strode off upon his way.

"So much for Mr. Henry Baker," said Holmes when he had closed the door behind him. "It is quite certain that he knows nothing whatever about the matter. Are you hungry, Watson?"

"Not particularly."

"Then I suggest that we turn our dinner into a supper and follow up this clue while it is still hot."

"By all means."

It was a bitter night, so we drew on our ulsters and wrapped cravats about our throats. Outside, the stars were shining coldly in a cloudless sky, and the breath of the passersby blew out into smoke like so many pistol shots. Our footfalls rang out crisply and loudly as we swung through the doctors' quarter, Wimpole Street, Harley Street, and so through Wigmore Street into Oxford Street. In a quarter of an hour we were in Bloomsbury at the Alpha Inn, which is a small public-house at the corner of one of the streets which runs down into Holborn. Holmes pushed open the door of the private bar and ordered two glasses of beer from the ruddy-faced, white-aproned landlord.

"Your beer should be excellent if it is as good as your geese," said he.

"My geese!" The man seemed surprised.

"Yes. I was speaking only half an hour ago to Mr. Henry Baker, who was a member of your goose club."

"Ah! Yes, I see. But you see, sir, them's not *our* geese."

"Indeed! Whose, then?"

"Well, I got the two dozen from a salesman in Covent Garden."

"Indeed? I know some of them. Which was it?"

"Breckinridge is his name."

"Ah! I don't know him. Well, here's your good health, landlord, and prosperity to your house. Good night.

"Now for Mr. Breckinridge," he continued, buttoning up his coat as we came out into the frosty air. "Remember, Watson, that though we have so homely a thing as a goose at one end of this chain, we have at the other a man who will certainly get seven years' penal servitude unless we can establish his innocence. It is possible that our inquiry may but confirm his guilt; but, in any case, we have a line of investigation which has been missed by the police, and which a singular chance has placed in our hands. Let us follow it out to the bitter end. Faces to the south, then!"

We passed across Holborn, down Endell Street, and so through a zigzag of slums to Covent Garden Market. One of the largest stalls bore the name of Breckinridge upon it, and the proprietor, a horsy-looking man, with a sharp face and trim side-whiskers, was helping a boy to put up the shutters.

"Good evening. It's a cold night," said Holmes.

The salesman nodded and shot a questioning glance at my companion.

"Sold out of geese, I see," continued Holmes, pointing at the bare slabs of marble.

"Let you have five hundred tomorrow morning."

"That's no good."

"Well, there are some on the stall with the gas-flare."

"Ah, but I was recommended to you."

"Who by?"

"The landlord of the Alpha."

"Oh, yes; I sent him a couple of dozen."

"Fine birds they were, too. Now where did you get them from?"

To my surprise the question provoked a burst of anger from the salesman.

"Now, then, mister," said he, with his head cocked and his arms akimbo, "what are you driving at? Let's have it straight, now."

"It is straight enough. I should like to know who sold you the geese which you supplied to the Alpha."

"Well, then, I shan't tell you."

"Oh, it is a matter of no importance; but I don't know why you should be so warm over such a trifle."

"Warm! You'd be as warm, maybe, if you were as pestered as I am. When I pay good money for a good article there should be an end of the business; but it's 'Where are the geese?' and 'Who did you sell the geese to?' and 'What will you take for the geese?' One would think they were the only geese in the world, to hear the fuss that is made over them."

"Well, I have no connection with any other people who have been making inquiries," said Holmes carelessly. "If you won't tell us, the bet is off, that is all. But I'm always ready to back my opinion on a matter of fowls, and I have a fiver on it that the bird I ate is country-bred."

"Well, then, you've lost your fiver, for it's town-bred," snapped the salesman.

"It's nothing of the kind."

"I say it is."

"I don't believe it."

"D'you think you know more about fowls than I, who have handled them ever since I was a nipper? I tell you, all those birds that went to the Alpha were town-bred."

"You'll never persuade me to believe that."

"Will you bet, then?"

"It's merely taking your money, for I know that I am right. But I'll have a sovereign on with you, just to teach you not to be obstinate."

The salesman chuckled grimly. "Bring me the books, Bill," said he.

The small boy brought round a small thin volume and a great greasy-backed one, laying them out together beneath the hanging lamp.

"Now, then, Mr. Cocksure," said the salesman, "I thought that I was out of geese, but before I finish you'll find that there is still one left in my shop. You see this little book?"

"Well?"

"That's the list of the folk from whom I buy. D'you see? Well, then, here on this page are the country folk, and the numbers after their names are where their accounts are in the big ledger. Now, then! You see this other page in red ink? Well, that is a list of my town suppliers. Now, look at that third name. Just read it out to me."

"Mrs. Oakshott, 117 Brixton Road—249," read Holmes.

"Quite so. Now turn that up in the ledger."

Holmes turned to the page indicated. "Here you are, 'Mrs. Oakshott, 117 Brixton Road, egg and poultry supplier.' "

"Now, then, what's the last entry?"

" 'December 22nd. Twenty-four geese at *7s. 6d.*' "

"Quite so. There you are. And underneath?"

" 'Sold to Mr. Windigate of the Alpha, at *12s.*' "

"What have you to say now?"

Sherlock Holmes looked deeply chagrined. He drew a sovereign from his pocket and threw it down upon the slab, turning away with the air of a man whose disgust is too deep for words. A few yards off he stopped under a lamppost and laughed in the hearty, noiseless fashion which was peculiar to him.

"When you see a man with whiskers of that cut and the 'Pink 'un' protruding out of his pocket, you can always draw him by a bet," said he. "I daresay that if I had put one hundred pounds down in front of him, that man would not have given me such complete information as was drawn from him by the idea that he was doing me on a wager. Well, Watson, we are, I fancy, nearing the end of our quest, and the only point which remains to be determined is whether we should go on to this Mrs. Oakshott tonight, or whether we should reserve it for tomorrow. It is clear from what that surly fellow said that there are others besides ourselves who are anxious about the matter, and I should—"

His remarks were suddenly cut short by a loud hubbub which broke out from the stall which we had just left. Turning round, we saw a little rat-faced fellow standing in the centre of the circle of yellow light which was thrown by the swinging lamp, while Breckinridge, the salesman, framed in the door of his stall, was shaking his fists fiercely at the cringing figure.

"I've had enough of you and your geese," he shouted. "I wish you were all at the devil together. If you come pestering me any more with your silly talk, I'll set the dog at you. You bring Mrs. Oakshott here and I'll answer her, but what have you to do with it? Did I buy the geese off you?"

"No; but one of them was mine all the same," whined the little man.

"Well, then, ask Mrs. Oakshott for it."

"She told me to ask you."

"Well, you can ask the King of Proosia, for all I care. I've had enough of it. Get out of this!" He rushed fiercely forward, and the inquirer flitted away into the darkness.

"Ha! This may save us a visit to Brixton Road," whispered Holmes.

"Come with me, and we will see what is to be made of this fellow." Striding through the scattered knots of people who lounged round the flaring stalls, my companion speedily overtook the little man and touched him upon the shoulder. He sprang round, and I could see in the gaslight that every vestige of colour had been driven from his face.

"Who are you, then? What do you want?" he asked in a quavering voice.

"You will excuse me," said Holmes blandly, "but I could not help overhearing the questions which you put to the salesman just now. I think that I could be of assistance to you."

"You? Who are you? How could you know anything of the matter?"

"My name is Sherlock Holmes. It is my business to know what other people don't know."

"But you can know nothing of this."

"Excuse me, I know everything of it. You are endeavouring to trace some geese which were sold by Mrs. Oakshott, of Brixton Road, to a salesman named Breckinridge, by him in turn to Mr. Windigate, of the Alpha, and by him to his club, of which Mr. Henry Baker is a member."

"Oh, sir, you are the very man whom I have longed to meet," cried the little fellow with outstretched hands and quivering fingers. "I can hardly explain to you how interested I am in this matter."

Sherlock Holmes hailed a four-wheeler which was passing. "In that case we had better discuss it in a cosy room rather than in this wind-swept marketplace," said he. "But pray tell me, before we go farther, who it is that I have the pleasure of assisting."

The man hesitated for an instant. "My name is John Robinson," he answered with a sidelong glance.

"No, no; the real name," said Holmes sweetly. "It is always awkward doing business with an alias."

A flush sprang to the white cheeks of the stranger. "Well, then," said he, "my real name is James Ryder."

"Precisely so. Head attendant at the Hotel Cosmopolitan. Pray step into the cab, and I shall soon be able to tell you everything which you would wish to know."

The little man stood glancing from one to the other of us with half-frightened, half-hopeful eyes, as one who is not sure whether he is on the verge of a windfall or of a catastrophe. Then he stepped into the cab, and in half an hour we were back in the sitting room at Baker Street.

Nothing had been said during our drive, but the high, thin breathing of our new companion, and the claspings and unclaspings of his hands, spoke of the nervous tension within him.

"Here we are!" said Holmes cheerily, as we filed into the room. "The fire looks very seasonable in this weather. You look cold, Mr. Ryder. Pray take the basket-chair. I will just put on my slippers before we settle this little matter of yours. Now, then! You want to know what became of those geese?"

"Yes, sir."

"Or rather, I fancy, of that goose. It was one bird, I imagine, in which you were interested—white, with a black bar across the tail."

Ryder quivered with emotion. "Oh, sir," he cried, "can you tell me where it went to?"

"It came here."

"Here?"

"Yes, and a most remarkable bird it proved. I don't wonder that you should take an interest in it. It laid an egg after it was dead—the bonniest, brightest little blue egg that ever was seen. I have it here in my museum."

Our visitor staggered to his feet and clutched the mantelpiece with his right hand. Holmes unlocked his strongbox and held up the blue carbuncle, which shone out like a star, with a cold, brilliant, many-pointed radiance. Ryder stood glaring with a drawn face, uncertain whether to claim or to disown it.

"The game's up, Ryder," said Holmes quietly. "Hold up, man, or you'll be into the fire! Give him an arm back into his chair, Watson. He's not got blood enough to go in for felony with impunity. Give him a dash of brandy. So! Now he looks a little more human. What a shrimp it is, to be sure!"

For a moment he had staggered and nearly fallen, but the brandy brought a tinge of colour into his cheeks, and he sat staring at his accuser.

"I have almost every link in my hands, and all the proofs which I could possibly need, so there is little which you need tell me. Still, that little may as well be cleared up to make the case complete. You had heard, Ryder, of this blue stone of the Countess of Morcar's?"

"It was Catherine Cusack who told me of it," said he in a crackling voice.

"I see—her ladyship's waiting-maid. Well, the temptation of sudden wealth so easily acquired was too much for you, as it has been for better men before you; but you were not very scrupulous in the means you used. It seems to me, Ryder, that there is the making of a very pretty villain in you. You knew that this man Horner, the plumber, had been concerned in some such matter before, and that suspicion would rest the more readily upon him. What did you do, then? You made some small job in my lady's room—you and your confederate Cusack—and you managed that he should be the man sent for. Then, when he had left, you rifled the jewel case, raised the alarm, and had this unfortunate man arrested. You then—"

Ryder threw himself down suddenly upon the rug and clutched at my companion's knees. "For God's sake, have mercy!" he shrieked. "Think of my father! Of my mother! It would break their hearts. I never went wrong before! I never will again. I swear it. I'll swear it on a Bible. Oh, don't bring it into court!"

"Get back into your chair!" said Holmes sternly. "It is very well to cringe and crawl now, but you thought little enough of this poor Horner in the dock for a crime of which he knew nothing."

"I will fly, Mr. Holmes. I will leave the country, sir. Then the charge against him will break down."

"Hum! We will talk about that. And now let us hear a true account of the next act. How came the stone into the goose, and how came the goose into the open market? Tell us the truth, for there lies your only hope of safety."

Ryder passed his tongue over his parched lips. "I will tell you it just as it happened, sir," said he. "When Horner had been arrested, it seemed to me that it would be best for me to get away with the stone at once, for I did not know at what moment the police might not take it into their heads to search me and my room. There was no place about the hotel where it would be safe. I went out, as if on some commission, and I made for my sister's house. She had married a man named Oakshott, and lived in Brixton Road, where she fattened fowls for the market. All the way there, every man I met seemed to me to be a policeman or a detective; and, for all that it was a cold night, the sweat was pouring down my face before I came to the Brixton Road. My sister asked me what was the matter, and why I was so pale; but I told her that I had been upset by the jewel robbery at the hotel. Then I went into the backyard and smoked a pipe, and wondered what it would be best to do.

"I had a friend once called Maudsley, who went to the bad, and has just been serving his time in Pentonville. One day he had met me, and fell into talk about the ways of thieves, and how they could get rid of what they stole. I knew that he would be true to me, for I knew one or two things about him; so I made up my mind to go right on to Kilburn, where he lived, and take him into my confidence. He would show me how to turn the stone into money. But how to get to him in safety? I thought of the agonies I had gone through in coming from the hotel. I might at any moment be seized and searched, and there would be the stone in my waistcoat pocket. I was leaning against the wall at the time and looking at the geese which were waddling about round my feet, and suddenly an idea came into my head which showed me how I could beat the best detective that ever lived.

"My sister had told me some weeks before that I might have the pick of her geese for a Christmas present, and I knew that she was always as good as her word. I would take my goose now, and in it I would carry my stone to Kilburn. There was a little shed in the yard, and behind this I drove one of the birds—a fine big one, white, with a barred tail. I caught it, and, prying its bill open, I thrust the stone down its throat as far as my finger could reach. The bird gave a gulp, and I felt the stone pass along its gullet and down into its crop. But the creature flapped and struggled, and out came my sister to know what was the matter. As I turned to speak to her the brute broke loose and fluttered off among the others.

" 'Whatever were you doing with that bird, Jem?' says she.

" 'Well,' said I, 'you said you'd give me one for Christmas, and I was feeling which was the fattest.'

" 'Oh,' says she, 'we've set yours aside for you—Jem's bird, we call it. It's the big white one over yonder. There's twenty-six of them, which makes one for you, and one for us, and two dozen for the market.'

" 'Thank you, Maggie,' says I; 'but if it is all the same to you, I'd rather have that one I was handling just now.'

" 'The other is a good three pounds heavier,' said she, 'and we fattened it expressly for you.'

" 'Never mind. I'll have the other, and I'll take it now,' said I.

" 'Oh, just as you like,' said she, a little huffed. 'Which is it you want, then?'

" 'That white one with the barred tail, right in the middle of the flock.'

" 'Oh, very well. Kill it and take it with you.'

"Well, I did what she said, Mr. Holmes, and I carried the bird all the way to Kilburn. I told my pal what I had done, for he was a man that it was easy to tell a thing like that to. He laughed until he choked, and we got a knife and opened the goose. My heart turned to water, for there was no sign of the stone, and I knew that some terrible mistake had occurred. I left the bird, rushed back to my sister's, and hurried into the backyard. There was not a bird to be seen there.

" 'Where are they all, Maggie?' I cried.

" 'Gone to the dealer's, Jem.'

" 'Which dealer's?'

" 'Breckinridge, of Covent Garden.'

" 'But was there another with a barred tail,' I asked, 'the same as the one I chose?'

" 'Yes, Jem; there were two barred-tailed ones, and I could never tell them apart.'

"Well, then, of course I saw it all, and I ran off as hard as my feet would carry me to this man Breckinridge; but he had sold the lot at once, and not one word would he tell me as to where they had gone. You heard him yourselves tonight. Well, he has always answered me like that. My sister thinks that I am going mad. Sometimes I think that I am myself. And now—and now I am myself a branded thief, without ever having touched the wealth for which I sold my character. God help me! God help me!" He burst into convulsive sobbing, with his face buried in his hands.

There was a long silence, broken only by his heavy breathing, and by the measured tapping of Sherlock Holmes's fingertips upon the edge of the table. Then my friend rose and threw open the door.

"Get out!" said he.

"What, sir! Oh, Heaven bless you!"

"No more words. Get out!"

And no more words were needed. There was a rush, a clatter upon the stairs, the bang of a door, and the crisp rattle of running footfalls from the street.

"After all, Watson," said Holmes, reaching up his hand for his clay pipe, "I am not retained by the police to supply their deficiencies. If Horner were in danger it would be another thing; but this fellow will not appear against him, and the case must collapse. I suppose that I am commuting a felony, but it is just possible that I am saving a soul. This fellow will not go wrong again; he is too terribly frightened. Send him to jail now, and you make him a jailbird for life. Besides, it is the season of forgiveness. Chance has put in our way a most singular and whimsical problem, and its solution is its own reward. If you will have the goodness to touch the bell, Doctor, we will begin another investigation, in which, also, a bird will be the chief feature."

THE MYSTERIOUS DEATH IN PERCY STREET

Baroness Orczy

Sedentariness was a consciously cultivated quality of many of the early British sleuths, as well as of American detectives made in their image. The epitome of the "armchair" detective is Baroness Orczy's Old Man in the Corner, who is almost never known to move from his table in a London tea shop. The de-emphasis on action in such stories in no way prevents masters of the form like Baroness Orczy from creating hair-raising suspense, however. Baroness Orczy is notable not only for devising the first armchair detective stories, but for writing the famous adventures of the Scarlet Pimpernel.

Miss Polly Burton had had many an argument with Mr. Richard Frobisher about that old man in the corner, who seemed far more interesting and deucedly more mysterious than any of the crimes over which he philosophized.

Dick thought, moreover, that Miss Polly spent more of her leisure time now in that A.B.C. shop than she had done in his own company before, and told her so, with that delightful air of sheepish sulkiness which the male creature invariably wears when he feels jealous and will not admit it.

Polly liked Dick to be jealous, but she liked that old scarecrow in the A.B.C. shop very much too, and though she made sundry vague promises from time to time to Mr. Richard Frobisher, she nevertheless drifted back instinctively day after day to the tea shop in Norfolk Street, Strand, and stayed there sipping coffee for as long as the man in the corner chose to talk.

On this particular afternoon she went to the A.B.C. shop with a fixed purpose, that of making him give her his views of Mrs. Owen's mysterious death in Percy Street.

The facts had interested and puzzled her. She had had countless arguments with Mr. Richard Frobisher as to the three great possible solutions of the puzzle—"Accident, Suicide, Murder?"

"Undoubtedly neither accident nor suicide," the old man said drily.

Polly was not aware that she had spoken. What an uncanny habit that creature had of reading her thoughts!

"You incline to the idea, then, that Mrs. Owen was murdered. Do you know by whom?"

He laughed, and drew forth the piece of string he always fidgeted with when unravelling some mystery.

"You would like to know who murdered that old woman?" he asked at last.

"I would like to hear your views on the subject," Polly replied.

"I have no views," he said. "No one can know who murdered the woman, since no one ever saw the person who did it. No one can give the faintest description of the mysterious man who alone could have committed that clever deed, and the police are playing a game of blind man's buff."

"But you must have formed some theory of your own," she persisted.

It annoyed her that the funny creature was obstinate about this point, and she tried to nettle his vanity.

"I suppose that as a matter of fact your original remark that 'there are no such things as mysteries' does not apply universally. There is a mystery—that of the death in Percy Street, and you, like the police, are unable to fathom it."

He pulled up his eyebrows and looked at her for a minute or two.

"Confess that that murder was one of the cleverest bits of work accomplished outside Russian diplomacy," he said with a nervous laugh. "I must say that were I the judge, called upon to pronounce sentence of death on the man who conceived that murder, I could not bring myself to do it. I would politely request the gentleman to enter our Foreign Office—we have need of such men. The whole *mise en scène* was truly artistic, worthy of its *milieu*—the Rubens Studios in Percy Street, Tottenham Court Road.

"Have you ever noticed them? They are only studios by name, and are merely a set of rooms in a corner house, with the windows slightly enlarged, and the rents charged accordingly in consideration of that additional five inches of smoky daylight, filtering through dusty windows. On the ground floor there is the order office of some stained-glass works, with a workshop in the rear, and on the first-floor landing a small room allotted to the caretaker, with gas, coal, and fifteen shillings a week, for which princely income she is deputed to keep tidy and clean the general aspect of the house.

"Mrs. Owen, who was the caretaker there, was a quiet, respectable woman, who eked out her scanty wages by sundry—mostly very meagre—tips doled out to her by impecunious artists in exchange for promiscuous domestic services in and about the respective studios.

"But if Mrs. Owen's earnings were not large, they were very regular, and she had no fastidious tastes. She and her cockatoo lived on her wages; and all the tips added up, and never spent, year after year, went to swell a very comfortable little account at interest in the Birkbeck Bank. This little account had mounted up to a very tidy sum, and the thrifty widow, or old maid—no one ever knew which she was—was generally referred to by the young artists of the Rubens Studios as a 'lady of means.' But this is a digression.

"No one slept on the premises except Mrs. Owen and her cockatoo. The rule was that one by one as the tenants left their rooms in the evening they took their respective keys to the caretaker's room. She would then, in the early morning, tidy and dust the studios and the office downstairs, lay the fire, and carry up coals.

"The foreman of the glass works was the first to arrive in the morning. He had a latchkey, and let himself in, after which it was the custom of the house that he should leave the street door open for the benefit of the other tenants and their visitors.

"Usually, when he came at about nine o'clock, he found Mrs. Owen busy about the house doing her work, and he had often a brief chat with her about the weather, but on this particular morning of February 2nd he neither saw nor heard her. However, as the shop had been tidied and the fire laid, he surmised that Mrs. Owen had finished her work earlier than usual, and thought no more about it. One by one the tenants of the studios turned up, and the day sped on without anyone's attention being drawn noticeably to the fact that the caretaker had not appeared upon the scene.

"It had been a bitterly cold night, and the day was even worse: a cutting northeasterly gale was blowing, there had been a great deal of snow during the night which lay quite thick on the ground, and at five o'clock in the afternoon, when the last glimmer of the pale winter daylight had disappeared, the confraternity of the brush put palette and easel aside and prepared to go home. The first to leave was Mr. Charles Pitt; he locked up his studio and, as usual, took his key into the caretaker's room.

"He had just opened the door when an icy blast literally struck him in the face; both the windows were wide open, and the snow and sleet were beating thickly into the room, forming already a white carpet upon the floor.

"The room was in semi-obscurity, and at first Mr. Pitt saw nothing, but instinctively realizing that something was wrong, he lit a match, and saw before him the spectacle of that awful and mysterious tragedy which has ever since puzzled both police and public. On the floor, already half covered by the drifting snow, lay the body of Mrs. Owen face downwards, in a nightgown, with feet and ankles bare, and these and her hands were of a deep purple colour; while in a corner of the room, hunched up with the cold, the body of the cockatoo lay stark and stiff.

"At first there was only talk of a terrible accident, the result of some inexplicable carelessness which perhaps the evidence at the inquest would help to elucidate.

"Medical assistance came too late; the unfortunate woman was indeed dead, frozen to death, inside her own room. Further examination showed that she had received a severe blow at the back of the head, which must have stunned her and caused her to fall, helpless, beside the open window. Temperature at five degrees below zero had done the rest. Detective-Inspector Howell discovered close to the window a wrought-iron gas bracket, the height of which corresponded exactly with the bruise which was at the back of Mrs. Owen's head.

"Hardly, however, had a couple of days elapsed when public curiosity was whetted by a few startling headlines, such as the halfpenny evening papers alone know how to concoct.

" 'The Mysterious Death in Percy Street.' 'Is It Suicide or Murder?' 'Thrilling Details—Strange Developments.' 'Sensational Arrest.'

"What had happened was simply this:

"At the inquest a few very curious facts connected with Mrs. Owen's life had come to light, and this had led to the apprehension of a young man of very respectable parentage on a charge of being concerned in the tragic death of the unfortunate caretaker.

"To begin with, it happened that her life, which in an ordinary way should have been very monotonous and regular, seemed, at any rate latterly, to have been more than usually chequered and excited. Every witness who had known her in the past concurred in the statement that since October last a great change had come over the worthy and honest woman.

"I happen to have a photo of Mrs. Owen as she was before this great change occurred in her quiet and uneventful life, and which led, as far as the poor soul was concerned, to such disastrous results.

"Here she is to the life," added the funny creature, placing the photo before Polly—"as respectable, as stodgy, as uninteresting as it is possible for a member of your charming sex to be; not a face, you will admit, to lead any youngster to temptation or to induce him to commit a crime.

"Nevertheless, one day all the tenants of the Rubens Studios were surprised and shocked to see Mrs. Owen, quiet, respectable Mrs. Owen, sallying forth at six o'clock in the afternoon, attired in an extravagant bonnet and a cloak trimmed with imitation astrakhan which—slightly open in front—displayed a gold locket and chain of astonishing proportions.

"Many were the comments, the hints, the bits of sarcasm levelled at the worthy woman by the frivolous confraternity of the brush.

"The plot thickened when from that day forth a complete change came over the worthy caretaker of the Rubens Studios. While she appeared day after day before the astonished gaze of the tenants and the scandalized looks of the neighbours, attired in new and extravagant dresses, her work was hopelessly neglected, and she was always 'out' when wanted.

"There was, of course, much talk and comment in various parts of the Rubens Studios on the subject of Mrs. Owen's 'dissipations.' The tenants began to put two and two together, and after a very little while the general consensus of opinion became firmly established that the honest caretaker's demoralization coincided week for week, almost day for day, with young Greenhill's establishment in No. 8 Studio.

"Everyone had remarked that he stayed much later in the evening than anyone else, and yet no one presumed that he stayed for purposes of work. Suspicions soon rose to certainty when Mrs. Owen and Arthur Greenhill were seen by one of the glass workmen dining together at Gambia's Restaurant in Tottenham Court Road.

"The workman, who was having a cup of tea at the counter, noticed particularly that when the bill was paid the money came out of Mrs. Owen's purse. The dinner had been sumptuous—veal cutlets, a cut from the joint, dessert, coffee, and liqueurs. Finally, the pair left the restaurant apparently very gay, young Greenhill smoking a choice cigar.

"Irregularities such as these were bound sooner or later to come to the ears and eyes of Mr. Allman, the landlord of the Rubens Studios; and a month after the New Year, without further warning, he gave her a week's notice to quit his house.

" 'Mrs. Owen did not seem the least bit upset when I gave her notice,' Mr. Allman declared in his evidence at the inquest; 'on the contrary, she told me that she had ample means, and had only worked recently for the sake of something to do. She added that she had plenty of friends who would look after her, for she had a nice little pile to leave to anyone who would know how to get the right side of her.'

"Nevertheless, in spite of this cheerful interview, Miss Bedford, the tenant of No. 6 Studio, had stated that when she took her key to the caretaker's room at six-thirty that afternoon she found Mrs. Owen in tears. The caretaker refused to be comforted, nor would she speak of her trouble to Miss Bedford.

"Twenty-four hours later she was found dead.

"The coroner's jury returned an open verdict, and Detective-Inspector Jones was charged by the police to make some enquiries about young Mr. Greenhill, whose intimacy with the unfortunate woman had been universally commented upon.

"The detective, however, pushed his investigations as far as the Birkbeck Bank. There he discovered that after her interview with Mr. Allman, Mrs. Owen had withdrawn what money she had on deposit, some eight hundred pounds, the result of twenty-five years' saving and thrift.

"But the immediate result of Detective-Inspector Jones's labours was that Mr. Arthur Greenhill, lithographer, was brought before the magistrate at Bow Street on the charge of being concerned in the death of Mrs. Owen.

"Now, you know as well as I do how the attitude of the young prisoner impressed the magistrate and police so unfavourably that, with every new witness brought forward, his position became more and more unfortunate. Yet he was a good-looking, rather coarsely built young fellow, with one of those awful Cockney accents which literally make one jump. But he looked painfully nervous, stammered at every word spoken, and repeatedly gave answers entirely at random.

"His father acted as lawyer for him, a rough-looking elderly man, who had the appearance of a country attorney rather than of a London solicitor.

"The police had built up a fairly strong case against the lithographer. Medical evidence revealed nothing new: Mrs. Owen had died from exposure, the blow at the back of the head not being sufficiently serious to cause anything but temporary disablement. When the medical officer had been called in, death had intervened for some time; it was quite impossible to say how long, whether one hour, or five, or twelve.

"The appearance and state of the room, when the unfortunate woman was found by Mr. Charles Pitt, were again gone over in minute detail. Mrs. Owen's clothes, which she had worn during the day, were folded neatly on a chair. The key of her cupboard was in the pocket of her dress. The door had been slightly ajar, but both the windows were wide open; one of them, which had the sash-line broken, had been fastened up most scientifically with a piece of rope.

"Mrs. Owen had obviously undressed preparatory to going to bed, and the magistrate very naturally soon made the remark how untenable the theory of an accident must be. No one in their five senses would undress with a temperature at below zero, and the windows wide open.

"After these preliminary statements the cashier of the Birkbeck was called and he related the caretaker's visit at the bank.

" 'It was then about one o'clock,' he stated. 'Mrs. Owen called and presented a check to self for eight hundred twenty-seven pounds, the amount of her balance. She seemed exceedingly happy and cheerful, and talked about needing plenty of cash, as she was going abroad to join her nephew, for whom she would in future keep house. I warned her about being sufficiently careful with so large a sum, and parting from it injudiciously, as women of her class are very apt to do. She laughingly declared that not only was she careful of it in the present, but meant to be so for the far-off future, for she intended to go that very day to a lawyer's office and to make a will.'

"The cashier's evidence was certainly startling in the extreme, since in the widow's room no trace of any kind was found of any money; against that, two of the notes handed over by the bank to Mrs. Owen on that day were cashed by young Greenhill on the very morning of her mysterious death. One was handed in by him to the West End Clothiers Company, in payment for a suit of clothes, and the other he changed at the Post Office in Oxford Street.

"After that all the evidence had of necessity to be gone through again on the subject of young Greenhill's intimacy with Mrs. Owen. He listened to it all with an air of the most painful nervousness; his cheeks were positively green, his lips seemed dry and parched, for he repeatedly passed his tongue over them, and when Constable E 18 deposed that at two A.M. on the morning of February 2nd he had seen the accused and spoken to him at the corner of Percy Street and Tottenham Court Road, young Greenhill all but fainted.

"The contention of the police was that the caretaker had been murdered and robbed during that night before she went to bed, that young Greenhill had done the murder, seeing that he was the only person known to have been intimate with the woman, and that it was, moreover, proved unquestionably that he was in the immediate neighbourhood of the Rubens Studios at an extraordinarily late hour of the night.

"His own account of himself, and of that same night, could certainly not be called very satisfactory. Mrs. Owen was a relative of his late mother's, he declared. He himself was a lithographer by trade, with a good deal of time and leisure on his hands. He certainly had employed some of that time in taking the old woman to various places of amusement. He had on more than one occasion suggested that she should give up menial work and come and live with him, but, unfortunately, she was a great deal imposed upon by her nephew, a man of the name of Owen, who exploited the good-natured woman in every possible way, and who had on more than one occasion made severe attacks upon her savings at the Birkbeck Bank.

"Severely cross-examined by the prosecuting counsel about this supposed relative of Mrs. Owen, Greenhill admitted that he did not know him—had, in fact, never seen him. He knew that his name was Owen, and that was all. His chief occupation consisted in sponging on the kind-hearted old woman, but he only went to see her in the evenings, when he presumably knew that she would be alone, and invariably after all the tenants of the Rubens Studios had left for the day.

"I don't know whether at this point it strikes you at all, as it did both magistrate and counsel, that there was a direct contradiction in this statement and the one made by the cashier of the Birkbeck on the subject of his last conversation with Mrs. Owen. 'I am going abroad to join my nephew, for whom I am going to keep house,' was what the unfortunate woman had said.

"Now Greenhill, in spite of his nervousness and at times contradictory answers, strictly adhered to his point, that there was a nephew in London who came frequently to see his aunt.

"Anyway, the sayings of the murdered woman could not be taken as evidence in law. Mr. Greenhill senior put the objection, adding: 'There may have been two nephews,' which the magistrate and the prosecution were bound to admit.

"With regard to the night immediately preceding Mrs. Owen's death, Greenhill stated that he had been with her to the theatre, had seen her home, and had had some supper with her in her room. Before he left her, at two A.M., she had of her own accord made him a present of ten pounds, saying: 'I am a sort of aunt to you, Arthur, and if you don't have it, Bill is sure to get it.'

"She had seemed rather worried in the early part of the evening, but later on she cheered up.

" 'Did she speak at all about this nephew of hers or about her money affairs?' asked the magistrate.

"Again the young man hesitated, but said, 'No, she did not mention either Owen or her money affairs.'

"If I remember rightly," added the old man in the corner, "for recollect I was not present, the case was here adjourned. But the magistrate would not grant bail. Greenhill was removed looking more dead than alive—though everyone remarked that Mr. Greenhill senior looked determined and not the least worried. In the course of his examination on behalf of his son, of the medical officer and one or two other witnesses, he had very ably tried to confuse them on the subject of the hour at which Mrs. Owen was last known to be alive.

"He made a very great point of the fact that the usual morning's work was done throughout the house when the inmates arrived. Was it conceivable, he argued, that a woman would do that kind of work overnight, especially as she was going to the theatre, and therefore would wish to dress in her smarter clothes? It certainly was a very nice point levelled against the prosecution, who promptly retorted: Just as conceivable as that a woman in those circumstances of life should, having done her work, undress beside an open window at nine o'clock in the morning with the snow beating into the room.

"Now it seems that Mr. Greenhill senior could produce any amount of witnesses who could help to prove a conclusive alibi on behalf of his son, if only some time subsequent to that fatal two A.M. the murdered woman had been seen alive by some chance passerby. Mr. Greenhill senior was an able man and an earnest one, and I fancy the magistrate felt some sympathy for his strenuous endeavours on his son's behalf. He granted a week's adjournment, which seemed to satisfy Mr. Greenhill completely.

"In the meanwhile the papers had talked of and almost exhausted the subject of the mystery in Percy Street. There had been, as you no doubt know from personal experience, innumerable arguments on the puzzling alternatives:

"Accident?

"Suicide?

"Murder?

"A week went by, and then the case against young Greenhill was resumed. Of course, the court was crowded. It needed no great penetration to remark at once that the prisoner looked more hopeful, and his father quite elated.

"Again a great deal of minor evidence was taken, and then came the turn of the defense. Mr. Greenhill called Mrs. Hall, confectioner, of Percy Street, opposite the Rubens Studios. She deposed that at eight o'clock in the morning of February 2nd, while she was tidying her shop window, she saw the caretaker of the Studios opposite, as usual, on her knees, her head and body wrapped in a shawl, cleaning her front steps. Her husband also saw Mrs. Owen, and Mrs. Hall remarked to her husband how thankful she was that her own shop had tiled steps, which did not need scrubbing on so cold a morning.

"Mr. Hall, confectioner, of the same address, corroborated this statement, and Mr. Greenhill, with absolute triumph, produced a third witness, Mrs. Martin, of Percy Street, who from her window on the second floor had, at seven-thirty A.M., seen the caretaker shaking mats outside her front door. The description this witness gave of Mrs. Owen's getup, with the shawl round her head, coincided point by point with that given by Mr. and Mrs. Hall.

"After that Mr. Greenhill's task became an easy one; his son was at home having his breakfast at eight o'clock that morning—not only himself but his servants would testify to that.

"The weather had been so bitter that the whole of that day young Greenhill had not stirred from his own fireside. Mrs. Owen was murdered after eight A.M. on that day, since she was seen alive by three people at that hour, therefore his son could not have murdered Mrs. Owen. The police must find the criminal elsewhere, or else bow to the opinion originally expressed by the public that Mrs. Owen had met with a terrible untoward accident, or that perhaps she may have wilfully sought her own death in that extraordinary and tragic fashion.

"Before young Greenhill was finally discharged, one or two witnesses were again examined, chief among these being the foreman of the glassworks. He had turned up at Rubens Studios at nine o'clock, and been in business all day. He averred positively that he did not specially notice any suspicious-looking individual crossing the hall that day. 'But,' he remarked with a smile, 'I don't sit and watch everyone who goes up and down stairs. I am too busy for that. The street door is always left open; anyone can walk in, up or down, who knows the way.'

"That there was a mystery in connection with Mrs. Owen's death—of that the police have remained perfectly convinced; whether young Greenhill held the key of that mystery or not they have never found out to this day.

"I could enlighten them as to the cause of the young lithographer's anxiety at the magisterial inquiry, but, I assure you, I do not care to do the work of the police for them. Why should I? Greenhill will never suffer from unjust suspicions. He and his father alone—besides myself—know in what a terribly tight corner he all but found himself.

"The young man did not reach home till nearly five o'clock that morning. His last train had gone; he had to walk, lost his way, and wandered about Hampstead for hours. Think what his position would have been if the worthy confectioners of Percy Street had not seen Mrs. Owen 'wrapped up in a shawl, on her knees, doing the front steps.'

"Moreover, Mr. Greenhill senior is a solicitor, who has a small office in John Street, Bedford Row. The afternoon before her death, Mrs. Owen had been to that office and had there made a will by which she left all her savings to young Arthur Greenhill, lithographer. Had that will been in other than paternal hands, it would have been proved, in the natural course of such things, and one other link would have been added to the chain which nearly dragged Arthur Greenhill to the gallows—'the link of a very strong motive.'

"Can you wonder that the young man turned livid, until such time as it was proved beyond a doubt that the murdered woman was alive hours after he had reached the safe shelter of his home.

"I saw you smile when I used the word 'murdered,' " continued the old man in the corner, growing quite excited now that he was approaching the dénouement of his story. "I know that the public, after the magistrate had discharged Arthur Greenhill, were quite satisfied to think that the mystery in Percy Street was a case of accident—or suicide."

"No," replied Polly, "there could be no question of suicide for two very distinct reasons."

He looked at her with some degree of astonishment. She supposed that he was amazed at her venturing to form an opinion of her own.

"And may I ask what, in your opinion, these reasons are?" he asked very sarcastically.

"To begin with, the question of money," she said. "Has any more of it been traced so far?"

"Not another five-pound note," he said with a chuckle; "they were all cashed in Paris during the Exhibition, and you have no conception how easy a thing that is to do, at any of the hotels or smaller *agents de change."*

"That nephew was a clever blackguard," she commented.

"You believe, then, in the existence of that nephew?"

"Why should I doubt it? Someone must have existed who was sufficiently familiar with the house to go about in it in the middle of the day without attracting anyone's attention."

"In the middle of the day?" he said with a chuckle.

"Any time after eight-thirty in the morning."

"So you, too, believe in the 'caretaker, wrapped up in a shawl,' cleaning her front steps?" he queried.

"But—"

"It never struck you, in spite of the training your interviews with me must have given you, that the person who carefully did all the work in the Rubens Studios, laid the fires, and carried up the coals, merely did it in order to gain time; in order that the bitter frost might really and effectually do its work, and Mrs. Owen not be missed until she was truly dead."

"But—" suggested Polly again.

"It never struck you that one of the greatest secrets of successful crime is to lead the police astray with regard to the *time* when the crime was committed.

"In this case the 'nephew,' since we admit his existence, would—even if he were ever found, which is doubtful—be able to prove as good an alibi as young Greenhill."

"But I don't understand—"

"How the murder was committed?" he said eagerly. "Surely you can see it all for yourself, since you admit the 'nephew'—a scamp, perhaps—who sponges on the good-natured woman. He terrorizes and threatens her, so much so that she fancies her money is no longer safe even in the Birkbeck Bank. Women of that class are apt at times to mistrust the Bank of England. Anyway, she withdraws her money. Who knows what she meant to do with it in the immediate future?

"In any case, she wishes to give it after her death to a young man whom she likes, and who has known how to win her good graces. That afternoon the nephew begs, entreats for more money; they have a row; the poor woman is in tears, and is only temporarily consoled by a pleasant visit at the theatre.

"At two o'clock in the morning young Greenhill parts from her. Two minutes later the nephew knocks at the door. He comes with a plausible tale of having missed his last train, and asks for 'a shakedown' somewhere in the house. The good-natured woman suggests a sofa in one of the studios, and then quietly prepares to go to bed. The rest is very simple and elementary. The nephew sneaks into his aunt's room, finds her standing in her nightgown; he demands money with threats of violence; terrified, she staggers, knocks her head against the gas bracket, and falls on the floor stunned, while the nephew seeks for her keys and takes possession of the eight hundred–odd pounds. You will admit that the subsequent *mise en scène* is worthy of a genius.

"No struggle, not the usual hideous accessories round a crime. Only the open windows, the bitter northeasterly gale, and the heavily falling snow—two silent accomplices, as silent as the dead.

"After that the murderer, with perfect presence of mind, busies himself in the house, doing the work which will insure that Mrs. Owen shall not be missed, at any rate, for some time. He dusts and tidies; some few hours later he even slips on his aunt's skirt and bodice, wraps his head in a shawl, and boldly allows those neighbours who are astir to see what they believe to be Mrs. Owen. Then he goes back to her room, resumes his normal appearance, and quietly leaves the house."

"He may have been seen."

"He undoubtedly *was* seen by two or three people, but no one thought anything of seeing a man leave the house at that hour. It was very cold, the snow was falling thickly, and as he wore a muffler round the lower part of his face, those who saw him would not undertake to know him again."

"That man was never seen nor heard of again?" Polly asked.

"He has disappeared off the face of the earth. The police are searching for him, and perhaps some day they will find him—then society will be rid of one of the most ingenious men of the age."

The old man had paused, absorbed in meditation. The young girl also was silent. Some memory too vague as yet to take a definite form was persistently haunting her; one thought was hammering away in her brain, and playing havoc with her nerves. That thought was the inexplicable feeling within her that there was something in connection with that hideous crime which she ought to recollect, something which—if she could only remember what it was—would give her the clue to the tragic mystery, and for once insure her triumph over this self-conceited and sarcastic scarecrow in the corner.

He was watching her through his great bone-rimmed spectacles, and she could see the knuckles of his bony hands, just above the top of the table, fidgeting, fidgeting, fidgeting, till she wondered if there existed another set of fingers in the world which would undo the knots his lean ones made in that tiresome piece of string.

Then suddenly—apropos of nothing, Polly *remembered*—the whole thing stood before her, short and clear like a vivid flash of lightning—Mrs. Owen lying dead in the snow beside her open window; one of them with a broken sash-line, tied up most scientifically with a piece of string. She remembered the talk there had been at the time about this improvised sash-line.

That was after young Greenhill had been discharged, and the question of suicide had been voted out.

Polly remembered that in the illustrated papers photographs appeared of this wonderfully knotted piece of string, so contrived that the weight of the frame could but tighten the knots, and thus keep the window open. She remembered that people deduced many things from that improvised sash-line, chief among these deductions being that the murderer was a sailor—so wonderful, so complicated, so numerous were the knots which secured that window frame.

But Polly knew better. In her mind's eye she saw those fingers, rendered doubly nervous by the fearful cerebral excitement, grasping at first mechanically, even thoughtlessly, a bit of twine with which to secure the window; then the ruling habit strongest through all, the girl could see it; the lean and ingenious fingers fidgeting, fidgeting with that piece of string, tying knot after knot, more wonderful, more complicated, than any she had yet witnessed.

"If I were you," she said, without daring to look into that corner where he sat, "I would break myself of the habit of perpetually making knots in a piece of string."

He did not reply, and at last Polly ventured to look up—the corner was empty, and through the glass door beyond the desk, where he had just deposited his few coppers, she saw the tails of his tweed coat, his extraordinary hat, his meagre, shrivelled-up personality, fast disappearing down the street.

Miss Polly Burton (of the *Evening Observer*) was married the other day to Mr. Richard Frobisher (of the *London Mail*). She has never set eyes on the old man in the corner from that day to this.

PERCIVAL BLAND'S PROXY

R. Austin Freeman

Meticulous about the scientific accuracy of his plots, Londoner R. Austin Freeman was, like Sir Arthur Conan Doyle, by training and early practice a medical doctor. In 1907, Freeman's first book was published, featuring a protagonist whose role as police doctor was to bring him into contact with many "scientifically" solvable mysteries. In many of the Dr. Thorndyke stories, plot is given more attention than characterization, but Freeman's characters are appealing nevertheless, and he must be credited as the founder of the scientific detective story.

PART I

Mr. Percival Bland was a somewhat uncommon type of criminal. In the first place, he really had an appreciable amount of common sense. If he had only had a little more, he would not have been a criminal at all. As it was, he had just sufficient judgment to perceive that the consequences of unlawful acts accumulate as the acts are repeated; to realise that the criminal's position must, at length, become untenable; and to take what he considered fair precautions against the inevitable catastrophe.

But in spite of these estimable traits of character and the precautions aforesaid, Mr. Bland found himself in rather a tight place and with a prospect of increasing tightness. The causes of this uncomfortable tension do not concern us, and may be dismissed with the remark that, if one perseveringly distributes flash Bank of England notes among the money changers of the Continent, there will come a day of reckoning when those notes are tendered to the exceedingly knowing old lady who lives in Threadneedle Street.

Mr. Bland considered uneasily the approaching storm cloud as he raked over the "miscellaneous property" in the salerooms of Messrs. Plimpton. He was a confirmed frequenter of auctions, as was not unnatural; for the criminal is essentially a gambler. And criminal and auction-frequenter have one quality in common: each hopes to get something of value without paying the market price for it.

So Percival turned over the dusty oddments and his own difficulties at one and the same time. The vital questions were: When would the storm burst? And would it pass by the harbour of refuge that he had been at such pains to construct? Let us inspect that harbour of refuge.

A quiet flat in the pleasant neighbourhood of Battersea bore a name-plate inscribed: Mr. Robert Lindsay; and the tenant was known to the porter and the charwoman who attended to the flat as a fair-haired gentleman who was engaged in the book trade as a travelling agent, and was consequently a good deal away from home. Now Mr. Robert Lindsay bore a distinct resemblance to Percival Bland; which was not surprising seeing that they were first cousins (or, at any rate, they said they were; and we may presume that they knew). But they were not very much alike. Mr. Lindsay had flaxen, or rather sandy, hair; Mr. Bland's hair was black. Mr. Bland had a mole under his left eye; Mr. Lindsay had no mole under his eye—but carried one in a small box in his waistcoat pocket.

At somewhat rare intervals the cousins called on one another; but they had the very worst of luck, for neither of them ever seemed to find the other at home. And what was even more odd was that whenever Mr. Bland spent an evening at home in his lodgings over the oil shop in Bloomsbury, Mr. Lindsay's flat was empty; and as sure as Mr. Lindsay was at home in his flat so surely were Mr. Bland's lodgings vacant for the time being. It was a queer coincidence, if anyone had noticed it; but nobody ever did.

However, if Percival saw little of his cousin, it was not a case of "out of sight, out of mind." On the contrary; so great was his solicitude for the latter's welfare that he not only had made a will constituting him his executor and sole legatee, but he had actually insured his life for no less a sum than three thousand pounds; and this will, together with the insurance policy, investment securities, and other necessary documents, he had placed in the custody of a highly respectable solicitor. All of which did him great credit. It isn't every man who is willing to take so much trouble for a mere cousin.

Mr. Bland continued his perambulations, pawing over the miscellaneous raffle from sheer force of habit, reflecting on the coming crisis in his own affairs, and on the provisions that he had made for his cousin Robert. As for the latter, they were excellent so far as they went, but they lacked definiteness and perfect completeness. There was the contingency of a "stretch," for instance; say fourteen years penal servitude. The insurance policy did not cover that. And, meanwhile, what was to become of the estimable Robert?

He had bruised his thumb somewhat severely in a screw-cutting lathe, and had abstractedly turned the handle of a bird-organ until politely requested by an attendant to desist, when he came upon a series of boxes containing, according to the catalogue, "a collection of surgical instruments, the property of a lately deceased practitioner." To judge by the appearance of the instruments, the practitioner must have commenced practice in his early youth and died at a very advanced age. They were an uncouth set of tools, of no value whatever excepting as testimonials to the amazing tenacity of life of our ancestors; but Percival fingered them over according to his wont, working the handle of a complicated brass syringe and ejecting a drop of greenish fluid onto the shirtfront of a dressy Hebrew (who requested him to "point the damn thing at thomeone elth nectht time"), opening musty leather cases, clicking off spring scarifiers, and feeling the edges of strange, crooked-bladed knives. Then he came upon a largish black box, which, when he raised the lid, breathed out an ancient and fishlike aroma and exhibited a collection of bones, yellow, greasy-looking, and spotted in places with mildew. The catalogue described them as "a complete set of human osteology"; but they were not an ordinary "student's set," for the bones of the hands and feet, instead of being strung together on catgut, were united by their original ligaments and were of an unsavoury brown colour.

"I thay, misther," expostulated the Hebrew, "shut that bocth. Thmellth like a blooming inquetht."

But the contents of the black box seemed to have a fascination for Percival. He looked in at those greasy remnants of mortality, at the brown and mouldy hands and feet and the skull that peeped forth eerily from the folds of a flannel wrapping; and they breathed out something more than that stale and musty odour. A suggestion—vague and general at first, but rapidly crystallising into distinct shape—seemed to steal out of the black box into his consciousness; a suggestion that somehow seemed to connect itself with his estimable cousin Robert.

For upwards of a minute he stood motionless, as one immersed in reverie, the lid poised in his hand and a dreamy eye fixed on the half-uncovered skull. A stir in the room roused him. The sale was about to begin. The members of the knock-out and other habitués seated themselves on benches around a long, baize-covered table; the attendants took possession of the first lots and opened their catalogues as if about to sing an introductory chorus; and a gentleman with a waxed moustache and a striking resemblance to his late Majesty, the third Napoleon, having ascended to the rostrum bespoke the attention of the assembly by a premonitory tap with his hammer.

How odd are some of the effects of a guilty conscience! With what absurd self-consciousness do we read into the minds of others our own undeclared intentions, when those intentions are unlawful! Had Percival Bland wanted a set of human bones for any legitimate purpose—such as anatomical study—he would have bought it openly and unembarrassed. Now, he found himself earnestly debating whether he should not bid for some of the surgical instruments, just for the sake of appearances; and there being little time in which to make up his mind—for the deceased practitioner's effects came first in the catalogue—he was already the richer by a set of cupping glasses, a tooth key, and an instrument of unknown use and diabolical aspect, before the fateful lot was called.

At length the black box was laid on the table, an object of obscene mirth to the knockers-out, and the auctioneer read the entry:

"Lot seventeen; a complete set of human osteology. A very useful and valuable set of specimens, gentlemen."

He looked around at the assembly majestically, oblivious of sundry inquiries as to the identity of the deceased and the verdict of the coroner's jury, and finally suggested five shillings.

"Six," said Percival.

An attendant held the box open and, chanting the mystic word "Loddle-men!" (which, being interpreted, meant "Lot, gentlemen") thrust it under the rather bulbous nose of the smart Hebrew; who remarked that "they 'ummed a bit too much to thoot him" and pushed it away.

"Going at six shillings," said the auctioneer, reproachfully; and as nobody contradicted him, he smote the rostrum with his hammer and the box was delivered into the hands of Percival on the payment of that modest sum.

Having crammed the cupping glasses, the tooth key, and the unknown instrument into the box, Percival obtained from one of the attendants a length of cord, with which he secured the lid. Then he carried his treasure out into the street and, chartering a four-wheeler, directed the driver to proceed to Charing Cross Station. At the station he booked the box in the cloakroom (in the name of Simpson) and left it for a couple of hours; at the expiration of which he returned and, employing a different porter, had it conveyed to a hansom, in which it was borne to his lodgings over the oil shop in Bloomsbury. There he, himself, carried it, unobserved, up the stairs and, depositing it in a large cupboard, locked the door and pocketed the key.

And thus was the curtain rung down on the first act.

The second act opened only a couple of days later, the office of callboy—to pursue the metaphor to the bitter end—being discharged by a Belgian police official who emerged from the main entrance to the Bank of England. What should have led Percival Bland into so unsafe a neighbourhood it is difficult to imagine, unless it was that strange fascination that seems so frequently to lure the criminal to places associated with his crime. But there he was within a dozen paces of the entrance when the officer came forth, and mutual recognition was instantaneous. Almost equally instantaneous was the self-possessed Percival's decision to cross the road.

It is not a nice road to cross. The old-fashioned horse driver would condescend to shout a warning to the indiscreet wayfarer. Not so the modern chauffeur, who looks stonily before him and leaves you to get out of the way of Juggernaut. He knows his "exonerating" coroner's jury. At the moment, however, the procession of Juggernauts was at rest; but Percival had seen the presiding policeman turn to move away and he darted across the fronts of the vehicles even as they started. The foreign officer followed. But in that moment the whole procession had got in motion. A motor omnibus thundered past in front of him; another was bearing down on him relentlessly. He hesitated, and sprang back; and then a taxicab, darting out from behind, butted him heavily, sending him sprawling in the road, whence he scrambled as best he could back onto the pavement.

Percival, meanwhile, had swung himself lightly onto the footboard of the first omnibus just as it was gathering speed. A few seconds saw him safely across at the Mansion House, and in a few more, he was whirling down Queen Victoria Street. The danger was practically over, though he took the precaution to alight at St. Paul's and, crossing to Newgate Street, board another westbound omnibus.

That night he sat in his lodgings turning over his late experience. It had been a narrow shave. That sort of thing mustn't happen again. In fact, seeing that the law was undoubtedly about to be set in motion, it was high time that certain little plans of his should be set in motion, too. Only, there was a difficulty; a serious difficulty. And as Percival thought round and round that difficulty his brows wrinkled and he hummed a soft refrain.

"Then is the time for disappearing,
Take a header—down you go—."

A tap at the door cut his song short. It was his landlady, Mrs. Brattle; a civil woman, and particularly civil just now. For she had a little request to make.

"It was about Christmas Night, Mr. Bland," said Mrs. Brattle. "My husband and me thought of spending the evening with his brother at Hornsey, and we were going to let the maid go home to her mother's for the night, if it wouldn't put you out."

"Wouldn't put me out in the least, Mrs. Brattle," said Percival.

"You needn't sit up for us, you see," pursued Mrs. Brattle, "if you'd just leave the side door unbolted. We shan't be home before two or three; but we'll come in quiet not to disturb you."

"You won't disturb me," Percival replied with a genial laugh. "I'm a sober man in general; but 'Christmas comes but once a year.' When once I'm tucked up in bed, I shall take a bit of waking on Christmas Night."

Mrs. Brattle smiled indulgently. "And you won't feel lonely, all alone in the house?"

"Lonely!" exclaimed Percival. "Lonely! With a roaring fire, a jolly book, a box of good cigars, and a bottle of sound port—ah, and a second bottle if need be. Not I."

Mrs. Brattle shook her head. "Ah," said she, "you bachelors! Well, well. It's a good thing to be independent," and with this profound reflection she smiled herself out of the room and descended the stairs.

As her footsteps died away Percival sprang from his chair and began excitedly to pace the room. His eyes sparkled and his face was wreathed with smiles. Presently he halted before the fireplace and, gazing into the embers, laughed aloud.

"Damn funny!" he said. "Deuced rich! Neat! Very neat! Ha! Ha!" And here he resumed his interrupted song:

"When the sky above is clearing,
When the sky above is clearing,
Bob up serenely, bob up serenely,
Bob up serenely from below!"

Which may be regarded as closing the first scene of the second act.

During the few days that intervened before Christmas, Percival went abroad but little; and yet he was a busy man. He did a little surreptitious shopping, venturing out as far as Charing Cross Road; and his purchases were decidedly miscellaneous. A porridge saucepan, a second-hand copy of *Gray's Anatomy*, a rabbit skin, a large supply of glue, and upwards of ten pounds of shin of beef, seems a rather odd assortment; and it was a mercy that the weather was frosty, for otherwise Percival's bedroom, in which these delicacies were deposited under lock and key, would have yielded odorous traces of its wealth.

But it was in the long evenings that his industry was most conspicuous; and then it was that the big cupboard with the excellent lever lock, which he himself had fixed on, began to fill up with the fruits of his labours. In those evenings the porridge saucepan would simmer on the hob with a rich lading of good Scotch glue, the black box of the deceased practitioner would be hauled forth from its hiding place, and the well-thumbed *Gray* laid open on the table.

It was an arduous business though; a stiffer task than he had bargained for. The right and left bones were so confoundedly alike, and the bones that joined were so difficult to fit together. However, the plates in *Gray* were large and very clear, so it was only a question of taking enough trouble.

His method of work was simple and practical. Having fished a bone out of the box, he would compare it with the illustrations in the book until he had identified it beyond all doubt, when he would tie on it a paper label with its name and side—right or left. Then he would search for the adjoining bone, and, having fitted the two together, would secure them with a good daub of glue and lay them in the fender to dry. It was a crude and horrible method of articulation that would have made a museum curator shudder. But it seemed to answer Percival's purpose—whatever that may have been—for gradually the loose "items" came together into recognisable members such as arms and legs, the vertebrae—which were, fortunately, strung in their order on a thick cord—were joined up into a solid backbone, and even the ribs, which were the toughest job of all, fixed on in some semblance of a thorax. It was a wretched performance. The bones were plastered with gouts of glue and yet would have broken apart at a touch. But, as we have said, Percival seemed satisfied, and as he was the only person concerned, there was nothing more to be said.

In due course, Christmas Day arrived. Percival dined with the Brattles at two, dozed after dinner, woke up for tea, and then, as Mrs. Brattle, in purple and fine raiment, came in to remove the tea tray, he spread out on the table the materials for the night's carouse. A quarter of an hour later, the side door slammed, and peering out of the window, he saw the shopkeeper and his wife hurrying away up the gaslit street towards the nearest omnibus route.

Then Mr. Percival Bland began his evening's entertainment; and a most remarkable entertainment it was, even for a solitary bachelor, left alone in a house on Christmas Night. First, he took off his clothing and dressed himself in a fresh suit. Then, from the cupboard, he brought forth the reconstituted "set of osteology," and, laying the various members on the table, returned to the bedroom, whence he presently reappeared with a large, unsavoury parcel which he had disinterred from a trunk. The parcel, being opened, revealed his accumulated purchases in the matter of shin of beef.

With a large knife, providently sharpened beforehand, he cut the beef into large, thin slices which he proceeded to wrap around the various bones that formed the "complete set"; whereby their nakedness was certainly mitigated though their attractiveness was by no means increased. Having thus "clothed the dry bones," he gathered up the scraps of offal that were left, to be placed presently inside the trunk. It was an extraordinary proceeding, but the next was more extraordinary still.

Taking up the newly clothed members one by one, he began very carefully to insinuate them into the garments that he had recently shed. It was a ticklish business, for the glued joints were as brittle as glass.

Very cautiously the legs were separately inducted, first into underclothing and then into trousers, the skeleton feet were fitted with the cast-off socks and delicately persuaded into the boots. The arms, in like manner, were gingerly pressed into their various sleeves and through the armholes of the waistcoat; and then came the most difficult task of all—to fit the garments to the trunk. For the skull and ribs, secured to the backbone with mere spots of glue, were ready to drop off at a shake; and yet the garments had to be drawn over them with the arms enclosed in the sleeves. But Percival managed it at last by resting his "restoration" in the big, padded armchair and easing the garments on inch by inch.

It now remained only to give the finishing touch; which was done by cutting the rabbit skin to the requisite shape and affixing it to the skull with a thin coat of stiff glue; and when the skull had thus been finished with a sort of crude, makeshift wig, its appearance was so appalling as even to disturb the nerves of the matter-of-fact Percival. However, this was no occasion for cherishing sentiment. A skull in an extemporised wig or false scalp might be, and in fact was, a highly unpleasant object; but so was a Belgian police officer.

Having finished the "restoration," Percival fetched the water jug from his bedroom, and, descending to the shop, the door of which had been left unlocked, tried the taps of the various drums and barrels until he came to the one which contained methylated spirit; and from this he filled his jug and returned to the bedroom. Pouring the spirit out into the basin, he tucked a towel round his neck and filling his sponge with spirit, proceeded very vigorously to wash his hair and eyebrows, and as, by degrees, the spirit in the basin grew dark and turbid, so did his hair and eyebrows grow lighter in colour until, after a final energetic rub with a towel, they had acquired a golden or sandy hue indistinguishable from that of the hair of his cousin Robert. Even the mole under his eye was susceptible to the changing conditions, for when he had wetted it thoroughly with spirit, he was able with the blade of a penknife, to peel it off as neatly as if it had been stuck on with spirit gum. Having done which, he deposited it in a tiny box which he carried in his waistcoat pocket.

The proceedings which followed were unmistakable as to their object. First he carried the basin of spirit through into the sitting room and deliberately poured its contents onto the floor by the armchair. Then, having returned the basin to the bedroom, he again went down to the shop, where he selected a couple of galvanised buckets from the stock, filled them with paraffin oil from one of the great drums, and carried them upstairs. The oil from one bucket he poured over the armchair and its repulsive occupant; the other bucket he simply emptied on the carpet, and then went down to the shop for a fresh supply.

When this proceeding had been repeated once or twice the entire floor and all the furniture were saturated, and such a reek of paraffin filled the air of the room that Percival thought it wise to turn out the gas. Returning to the shop, he poured a bucketful of oil over the stack of bundles of firewood, another over the counter and floor, and a third over the loose articles on the walls and hanging from the ceiling. Looking up at the latter, he now perceived a number of greasy patches where the oil had soaked through from the floor above, and some of these were beginning to drip onto the shop floor.

He now made his final preparations. Taking a bundle of "Wheel" fire lighters, he made a small pile against the stack of firewood. In the midst of the fire lighters he placed a ball of string saturated in paraffin; and in the central hole of the ball he stuck a half-dozen diminutive Christmas candles. This mine was now ready. Providing himself with a stock of fire lighters, a few balls of paraffined string, and a dozen or so of the little candles, he went upstairs to the sitting-room, which was immediately above the shop. Here, by the glow of the fire, he built up one or two piles of fire lighters around and partly under the armchair, placed the balls of string on the piles, and stuck two or three bundles in each ball. Everything was now ready. Stepping into the bedroom, he took from the cupboard a spare overcoat, a new hat, and a new umbrella—for he must leave his old hats, coat, and umbrella in the hall. He put on the coat and hat, and, with the umbrella in his hand, returned to the sitting room.

Opposite the armchair he stood awhile, irresolute, and a pang of horror shot through him. It was a terrible thing that he was going to do; a thing the consequences of which no one could foresee. He glanced furtively at the awful shape that sat huddled in the chair, its horrible head all awry and its rigid limbs sprawling in hideous, grotesque deformity. It was but a dummy, a mere scarecrow; but yet, in the dim firelight, the grisly face under that horrid wig seemed to leer intelligently, to watch him with secret malice out of its shadowy eye sockets, until he looked away with clammy skin and a shiver of half-superstitious terror.

But this would never do. The evening had run out, consumed by these engrossing labours; it was nearly eleven o'clock, and high time for him to be gone. For if the Brattles should return prematurely he was lost. Pulling himself together with an effort, he struck a match and lit the little candles one after the other. In a quarter of an hour or so, they would have burned down to the balls of string, and then—

He walked quickly out of the room; but at the door he paused for a moment to look back at the ghastly figure, seated rigidly in the chair with the lighted candles at its feet, like some foul fiend appeased by votive fires. The unsteady flames threw flickering shadows on its face that made it seem to mow and gibber and grin in mockery of all his care and caution. So he turned and tremblingly ran down the stairs—opening the staircase window as he went. Running into the shop, he lit the candles there and ran out again, shutting the door after him.

Secretly and guiltily he crept down the hall, and opening the door a few inches peered out. A blast of icy wind poured in with a light powdering of dry snow. He opened his umbrella, flung open the door, looked up and down the empty street, stepped out, closed the door softly, and strode away over the whitening pavement.

Part II

It was one of the axioms of medico-legal practice laid down by my colleague, John Thorndyke, that the investigator should be constantly on his guard against the effects of suggestion. Not only must all prejudices and preconceptions be avoided, but when information is received from outside, the actual, undeniable facts must be carefully sifted from the inferences which usually accompany them. Of the necessity of this precaution our insurance practice furnished an excellent instance in the case of the fire at Mr. Brattle's oil shop.

The case was brought to our notice by Mr. Stalker of the "Griffin" Fire and Life Insurance Society a few days after Christmas. He dropped in, ostensibly to wish us a Happy New Year, but a discreet pause in the conversation on Thorndyke's part elicited a further purpose.

"Did you see the account of that fire in Bloomsbury?" Mr. Stalker asked.

"The oil shop? Yes. But I didn't note any details, excepting that a man was apparently burnt to death and that the affair happened on the twenty-fifth of December."

"Yes, I know," said Mr. Stalker. "It seems uncharitable, but one can't help looking a little askance at these quarter-day fires. And the date isn't the only doubtful feature in this one; the Divisional Officer of the Fire Brigade, who has looked over the ruins, tells me that there are some appearances suggesting that the fire broke out in two different places—the shop and the first-floor room over it. Mind you, he doesn't say that it actually did. The place is so thoroughly gutted that very little is to be learned from it; but that is his impression; and it occurred to me that if you were to take a look at the ruins, your radiographic eye might detect something that he had overlooked."

"It isn't very likely," said Thorndyke. "Every man to his trade. The Divisional Officer looks at a burnt house with an expert eye, which I do not. My evidence would not carry much weight if you were contesting the claim."

"Perhaps not," replied Mr. Stalker, "and we are not anxious to contest the claim unless there is manifest fraud. Arson is a serious matter."

"It is wilful murder in this case," remarked Thorndyke.

"I know," said Stalker. "And that reminds me that the man who was burnt happens to have been insured in our office, too. So we stand a double loss."

"How much?" asked Thorndyke.

"The dead man, Percival Bland, had insured his life for three thousand pounds."

Thorndyke became thoughtful. The last statement had apparently made more impression on him than the former ones.

"If you want me to look into the case for you," said he, "you had better let me have all the papers connected with it, including the proposal forms."

Mr. Stalker smiled. "I thought you would say that—know you of old, you see—so I slipped the papers in my pocket before coming here."

He laid the documents on the table and asked: "Is there anything that you want to know about the case?"

"Yes," replied Thorndyke. "I want to know all that you can tell me."

"Which is mighty little," said Stalker; "but such as it is, you shall have it.

"The oil shop man's name is Brattle and the dead man, Bland, was his lodger. Bland appears to have been a perfectly steady, sober man in general; but it seems that he had announced his intention of spending a jovial Christmas Night and giving himself a little extra indulgence. He was last seen by Mrs. Brattle at about half-past six, sitting by a blazing fire, with a couple of unopened bottles of port on the table and a box of cigars. He had a book in his hand and two or three newspapers lay on the floor by his chair. Shortly after this, Mr. and Mrs. Brattle went out, on a visit to Hornsey, leaving him alone in the house."

"Was there no servant?" asked Thorndyke.

"The servant had the day and night off duty to go to her mother's. That, by the way, looks a trifle fishy. However, to return to the Brattles; they spent the evening at Hornsey and did not get home until past three in the morning, by which time their house was a heap of smoking ruins. Mrs. Brattle's idea is that Bland must have drunk himself sleepy, and dropped one of the newspapers into the fender, where a chance cinder may have started the blaze. Which may or may not be the true explanation. Of course, a habitually sober man can get pretty mimsey on two bottles of port."

"What time did the fire break out?" asked Thorndyke.

"It was noticed about half-past eleven that flames were issuing from one of the chimneys, and the alarm was given at once. The first engine arrived ten minutes later, but, by that time, the place was roaring like a furnace. Then the water plugs were found to be frozen hard, which caused some delay; in fact, before the engines were able to get to work the roof had fallen in, and the place was a mere shell. You know what an oil-shop is, when once it gets a fair start."

"And Mr. Bland's body was found in the ruins, I suppose?"

"Body!" exclaimed Mr. Stalker; "there wasn't much body! Just a few charred bones, which they dug out of the ashes the next day."

"And the question of identity?"

"We shall leave that to the coroner. But there really isn't any question. To begin with, there was no one else in the house; and then the remains were found mixed up with the springs and castors of the chair that Bland was sitting in when he was last seen. Moreover, there were found, with the bones, a pocketknife, a bunch of keys, and a set of steel waistcoat buttons, all identified by Mrs. Brattle as belonging to Bland.

She noticed the cut-steel buttons on his waistcoat when she wished him 'good night.' "

"By the way," said Thorndyke, "was Bland reading by the light of an oil lamp?"

"No," replied Stalker. "There was a two-branch gasalier with a porcelain shade to one burner, and he had the burner alight when Mrs. Brattle left."

Thorndyke reflectively picked up the proposal form and, having glanced through it, remarked: "I see that Bland is described as unmarried. Do you know why he insured his life for this large amount?"

"No; we assumed that it was probably in connection with some loan that he had raised. I learn from the solicitor who notified us of the death that the whole of Bland's property is left to a cousin—a Mr. Lindsay, I think. So the probability is that this cousin had lent him money. But it is not the life claim that is interesting us. We must pay that in any case. It is the fire claim that we want you to look into."

"Very well," said Thorndyke; "I will go round presently and look over the ruins, and see if I can detect any substantial evidence of fraud."

"If you would," said Mr. Stalker, rising to take his departure, "we should be very much obliged. Not that we shall probably contest the claim in any case."

When he had gone, my colleague and I glanced through the papers, and I ventured to remark: "It seems to me that Stalker doesn't quite appreciate the possibilities of this case."

"No," Thorndyke agreed. "But, of course, it is an insurance company's business to pay, and not to boggle at anything short of glaring fraud. And we specialists, too," he added with a smile, "must beware of seeing too much. I suppose that, to a rhinologist, there is hardly such a thing as a healthy nose—unless it is his own—and the uric acid specialist is very apt to find the firmament studded with dumbbell crystals. We mustn't forget that normal cases do exist, after all."

"That is true," said I; "but, on the other hand, the rhinologist's business is with the unhealthy nose, and our concern is with abnormal cases."

Thorndyke laughed. " 'A Daniel come to judgment,' " said he. "But my learned friend is quite right. Our function is to pick holes. So let us pocket the documents and wend Bloomsbury way. We can talk the case over as we go."

We walked an easy pace, for there was no hurry, and a little preliminary thought was useful. After a while, as Thorndyke made no remark, I reopened the subject.

"How does the case present itself to you?" I asked.

"Much as it does to you, I expect," he replied. "The circumstances invite inquiry, and I do not find myself connecting them with the shopkeeper. It is true that the fire occurred on quarter-day; but there is nothing to show that the insurance will do more than cover the loss of stock, chattels, and the profits of trade. The other circumstances are much more suggestive. Here is a house burned down and a man killed. That man was insured for three thousand pounds, and consequently, some person stands to gain by his death to that amount. The whole set of circumstances is highly favourable to the idea of homicide. The man was alone in the house when he died; and the total destruction of both the body and its surroundings seems to render investigation impossible. The cause of death can only be inferred; it cannot be proved; and the most glaring evidence of a crime will have vanished utterly. I think that there is a quite strong prima facie suggestion of murder. Under the known conditions, the perpetration of a murder would have been easy, it would have been safe from detection, and there is an adequate motive.

"On the other hand, suicide is not impossible. The man might have set fire to the house and then killed himself by poison or otherwise. But it is intrinsically less probable that a man should kill himself for another person's benefit than that he should kill another man for his own benefit.

"Finally, there is the possibility that the fire and the man's death were the result of accident; against which is the official opinion that the fire started in two places. If this opinion is correct, it establishes, in my opinion, a strong presumption of murder against some person who may have obtained access to the house."

This point in the discussion brought us to the ruined house, which stood at the corner of two small streets. One of the firemen in charge admitted us, when we had shown our credentials, through a temporary door and down a ladder into the basement, where we found a number of men treading gingerly, ankle deep in white ash, among a litter of charred woodwork, fused glass, warped and broken china, and more or less recognisable metal objects.

"The coroner and the jury," the fireman explained, "come to view the scene of the disaster." He introduced us to the former, who bowed stiffly and continued his investigations.

"These," said the other fireman, "are the springs of the chair that the deceased was sitting in. We found the body—or rather the bones—lying among them under a heap of hot ashes; and we found the buttons of his clothes and the things from his pockets among the ashes, too. You'll see them in the mortuary with the remains."

"It must have been a terrific blaze," one of the jurymen remarked. "Just look at this, sir," and he handed to Thorndyke what looked like part of a gas-fitting, of which the greater part was melted into shapeless lumps and the remainder encrusted with fused porcelain.

"That," said the fireman, "was the gasalier of the first-floor room, where Mr. Bland was sitting. Ah! you won't turn that tap, sir; nobody'll ever turn that tap again."

Thorndyke held the twisted mass of brass towards me in silence, and glancing up the blackened walls, remarked: "I think we shall have to come here again with the Divisional Officer, but meanwhile, we had better see the remains of the body. It is just possible that we may learn something from them."

He applied to the coroner for the necessary authority to make the inspection, and, having obtained a rather ungracious and grudging permission to examine the remains when the jury had "viewed" them, began to ascend the ladder.

"Our friend would have liked to refuse permission," he remarked when we had emerged into the street, "but he knew that I could and should have insisted."

"So I gathered from his manner," said I. "But what is he doing here? This isn't his district."

"No; he is acting for Bettsford, who is laid up just now; and a very poor substitute he is. A non-medical coroner is an absurdity in any case, and a coroner who is hostile to the medical profession is a public scandal. By the way, that gas tap offers a curious problem. You noticed that it was turned off?"

"Yes."

"And consequently that the deceased was sitting in the dark when the fire broke out. I don't see the bearing of the fact, but it is certainly rather odd. Here is the mortuary. We had better wait and let the jury go in first."

We had not long to wait. In a couple of minutes or so the "twelve good men and true" made their appearance with a small attendant crowd of ragamuffins. We let them enter first, and then we followed. The mortuary was a good-sized room, well lighted by a glass roof, and having at its centre a long table, on which lay the shell containing the remains. There was also a sheet of paper on which had been laid out a set of blackened steel waistcoat buttons, a bunch of keys, a steel-handled pocketknife, a steel-cased watch on a partly fused rolled-gold chain, and a pocket corkscrew. The coroner drew the attention of the jury to these objects, and then took possession of them, that they might be identified by witnesses. And meanwhile the jurymen gathered round the shell and stared shudderingly at its gruesome contents.

"I am sorry, gentlemen," said the coroner, "to have to subject you to this painful ordeal. But duty is duty. We must hope, as I think we may, that this poor creature met a painless, if in some respects a rather terrible, death."

At this point, Thorndyke, who had drawn near to the table, cast a long and steady glance down into the shell, and immediately his ordinarily rather impassive face seemed to congeal; all expression faded from it, leaving it as immovable and uncommunicative as the granite face of an Egyptian statue. I knew the symptom of old and began to speculate on its present significance.

"Are you taking any medical evidence?" he asked.

"Medical evidence!" the coroner repeated, scornfully. "Certainly not, sir! I do not waste the public money by employing so-called experts to tell the jury what each of them can see quite plainly for himself. I imagine," he added, turning to the foreman, "that you will not require a learned doctor to explain to you how that poor fellow met his death?" And the foreman, glancing askance at the skull, replied, with a pallid and sickly smile, that he "thought not."

"Do you, sir," the coroner continued, with a dramatic wave of the hand towards the plain coffin, "suppose that we shall find any difficulty in determining how that man came by his death?"

"I imagine," replied Thorndyke, without moving a muscle, or, indeed, appearing to have any muscles to move, "I imagine you will find no difficulty whatever."

"So do I," said the coroner.

"Then," retorted Thorndyke, with a faint, inscrutable smile, "we are, for once, in complete agreement."

As the coroner and jury retired, leaving my colleague and me alone in the mortuary, Thorndyke remarked:

"I suppose this kind of farce will be repeated periodically so long as these highly technical medical inquiries continue to be conducted by lay persons."

I made no reply, for I had taken a long look into the shell, and was lost in astonishment.

"But my dear Thorndyke!" I exclaimed. "What on earth does it mean? Are we to suppose that a woman can have palmed herself off as a man on the examining medical officer of a London Life Assurance Society?"

Thorndyke shook his head. "I think not," said he. "Our friend, Mr. Bland, may conceivably have been a woman in disguise, but he certainly was not a Negress."

"A Negress!" I gasped. "By Jove! So it is. I hadn't looked at the skull. But that only makes the mystery more mysterious. Because, you remember, the body was certainly dressed in Bland's clothes."

"Yes, there seems to be no doubt about that. And you may have noticed, as I did," Thorndyke continued drily, "the remarkably fireproof character of the waistcoat buttons, watch case, knife handle, and other identifiable objects."

"But what a horrible affair!" I exclaimed. "The brute must have gone out and enticed some poor devil of a Negress into the house, have murdered her in cold blood, and then deliberately dressed the corpse in his own clothes! It is perfectly frightful!"

Again Thorndyke shook his head. "It wasn't as bad as that, Jervis," said he, "though I must confess that I feel strongly tempted to let your hypothesis stand. It would be quite amusing to put Mr. Bland on trial for the murder of an unknown Negress, and let him explain the facts himself. But our reputation is at stake. Look at the bones again and a little more critically. You very probably looked for the sex first; then you looked for racial characteristics. Now carry your investigations a step further."

"There is the stature," said I. "But that is of no importance, as these are not Bland's bones. The only other point that I notice is that the fire seems to have acted very unequally on the different parts of the body."

"Yes," agreed Thorndyke, "and that is the point. Some parts are more burnt than others; and the parts which are burnt most are the wrong parts. Look at the backbone, for instance. The vertebrae are as white as chalk. They are mere masses of bone ash. But, of all parts of the skeleton, there is none so completely protected from fire as the backbone, with the great dorsal muscles behind, and the whole mass of the viscera in front. Then look at the skull. Its appearance is quite inconsistent with the suggested facts. The bones of the face are bare and calcined and the orbits contain not a trace of the eyes or other structures; and yet there is a charred mass of what may or may not be scalp adhering to the crown. But the scalp, as the most exposed and the thinnest covering, would be the first to be destroyed, while the last to be consumed would be the structures about the jaws and the base, of which, you see, not a vestige is left."

Here he lifted the skull carefully from the shell, and, peering in through the great foramen at the base, handed it to me.

"Look in," he said, "through the Foramen Magnum—you will see better if you hold the orbits towards the skylight—and notice an even more extreme inconsistency with the supposed conditions. The brain and membranes have vanished without leaving a trace. The inside of the skull is as clean as if it had been macerated. But this is impossible. The brain is not only protected from the fire; it is also protected from contact with the air. But without access of oxygen, although it might become carbonised, it could not be consumed. No, Jervis; it won't do."

I replaced the skull in the coffin and looked at him in surprise.

"What is it that you are suggesting?" I asked.

"I suggest that this was not a body at all, but merely a dry skeleton."

"But," I objected, "what about those masses of what looks like charred muscle adhering to the bones?"

"Yes," he replied, "I have been noticing them. They do, as you say, look like masses of charred muscle. But they are quite shapeless and structureless; I cannot identify a single muscle or muscular group; and there is not a vestige of any of the tendons. Moreover, the distribution is false. For instance, will you tell me what muscle you think that is?"

He pointed to a thick, charred mass on the inner surface of the left tibia or shinbone. "Now this portion of the bone—as many a hockey player has had reason to realise—has no muscular covering at all. It lies immediately under the skin."

"I think you are right, Thorndyke," said I. "That lump of muscle in the wrong place gives the whole fraud away. But it was really a rather smart dodge. This fellow Bland must be an ingenious rascal."

"Yes," agreed Thorndyke; "but an unscrupulous villain too. He might have burned down half the street and killed a score of people. He'll have to pay the piper for this little frolic."

"What shall you do now? Are you going to notify the coroner?"

"No; that is not my business. I think we will verify our conclusions and then inform our clients and the police. We must measure the skull as well as we can without callipers, but it is, fortunately, quite typical. The short, broad, flat nasal bones, with the 'Simian groove,' and those large strong teeth, worn flat by hard and gritty food, are highly characteristic." He once more lifted out the skull, and, with a spring tape, made a few measurements, while I noted the lengths of the principal long bones and the width across the hips.

"I make the cranial-nasal index 55–1," said he, as he replaced the skull, "and the cranial index about 72, which are quite representative numbers; and, as I see that your notes show the usual disproportionate length of arm and the characteristic curve of the tibia, we may be satisfied. But it is fortunate that the specimen is so typical. To the experienced eye, racial types have a physiognomy which is unmistakable on mere inspection. But you cannot transfer the experienced eye. You can only express personal conviction and back it up with measurements.

"And now we will go and look in on Stalker, and inform him that his office has saved three thousand pounds by employing us. After which it will be Westward Ho! for Scotland Yard, to prepare an unpleasant little surprise for Mr. Percival Bland."

There was joy among the journalists on the following day. Each of the morning papers devoted an entire column to an unusually detailed account of the inquest on the late Percival Bland—who, it appeared, met his death by misadventure—and a verbatim report of the coroner's eloquent remarks on the danger of solitary fireside tippling, and the stupefying effects of port wine. An adjacent column contained an equally detailed account of the appearance of the deceased at Bow Street Police Court to answer complicated charges of arson, fraud, and forgery; while a third collated the two accounts with gleeful commentaries.

Mr. Percival Bland, alias Robert Lindsay, now resides on the breezy uplands of Dartmoor, where, in his abundant leisure, he no doubt regrets his misdirected ingenuity. But he has not laboured in vain. To the Lord Chancellor he has furnished an admirable illustration of the danger of appointing lay coroners; and to me an unforgettable warning against the effects of suggestion.

THE NEW HAT

Thomas Burke

Thomas Burke's best-known work is the short story "The Hands of Mr. Ottermole," which some critics cite as the best mystery short story ever written. Because that piece has been so widely anthologized, we've included here one of the author's lesser-known stories, a tale in which the terror centers around three cruel relationships and the awful power of suggestion. Thomas Burke's first popular success, a collection of stories entitled Limehouse Nights, *was set in London's Chinatown, a district whose underworld he depicted brillantly.*

Old Mrs. Manvers was wheeled each morning in her chair from a street in Cyprus to her "pitch" near the Woolwich ferry; and there year by year she sat, moping and hating. She was gaunt and grizzled, and her face was soft. Her outer clothing, and those parts of the inner that were visible, were dulled with usage. She was muffled in two or three worn coats, a woollen scarf, and woollen mittens. Her arms were long, and her hands, that for years had performed no heavy task, were large and shapeless. People first seeing her thought of November the Fifth, and then felt ashamed of themselves.

In this wooden chair she lived and ate and slept. Day by day she sat at her corner, collecting casual coins and small comforts from the workers she knew, and sometimes making a sale from the tray of matches, collar studs, and bootlaces which she carried on the arm of her chair; and morning and evening her niece, Daisy, wheeled her out and home. Daisy was brisk, bright-coloured, and strong, and Mrs. Manvers hated her. She hated her for being whole and strong, and so stressing her aunt's deformity and the deformity of her aunt's boy, who went on crutches. For the boy she had infinite pity and love; indeed, all things, human and animal, that were maimed or misshapen, won from her warm looks and sympathy. But health and grace, wherever she saw them, whether immediately about her, or in pictures, in men or children or horses, filled her with a longing to seize them and grind them beneath her feet.

What she couldn't do to them she could do to Daisy. Daisy was on the spot, at her hand. Through Daisy she could make her protest to the world, and she did. Week by week she noted with appreciation the slow crushing of the spirit, the drooping of her gaiety, the abatement of her step. To cloud Daisy's beauty with distress and mortification was her challenge to things as they are, and as often as Daisy wilted under her words she knew satisfaction. At evenings she would sit propped in her chair in their two-room home, and encourage the boy, Johnny, and prompt him in tauntings, and chuckle at Daisy's discomfiture; and at any attempt on Daisy's part to retort, she would curse her and cuff her.

Under three years of this Daisy wilted in patience. There was nothing else that she could do. Her offenders were safe, beyond requital. They could go to any length and she could make no effective return; for they were cripples. That word quieted in her all anger and indignation. She could not use her fluent physical power against them. She could not lift her voice against them. They were helpless, dependent upon her for every small business of the day. She could not resist their whims. She could not bring herself to the cruelty of abandoning them. Too, she knew no other life and no other people. She had here enough to eat and a place to sleep in, and the timid heart craves always the familiar scene and the known faces, though these faces be unkind. So she remained.

Often she looked at the old woman as she sat forlorn in her chair, fondling her son and crooning over him; and often she wished them dead. Of the hopes and desires and dreams that, thwarted, had turned the old woman's heart sour, Daisy was not of an age to guess. She saw her aunt and the boy only as her cruel captors; the weak triumphant over the strong; and the bonds by which they held her were their own deformities. . . .

That Monday evening she had got the old woman home, and had gone out to buy a few scraps for supper. In the street she met the Flanagan boy, and Johnny and the old woman waited and waited, tempers fuming and rising. Suddenly, Johnny, at the window, cried to his mother: "I can see 'er down there. With that Flanagan." And his mother said, "Ah—that's all she thinks of. Gadding about and flirting. We c'n starve f'r all she cares. There's 'er noo 'at she's just brought 'ome from the Club."

Johnny had an idea. Bursting with it, he leaned from the window and shouted to Daisy, "Day-zee! We want our supper. 'F you don' come up, I'll—I'll get yer noo 'at and smash it!" He turned to his mother. "Ah—that's moved her. I done it."

Flustered and petulant, Daisy came in. Without waiting to take off her coat she set about preparing the meal. But her heart was not in the job. It was adrift with the Flanagan boy.

Johnny sat on the step of his mother's chair. "How much longer? Don't hurry up, I'll—smash yer 'at."

The new hat, bought from subscriptions to the factory Club, hung on a peg behind the door. With a hop and a skip he got it. Daisy, at the fireplace, swung round. "Eh? Here—Johnny—you leave that alone. Johnny—you dare. *Johnny!*" Her face went white. She saw her hard-won treasure, this piece of beauty wrought for the gladdening of the Flanagan boy, in brutal hands. "Now—Johnny—put it down. There's a good boy."

"I ain't a good boy!"

"No, but—Johnny . . ." She was approaching him with hands out. "Now—give it me."

He hopped away and waved it. "Git the supper, then."

"I'm getting the supper, ain't I? Now, Johnny. Put it down."

"Supper first. Then you can 'ave it."

"Now don't be silly." She stood before him, wheedling. "Johnny! Don't be nasty, now. You'll have your supper in a tick."

"I could smash it, yeh know. Wouldn't take me long, neither. Ain't much of it. Bin waiting nearly an hour we 'ave."

Despairing of words, she made a grab at it. He put it behind him with "Yeah!" She stood over him, dodging round him, furious, impotent. He grinned. "Go on—'it me."

Her aunt growled at her. "Leave the boy alone and git the supper."

"But he's got my hat." She was near tears now. "Auntie, make him give me my hat."

"Leave 'im alone, d'y'ear? Tormenting the boy. You and yer 'at. All you think of is dressing up fer the boys, while we have to sit 'ere—"

"I know. But make him give me my hat. . . . Come on, Johnny. I'll get yeh something hot. Something nice."

Johnny stood swinging the hat, grinning. Then the grin faded and the mouth went vicious. "Urr—that's what you say now. Fat lot you cared when you was down there wi' Jimmy Flanagan. Nearly an hour. And me and Mum nearly starving. Urr!"

A snap—and his fingers had the ribbon off. A rip—and the brim came away from the crown. At the first sound Daisy flew at him. In the shock of the moment she forgot his crippled state; forgot everything but the crowding afflictions of her situation and the accumulated distresses of the day. They struggled. The hat went down and he stamped upon it with his one sound foot. Then, no longer Daisy, but a suffering organism, unconscious of what she was doing, she struck him in the face. The crutch slipped, and he went down. His head made a noise on the floor. He lay there howling.

For a moment the three of them were stupid with shock. It was as though a kitten had changed before their eyes into a grown tiger. The old woman snarled and tried to heave herself from the chair and fall upon the girl. Johnny picked himself up and ran to the next room. Daisy, blind with tears, stooped over the remnants of her treasure, gathered them up, and hugged them. Then she became aware of her aunt's voice.

"Come 'ere, you—come 'ere!"

For the first time in her life she ignored the command. She was possessed. She drew back to the wall, and cried between sobs: "Shan't. You can't make me neither. Stood about enough o' you two. All these years. I'm fed up. All I done for you. . . . And now . . . my hat . . ."

The old woman ground words at her through her teeth. "Urr—you beauty. You strike my boy, you—you— Cripple-boy and all. You little bitch! Urr—if I could get at you."

Daisy stood away, arms down, hands clenched, and gave hysterical defiance. "Smashing my hat. . . . Don't care if I did hit him. Serve him right. . . . I wish I was dead. Couple o' beasts—that's what you are. Both of yeh. You—you—you old hag." And grimacing and sobbing she ran upon the old woman and struck the big red face. For a moment her aunt said nothing, and the girl's fury died. "There! You made me. Oh, my God, you made me hit you."

The old woman spoke at last in a whine. "You beauty. You little devil. Striking two 'elpless cripples. You beauty. Come 'ere!" She snapped the last words, and Daisy flew to the window, crying, "No—

no. I'll throw meself out first." And stood there, hands over her face, sobbing with hate.

"Come 'ere at once."

"Shan't."

"All right, me lady. You wait."

For a full minute there was no sound but Daisy's sobs and Johnny whimpering in the next room. Then, just as balance was returning to her, she heard a new noise, and dropped her hands and lifted her head. She screamed. The old woman's hands were on the wheels of the chair, and the chair was coming towards her.

The chair had almost penned her in the corner by the window when with a quick turn she dodged to the farther wall. The woman backed the chair, and came at her again. She made a dash for the door, but a sudden twist on the wheels brought the chair across it. Daisy thrust out her arms and turned again for the wall. Twice round the room they went, rumbling and gasping. The old woman swore in ejaculations. On the second round Daisy dodged towards the inner room, but there her way was barred. Johnny stood there with lifted crutch. As she fell back from him, the chair came near her. She turned, and as she turned Johnny hopped forward and pushed her. She fell against and across the chair. The old woman grabbed her. "Gotcher! Now! Now what yeh gotter say—eh?"

All that night she lay awake, and her young mind wandered. Ideas and emotions that she had long repelled were now welcomed. The woman and boy passed from her consciousness as persons: They became symbols of all things mean and malignant; and the hat became a symbol of spiritual grace. Something in her had died during that struggle, and a new personality had arisen possessed by memory of beauty broken. Running away or self-destruction were no longer thought of. Hate now held her. She wanted to direct upon her aunt the force of her hate; to compel her aunt's recognition of her as an enemy to be feared. She wanted her aunt to suffer as she had suffered. She wanted to shower blows upon that ragged head. . . .

Next morning, sick at heart and sullen of face, Daisy was preparing her for the journey to her "pitch"—hating her behind tight lips—when, from the street, came a sudden chorus of voices that rose without pause to a roar. Both started.

"Dock strikers," said the old woman. "They said there'd be a shindy today."

The noise outside grew swiftly: savage cries, commanding voices, contesting feet, the noise of the jungle animal—Mob. Daisy went to the window. "Oo-er. It's a riot. Police, too. On horseback. One of 'em's got a sword. They're going for the crowd. We can't go out yet." She stood wide-eyed at the window, and the old woman had to shout twice before Daisy heard her. "What?"

"I said: Where's Johnny?"

"Johnny? I dunno. He went out."

"Out? Out where? Go'n fetch 'im in, then. Quick. Don't stand there."

"Go out there? I can't. The crowd's right against the door."

"Right against the door? And Johnny out there?" The old woman waved her arms to command, but Daisy's face was pressed to the window.

"Oh! Listen!"

The roar of voices and the clatter of hoofs came to them in shudders. There was a crash of glass and a big scream. Daisy gave it an echo and clasped her hands. "Oh. Oh. They're riding 'em down. They're riding 'em down. Oh, my God! Oh—Auntie!"

"What is it? What's going on?"

"Oh, look—look!"

"What is it? Wheel me up!"

Daisy did not hear. She pointed through the window, stammering: "Johnny! Johnny!"

"What about it? What is it?" She groaned and twisted herself.

"Johnny—he's out there. In the thick of it. Oh, the noise—like wild animals they are."

The old woman babbled and fumbled with the wheels of her chair. "Go down to 'im, then. Go down to 'im. Or lemme go down. Wheel me down."

"I daren't. I couldn't. They're fighting each other now. Listen."

"Lemme go down. They won't 'urt me. Lemme get my boy. Oh . . . Daisy. . . . Come an' get me down."

"No—no. You mustn't. You couldn't do anything. I'll call him." She lifted the window and called: "Johnny! Johnny!" She turned to the room. "He's heard me. He's looking up. But he can't move. He's wedged in. The police are shoving 'em about."

The old woman gripped the chair arms and struggled to use her limbs and made noises. "Lemme go down!"

"It ain't no use. You can't get out. They're right on the door. Police've got their truncheons out. . . . Oo! There's a man down. They're all on top of him. I can't see Johnny. Not now. . . . Yes, I can. They're all running. And the police after 'em. Oo! There's a man picked Johnny up—running with him. Oo! Oh, my God—he's—he's down. Listen—they're mad. They're mad. He can't get up. The crowd's coming back. They got sticks and stones. They're just on Johnny now. The police are on 'em."

"Lemme come to the window, then. Oh, Daisy, Daisy. Lemme see. Go down to 'em. Get my Johnny."

"It's no good. You can't. Better keep away. It's too awful."

With swift movements the old woman turned the spokes of the wheels and brought herself near to Daisy. But she was too low to see from the window. "Lift me up."

"No. There's things going on there. . . . They won't hurt Johnny. You best not look."

"I must. I must. Oh, lift me up." She scrabbled with her fingers at the sill and drew herself up. From the jungle below came another scream. "I can't see him. I can't see him."

"He was there just now. Where that policeman is. There he is! Trying to run away. He's—oh, my God, he's down again. The horses are over him. They're going this way and that."

"Oh, lemme go down. Oh, my legs. Lemme die with my Johnny. Daisy! I won't be harsh with yeh no more. There's something happened to him. I know there has." She was whimpering now and slipped back into the chair. Her head sagged. She stretched her arms to the window. "My boy!"

Daisy was repeating: "It's no good. You can't—" when she ran from the window to the bed crying: "Oh, my God."

The old woman moaned. "What did yeh see, Daisy? Oh, tell us."

Daisy got up, choking and white, and waved to the street. "Johnny. I saw him. I can't tell yeh what I saw. Under the horses. You can't see him, though. Don't try to. Don't look. It's too awful. When they moved away, I saw him, and—"

The old woman shot upward in the chair. Her eyes stared. Her mouth made noises. Daisy, clasping herself, drew away and looked again through the window, and swung back from it and stood over her aunt. With flying hands she pointed her words. "They've just cleared. And I saw him. Only I didn't really see him. Where he'd been standing there was only—only—Oh!" She flew to the bed and covered her face in the pillow and tried to shut from her ears the noise of the strikers and their enemies, and the gurgling of her aunt.

They stayed so for some minutes; then, following a sharp break in her aunt's voice, she was sensible of a curious stillness in the room. She got up and went to the chair. The head had fallen to one side. The eyes were fixed. She put a hand to her aunt's breast. The old woman was dead.

Then she looked up and breathed heavily and stretched her arms, and turned idly to the window.

Two minutes later there was peace. The battle shifted to the main road, and its noise came in faint splashes to the room. A minute later and through the silence came a stumble and a hop and a noisy clatter of crutch on the floor.

"Ullo, Daisy. Cuh! Ain't half bin a rumpus outside. I see it all. I was at Flanagan's and they took me upstairs to a window. I see it all."

"I know. I saw you there. The row's upset your mother. I think it's done for her. You better go and find a doctor somewhere."

THE MAN IN THE PASSAGE

G. K. Chesterton

G. K. Chesterton was an established critic and dramatist before he turned his hand to mystery writing in 1905. The cases of his most famous detective, an unobtrusive Catholic priest called Father Brown, usually involve an apparent metaphysical mystery, for which his sleuth finds an all too worldly solution. Chesterton delights in presenting paradoxes of human psychology in his fiction. He never wrote a novel featuring Father Brown, but the character appears in six short-story collections.

Two men appeared simultaneously at the two ends of a sort of passage running along the side of the Apollo Theatre in the Adelphi. The evening daylight in the streets was large and luminous, opalescent and empty. The passage was comparatively long and dark, so each man could see the other as a mere black silhouette at the other end. Nevertheless, each man knew the other, even in that inky outline, for they were both men of striking appearance, and they hated each other.

The covered passage opened at one end on one of the steep streets of the Adelphi, and at the other on a terrace overlooking the sunset-coloured river. One side of the passage was a blank wall, for the building it supported was an old, unsuccessful theatre restaurant, now shut up. The other side of the passage contained two doors, one at each end. Neither was what was commonly called the stage door; they were a sort of special and private stage doors, used by very special performers, and in this case by the star actor and actress in the Shakespearean performance of the day. Persons of that eminence often like to have such private exits and entrances, for meeting friends or avoiding them.

The two men in question were certainly two such friends, men who evidently knew the doors and counted on their opening, for each approached the door at the upper end with equal coolness and confidence. Not, however, with equal speed; but the man who walked fast was the man from the other end of the tunnel, so they both arrived before the secret stage door almost at the same instant. They saluted each other with civility, and waited a moment before one of them, the sharper walker, who seemed to have the shorter patience, knocked at the door.

In this and everything else each man was opposite and neither could be called inferior. As private persons, both were handsome, capable, and popular. As public persons, both were in the first public rank. But everything about them, from their glory to their good looks, was of a diverse and incomparable kind. Sir Wilson Seymour was the kind of man whose importance is known to everybody who knows. The more you mixed with the innermost ring in every polity or profession, the more often you met Sir Wilson Seymour. He was the one intelligent man on twenty unintelligent committees—on every sort of subject, from the reform of the Royal Academy to the project of bimetallism for Greater Britain. In the arts especially he was omnipotent. He was so unique that nobody could quite decide whether he was a great aristocrat who had taken up art, or a great artist whom the aristocrats had taken up. But you could not meet him for five minutes without realizing that you had really been ruled by him all your life.

His appearance was "distinguished" in exactly the same sense; it was at once conventional and unique. Fashion could have found no fault with his high silk hat; yet it was unlike anyone else's hat—a little higher, perhaps, and adding something to his natural height. His tall, slender figure had a slight stoop, yet it looked the reverse of feeble. His hair was silver-gray, but he did not look old; it was worn longer than the common, yet he did not look effeminate; it was curly, but it did not look curled. His carefully pointed beard made him look more manly and militant rather than otherwise, as it does in those old admirals of Velasquez with whose dark portraits his house was hung. His gray gloves were a shade bluer, his silver-knobbed cane a shade longer than scores of such gloves and canes flapped and flourished about the theatres and the restaurants.

The other man was not so tall, yet would have struck nobody as short, but merely as strong and handsome. His hair also was curly, but fair and cropped close to a strong, massive head—the sort of head you break a door with, as Chaucer said of the Miller's. His military moustache and the carriage of his shoulders showed him a soldier, but he had a pair of those peculiar, frank, and piercing blue eyes which are more common in sailors. His face was somewhat square, his jaw was square; his shoulders were square, even his jacket was square. Indeed, in the wild school of caricature then current, Mr. Max Beerbohm had represented him as a proposition in the fourth book of Euclid.

For he also was a public man, though with quite another sort of success. You did not have to be in the best society to have heard of Captain Cutler, of the siege of Hong Kong and the great march across China. You could not get away from hearing of him wherever you were; his portrait was on every other postcard; his maps and battles in every other illustrated paper; songs in his honour in every other music-hall turn or on every other barrel organ. His fame, though probably more temporary, was ten times more wide, popular, and spontaneous than the other man's. In thousands of English homes he appeared enormous above England, like Nelson. Yet he had infinitely less power in England than Sir Wilson Seymour.

The door was opened to them by an aged servant or "dresser," whose broken-down face and figure and black, shabby coat and trousers contrasted queerly with the glittering interior of the great actress's dressing room. It was fitted and filled with looking glasses at every angle of refraction, so that they looked like the hundred facets of one huge diamond—if one could get inside a diamond. The other features of luxury—a few flowers, a few coloured cushions, a few scraps of stage costume—were multiplied by all the mirrors into the madness of the Arabian Nights, and danced and changed places perpetually as the shuffling attendant shifted a mirror outwards or shot one back against the wall.

They both spoke to the dingy dresser by name, calling him Parkinson, and asking for the lady as Miss Aurora Rome. Parkinson said she was in the other room, but he would go and tell her. A shade crossed the brow of both visitors; for the other room was the private room of the great actor with whom Miss Aurora was performing, and she was of the kind that does not inflame admiration without inflaming jealousy. In about half a minute, however, the inner door opened, and she entered as she always did, even in private life, so that the very silence seemed to be a roar of applause, and one well deserved. She was clad in a somewhat strange garb of peacock green and peacock blue satins, that gleamed like blue and green metals, such as delight children and esthetes, and her heavy, hot brown hair framed one of those magic faces which are dangerous to all men, but especially to boys and to men growing gray. In company with her male colleague, the great American actor, Isidore Bruno, she was producing a particularly poetical and fantastic interpretation of *Midsummer Night's Dream,* in which the artistic prominence was given to Oberon and Titania, or in other words to Bruno and herself.

Set in dreamy and exquisite scenery, and moving in mystical dances, the green costume, like burnished beetle wings, expressed all the elusive individuality of an elfin queen. But when personally confronted in what was still broad daylight, a man looked only at her face.

She greeted both men with the beaming and baffling smile which kept so many males at the same just dangerous distance from her. She accepted some flowers from Cutler, which were as tropical and expensive as his victories; and another sort of present from Sir Wilson Seymour, offered later on and more nonchalantly by that gentleman. For it was against his breeding to show eagerness, and against his conventional unconventionality to give anything so obvious as flowers. He had picked up a trifle, he said, which was rather a curiosity; it was an ancient Greek dagger of the Mycenean Epoch, and might have been well worn in the time of Theseus and Hippolyta. It was made of brass like all the Heroic weapons, but, oddly enough, sharp enough to prick anyone still. He had really been attracted to it by the leaflike shape; it was as perfect as a Greek vase. If it was of any interest to Miss Rome or could come in anywhere in the play, he hoped she would—

The inner door burst open and a big figure appeared, who was more of a contrast to the explanatory Seymour than even Captain Cutler. Nearly six-foot-six, and of more than theatrical thews and muscles, Isidore Bruno, in the gorgeous leopard skin and golden-brown garments of Oberon, looked like a barbaric god. He leaned on a sort of hunting spear, which across a theatre looked a slight, silvery wand, but which in the small and comparatively crowded room looked as plain as a pikestaff—and as menacing. His vivid, black eyes rolled volcanically, his bronze face, handsome as it was, showed at that moment a combination of high cheekbones with set white teeth, which recalled certain American conjectures about his origin in the Southern plantations.

"Aurora," he began, in that deep voice like a drum of passion that had moved so many audiences, "will you—"

He stopped indecisively because a sixth figure had suddenly presented itself just inside the doorway—a figure so incongruous in the scene as to be almost comic. It was a very short man in the black uniform of the Roman secular clergy, and looking (especially in such a presence as Bruno's and Aurora's) rather like the wooden Noah out of an ark. He did not, however, seem conscious of any contrast, but said with dull civility, "I believe Miss Rome sent for me."

A shrewd observer might have remarked that the emotional temperature rather rose at so unemotional an interruption. The detachment of a professional celibate seemed to reveal to the others that they stood round the woman as a ring of amorous rivals; just as a stranger coming in with frost on his coat will reveal that a room is like a furnace. The presence of the one man who did not care about her increased Miss Rome's sense that everybody else was in love with her, and each in a somewhat dangerous way: the actor with all the appetite of a savage and a spoiled child; the soldier with all the simple selfishness of a man of will rather than mind; Sir Wilson with that daily hardening concentration with which old hedonists take to a hobby; nay, even the abject Parkinson, who had known her before her triumphs, and who followed her about the room with eyes or feet, with the dumb fascination of a dog.

A shrewd person might also have noted a yet odder thing. The man like a black wooden Noah (who was not wholly without shrewdness) noted it with a considerable but contained amusement. It was evident that the great Aurora, though by no means indifferent to the admiration of the other sex, wanted at this moment to get rid of all the men who admired her and be left alone with the man who did not—did not admire her in that sense, at least; for the little priest did admire and even enjoy the firm feminine diplomacy with which she set about her task. There was, perhaps, only one thing that Aurora Rome was clever about, and that was one half of humanity—the other half. The little priest watched, like a Napoleonic campaign, the swift precision of her policy for expelling all while banishing none. Bruno, the big actor, was so babyish that it was easy to send him off in brute sulks, banging the door. Cutler, the British officer, was pachydermatous to ideas, but punctilious about behaviour. He would ignore all hints, but he would die rather than ignore a definite commission from a lady. As to old Seymour, he had to be treated differently; he had to be left to the last. The only way to move him was to appeal to him in confidence as an old friend, to let him into the secret of the clearance. The priest did really admire Miss Rome as she achieved all these three objects in one selected action.

She went across to Captain Cutler and said in her sweetest manner, "I shall value all these flowers because they must be your favourite flowers. But they won't be complete, you know, without *my* favourite flower. *Do* go over to that shop around the corner and get me some lilies-of-the-valley and then it will be *quite lovely."*

The first object of her diplomacy, the exit of the enraged Bruno, was at once achieved. He had already handed his spear in a lordly style like a sceptre to the piteous Parkinson, and was about to assume one of the cushioned seats like a throne. But at this open appeal to his rival there glowed in his opal eyeballs all the sensitive insolence of the slave; he knotted his enormous brown fists for an instant, and then, dashing open the door, disappeared into his own apartments beyond. But meanwhile Miss Rome's experiment in mobilizing the British Army had not succeeded so simply as seemed probable. Cutler had indeed risen stiffly and suddenly, and walked towards the door, hatless, as if at a word of command. But perhaps there was something ostentatiously elegant about the languid figure of Seymour leaning against one of the looking glasses, that brought him up short at the entrance, turning his head this way and that like a bewildered bulldog.

"I must show this stupid man where to go," said Aurora in a whisper to Seymour, and ran out to the threshold to speed the parting guest.

Seymour seemed to be listening, elegant and unconscious as was his posture, and he seemed relieved when he heard the lady call out some last instructions to the captain, and then turn sharply and run laughing down the passage towards the other end, the end on the terrace above the Thames. Yet a second or two after, Seymour's brow darkened again. A man in his position has so many rivals, and he remembered that at the other end of the passage was the corresponding entrance to

Bruno's private room. He did not lose his dignity; he said some civil words to Father Brown about the revival of Byzantine architecture in the Westminster Cathedral, and then, quite naturally, strolled out himself into the upper end of the passage. Father Brown and Parkinson were left alone, and they were neither of them men with a taste for superfluous conversation. The dresser went round the room, pulling out looking glasses and pushing them in again, his dingy dark coat and trousers looking all the more dismal since he was still holding the festive fairy spear of King Oberon. Every time he pulled out the frame of a new glass, a new black figure of Father Brown appeared; the absurd glass chamber was full of Father Browns, upside down in the air like angels, turning somersaults like acrobats, turning their backs to everybody like very rude persons.

Father Brown seemed quite unconscious of this cloud of witnesses, but followed Parkinson with an idly attentive eye till he took himself and his absurd spear into the farther room of Bruno. Then he abandoned himself to such abstract meditations as always amused him—calculating the angles of the mirrors, the angles of each refraction, the angle at which each must fit into the wall . . . when he heard a strong but strangled cry.

He sprang to his feet and stood rigidly listening. After the same instant Sir Wilson Seymour burst back into the room, white as ivory. "Who's that man in the passage?" he cried. "Where's that dagger of mine?"

Before Father Brown could turn in his heavy boots, Seymour was plunging about the room looking for the weapon. And before he could possibly find that weapon or any other, a brisk running of feet broke upon the pavement outside, and the square face of Cutler was thrust into the same doorway. He was still grotesquely grasping a bunch of lilies-of-the-valley. "What's this?" he cried. "What's that creature down the passage? Is this some of your tricks?"

"My tricks!" exclaimed his pale rival, and made a stride towards him.

In the instant of time in which all this happened, Father Brown stepped out into the top of the passage, looked down it, and at once walked briskly towards what he saw.

At this the other two men dropped their quarrel and darted after him, Cutler calling out, "What are you doing? Who are you?"

"My name is Brown," said the priest sadly, as he bent over something and straightened himself again. "Miss Rome sent for me, and I came as quickly as I could. I have come too late."

The three men looked down, and in one of them at least the life died in that late light of afternoon. It ran along the passage like a path of gold, and in the midst of it Aurora Rome lay lustrous in her robes of green and gold, with her dead face turned upwards. Her dress was torn away as in a struggle, leaving the right shoulder bare, but the wound from which the blood was welling was on the other side. The brass dagger lay flat and gleaming a yard or so away.

There was a blank stillness for a measurable time; so that they could hear far off a flower girl's laugh outside Charing Cross, and someone whistling furiously for a taxicab in one of the streets off the Strand. Then the captain, with a movement so sudden that it might have been passion or playacting, took Sir Wilson Seymour by the throat.

Seymour looked at him steadily without either fight or fear. "You need not kill me," he said, in a voice quite cold. "I shall do that on my own account."

The captain's hand hesitated and dropped; and the other added with the same icy candor, "If I find I haven't the nerve to do it with that dagger, I can do it in a month with drink."

"Drink isn't good enough for me," replied Cutler, "but I'll have blood for this before I die. Not yours—but I think I know whose."

And before the others could appreciate his intention he snatched up the dagger, sprang at the other door at the lower end of the passage, burst it open, bolt and all, and confronted Bruno in his dressing room. As he did so, old Parkinson tottered in his wavering way out of the door and caught sight of the corpse lying in the passage. He moved shakily towards it; looked at it weakly with a working face; then moved shakily back into the dressing room again, and sat down suddenly on one of the richly cushioned chairs. Father Brown instantly ran across to him, taking no notice of Cutler and the colossal actor, though the room already rang with their blows and they began to struggle for the dagger. Seymour, who retained some practical sense, was whistling for the police at the end of the passage.

When the police arrived it was to tear the two men from an almost apelike grapple; and, after a few formal inquiries, to arrest Isidore Bruno upon a charge of murder, brought against him by his furious opponent. The idea that the great national hero of the hour had arrested a wrongdoer with his own hand doubtless had its weight with the police, who are not without elements of the journalist. They treated Cutler with a certain solemn attention, and pointed out that he had got a slight slash on the hand. Even as Cutler bore him back across tilted chair and table, Bruno had twisted the dagger out of his grasp and disabled him just below the wrist. The injury was really slight, but till he was removed from the room the half-savage prisoner stared at the running blood with a steady smile.

"Looks a cannibal sort of chap, don't he?" said the constable confidentially to Cutler.

Cutler made no answer, but said sharply a moment after, "We must attend to the . . . the death . . ." and his voice escaped from articulation.

"The two deaths," came in the voice of the priest from the farther side of the room. "This poor fellow was gone when I got across to him." And he stood looking down at old Parkinson, who sat in a black huddle on the gorgeous chair. He also had paid his tribute, not without eloquence, to the woman who had died.

The silence was first broken by Cutler, who seemed not untouched by a rough tenderness. "I wish I was him," he said huskily. "I remember he used to watch her wherever she walked more than—anybody. She was his air, and he's dried up. He's just dead."

"We are all dead," said Seymour, in a strange voice, looking down the road.

They took leave of Father Brown at the corner of the road, with some random apologies for any rudeness they might have shown. Both their faces were tragic, but also cryptic.

The mind of the little priest was always a rabbit warren of wild thoughts that jumped too quickly for him to catch them. Like the white tail of a rabbit, he had the vanishing thought that he was certain of their grief, but not so certain of their innocence.

"We had better all be going," said Seymour heavily. "We have done all we can to help."

"Will you understand my motives," asked Father Brown quietly, "if I say you have done all you can to hurt?"

They both started as if guiltily, and Cutler said sharply, "To hurt?"

"To hurt yourselves," answered the priest. "I would not add to your troubles if it weren't common justice to warn you. You've done nearly everything you could do to hang yourselves, if this actor should be acquitted. They'll be sure to subpoena me; I shall be bound to say that after the cry was heard each of you rushed into the room in a wild state and began quarrelling about a dagger. As far as my words on oath can go, either of you might have done it. You hurt yourselves with that; and then Captain Cutler must hurt himself with the dagger."

"Hurt myself!" exclaimed the captain, with contempt. "A silly little scratch."

"Which drew blood," replied the priest, nodding. "We know there's blood on the brass now. And so we shall never know whether there was blood on it before."

There was a silence; and then Seymour said, with an emphasis quite alien to his daily accent, "But I saw a man in the passage."

"I know you did," answered the cleric Brown, with a face of wood; "so did Captain Cutler. That's what seems so improbable."

Before either could make sufficient sense of it even to answer, Father Brown had politely excused himself and gone stumping up the road with his stumpy old umbrella.

As modern newspapers are conducted, the most honest and most important news is the police news. If it be true that in the twentieth century more space was given to murder than to politics, it was for the excellent reason that murder is a more serious subject. But even this would hardly explain the enormous omnipresence and widely distributed detail of "The Bruno Case," or "The Passage Mystery," in the Press of London and the provinces. So vast was the excitement that for some weeks the Press really told the truth; and the reports of examination and cross-examination, if interminable, even if intolerable, are at least reliable. The true reason, of course, was the coincidence of persons. The victim was a popular actress; the accused a popular actor; and the accused had been caught red-handed, as it were, by the most popular soldier of the patriotic season. In those extraordinary circumstances the Press was paralyzed into probity and accuracy; and the rest of this somewhat singular business can practically be recorded from the reports of Bruno's trial.

The trial was presided over by Mr. Justice Monkhouse, one of those who are jeered at as humorous judges, but who are generally much more serious than the serious judges, for their levity comes from a living impatience of professional solemnity; while the serious judge is really filled with frivolity, because he is filled with vanity. All the chief actors being of a worldly importance, the barristers were well balanced; the prosecutor for the Crown was Sir Walter Cowdray, a heavy but weighty advocate of the sort that knows how to seem English and trustworthy, and how to be rhetorical with reluctance. The prisoner was defended by Mr. Patrick Butler, K.C., who was mistaken for a mere *flâneur* by those who misunderstand the Irish character—and those who had not been examined by him. The medical evidence involved no contradictions, the doctor whom Seymour had summoned on the spot agreeing with the eminent surgeon who had later examined the body. Aurora Rome had been stabbed with some sharp instrument such as a knife or dagger; some instrument, at least, of which the blade was short. The wound was just over the heart, and she had died instantly. When the first doctor saw her she could hardly have been dead for twenty minutes. Therefore, when Father Brown found her, she could hardly have been dead for three.

Some official detective evidence followed, chiefly concerned with the presence or absence of any proof of a struggle; the only suggestion of this was the tearing of the dress at the shoulder, and this did not seem to fit in particularly well with the direction and finality of the blow. When these details had been supplied, though not explained, the first of the important witnesses was called.

Sir Wilson Seymour gave evidence as he did everything else that he did at all—not only well, but perfectly. Though himself much more of a public man than the judge, he conveyed exactly the fine shade of self-effacement before the King's Justice; and though everyone looked at him as they would at the Prime Minister or the Archbishop of Canterbury, they could have said nothing of his part in it but that it was that of a private gentleman, with an accent on the noun. He was also refreshingly lucid, as he was on the committees. He had been calling on Miss Rome at the theatre; he had met Captain Cutler there; they had been joined for a short time by the accused, who had then returned to his own dressing room; they had then been joined by a Roman Catholic priest, who asked for the deceased lady and said his name was Brown. Miss Rome had then gone just outside the theatre to the entrance of the passage, in order to point out to Captain Cutler a flower shop at which he was to buy her some more flowers; and the witness had remained in the room, exchanging a few words with the priest. He had then distinctly heard the deceased, having sent the captain on his errand, turn round laughing and run down the passage towards its other end, where was the prisoner's dressing room. In idle curiosity as to the rapid movements of his friends, he had strolled out to the head of the passage himself and looked down it towards the prisoner's door. Did he see anything in the passage? Yes, he saw something in the passage.

Sir Walter Cowdray allowed an impressive interval, during which the witness looked down, and for all his usual composure seemed to have more than his usual pallor. Then the barrister said in a lower voice, which seemed at once sympathetic and creepy, "Did you see it distinctly?"

Sir Wilson Seymour, however moved, had his excellent brains in full working order. "Very distinctly as regards its outline, but quite indistinctly—indeed not at all—as regards the details inside the outline. The passage is of such length that anyone in the middle of it appears quite black against the light at the other end." The witness lowered his steady eyes once more and added, "I had noticed the fact before, when Captain Cutler first entered it." There was another silence, and the judge leaned forward and made a note.

"Well," said Sir Walter patiently, "what was the outline like? Was it, for instance, like the figure of the murdered woman?"

"Not in the least," answered Seymour quietly.

"What did it look to you like?"

"It looked to me," replied the witness, "like a tall man."

Everyone in court kept his eyes riveted on his pen or his umbrella handle or his book or his boots or whatever he happened to be looking at. They seemed to be holding their eyes away from the prisoner by main force; but they felt his figure in the dock, and they felt it as gigantic. Tall as Bruno was to the eye, he seemed to swell taller and taller when all eyes had been torn away from him.

Cowdray was resuming his seat with his solemn face, smoothing his black silk robes and white silk whiskers. Sir Wilson was leaving the witness box, after a few final particulars to which there were many other witnesses, when the counsel for the defense sprang up and stopped him.

"I shall only detain you a moment," said Mr. Butler, who was a rustic-looking person with red eyebrows and an expression of partial slumber. "Will you tell his lordship how you knew it was a man?"

A faint, refined smile seemed to pass over Seymour's features. "I'm afraid it is the vulgar test of trousers," he said. "When I saw daylight between the long legs I was sure it was a man, after all."

Butler's sleepy eyes opened as suddenly as some silent explosion. "After all!" he repeated slowly. "So you did think first it was a woman?" The red brows quivered.

Seymour looked troubled for the first time. "It is hardly a point of fact," he said, "but if his lordship would like me to answer for my impression, of course I shall do so. There was something about the thing that was not exactly a woman and yet was not quite a man; somehow the curves were different. And it had something that looked like long hair."

"Thank you," said Mr. Butler, K.C., and sat down suddenly, as if he had got what he wanted.

Captain Cutler was a far less plausible and composed witness than Sir Wilson, but his account of the opening incidents was solidly the same. He described the return of Bruno to his dressing room, the dispatching of himself to buy a bunch of lilies-of-the-valley, his return to the upper end of the passage, the thing he saw in the passage, his suspicion of Seymour, and his struggle with Bruno. But he could give little artistic assistance about the black figure that he and Seymour had seen. Asked about its outline, he said he was no art critic—with a somewhat too obvious sneer at Seymour. Asked if it was a man or a woman, he said it looked more like a beast—with a too obvious snarl at the prisoner. But the man was plainly shaken with sorrow and sincere anger, and Cowdray quickly excused him from confirming facts that were already fairly clear.

The defending counsel also was again brief in his cross-examination; although (as was his custom) even in being brief, he seemed to take a long time about it. "You used a rather remarkable expression," he said, looking at Cutler sleepily. "What do you mean by saying that it looked more like a beast than a man or a woman?"

Cutler seemed seriously agitated. "Perhaps I oughtn't to have said that," he said, "but when the brute has huge humped shoulders like a chimpanzee, and bristles sticking out of its head like a pig—"

Mr. Butler cut short his curious impatience in the middle. "Never mind whether its hair was like a pig's," he said. "Was it like a woman's?"

"A woman's!" cried the soldier. "Great Scott, no!"

"The last witness said it was," commented the counsel, with unscrupulous swiftness. "And did the figure have any of those serpentine and semi-feminine curves to which eloquent allusion has been made? No? No feminine curves? The figure, if I understand you, was rather heavy and square than otherwise?"

"He may have been bending forward," said Cutler, in a hoarse and rather faint voice.

"Or again, he may not," said Mr. Butler, and sat down suddenly for the second time.

The third witness called by Sir Walter Cowdray was the little Catholic clergyman, so little compared with the others that his head seemed hardly to come above the box, so that it was like cross-examining a child. But unfortunately Sir Walter had somehow got it into his head (mostly by some ramifications of his family's religion) that Father Brown was on the side of the prisoner, because the prisoner was wicked and foreign and even partly black. Therefore, he took Father Brown up sharply whenever that proud pontiff tried to explain anything; and told him to answer yes or no, and merely tell the plain facts. When Father Brown began, in his simplicity, to say who he thought the man in the passage was, the barrister told him that he did not want his theories.

"A black shape was seen in the passage. And you say you saw the black shape. Well, what shape was it?"

Father Brown blinked as under rebuke; but he had long known the literal nature of obedience. "The shape," he said, "was short and thick, but had two sharp, black projections curved upwards on each side of the head or top, rather like horns, and—"

"Oh, the devil with horns, no doubt," ejaculated Cowdray, sitting down in triumphant jocularity.

"No," said the priest dispassionately. "I know who it was."

Those in court had been wrought up to an irrational but real sense of some monstrosity. They had forgotten the figure in the dock and thought only of the figure in the passage. And the figure in the passage, described by three capable and respectable men who had all seen it, was a shifting nightmare: One called it a woman, and the other a beast, and the other a devil . . .

The judge was looking at Father Brown with level and piercing eyes. "You are a most extraordinary witness," he said, "but there is something about you that makes me think you are trying to tell the truth. Well, who was the man you saw in the passage?"

"He was myself," said Father Brown.

Butler, K.C., sprang to his feet in an extraordinary stillness, and said quite calmly, "Your lordship will allow me to cross-examine?" And then, without stopping, he shot at Brown the apparently disconnected question, "You have heard about this dagger; you know the experts say the crime was committed with a short blade?"

"A short blade," assented Brown, nodding solemnly like an owl, "but a very long hilt."

Before the audience could quite dismiss the idea that the priest had really seen himself doing murder with a short dagger with a long hilt (which seemed somehow to make it more horrible), he had himself hurried on to explain.

"I mean daggers aren't the only things with short blades. Spears have short blades. And spears catch at the end of the steel just like daggers, if they're that sort of fancy spear they have in theatres; like the spear poor old Parkinson killed his wife with, just when she'd sent for me to settle their family troubles—and I came just too late, God forgive me! But he died penitent—he just died of being penitent. He couldn't bear what he'd done."

The general impression in court was that the little priest, who was gabbling away, had literally gone mad in the box. But the judge still looked at him with bright and steady eyes of interest; and the counsel for the defense went on with his questions, unperturbed.

"If Parkinson did it with that pantomine spear," asked Butler, "he must have thrust from four yards away. How do you account for signs of struggle, like the dress dragged off the shoulder?" He had slipped into treating this mere witness as an expert; but no one noticed it now.

"The poor lady's dress was torn," said the witness, "because it was caught in a panel that slid to just behind her. She struggled to free herself, and as she did so Parkinson came out of the prisoner's room and lunged with the spear."

"A panel?" repeated the barrister in a curious voice.

"It was a looking glass on the other side," explained Father Brown. "When I was in the dressing room I noticed that some of them could probably be slid out into the passage."

There was another vast and unnatural silence, and this time it was the judge who spoke. "So you really mean that, when you looked down that passage, the man you saw was yourself—in a mirror?"

"Yes, my lord; that was what I was trying to say," said Brown, "but they asked me for the shape; and our hats have corners just like horns, and so I—"

The judge leaned forward, his old eyes yet more brilliant, and said in specially distinct tones, "Do you really mean to say that when Sir Wilson Seymour saw that wild what-you-call-him with curves and a woman's hair and a man's trousers, what he saw was Sir Wilson Seymour?"

"Yes, my lord," said Father Brown.

"And you mean to say that when Captain Cutler saw that chimpanzee with humped shoulders and hog's bristles, he simply saw himself?"

"Yes, my lord."

The judge leaned back in his chair with a luxuriance in which it was hard to separate the cynicism and the admiration. "And can you tell us why," he asked, "you should know your own figure in a looking glass, when two such distinguished men don't?"

Father Brown blinked even more painfully than before; then he stammered, "Really, my lord, I don't know . . . unless it's because I don't look at it so often."

THE RAPE OF THE SHERLOCK

A. A. Milne

American readers may be unaware that A. A. (Alan Alexander) Milne was not only the creator of the beloved children's classics featuring Winnie the Pooh but the author of adult mysteries. Milne played an important role in developing a subgenre of the detective story that would flourish later on both sides of the Atlantic: the comic mystery story. Even a piece as short as the following displays his comedic gift.

It was in the summer of last June that I returned unexpectedly to our old rooms in Baker Street. I had that afternoon had the unusual experience of calling on a patient, and in my nervousness and excitement had lost my clinical thermometer down his throat. To recover my nerve I had strolled over to the old place, and was sitting in my armchair thinking of my ancient wound, when all at once the door opened, and Holmes glided wistfully under the table. I sprang to my feet, fell over the Persian slipper containing the tobacco, and fainted. Holmes got into his dressing gown and brought me to.

"Holmes," I cried, "I thought you were dead."

A spasm of pain shot across his mobile brow.

"Couldn't you trust me better than that?" he asked, sadly. "I will explain. Can you spare me a moment?"

"Certainly," I answered. "I have an obliging friend who would take my practice for that time."

He looked keenly at me for answer. "My dear, dear Watson," he said, "you have lost your clinical thermometer."

"My dear Holmes—" I began, in astonishment.

He pointed to a fairly obvious bulge in his throat.
"I was your patient," he said.
"Is it going still?" I asked, anxiously.
"Going fast," he said, in a voice choked with emotion.
A twinge of agony dashed across his mobile brow. (Holmes's mobility is a byword in military Clubs.) In a little while the bulge was gone.
"But why, my dear Holmes—"
He held up his hand to stop me, and drew out an old chequebook.
"What would you draw from that?" he asked.
"The balance," I suggested, hopefully.
"What conclusion, I meant," he snapped.
I examined the cheque-book carefully. It was one on Lloyd's Bank, half-empty, and very, very old. I tried to think what Holmes would have deduced, but with no success. At last, determined to have a dash for my money, I said:
"The owner is a Welshman."
Holmes smiled, picked up the book, and made the following rapid diagnosis of the case:
"He is a tall man, right-handed, and a good boxer; a genius on the violin, with an unrivalled knowledge of criminal London, extraordinary powers of perception, a perfectly enormous brain; and, finally, he has been hiding for some considerable time."
"Where?" I asked, too interested to wonder how he had deduced so much from so little.
"In Portland."
He sat down, snuffed the ash of my cigar, and remarked:
"Ah! Flor—de—Dindigul—I—see,—do—you—follow—me—Watson?" Then, as he pulled down his *Encyclopaedia Britannica* from its crate, he added:
"It is my own chequebook."
"But Moriarty?" I gasped.
"There is no such man," he said. "It is merely the name of a soup."

THE MYSTERY OF THE BAGDAD CHEST

Agatha Christie

Hercule Poirot, perhaps the most beloved creation of an English mystery writer after Sherlock Holmes, was not, of course, an Englishman. A World War I refugee from Belgium, and a former member of the Belgian police, Poirot, in his foreignness, accentuates the Britishness of the society that surrounds him. If Poirot's Continental tastes and manners sometimes appear slightly comic, they only serve to confirm the essential soundness of all that is English. Poirot was the hero of Christie's first book, The Mysterious Affair at Styles, *and she continued to write about him for more than fifty years.*

The words made a catchy headline, and I said as much to my friend, Hercule Poirot. I knew none of the persons involved. My interest was merely the dispassionate one of the man in the street. Poirot agreed.

"Yes, it has a flavour of the Oriental, of the mysterious. The chest may very well have been a sham Jacobean one from the Tottenham Court Road; nonetheless, the reporter who thought of naming it the Bagdad Chest was happily inspired. The word 'Mystery' is also thoughtfully placed in juxtaposition, though I understand there is very little mystery about the case."

"Exactly. It is all rather horrible and macabre, but it is not mysterious."

"Horrible and macabre," repeated Poirot thoughtfully.

"The whole idea is revolting," I said, rising to my feet and pacing up and down the room. "The murderer kills this man—his friend—shoves him into the chest, and half an hour later is dancing in that same room with the wife of his victim. Think! If she had imagined for one moment—"

"True," said Poirot thoughtfully. "That much-vaunted possession, a woman's intuition—it does not seem to have been working."

"The party seems to have gone off very merrily," I said with a slight shiver. "And all that time, as they danced and played poker, there was a dead man in the room with them. One could write a play about such an idea."

"It has been done," said Poirot. "But console yourself, Hastings," he added kindly. "Because a theme has been used once, there is no reason why it should not be used again. Compose your drama."

I had picked up the paper and was studying the rather blurred reproduction of a photograph.

"She must be a beautiful woman," I said slowly. "Even from this, one gets an idea."

Below the picture ran the inscription:

A RECENT PORTRAIT OF MRS. CLAYTON,
THE WIFE OF THE MURDERED MAN

Poirot took the paper from me.

"Yes," he said. "She is beautiful. Doubtless she is of those born to trouble the souls of men."

He handed the paper back to me with a sigh.

"Dieu merci, I am not of an ardent temperament. It has saved me from many embarrassments. I am duly thankful."

I do not remember that we discussed the case further. Poirot displayed no special interest in it at the time. The facts were so clear, there was so little ambiguity about them, that discussion seemed merely futile.

Mr. and Mrs. Clayton and Major Rich were friends of fairly long standing. On the day in question, the tenth of March, the Claytons had accepted an invitation to spend the evening with Major Rich. At about seven-thirty, however, Clayton explained to another friend, a Major Curtiss, with whom he was having a drink, that he had been unexpectedly called to Scotland and was leaving by the eight o'clock train.

"I'll just have time to drop in and explain to old Jack," went on Clayton. "Marguerita is going, of course. I'm sorry about it, but Jack will understand how it is."

Mr. Clayton was as good as his word. He arrived at Major Rich's rooms about twenty to eight. The major was out at the time, but his manservant, who knew Mr. Clayton well, suggested that he come in and wait. Mr. Clayton said that he had not time, but that he would come in and write a note. He added that he was on his way to catch a train.

The valet accordingly showed him into the sitting room.

About five minutes later Major Rich, who must have let himself in without the valet hearing him, opened the door of the sitting room, called his man, and told him to go out and get some cigarettes. On his return the man brought them to his master, who was then alone in the sitting room. The man naturally concluded that Mr. Clayton had left.

The guests arrived shortly afterward. They comprised Mrs. Clayton, Major Curtiss, and a Mr. and Mrs. Spence. The evening was spent dancing to the phonograph and playing poker. The guests left shortly after midnight.

The following morning, on coming to do the sitting room, the valet was startled to find a deep stain discolouring the carpet below and in front of a piece of furniture which Major Rich had brought from the East and which was called the Bagdad Chest.

Instinctively the valet lifted the lid of the chest and was horrified to find inside the doubled-up body of a man who had been stabbed to the heart.

Terrified, the man ran out of the flat and fetched the nearest policeman. The dead man proved to be Mr. Clayton. The arrest of Major Rich followed very shortly afterward. The major's defense, it was understood, consisted of a sturdy denial of everything. He had not seen Mr. Clayton the preceding evening and the first he had heard of his going to Scotland had been from Mrs. Clayton.

Such were the bald facts of the case. Innuendoes and suggestions naturally abounded. The close friendship and intimacy of Major Rich and Mrs. Clayton were so stressed that only a fool could fail to read between the lines. The motive of the crime was plainly indicated.

Long experience had taught me to make allowance for baseless calumny. The motive suggested might, for all the evidence, be entirely nonexistent. Some other reason might have precipitated the crime. But one thing did stand out clearly—that Rich was the murderer.

As I say, the matter might have rested there had it not happened that Poirot and I were due at a party given by Lady Chitterton that night.

Poirot, while bemoaning social engagements and declaring a passion for solitude, really enjoyed these affairs enormously. To be made a fuss of and treated as a lion suited him to the ground.

On occasions he positively purred! I have seen him blandly receiving the most outrageous compliments as no more than his due, and uttering the most blatantly conceited remarks, such I can hardly bear to set down.

Sometimes he would argue with me on the subject.

"But, my friend, I am not an Anglo-Saxon. Why should I play the hypocrite? *Si, si,* that is what you do, all of you. The airman who has made a difficult flight, the tennis champion—they look down their noses, they mutter inaudibly that 'it is nothing.' But do they really think that themselves? Not for a moment. They would admire the exploit in someone else. So, being reasonable men, they admire it in themselves. But their training prevents them from saying so.

"Me, I am not like that. The talents that I possess—I would salute them in another. As it happens, in my own particular line, there is no one to touch me. *C'est dommage!* As it is, I admit freely and without the hypocrisy that I am a great man. I have the order, the method, and the psychology in an unusual degree. I am, in fact, Hercule Poirot! Why should I turn red and stammer and mutter into my chin that really I am very stupid? It would not be true."

"There is certainly only one Hercule Poirot," I agreed—not without a spice of malice, of which, fortunately, Poirot remained quite oblivious.

Lady Chitterton was one of Poirot's most ardent admirers. Starting from the mysterious conduct of a Pekingese, he had unravelled a chain which led to a noted burglar and housebreaker. Lady Chitterton had been loud in his praises ever since.

To see Poirot at a party was a great sight. His faultless evening clothes, the exquisite set of his white tie, the exact symmetry of his hair parting, the sheen of pomade on his hair, and the tortured splendour of his famous moustache—all combined to paint the perfect picture of an inveterate dandy. It was hard, at these moments, to take the man seriously.

It was about half-past eleven when Lady Chitterton, bearing down on us, whisked Poirot neatly out of an admiring group, and carried him off—I need hardly say, with myself in tow.

"I want you to go into my little room upstairs," said Lady Chitterton rather breathlessly as soon as she was out of earshot of her other guests. "You know where it is, M. Poirot. You'll find someone there who needs your help very badly—and you will help her, I know. She's one of my dearest friends—so don't say no."

Energetically leading the way as she talked, Lady Chitterton flung open a door, exclaiming as she did so, "I've got him, Marguerita darling. And he'll do anything you want. You *will* help Mrs. Clayton, won't you, M. Poirot?"

And taking the answer for granted, she withdrew with the same energy that characterized all her movements.

Mrs. Clayton had been sitting in a chair by the window. She rose now and came toward us. Dressed in deep mourning, the dull black showed up her fair colouring. She was a singularly lovely woman, and there was about her a simple childlike candour which made her charm quite irresistible.

"Alice Chitterton is so kind," she said. "She arranged this. She said you would help me, M. Poirot. Of course I don't know whether you will or not—but I hope you will."

She had held out her hand and Poirot had taken it. He held it now for a moment or two while he stood scrutinizing her closely. There was nothing ill bred in his manner. It was more the kind but searching look that a famous consultant gives a new patient as the latter is ushered into his presence.

"Are you sure, madame," he said at last, "that I can help you?"

"Alice says so."

"Yes, but I am asking you."

"I don't know what you mean."

"What is it, madame, that you want me to do?"

"You—you—know who I am?" she asked.

"Assuredly."

"Then you can guess what it is I am asking you to do, M. Poirot—Captain Hastings"—I was gratified that she realized my identity—"Major Rich did *not* kill my husband."

"Why not?" Poirot asked.

"I beg your pardon?"

Poirot smiled at her slight discomfiture.

"I said, 'Why not?' " he repeated.

"I'm not sure that I understand."

"Yet it is very simple. The police—the lawyers—they will all ask the same question: Why did Major Rich kill M. Clayton? I ask the opposite. I ask you, madame, why did Major Rich *not* kill Major Clayton?"

"You mean—why I'm so sure? Well, but I *know*. I know Major Rich so well."

"You know Major Rich so well," repeated Poirot tonelessly.

The colour flamed into her cheeks.

"Yes, that's what they'll say, what they'll think! Oh, I know!"

"C'est vrai. That is what they will ask you about—how well you knew Major Rich. Perhaps you will speak the truth, perhaps you will lie. It is very necessary for a woman to lie sometimes. Women must defend themselves—and the lie, it is a good weapon. But there are three people, madame, to whom a woman should speak the truth. To her father confessor, to her hairdresser, and to her private detective—if she trusts him. Do you trust me, madame?"

Marguerita Clayton drew a deep breath. "Yes," she said. "I do. I must," she added.

"Then, how well do you know Major Rich?"

She looked at him for a moment in silence, then she raised her chin defiantly.

"I will answer your question. I loved Jack from the first moment I saw him—two years ago. Lately I think—I believe—he has come to love me. But he has never said so."

"Epatant!" said Poirot. "You have saved me a good quarter of an hour by coming to the point without beating the bush. You have good sense. Now did your husband suspect your feelings?"

"I don't know," said Marguerita slowly. "I thought—lately—that he might. His manner has been different. . . . But that may have been merely my fancy."

"Nobody else knew?"

"I do not think so."

"And—pardon me, madame—you did not love your husband?"

There were, I think, very few women who would have answered that question as simply as this woman did. They would have tried to explain their feelings.

Marguerita Clayton said quite simply, "No."

"Bien. Now we know where we are. According to you, madame, Major Rich did not kill your husband, but you realize that all the evi-

dence points to his having done so. Are you aware, privately, of any flaw in that evidence?"

"No. I know nothing."

"When did your husband first inform you of his visit to Scotland?"

"Just after lunch. He said it was a bore, but he'd have to go. Something to do with land values, he said."

"And after that?"

"He went out—to his club, I think. I—I didn't see him again."

"Now as to Major Rich—what was his manner that evening? Just as usual?"

"Yes, I think so."

"You are not sure?"

Marguerita wrinkled her brows.

"He was a little constrained. With me—not with the others. But I thought I knew why that was. You understand? I am sure the constraint or—or—absent-mindedness perhaps describes it better—had nothing to do with Edward. He was surprised to hear that Edward had gone to Scotland, but not unduly so."

"And nothing else unusual occurs to you in connection with that evening?"

Marguerita thought.

"No, nothing whatever."

"You noticed the chest?"

She shook her head with a little shiver.

"I don't even remember it—or what it was like. We played poker most of the evening."

"Who won?"

"Major Rich. I had very bad luck, and so did Major Curtiss. The Spences won a little, but Major Rich was the chief winner."

"The party broke up—when?"

"About half-past twelve, I think. We all left together."

"Ah!"

Poirot remained silent, lost in thought.

"I wish I could be more helpful to you," said Mrs. Clayton. "I seem to be able to tell you so little."

"About the present—yes. What about the past, madame?"

"The past?"

"Yes. Have there not been incidents?"

She flushed.

"You mean that dreadful little man who shot himself. It wasn't my fault, M. Poirot. Indeed it wasn't."

"It was not precisely of that incident that I was thinking."

"That ridiculous duel? But Italians do fight duels. I was so thankful the man wasn't killed."

"It must have been a relief to you," agreed Poirot gravely.

She was looking at him doubtfully. He rose and took her hand in his.

"I shall not fight a duel for you, madame," he said. "But I will do what you have asked me. I will discover the truth. And let us hope that your instincts are correct—that the truth will help and not harm you."

Our first interview was with Major Curtiss. He was a man of about forty, of soldierly build, with very dark hair and a bronzed face. He had known the Claytons for some years and Major Rich also. He confirmed the press reports.

Clayton and he had had a drink together at the club just before half-past seven, and Clayton had then announced his intention of looking in on Major Rich on his way to Euston.

"What was Mr. Clayton's manner? Was he depressed or cheerful?"

The major considered. He was a slow-spoken man.

"Seemed in fairly good spirits," he said at last.

"He said nothing about being on bad terms with Major Rich?"

"Good Lord, no. They were pals."

"He didn't object to his wife's friendship with Major Rich?"

The major became very red in the face.

"You've been reading those damned newspapers, with their hints and lies. Of course he didn't object. Why, he said to me, 'Marguerita's going, of course.' "

"I see. Now during the evening—the manner of Major Rich—was that much as usual?"

"I didn't notice any difference."

"And madame? She, too, was as usual?"

"Well," he reflected, "now I come to think of it, she was a bit quiet. You know, thoughtful and faraway."

"Who arrived first?"

"The Spences. They were there when I got there. As a matter of fact, I'd called round for Mrs. Clayton, but found she'd already started. So I got there a bit late."

"And how did you amuse yourselves? You danced? You played the cards?"

"A bit of both. Danced first."

"There were five of you?"

"Yes, but that's all right, because I don't dance. I put on the records and the others danced."

"Who danced most with whom?"

"Well, as a matter of fact, the Spences like dancing together. They've got a sort of craze on it—fancy steps and all that."

"So that Mrs. Clayton danced mostly with Major Rich?"

"That's about it."

"And then you played poker?"

"Yes."

"And when did you leave?"

"Oh, quite early. A little after midnight."

"Did you all leave together?"

"Yes. As a matter of fact, we shared a taxi, dropped Mrs. Clayton first, then me, and the Spences took it on to Kensington."

Our next visit was to Mr. and Mrs. Spence. Only Mrs. Spence was at home, but her account of the evening tallied with that of Major Curtiss except that she displayed a slight acidity concerning Major Rich's luck at cards.

Earlier in the morning Poirot had had a telephone conversation with Inspector Japp, of Scotland Yard. As a result, we arrived at Major Rich's rooms and found his manservant, Burgoyne, expecting us.

The valet's evidence was precise and clear.

Mr. Clayton had arrived at twenty minutes to eight. Unluckily Major Rich had just that very minute gone out. Mr. Clayton had said that he couldn't wait, as he had to catch a train, but he would just scrawl a note. He accordingly went into the sitting room to do so. Burgoyne had not actually heard his master come in, as he was running the bath, and Major Rich, of course, let himself in with his own key.

In the valet's opinion it was about ten minutes later that Major Rich called him and sent him out for cigarettes. No, he had not gone into the sitting room. Major Rich had stood in the doorway. He had returned with the cigarettes five minutes later and on this occasion he had gone into the sitting room, which was then empty, save for his master, who was standing by the window smoking.

His master had inquired if his bath were ready and on being told it was, had proceeded to take it. He, Burgoyne, had not mentioned Mr. Clayton, as he assumed that his master had found Mr. Clayton there and let him out himself. His master's manner had been precisely the same as usual. He had taken his bath, changed, and shortly after, Mr. and Mrs. Spence had arrived, to be followed by Major Curtiss and Mrs. Clayton.

It had not occurred to him, Burgoyne explained, that Mr. Clayton might have left before his master's return. To do so, Mr. Clayton would have had to bang the front door behind him, and that the valet was sure he would have heard.

Still in the same impersonal manner, Burgoyne proceeded to his finding of the body. For the first time my attention was directed to the fatal chest. It was a good-sized piece of furniture standing against the wall next to the phonograph cabinet. It was made of some dark wood and plentifully studded with brass nails. The lid opened simply enough. I looked in and shivered. Though well scrubbed, ominous stains remained.

Suddenly Poirot uttered an exclamation. "Those holes there—they are curious. One would say that they had been newly made."

The holes in question were at the back of the chest against the wall. There were four of them, about a quarter of an inch in diameter.

Poirot bent down to examine them, looking inquiringly at the valet.

"It's certainly curious, sir. I don't remember ever seeing those holes in the past, though maybe I wouldn't notice them."

"It makes no matter," said Poirot.

Closing the lid of the chest, he stepped back into the room until he was standing with his back against the window. Then he suddenly asked a question.

"Tell me," he said. "When you brought the cigarettes into your master that night, was there not something out of place in the room?"

Burgoyne hesitated for a minute, then with some slight reluctance he replied, "It's odd your saying that, sir. Now you come to mention it, there was. That screen there that cuts off the draught from the bedroom door—it was moved a bit more to the left."

"Like this?"

Poirot darted nimbly forward and pulled at the screen. It was a handsome affair of painted leather. It already slightly obscured the view of the chest, and as Poirot adjusted it, it hid the chest altogether.

"That's right, sir," said the valet. "It was like that."

"And the next morning?"

"It was still like that. I remember. I moved it away and it was then I saw the stain. The carpet's gone to be cleaned, sir. That's why the boards are bare."

Poirot nodded.

"I see," he said. "Thank you."

He placed a crisp piece of paper in the valet's palm.

"Thank you, sir."

"Poirot," I said when we were out in the street, "that point about the screen—is that a point helpful to Rich?"

"It is a further point against him," said Poirot ruefully. "The screen hid the chest from the room. It also hid the stain on the carpet. Sooner or later the blood was bound to soak through the wood and stain the carpet. The screen would prevent discovery for the moment. Yes—but there is something I do not understand. The valet, Hastings, the valet."

"What about the valet? He seemed a most intelligent fellow."

"As you say, most intelligent. Is it credible, then, that Major Rich failed to realize that the valet would certainly discover the body in the morning? Immediately after the deed he had no time for anything—granted. He shoves the body into the chest, pulls the screen in front of it, and goes through the evening hoping for the best. But after the guests are gone? Surely, then is the time to dispose of the body."

"Perhaps he hoped the valet wouldn't notice the stain?"

"That, *mon ami,* is absurd. A stained carpet is the first thing a good servant would be bound to notice. And Major Rich, he goes to bed and snores there comfortably and does nothing at all about the matter. Very remarkable and interesting, that."

"Curtiss might have seen the stains when he was changing the records the night before?" I suggested.

"That is unlikely. The screen would throw a deep shadow just there. No, but I begin to see. Yes, dimly I begin to see."

"See what?" I asked eagerly.

"The possibilities, shall we say, of an alternative explanation. Our next visit may throw light on things."

Our next visit was to the doctor who had examined the body. His evidence was a mere recapitulation of what he had already given at the inquest. Deceased had been stabbed to the heart with a long thin knife something like a stiletto. The knife had been left in the wound. Death had been instantaneous. The knife was the property of Major Rich and usually lay on his writing table. There were no fingerprints on it, the doctor understood. It had been either wiped or held in a handkerchief. As regards time, any time between seven and nine seemed indicated.

"He could not, for instance, have been killed after midnight?" asked Poirot.

"No. That I can say. Ten o'clock at the outside—but seven-thirty to eight seems clearly indicated."

"There *is* a second hypothesis possible," Poirot said when we were back home. "I wonder if you see it, Hastings. To me it is very plain, and I only need one point to clear up the matter for good and all."

"It's no good," I said. "I don't see it."

"But make an effort, Hastings. Make an effort."

"Very well," I said. "At seven-forty Clayton is alive and well. The last person to see him alive is Rich—"

"So we assume."

"Well, isn't it so?"

"You forget, *mon ami,* that Major Rich denies that. He states explicitly that Clayton was gone when he came in."

"But the valet says that he would have heard Clayton leave because of the bang of the door. And also, if Clayton had left, when did he return? He couldn't have returned after midnight because the doctor says positively that he was dead at least two hours before that. That only leaves one alternative."

"Yes, *mon ami?*" said Poirot.

"That in the five minutes Clayton was alone in the sitting room, someone else came in and killed him. But there we have the same objection. Only someone with a key could come in without the valet's knowing, and in the same way the murderer on leaving would have had to bang the door, and that again the valet would have heard."

"Exactly," said Poirot. "And therefore—"

"And therefore—nothing," I said. "I can see no other solution."

"It is a pity," murmured Poirot. "And it is really so exceedingly simple—as the clear blue eyes of Madame Clayton."

"You really believe—"

"I believe nothing—until I have got proof. One little proof will convince me."

He took up the telephone and called Inspector Japp at Scotland Yard.

Twenty minutes later we were standing before a little heap of assorted objects laid out on a table. They were the contents of the dead man's pockets.

There was a handkerchief, a handful of loose change, a pocketbook containing three pounds ten shillings, a couple of bills, and a worn snapshot of Marguerita Clayton. There was also a pocketknife, a gold pencil, and a cumbersome wooden tool.

It was on this last that Poirot swooped. He unscrewed it and several small blades fell out.

"You see, Hastings, a gimlet and all the rest of it. Ah, it would be a matter of a very few minutes to bore a few holes in the chest with this."

"Those holes we saw?"

"Precisely."

"You mean it was Clayton who bored them himself?"

"Mais, oui—mais, oui! What did they suggest to you, those holes? They were not to *see* through, because they were at the back of the chest. What were they for, then? Clearly for air. But you do not make air holes for a dead body—so clearly they were *not* made by the murderer. They suggest one thing—and one thing only—that a man was going to *hide* in that chest.

"And at once, on that hypothesis, things become intelligible. Mr. Clayton is jealous of his wife and Rich. He plays the old, old trick of pretending to go away. He watches Rich go out, then he gains admission, is left alone to write a note, quickly bores those holes, and then hides inside the chest. His wife is coming there that night. Possibly Rich will put the others off, possibly she will remain after the others have gone, or pretend to go and return. Whatever it is, Clayton will *know*. Anything is preferable to the ghastly suspicion he is enduring."

"Then you mean that Rich killed him *after* the others had gone? But the doctor said that was impossible."

"Exactly. So you see, Hastings, he must have been killed *during* the evening."

"But everyone was in the room!"

"Precisely," said Poirot gravely. "You see the beauty of that? 'Everyone was in the room.' What an alibi! What sangfroid—what nerve—what audacity!"

"I still don't understand."

"Who went behind that screen to wind up the phonograph and

change the records? The phonograph and the chest were side by side, remember. The others are dancing—the phonograph is playing. And the man who does not dance lifts the lid of the chest and thrusts the knife he has just slipped into his sleeve deep into the body of the man who was hiding there."

"Impossible! The man would cry out."

"Not if he were drugged first."

"Drugged?"

"Yes. Who did Clayton have a drink with at seven-thirty? Ah! Now you see. Curtiss! Curtiss has inflamed Clayton's mind with suspicions against his wife and Rich. Curtiss suggests this plan—the visit to Scotland, the concealment in the chest, the final touch of moving the screen. Not so that Clayton can raise the lid a little and get relief—no, so that he, Curtiss, can raise the lid of that chest unobserved.

"The plan is Curtiss's, and observe the beauty of it, Hastings. If Rich had observed that the screen was out of place and moved it back—well, no harm is done. He can make another plan. Clayton hides in the chest, the mild narcotic that Curtiss had administered takes effect. He sinks into unconsciousness. Curtiss lifts up the lid and strikes—and the phonograph goes on playing, 'Walking My Baby Back Home.'"

I found my voice. "Why? But why?"

Poirot shrugged. "Why did a man shoot himself? Why did two Italians fight a duel? Curtiss is of a dark passionate temperament. He wanted Marguerita Clayton. With her husband and Rich out of the way, she would, or so he thought, turn to him."

He added musingly, "These simple childlike women—they are very dangerous. But *mon Dieu!* What an artistic masterpiece! It goes to my heart to hang a man like that. I may be a genius myself, but I am capable of recognizing genius in other people. A perfect murder, *mon ami.* I, Hercule Poirot, say it to you. A perfect murder. *Epatant!*"

STRIDING FOLLY

Dorothy L. Sayers

The aristocratic detective finds its most interesting embodiment in the stories of Dorothy L. Sayers and her Oxford-educated sleuth, Lord Peter Wimsey. Like many of the very first fictional detectives, Wimsey is something of an eccentric, although his affectations do at least have roots in mannerisms and dress that were then common to Oxford and to Wimsey's class. Wimsey provided a vehicle for Sayers, one of the first female graduates of Oxford University, and a distinguished translator and poet, to explore interests wider than those of other detective writers. Wimsey doesn't appear until late in "Striding Folly," but he still manages to play expertly the part of the great detective.

"Shall I expect you next Wednesday for our game as usual?" asked Mr. Mellilow.

"Of course, of course," replied Mr. Creech. "Very glad there's no ill feeling, Mellilow. Next Wednesday as usual. Unless . . ." His heavy face darkened for a moment, as though at some disagreeable recollection. "There may be a man coming to see me. If I'm not here by nine, don't expect me. In that case, I'll come on Thursday."

Mr. Mellilow let his visitor out through the French window and watched him across the lawn to the wicket-gate leading to the Hall grounds. It was a clear October night, with a gibbous moon going down the sky. Mr. Mellilow slipped on his galoshes (for he was careful of his health and the grass was wet) and himself went down past the sundial and the fishpond and through the sunk garden till he came to the fence that bounded his tiny freehold on the southern side. He leaned his arms on the rail and gazed across the little valley at the tumbling river and the wide slope beyond, which was crowned, at a mile's distance, by the ridiculous stone tower known as the Folly. The valley, the slope, and the tower all belonged to Striding Hall. They lay there, peaceful and lovely in the moonlight, as though nothing could ever disturb their fantastic solitude. But Mr. Mellilow knew better.

He had bought the cottage to end his days in, thinking that here was a corner of England the same yesterday, today, and forever. It was strange that he, a chess player, should not have been able to see three moves ahead. The first move had been the death of the old squire. The second had been the purchase by Creech of the whole Striding property. Even then, he had not been able to see why a rich businessman—unmarried and with no rural interests—should have come to live in a spot so remote. True, there were three considerable towns at a few miles' distance, but the village itself was on the road to nowhere. Fool! he had forgotten the Grid! It had come, like a great, ugly chess rook swooping from an unconsidered corner, marching over the country, straddling four, six, eight parishes at a time, planting hideous pylons to mark its progress, and squatting now at Mr. Mellilow's very door.

For Creech had just calmly announced that he was selling the valley to the electrical company; and there would be a huge power plant on the river and workmen's bungalows on the slope, and then Development—which, to Mr. Mellilow, was another name for the devil. It was ironical that Mr. Mellilow, alone in the village, had received Creech with kindness, excusing his vulgar humour and insensitive manners, because he thought Creech was lonely and believed him to be well-meaning, and because he was glad to have the kind of neighbour who could give him a weekly game of chess.

Mr. Mellilow came in sorrowful, and restored his galoshes to their usual resting place on the veranda by the French window. He put the chessmen away and the cat out and locked up the cottage—for he lived quite alone, with a woman coming in by the day.

Then he went up to bed with his mind full of the Folly, and presently he fell asleep and dreamed.

He was standing in a landscape whose style seemed very familiar to him. There was a wide plain, intersected with hedgerows, and crossed in the middle distance by a river, over which was a small stone bridge. Enormous blue-black thunderclouds hung heavy overhead, and the air had the electric stillness of something stretched to snapping point. Far off, beyond the river, a livid streak of sunlight pierced the clouds and lit up with theatrical brilliance a tall, solitary tower. The scene had a curious unreality, as though of painted canvas. It was a picture, and he had an odd conviction that he recognized the handling and could put a name to the artist. "Smooth and tight," were the words that occurred to him. And then, "It's bound to break before long." And then, "I ought not to have come out without my galoshes."

It was important, it was imperative that he should get to the bridge. But the faster he walked, the greater the distance grew, and without his galoshes the going was very difficult. Sometimes he was bogged to the knee, sometimes he floundered on steep banks of shifting shale; and the air was not merely oppressive—it was *hot* like the inside of an oven. He was running now, with the breath labouring in his throat, and when he looked up he was astonished to see how close he was to the tower. The bridge was fantastically small, dwindled to a pinpoint on the horizon, but the tower fronted him just across the river, and close on his right was a dark wood, which had not been there before.

Something flickered on the wood's edge, out and in again, shy and swift as a rabbit; and now the wood was between him and the bridge, and the tower behind it, still glowing in that unnatural streak of sunlight. He was at the river's brink, but the bridge was nowhere to be seen—and the tower, the tower was moving. It had crossed the river. It had taken the wood in one gigantic leap. It was no more than fifty yards off, immensely high, shining, and painted. Even as he ran, dodging and twisting, it took another field in its stride, and when he turned to flee it was there before him. It was a double tower—twin towers—a tower and its mirror image, advancing with a swift and awful stealth from either side to crush him. He was pinned now between them, panting. He saw their smooth, yellow sides tapering up to heaven, and about their feet went a monstrous stir, like the quiver of a crouching cat.

Then the low sky burst like a sluice and through the drench of the rain he leaped at a doorway in the foot of the tower before him and found himself climbing the familiar stair of Striding Folly. "My galoshes will be here," he said, with a passionate sense of relief. The lightning stabbed suddenly through a loophole and he saw a black crow lying dead upon the stairs. Then thunder . . . like the rolling of drums. . . .

Mr. Mellilow, finishing his supper on the following Wednesday, rather hoped that Mr. Creech would not come. He had thought a good deal during the week about the electric-power scheme, and the more he thought about it, the less he liked it. He had discovered another thing which had increased his dislike. Sir Henry Hunter, who owned a good deal of land on the other side of the market town, had, it appeared, offered the company a site more suitable than Striding in every way and on extremely favourable terms. The choice of Striding seemed inexplicable, unless on the supposition that Creech had bribed the surveyor. Sir Henry voiced his suspicions without any mincing of words. He admitted, however, that he could prove nothing.

"But he's crooked," he said. "I have heard things about him in Town. Other things. Ugly rumours."

Mr. Mellilow suggested that the deal might not, after all, go through.

"You're an optimist," said Sir Henry. "Nothing stops a fellow like Creech. Except death. He's a man with enemies. . . ." He broke off, adding darkly: "Let's hope he breaks his neck one of these days—and the sooner the better."

Mr. Mellilow was uncomfortable. He did not like to hear about crooked transactions. Businessmen, he supposed, were like that; but if they were, he would rather not play games with them. It spoiled things, somehow. Better, perhaps, not to think too much about it. He took up the newspaper, determined to occupy his mind, while waiting for Creech, with that day's chess problem. White to play and mate in three.

He had just become pleasantly absorbed when a knock came at the front door. Creech? As early as eight o'clock? Surely not. And in any case, he would have come by the lawn and the French window. But who else would visit the cottage of an evening? Rather disconcerted, he rose to let the visitor in. But the man who stood on the threshold was a stranger.

"Mr. Mellilow?"

"Yes, my name is Mellilow. What can I do for you?"

(A motorist, he supposed, inquiring his way or wanting to borrow something.)

"Ah! that is good. I have come to play chess with you."

"To play chess?" repeated Mr. Mellilow, astonished.

"Yes; I am a commercial traveller. My car has broken down in the village. I have to stay at the inn, and I ask the good Potts if there is anyone who can give me a game of chess to pass the evening. He tells me Mr. Mellilow lives here and plays well. Indeed, I recognize the name. Have I not read *Mellilow on Pawn-Play*? It is yours, no?"

Rather flattered, Mr. Mellilow admitted the authorship of this little work.

"So. I congratulate you. And you will do me the favour to play with me, hey? Unless I intrude, or you have company."

"No," said Mr. Mellilow. "I am more or less expecting a friend, but he won't turn up till nine and perhaps he won't come at all."

"If he come, I go," said the stranger. "It is very good of you." He had somehow oozed his way into the house without any direct invitation and was removing his hat and overcoat. He was a big man with a short, thick, curly beard and tinted spectacles, and he spoke in a deep voice with a slight foreign accent. "My name," he added, "is Czorny. I represent Messrs. Carter & Grandee of Farringdon Street, the manufacturers of electrical fittings."

He grinned widely, and Mr. Mellilow's heart contracted. Such haste seemed almost indecent. Before the site was even taken! He felt an unreasonable resentment against this harmless man. Then he rebuked himself. It was not the man's fault. "Come in," he said, with more cordiality in his voice than he really felt, "I shall be very glad to give you a game."

"I am very grateful," said Mr. Czorny, squeezing his great bulk through into the sitting room. "Ha! you are working out the *Record*'s three-mover. It is elegant but not profound. You will not take long to break his back. You permit that I disturb?"

Mr. Mellilow nodded, and the stranger began to arrange the board for play.

"You have hurt your hand?" inquired Mr. Mellilow.

"It is nothing," replied Mr. Czorny, turning back the glove he wore and displaying a quantity of sticking-plaster. "I break my knuckles trying to start the car. She kick me. Bah! A trifle. I wear a glove to protect him. So, we begin?"

"Won't you have something to drink first?"

"No, no, thank you very much. I have refreshed myself already at the inn. Too many drinks are not good. But do not let that prevent you."

Mr. Mellilow helped himself to a modest whiskey and soda and sat down to the board. He won the draw and took the white pieces, playing his king's pawn to king's fourth.

"So!" said Mr. Czorny, as the next few moves and counter-moves followed their prescribed course, "the *giuoco piano,* hey? Nothing spectacular. We try the strength. When we know what we have each to meet, then the surprises will begin."

The first game proceeded cautiously. Whoever Mr. Czorny might be, he was a sound and intelligent player, not easily stampeded into indiscretions. Twice Mr. Mellilow baited a delicate trap; twice, with a broad smile, Mr. Czorny stepped daintily out between the closing jaws. The third trap was set more carefully. Gradually, and fighting every step of the way, black was forced behind his last defenses. Yet another five minutes, and Mr. Mellilow said gently: "Check"; adding, "and mate in four." Mr. Czorny nodded. "That was good." He glanced at the clock. "One hour. You give me my revenge, hey? Now we know one another. Now we shall see."

Mr. Mellilow agreed. Ten minutes past nine. Creech would not come now. The pieces were set up again. This time, Mr. Czorny took white, opening with the difficult and dangerous Steinitz gambit. Within a few minutes Mr. Mellilow realized that, up till now, his opponent had been playing with him in a double sense. He experienced that eager and palpitating excitement which attends the process of biting off more than one can chew. By half-past nine, he was definitely on the defensive; at a quarter to ten, he thought he spied a way out; five minutes later, Mr. Czorny said, suddenly, "It grows late; we must begin to push a little," and thrust forward a knight, leaving his queen *en prise*.

Mr. Mellilow took prompt advantage of the oversight—and became aware, too late, that he was menaced by the advance of a white rook.

Stupid! How had he come to overlook that? There was an answer, of course . . . but he wished the little room were not so hot and that the stranger's eyes were not so inscrutable behind the tinted glasses. If he could maneuvre his king out of harm's way for the moment and force his pawn through, he had still a chance. The rook moved in upon him as he twisted and dodged; it came swooping and striding over the board, four, six, eight squares at a time; and now the second white rook had darted out from its corner; they were closing in upon him—a double castle, twin castles, a castle and its mirror image: Oh Lord, it was his dream of striding towers, smooth and yellow and painted. Mr. Mellilow wiped his forehead.

"Check!" said Mr. Czorny. And again, "Check!" And then, "Checkmate!"

Mr. Mellilow pulled himself together. This would never do. His heart was thumping as though he had been running a race. It was ridiculous to be so much overwrought by a game of chess, and if there was one kind of man in the world that he despised, it was a bad loser. The stranger was uttering some polite commonplace—he could not tell what—and replacing the pieces in their box.

"I must go now," said Mr. Czorny. "I thank you very much for the pleasure you have so kindly given me. . . . Pardon me, you are a little unwell?"

"No, no," said Mr. Mellilow. "It is the heat of the fire and the lamp. I have enjoyed our games very much. Won't you take anything before you go?"

"No, I thank you. I must be back before the good Potts locks me out. Again, my hearty thanks."

He grasped Mr. Mellilow's hand in his gloved grip and strode quickly into the hall. In another moment he had seized hat and coat and was gone. His footsteps died away along the cobbled path.

Mr. Mellilow returned to the sitting room. A curious episode; he could scarcely believe that it had really happened. There lay the empty board, the pieces in their box, the *Record* on the old oak chest with a solitary tumbler beside it; he might have dozed off and dreamed the whole thing, for all the trace the stranger's visit had left. Certainly the room was very hot. He threw the French window open. A lopsided moon had risen, checkering the valley and the slope beyond with patches of black and white. High up, and distant, the Folly made a pale streak upon the sky. Mr. Mellilow thought he would walk down to the bridge to clear his head. He groped in the accustomed corner for his galoshes. They were not there. "Where on earth has that woman put them?" muttered Mr. Mellilow. And he answered himself, irrationally but with complete conviction, "My galoshes are left up at the Folly."

His feet seemed to move of their own accord. He was through the garden now, walking quickly down the field to the little wooden footbridge. His galoshes were at the Folly. It was imperative that he should fetch them back; the smallest delay would be fatal. "This is ridiculous," thought Mr. Mellilow to himself. "It is that foolish dream running in my head. Mrs. Gibbs must have taken them away to clean them. But while I am here, I may as well go on; the walk will do me good."

The power of the dream was so strong upon him that he was almost surprised to find the bridge in its accustomed place. He put his hand on the rail and was comforted by the roughness of the untrimmed bark. Half a mile uphill now to the Folly. Its smooth sides shone in the moonlight, and he turned suddenly, expecting to see the double image striding the fields behind him. Nothing so sensational was to be seen, however. He breasted the slope with renewed courage. Now he stood close beneath the tower—and with a little shock he saw that the door at its base stood open.

He stepped inside, and immediately the darkness was all about him like a blanket. He felt with his foot for the stair and groped his way up between the newel and the wall. Now in gloom, now in the gleam of a loophole, the spiral seemed to turn endlessly. Then, as his head rose into the pale glimmer of the fourth window, he saw a shapeless blackness sprawled upon the stair. With a sudden dreadful certainty that *this* was what he had come to see, he mounted further and stooped over it. Creech was lying there, dead. Close beside the body lay a pair of galoshes. As Mr. Mellilow moved to pick them up, something rolled beneath his foot. It was a white chess rook. . . .

The police surgeon said that Creech had been dead since about nine o'clock. It was proved that at eight-fifty he had set out towards the wicket-gate to play chess with Mr. Mellilow. And in the morning light the prints of Mr. Mellilow's galoshes were clear, leading down the gravelled path on the far side of the lawn, past the sundial and the fishpond, and through the sunk garden and so over the muddy field and the footbridge, and up the slope to the Folly. Deep footprints they were, and close together, such as a man might make who carried a monstrous burden. A good mile to the Folly and half of it uphill. The doctor looked inquiringly at Mr. Mellilow's spare form.

"Oh, yes," said Mr. Mellilow. "I could have carried him. It's a matter of knack, not strength. You see"—he blushed faintly—"I'm not really a gentleman. My father was a miller and I spent my whole boyhood carrying sacks. Only I was always fond of my books, and so I managed to educate myself and earn a little money. It would be silly to pretend I couldn't have carried Creech. But I didn't do it, of course."

"It's unfortunate," said the superintendent, "that we can't find no trace of this man Czorny." His voice was the most unpleasant Mr. Mellilow had ever heard—a skeptical voice with an edge like a saw. "He never come down to the Feathers, that's a certainty. Potts never set eyes on him, let alone sent him up here with a tale about chess. Nor nobody saw no car neither. An odd gentleman this Mr. Czorny seems to have been. No footmarks to the front door? Well, it's cobbles, so you wouldn't expect none. That his glass of whiskey by any chance, sir? . . . Oh? he wouldn't have a drink, wouldn't he? Ah! And you played two games of chess in this very room? Ah! very absorbing pursoot, so I'm told. You didn't hear poor Mr. Creech come up the garden last night, did you?"

"The window was shut," said Mr. Mellilow, "and the curtains drawn. And Mr. Creech always walked straight over the grass from the wicket-gate."

"H'm!" said the superintendent. "So he comes, or somebody comes, right up onto the veranda and sneaks a pair of galoshes; and you and this Mr. Czorny are so occupied you don't hear nothing."

"Come, Superintendent," said the chief constable, who was sitting on Mr. Mellilow's oak chest and looked rather uncomfortable. "I don't think that's impossible. The man might have worn tennis shoes or something. How about fingerprints on the chessmen?"

"He wore a glove on his right hand," said Mr. Mellilow unhappily. "I remember that he didn't use his left hand at all—not even when taking a piece."

"A very remarkable gentleman," said the superintendent again. "No fingerprints, no footprints, no drinks, no eyes visible, no features to speak of, pops in and out without leaving no trace—a kind of vanishing gentleman." Mr. Mellilow made a helpless gesture. "These the chessmen you was using?" Mr. Mellilow nodded, and the superintendent turned the box upside-down upon the board, carefully extending a vast enclosing paw to keep the pieces from rolling away. "Let's see. Two big 'uns with crosses on the top and two big 'uns with spikes. Four chaps with split-open 'eads. Four 'orses. Two black 'uns—what d'you call these? Rooks, eh? Look more like churches to me. One white church—rook if you like. What's gone with the other one? Or don't these rook-affairs go in pairs like the rest?"

"They must be both there," said Mr. Mellilow. "He was using two white rooks in the endgame. He mated me with them—I remember. . . ."

He remembered only too well. The dream and the double castle moving to crush him. He watched the superintendent feeling in his pocket and suddenly knew the name of the terror that had flickered in and out of the black wood.

The superintendent set down the white rook that had lain by the corpse at the Folly. Colour, height, and weight matched with the rook on the board.

"Staunton men," said the chief constable, "all of a pattern."

But the superintendent, with his back to the French window, was watching Mr. Mellilow's gray face.

"He must have put it in his pocket," said Mr. Mellilow. "He cleared the pieces away at the end of the game."

"But he couldn't have taken it up to Striding Folly," said the superintendent, "nor he couldn't have done the murder, by your own account."

"Is it possible that you carried it up to the Folly yourself," asked the chief constable, "and dropped it there when you found the body?"

"The gentleman has said that he saw this man Czorny put it away," said the superintendent.

They were watching him now, all of them. Mr. Mellilow clasped his head in his hands. His forehead was drenched. "Something must break soon," he thought.

Like a thunderclap there came a blow on the window; the superintendent leaped nearly out of his skin.

"Lord, my lord!" he complained, opening the window and letting a gust of fresh air into the room, "how you startled me!"

Mr. Mellilow gasped. Who was this? His brain wasn't working properly. That friend of the chief constable's, of course, who had disappeared somehow during the conversation. Like the bridge in his dream. Disappeared. Gone out of the picture.

"Absorbin' game, detectin'," said the chief constable's friend. "Very much like chess. People come creepin' right up onto the veranda and you never even notice them. In broad daylight, too. Tell me, Mr. Mellilow—what made you go up last night to the Folly?"

Mr. Mellilow hesitated. This was the point in his story that he had made no attempt to explain. Mr. Czorny had sounded unlikely enough; a dream about galoshes would sound more unlikely still.

"Come now," said the chief constable's friend, polishing his monocle on his handkerchief and replacing it with an exaggerated lifting of the eyebrows. "What was it? Woman, woman, lovely woman? Meet me by moonlight and all that kind of thing?"

"Certainly not," said Mr. Mellilow indignantly. "I wanted a breath of fresh—" He stopped, uncertainly. There was something in the other man's childish-foolish face that urged him to speak the reckless truth. "I had a dream," he said.

The superintendent shuffled his feet, and the chief constable crossed one leg awkwardly over the other.

"Warned of God in a dream," said the man with the monocle, unexpectedly. "What did you dream of?" He followed Mr. Mellilow's glance at the board. "Chess?"

"Of two moving castles," said Mr. Mellilow, "and the dead body of a black crow."

"A pretty piece of fused and inverted symbolism," said the other. "The dead body of a black crow becomes a dead man with a white rook."

"But that came afterwards," said the chief constable.

"So did the endgame with the two rooks," said Mr. Mellilow.

"Our friend's memory works both ways," said the man with the monocle, "like the White Queen's. She, by the way, could believe as many as six impossible things before breakfast. So can I. Pharaoh, tell your dream."

"Time's getting on, Wimsey," said the chief constable.

"Let time pass," retorted the other, "for, as a great chess player observed, it helps more than reasoning."

"What player was that?" demanded Mr. Mellilow.

"A lady," said Lord Peter Wimsey, "who played with living men and mated kings, popes, and emperors."

"Oh," said Mr. Mellilow. "Well—" He told his tale from the beginning, making no secret of his grudge against Creech and his nightmare fancy of the striding electric pylons. "I think," he said, "that was what gave me the dream." And he went on to his story of the galoshes, the bridge, the moving towers, and death on the stairs at the Folly.

"An exceedingly lucky dream for you," said Wimsey. "But I see now why they chose you. Look! It is all clear as daylight. If you had had no dream—if the murderer had been able to come back later and replace your galoshes—if someone else had found the body in the morning with the chess rook beside it and your tracks leading back and home again, that might have been mate in one move. There are two men to look for, Superintendent. One of them belongs to Creech's household, for he knew that Creech came every Wednesday through the wicket-gate to play chess with you; and he knew that Creech's chessmen and yours were twin sets. The other was a stranger—probably the man whom Creech half-expected to call upon him. One lay in wait for Creech and strangled him near the wicket-gate as he arrived; fetched your galoshes from the veranda, and carried the body down to the Folly. And the other came here in disguise to hold you in play and give you an alibi that no one could believe. The one man is strong in his hands and strong in the back—a sturdy, stocky man with feet no bigger than yours. The other is a big man, with noticeable eyes and probably clean-shaven, and he plays brilliant chess. Look among Creech's enemies for those two men and ask them where they were between eight o'clock and ten-thirty last night."

"Why didn't the strangler bring back the galoshes?" asked the chief constable.

"Ah!" said Wimsey; "that was where the plan went wrong. I think he waited up at the Folly to see the light go out in the cottage. He thought it would be too great a risk to come up twice onto the veranda while Mr. Mellilow was there."

"Do you mean," asked Mr. Mellilow, "that he was there, *in* the Folly, watching me, when I was groping up those black stairs?"

"He may have been," said Wimsey. "But probably, when he saw you coming up the slope, he knew that things had gone wrong and fled away in the opposite direction, to the high road that runs behind the Folly. Mr. Czorny, of course, went, as he came, by the road that passes Mr. Mellilow's door, removing his disguise in the nearest convenient place."

"That's all very well, my lord," said the superintendent, "but where's the proof of it?"

"Everywhere," said Wimsey. "Go and look at the tracks again. There's one set going outwards in galoshes, deep and short, made when the body was carried down. One made later, in walking shoes, which is Mr. Mellilow's track going outwards towards the Folly. And the third is Mr. Mellilow again, coming back, the track of a man running very fast. Two out and only one in. Where is the man who went out and never came back?"

"Yes," said the superintendent doggedly. "But suppose Mr. Mellilow made that second lot of tracks himself to put us off the scent, like? I'm not saying he did, mind you, but why couldn't he have?"

"Because," said Wimsey, "he had no time. The in-and-out tracks left by the shoes were made *after* the body was carried down. There is no other bridge for three miles on either side, and the river runs waist-deep. It can't be forded; so it must be crossed by the bridge. But at half-past ten Mr. Mellilow was in the Feathers, on *this* side of the river, ringing up the police. It couldn't be done, Super, unless he had wings. The bridge is there to prove it; for the bridge was crossed three times only."

"The bridge," said Mr. Mellilow, with a great sigh. "I knew in my dream there was something important about that. I knew I was safe if only I could get to the bridge."

YOU CAN'T HANG TWICE

Anthony Gilbert

The climate of the British Isles is tailor-made for mystery, for under the enshrouding fogs all manner of nefarious doings may take place outside the sharp eye of the law. For a story with an assisting fog we turn to Anthony Gilbert, a writer whose true identity, Lucy Beatrice Malleson, Ellery Queen revealed to readers in 1946. The following adventure is the first in a series of short stories the pseudonymous novelist wrote featuring Cockney lawyer Arthur Crook. It took second place in Ellery Queen's worldwide short-story contest in 1946, and is an example of the "inverted" type of detective story invented by Gilbert's predecessor, R. Austin Freeman.

The mist that had been creeping up from the river during the early afternoon had thickened into a grey blanket of fog by twilight, and by the time Big Ben was striking nine and people all over England were turning on their radio sets for the news, it was so dense that Arthur Crook, opening the window of his office at 123 Bloomsbury Street and peering out, felt that he was poised over chaos. Not a light, not an outline, was visible; below him, the darkness was like a pit. Only his sharp ears caught, faint and far away, the uncertain footfall of a benighted pedestrian and the muffled hooting of a motorist ill-advised enough to be caught abroad by the weather.

"An ugly night," reflected Arthur Crook, staring out over the invisible city. "As bad a night as I remember." He shut the window down. "Still," he added, turning back to the desk where he had been working for the past twelve hours, "it all makes for employment. Fogs mean work for the doctor, for the ambulance driver, for the police and the mortician, for the daring thief and the born wrong 'un."

Yes, and work, too, for men like Arthur Crook, who catered specially for the lawless and the reckless and who was known in two continents as the Criminals' Hope and the Judges' Despair.

And even as these thoughts passed through his mind, the driver was waiting, unaware of what the night was to hold, the victim crept out under cover of darkness from the rabbit-hutch-cum-bath that he called his flat, and his enemy watched unseen but close at hand.

In his office, Mr. Crook's telephone began to ring.

The voice at the other end of the line seemed a long way off, as though that also were muffled by the fog, but Crook, whose knowledge of men was wide and who knew them in all moods, realized that the fellow was ridden by fear.

"Mr. Crook," whispered the voice, and he heard the pennies fall as the speaker pressed Button B. "I was afraid it would be too late to find you . . ."

"When I join the forty-hour-a-week campaign I'll let the world know," said Crook affably. "I'm one of those chaps you read about. Time doesn't mean a thing to me. And in a fog like this it might just as well be nine o'clock in the morning as nine o'clock at night."

"It's the fog that makes it possible for me to call you at all," said the voice mysteriously. "You see, in the dark, one hopes he isn't watching."

Hell, thought Crook disappointedly. Just another case of persecution mania, but he said patiently enough, "What is it? Someone on your tail?"

His correspondent seemed sensitive to his change of mood. "You think I'm imagining it? I wish to Heaven I were. But it's not just that I'm convinced I'm being followed. Already he's warned me three times. The last time was tonight."

"How does he warn you?"

"He rings up my flat and each time he says the same thing. 'Is that you, Smyth? Remember—silence is golden,' and then he rings off again."

"On my Sam," exclaimed Crook, "I've heard of better gags at a kids' party. Who is your joking friend?"

"I don't know his name," said the voice, and now it sounded further away than ever, "but—he's the man who strangled Isobel Baldry."

Everyone knows about quick-change artists, how they come onto the stage in a cutaway coat and polished boots, bow, go off and before you can draw your breath they're back in tinsel tights and a tinfoil halo. You can't think how it can be done in the time, but no quick-change artist was quicker than Mr. Crook when he heard that. He became a totally different person in the space of a second.

"Well, now we are going places," he said, and his voice was as warm as a fire that's just been switched on. "What did you say your name was?"

"Smyth."

"If that's the way you want it. . . ."

"I don't. I'd have liked a more distinguished name. I did the best I could spelling it with a Y, but it hasn't helped much. I was one of the guests at the party that night. You don't remember, of course. I'm not the sort of man people do remember. She didn't. When I came to her house that night she thought I'd come to check the meter or something. She'd never expected me to turn up. She'd just said, 'You must come in one evening. I'm always at home on Fridays,' and I thought she just meant two or three people at most. . . ."

"Tête-à-tête with a tigress," said Crook. "What are you anyhow? A lion-tamer?"

"I work for a legal firm called Wilson, Wilson, and Wilson. I don't know if it was always like that on Fridays, but the house seemed full of people when I arrived and—they were all the wrong people, wrong for me, I mean. They were quite young and most of them were either just demobilized or were waiting to come out. Even the doctor had been in the Air Force. They all stared at me as if I had got out of a cage. I heard one say, He looks as if he had been born in a bowler hat and striped p-pants. They just thought I was a joke."

And not much of one at that, thought Mr. Crook unsympathetically.

"But as it happens, the joke's on them," continued the voice, rising suddenly. "Because I'm the only one who knows that Tom Merlin isn't guilty."

"Well, *I* know," Mr. Crook offered mildly, "because I'm defendin' him, and I only work for the innocent. And the young lady knows or she wouldn't have hauled me into this—the young lady he's going to marry, I mean. And of course the real murderer knows. So that makes four of us. Quite a team. Suppose you tell us how you know?"

"Because I was behind the curtain when *he* came out of the Turret Room. He passed me so close I could have touched him, though of course I couldn't see him because the whole house was dark, because of this game they were playing, the one called Murder. I didn't know then that a crime had been committed, but when the truth came out I realized he must have come out of the room where she was, because there was no other place he could have come from."

"Look," said Mr. Crook, "just suppose I've never heard this story before." And probably he hadn't heard this one, he reflected. "Start from page one and just go through to the end. Why were you behind the curtain?"

"I was hiding—not because of the game, but because I—oh, I was so miserable. I ought never to have gone. It wasn't my kind of party. No one paid any attention to me except to laugh when I did anything wrong. If it hadn't been for Mr. Merlin I wouldn't even have had a drink. And he was just sorry for me. I heard him say to the doctor, Isobel ought to remember everyone's human, and the doctor—Dr. Dunn—said, it's a bit late in the day to expect that."

"Sounds a dandy party," said Crook.

"It was—terrible. I couldn't understand why all the men seemed to be in love with her. But they were. She wasn't specially goodlooking, but they behaved as though there was something about her that made everyone else unimportant."

Crook nodded over the head of the telephone. That was the dead woman's reputation. A courtesan manqué—that's how the press had described her. Born in the right period she'd have been a riot. As it was, she didn't do so badly, even in 1945.

"It had been bad enough before," the voice went on. "We'd had charades, and of course I'm no good at that sort of thing. The others were splendid. One or two of them were real actors on the stage, and even the others seemed to have done amateur theatricals half their lives. And how they laughed at me—till they got bored because I was so stupid. They stopped after a time, though I offered to drop out and just be audience; and then I wanted to go back, but Miss Baldry said how could I when she was three miles from a station and no one else was going yet? I could get a lift later. Murder was just as bad as the rest, worse in a way, because it was dark, and you never knew who you might bump into. I bumped right into her and Tom Merlin once. He was telling her she better be careful, one of these days she'd get her neck broken, and she laughed and said, Would you like to do it, Tom? And then she laughed still more and asked him if he was still thinking of that dreary little number—that's what she called her—he'd once thought he might marry. And asked him why he didn't go back, if he wanted to? It was most uncomfortable. I got away and found a window onto the flat roof, what they call the leads. I thought I'd stay there till the game was over. But I couldn't rest even there, because after a minute Mr. Merlin came out in a terrible state, and I was afraid of being seen, so I crept round in the shadows and came into the house through another window. And that's how I found myself in the Turret Room."

"Quite the little Lord Fauntleroy touch," observed Crook, admiringly. "Well?"

"Though, of course, all the lights were out, the moon was quite bright and I could see the blue screen and I heard a sound and I guessed Miss Baldry was hidden there. For a minute I thought I'd go across and find her and win the game, but another second and I realized that there was someone—a man—with her."

"But you don't know who?"

"No."

"Tough," said Crook. "Having a good time, were they?"

"I don't know about a good time. I think the fact is everyone had been drinking rather freely, and they were getting excited, and I never liked scenes—I haven't a very strong stomach, I'm afraid—so I thought I'd get out. They were so much engrossed in one another—You have it coming to you, Isobel—I heard him say. I got out without them hearing me—I did fire-watching, you know, and one learns to move quietly."

"Quite right," assented Crook. "No sense startling a bomb. Well?"

"I went down a little flight of stairs and onto a landing, and I thought I heard feet coming up, so I got behind the curtain. I was terrified someone would discover me, but the feet went down again and I could hear whispers and laughter—everything you'd expect at a party. They were all enjoying themselves except me."

"And Isobel, of course," suggested Crook.

"She had been—till then. Well, I hadn't been behind the curtain for very long when the door of the Turret Room shut very gently, and someone came creeping down. He stopped quite close to me as if he were leaning over the staircase making sure no one would see him come down. I scarcely dared breathe—though, of course, I didn't know then there had been a murder—and after a minute I heard him go down. The next thing I heard was someone coming up, quickly, and going up the stairs and into the Turret Room. I was just getting ready to come out when I heard a man calling, Norman! Norman! For Pete's sake . . . and Dr. Dunn—he was the R.A.F. doctor, but of course you know that—called out, I'm coming. Where are you? And the first man—it was Andrew Tatham, the actor, who came out of the Army after Dunkirk—said, Keep the women out. An appalling thing's happened."

"And, of course, the women came surgin' up like the sea washin' round Canute's feet?"

"A lot of people came up, and I came out from my hiding place and joined them, but the door of the Turret Room was shut, and after a minute Mr. Tatham came out and said, We'd better all go down. There's been an accident, and Dr. Dunn joined him and said, What's the use of telling them that? They'll have to know the truth. Isobel's been murdered, and we're all in a spot."

"And when did it strike you that you had something to tell the police?" enquired Crook drily.

"Not straight away. I—I was very shocked myself. Everyone began to try and remember where they'd been, but, of course, in the dark, no one could really prove anything. I said, I was behind that curtain. I wasn't really playing, but no one listened. I might have been the invisible man. And then one of the girls said, Where's Tom? and Mr. Tatham said, That's queer. Hope to Heaven he hasn't been murdered, too. But he hadn't, of course. He joined us after a minute and said, A good time being had by all? and one of the girls, the one they called Phoebe, went into hysterics. Then Mr. Tatham said, Where on earth have you been? and he said he was on the leads. He wasn't playing either. They all looked either surprised or—a bit disbelieving, and Dr. Dunn said, But if you were on the leads you must have heard something, and he said, Only the usual row. Why? Have we had a murder? And Mr. Tatham said, Stop it, you fool. And then he began to stare at all of us, and said, Tell me, what is it? Why are you looking like that? So then they told him. Some of them seemed to think he must have heard noises, but Dr. Dunn said that if whoever was responsible knew his onions there needn't be enough noise to attract a man at the farther end of the flat roof, particularly as he'd expect to hear a good deal of movement and muttering and so on."

"And when the police came—did you remember to tell them about the chap who'd come out of the Turret Room? Or did you have some special reason for keeping it dark?"

"I—I'm afraid I rather lost my head. You see, I was planning exactly what I'd say when it occurred to me that nobody else had admitted going into that room at all, and I hadn't an atom of proof that my story was true, and—it isn't as if I knew who the man was. . . ."

"You know," said Crook, "it looks like I'll be holding your baby when I'm through with Tom Merlin's."

"I didn't see I could do any good," protested Mr. Smyth. "And then they arrested Mr. Merlin and I couldn't keep silent any longer. Because it seemed to me that though I couldn't tell them the name of the murderer or even prove that Mr. Merlin was innocent, a jury wouldn't like to bring in a verdict of guilty when they heard what I had to say."

"Get this into your head," said Crook sternly. "They won't bring in a verdict of guilty in any circumstances. I'm lookin' after Tom Merlin, so he won't be for the high jump this time. But all the same, you and me have got to get together. Just where do you say you are?"

"On the Embankment—in a call-box."

"Well, what's wrong with you coming along right now?"

"In this fog?"

"I thought you said the fog made it safer."

"Safer to telephone, because the box is quite near my flat." He broke suddenly into a queer convulsive giggle. "Though as a matter of fact I began to think the stars in their courses were against me, when I found I only had one penny. Luckily, there was one in my pocket—I keep one there for an evening paper—"

"Keep that bit for your memoirs," Crook begged him. "Now all you've got to do is proceed along the Embankment. . . ."

"The trams have stopped."

"Don't blame 'em," said Crook.

"And I don't know about the trains, but I wouldn't dare travel by Underground in this weather, and though I think there was one taxi a little while ago . . ."

"Listen!" said Crook. "You walk like I told you till you come to Charing Cross. You can't fall off the Embankment, and if there's no traffic nothing can run you down. The tubes are all right, and from Charing Cross to Russell Square is no way at all. Change at Leicester Square. Got that? You can be in my office within twenty-five minutes. I'm only three doors from the station."

"Wouldn't tomorrow . . . ?" began Smyth, but Crook said, "Not it.

You might have had another warning by tomorrow and this time it might be a bit more lethal than an anonymous telephone message. Now, don't lose heart. It's like going to the dentist. Once it's done, it's over for six months. So long as X thinks you're huggin' your guilty secret to your own buzoom you're a danger to him. Once you've spilt the beans you're safe."

"It's a long way to Charing Cross," quavered the poor little rabbit.

"No way at all," Crook assured him. "And never mind about the trams and the taxicabs. You might be safer on your own feet at that."

Thus is many a true word spoken in jest.

"And now," ruminated Mr. Crook, laying the telephone aside and looking at the great pot-bellied watch he drew from his pocket, "first, how much of that story is true? and second, how much are the police going to believe? If he was a pal of Tom Merlin's, that's just the sort of story he would tell, and if it's all my eye and Betty Martin, he couldn't have thought of a better. It don't prove Tom's innocent, but as he says, it's enough to shake the jury."

It was also, of course, the sort of story a criminal might tell, but in that case he'd have told it at once. Besides, even the optimistic Mr. Crook couldn't suspect Mr. Smyth of the murder. He wasn't the stuff of which murderers are made.

"No personality," decided Crook. "Black tie, wing collar, umbrella, and briefcase, the eight-ten every weekday— Yes, Mr. Brown. Certainly, Mr. Jones. I will attend to that, Mr. Robinson. Back on the six-twelve regular as clockwork, a newsreel or pottering with the window boxes on Saturday afternoons, long lie-in on Sunday"—that was his program until the time came for his longest lie-in of all.

And at that moment neither Mr. Smyth nor Arthur Crook had any notion how near that was.

Crook looked at his watch. "Five minutes before the balloon goes up," he observed. It went up like an actor taking his cue. At the end of five minutes the telephone rang again.

As he made his snail's pace of a way towards Charing Cross, Mr. Smyth was rehearsing feverishly the precise phrases he would use to Mr. Crook. He was so terrified of the coming interview that only a still greater terror could have urged him forward. For there was nothing of the hero about him. The services had declined to make use of him during the war, and it had never occurred to him to leave his safe employment and volunteer for anything in the nature of war work. Fire-watching was compulsory.

"The fact is, I wasn't born for greatness," he used to assure himself. "The daily round, the common task . . . I never wanted the limelight." But it looked as though that was precisely what he was going to get. For the hundredth time he found himself wishing he had never met Isobel Baldry, or, having met her, had never obeyed the mad impulse which made him look up the number she had given him and virtually invite himself to her party. The moment he arrived he knew she had never meant him to accept that invitation.

The darkness seemed full of eyes and ears. He stopped suddenly to see whether he could surprise stealthy footsteps coming after him, but he heard only the endless lapping of black water against the Embankment, the faint noise of the police launch going downstream, and above both these sounds, the frenzied beating of his own heart. He went on a little way, then found to his horror that he could not move. In front of him the darkness seemed impenetrable; behind him the atmosphere seemed to close up like a wall, barring his retreat. He was like someone coming down the side of a sheer cliff who suddenly finds himself paralyzed, unable to move a step in either direction. He didn't know what would have happened, but at that moment a car came through the fog travelling at what seemed to him dangerous speed. It was full of young men, the prototype of those he had met at Isobel Baldry's ill-starred party. They were singing as they went. That gave him a fresh idea, and without moving he began to call, "Taxi! Taxi!" Someone in the car heard him and leaned out to shout, "No soap, old boy," but now panic had him in its grip. And it seemed as if then his luck changed. Another vehicle came more slowly through the darkness.

"Taxi!" he called, and to his relief he heard the car stop.

Relief panted in his voice. "I want to go to Bloomsbury Street. Number 123. Do you know it?"

"Another client for Mr. Cautious Crook." The driver gave a huge chuckle. "Well, well."

"You—you mean you know him?"

"All the men on the night shift know about Mr. Crook. Must work on a night shift 'imself, the hours 'e keeps."

"You mean—his clients prefer to see him at night?" He was startled.

"Yerss. Not so likely to be reckernized by a rozzer, see? Oh, 'e gets a queer lot. Though this is the first time I've bin asked to go there in a fog like this." His voice sounded dubious. "Don't see 'ow it can be done, guvnor."

"But you must. It's most important. I mean, he's expecting me."

"Sure? On a night like this? You should worry."

"But—I've only just telephoned him." Now it seemed of paramount importance that he should get there by hook or crook.

"Just like that. Lumme, you must be in a 'urry."

"I am. I—I don't mind making it worth your while . . ." It occurred to him that to the driver this sort of conversation might be quite an ordinary occurrence. He hadn't realized before the existence of a secret life dependent on the darkness.

"Cost yer a quid," the driver said promptly.

"A pound?" He was shocked.

"Mr. Crook wouldn't be flattered to think you didn't think 'im worth a quid," observed the driver.

Mr. Smyth made up his mind. "All right."

"Sure you've got it on you?"

"Yes. Oh, I see." He saw that the man intended to have the pound before he started on the journey, and he fumbled for his shabby shiny note-case and pulled out the only pound it held and offered it to the driver. Even in the fog the driver didn't miss it. He snapped on the light inside the car for an instant to allow Mr. Smyth to get in, then put it off again, and his fare sank sprawling on the cushions. The driver's voice came to him faintly as he started up the engine.

"After all, guvnor, a quid's not much to save yer neck."

He started. His neck? His neck wasn't in danger. No one thought he'd murdered Isobel Baldry. But the protest died even in his heart within a second. Not his neck but his life—that was what he was paying a pound to save. Now that the car was on its way he knew a pang of security. He was always nervous about journeys, thought he might miss the train, get into the wrong one, find there wasn't a seat. Once the journey started he could relax. He thought about the coming interview; he was pinning all his faith on Arthur Crook. He wouldn't be scared; the situation didn't exist that could scare such a man. And perhaps, he reflected, lulling himself into a false security, Mr. Crook would laugh at his visitor's fears. That's just what I wanted, he'd say. You've solved the whole case for me, provided the missing link. Justice should be grateful to you, Mr. Smyth. . . . He lost himself in a maze of prefabricated dreams.

Suddenly he realized that the cab, which had been crawling for some time, had now drawn to a complete standstill. The driver got down and opened the door.

"Sorry, sir, this perishin' fog. Can't make it, after all."

"You mean, you can't get there?" He sounded incredulous.

"It's my neck as well as yours," the driver reminded him.

"But—I must—I mean are you sure it's impossible? If we go very slowly . . ."

"If we go much slower we'll be proceedin' backwards. Sorry, guvnor, but there's only one place we'll make tonight if we go any further and that's Kensal Green. Even Mr. Crook can't help you once you're there."

"Then—where are we now?"

"We ain't a 'undred miles from Charing Cross," returned the driver cautiously. "More than that I wouldn't like to say. But I'm not taking the cab no further in this. If any mug likes to try pinchin' it 'e's welcome."

Reluctantly Mr. Smyth crawled out into the black street; it was bitterly cold and he shivered.

"I'll 'ave to give you that quid back," said the driver, wistfully.

"Well, you didn't get me to Bloomsbury Street, did you?" He supposed he'd have to give the fellow something for his trouble. He put out one hand to take the note and shoved the other into the pocket where he kept his change. Then it happened, with the same shocking suddenness as Isobel Baldry's death. His fingers had just closed on the note when something struck him with appalling brutality. Automatically he grabbed harder, but it wasn't any use; he couldn't hold it. Besides, other blows followed the first. A very hail of blows in fact, accompanied by shock and sickening pain and a sense of the world ebbing away. He didn't really appreciate what had happened; there was too little time. Only as he staggered and his feet slipped on the wet leaves of the gutter, so that he went down for good, he thought, the darkness closing on his mind forever, "I thought it was damned comfortable for a taxi."

It was shortly after this that Arthur Crook's telephone rang for the second time, and a nervous voice said, "This is Mr. Smyth speaking. I'm sorry I can't make it. I—this fog's too thick. I'll get lost. I'm going right back."

"That's all right," said Crook heartily. "Don't mind me. Don't mind Tom Merlin. We don't matter."

"If I get knocked down in the fog and killed it won't help either of you," protested the voice.

"Come to that, I daresay I won't be any worse off if you are."

"But—you can't do anything tonight."

"If I'm goin' to wait for you I shan't do anything till Kingdom Come."

"I—I'll come tomorrow. It won't make any difference really."

"We've had all this out before," said Crook. "I was brought up strict. Never put off till tomorrow what you can do today."

"But I can't—that's what I'm telling you. I'll come—I'll come at nine o'clock tomorrow."

"If he lets you," said Crook darkly.

"He?"

"He might be waiting for you on the doorstep. You never know. Where are you, by the way?"

"In a call-box."

"I know that. I heard the pennies drop. But where?"

"On the Embankment."

"What's the number?"

"It's a call-box, I tell you."

"Even call-boxes have numbers."

"I don't see . . ."

"Not trying to hide anything from me, Smyth, are you?"

"Of course not. It's Fragonard 1511."

"That's the new Temple exchange. You must have overshot your mark."

"Oh? Yes. I mean, have I?"

"You were coming from Charing Cross. You've walked a station too far."

"It's this fog. I thought—I thought it was Charing Cross just over the road."

"No bump of locality," suggested Crook kindly.

"I can't lose my way if I stick to the Embankment. I'm going straight back to Westminster and let myself into my flat, and I'll be with you without fail at nine sharp tomorrow."

"Maybe," said Crook pleasantly. "Happy dreams." He rang off. "Picture of a gentleman chatting to a murderer," he announced. "Must be a dog's life, a murderer's. So damned lonely. And dangerous. You can't trust anyone, can't confide in anyone, can't even be sure of yourself. One slip and you're finished. One admission of something only the murderer can know and it's the little covered shed for you one of these cold mornings. Besides, you can't guard from all directions at once, and how was the chap who's just rung me to know that Smyth only had two coppers on him when he left his flat tonight, and so he couldn't have put through a second call?"

The inference was obvious. Someone wanted Mr. Crook to believe that Smyth had gone yellow and that was why he hadn't kept his date. Otherwise—who knew?—if the mouse wouldn't come to Mahomet, Mahomet might go looking for the mouse. And later, when the fog had dispersed, some early workman or street cleaner, perhaps even a bobby, would stumble over a body on the Embankment, and he—Crook—would come forward with his story and it would be presumed that the chap had been bowled over in the dark—or even manhandled for the sake of any valuables he might carry. Crook remembered his earlier thought—work for the doctor, for the ambulance driver, for the mortician—and for Arthur Crook. Somewhere at this instant Smyth lay, deprived forever of the power of passing on information, rescuing an innocent man, helping to bring a guilty one to justice, somewhere between Temple Station and Westminster Bridge.

"And my bet 'ud be Temple Station," Crook told himself.

It was a fantastic situation. He considered for a moment ringing the police and telling them the story, but the police are only interested in crimes after they've been committed, and a murder without a corpse just doesn't make sense to them at all. So, decided Mr. Crook, he'd do all their spadework for them, find the body, and then sit back and see how they reacted to that. He locked his office, switched off the lights, and came tumbling down the stairs like a sack of coals. It was his boast that he was like a cat and could see in the dark, but even he took his time getting to Temple Station. Purely as a precaution he pulled open the door of the telephone booth nearby and checked the number. As he had supposed, it was Fragonard 1511.

There was a chance, of course, that X had heaved the body over the Embankment, but Crook was inclined to think not. To begin with, you couldn't go dropping bodies into the Thames without making a splash of some sort, and you could never be sure that the Thames police wouldn't be passing just then. Besides, even small bodies are heavy, and there might be blood. Better on all counts to give the impression of a street accident. Crook had known of cases where men had deliberately knocked out their victims and then ridden over them in cars. Taking his little sure-fire pencil torch from his pocket, Crook began his search. His main fear wasn't that he wouldn't find the body, but that some interfering constable would find him before that happened. And though he had stood up to bullets and blunt instruments in his time, he knew that no career can stand against ridicule. He was working slowly along the Embankment, wondering if the fog would ever lift, when the beam of his torch fell on something white a short distance above the ground. This proved to be a handkerchief tied to the arm of one of the Embankment benches. It was tied hard in a double knot, with the ends spread out, as though whoever put it there wanted to be sure of finding it again. He looked at it for a minute before its obvious significance occurred to him. Why did you tie a white cloth to something in the dark? Obviously to mark a place. If you didn't, on such a night, you'd never find your way back. What he still didn't know was why whoever had put out Smyth's light should want to come back to the scene of the crime. For it was Smyth's handkerchief. He realized that as soon as he had untied it and seen the sprawling letters "Smyth" in one corner. There was something peculiarly grim about a murderer taking his victim's handkerchief to mark the spot of the crime. After that it didn't take him long to find the body. It lay in the gutter, the blood on the crushed forehead black in the bright torchlight, the face dreadful in its disfigurement and dread. Those who talked of the peace of death ought to see a face like that; it might quiet them a bit, thought Mr. Crook grimly. He'd seen death so often you'd not have expected him to be squeamish, but he could wish that someone else had found Mr. Smyth.

Squatting beside the body like a busy little brown elephant, he went through the pockets. He'd got to find out what the murderer had taken that he had to return. Of course, someone else might have found the body and left the handkerchief but an innocent man, argued Crook, would have left his own. You'd have to be callous to take things off the body of a corpse. There wasn't much in the dead man's pockets: a note-case with some ten-shilling notes in it, a season ticket, some loose cash, an old-fashioned turnip watch—that was all. No matches, no cigarettes, of course no handkerchief.

"What's missing?" wondered Mr. Crook, delving his hands into his own pockets and finding there watch, coin purse, note-case, identity card, tobacco pouch, latchkey. . . . "That's it," said Mr. Crook. "He hasn't got a key. But he talked of going back and letting himself in, so he had a key. . . ." There was the chance that it might have fallen out of his pocket, but though Crook sifted through the damp sooty leaves he found nothing; he hadn't expected to, anyhow. There were only two reasons why X should have wanted to get into the flat. One was that he believed Smyth had some evidence against him and he meant to lay hands on it; the other was to fix an alibi showing that the dead man was alive at, say, ten-thirty, at which hour, decided Mr. Crook, the murderer would have fixed an alibi for himself. He instantly cheered up. The cleverest criminal couldn't invent an alibi that an even cleverer man couldn't disprove.

He straightened himself, and as he did so he realized that the corpse had one of its hands folded into a fist; it was a job to open the fingers, but when he had done so he found a morsel of tough white paper with a greenish blur on the torn edge. He recognized that all right, and in defiance of anything the police might say he put the paper into his pocketbook. The whole world by this time seemed absolutely deserted; every now and again a long melancholy hoot came up from the river from some benighted tug or the sirens at the mouth of the estuary echoed faintly through the murk; but these were other-worldly sounds that increased rather than dispelled the deathlike atmosphere. As to cause of death, his guess would be a spanner. A spanner is a nice anonymous weapon, not too difficult to procure, extraordinarily difficult to identify. Only fools went in for fancy weapons like sword-sticks and Italian knives and loaded riding crops, all of which could be traced pretty easily to the owners. In a critical matter like murder it's safer to leave these to the backroom boys and stick to something as common as dirt. Crook was pretty common himself, and, like dirt, he stuck.

"The police are going to have a treat tonight," he told himself, making a beeline for the telephone. His first call was to the dead man's flat, and at first he thought his luck was out. But just when he was giving up hope he could hear the receiver being snatched off and a breathless voice said, "Yes?"

"Mr. Smyth? Arthur Crook here. Just wanted to be sure you got back safely."

"Yes. Yes. But only just. I decided to walk after all."

"Attaboy!" said Mr. Crook. "Don't forget about our date tomorrow."

"Nine o'clock," said the voice. "I will be there."

Mr. Crook hung up the receiver. What a liar you are, he said, and then at long last he dialed 999.

The murderer had resolved to leave nothing to chance. After his call to Mr. Crook's office he came back to the waiting car and drove as fast as he dared back to the block of flats where he lived. At this hour the man in charge of the car park would have gone off duty, and on such a night there was little likelihood of his encountering anyone else. Carefully he ran the car into an empty space and went over it carefully with a torch. He hunted inside in case there should be any trace there of the dead man, but there was none. He had been careful to do all the opening and closing of doors, so there was no fear of fingerprints, but when he went over the outside of the car his heart jumped into his mouth when he discovered blood marks on the righthand passenger door. He found an old rag and carefully polished them off, depositing the rag in a corner at the further end of the car park. This unfortunately showed up the stains of mud and rain on the rest of the body, but he hadn't time to clean all the paintwork; there was still a lot to be done and, as he knew, there is a limit to what a man's nervous system can endure. Locking the car, he made his way round to the entrance of the flats. The porter was just going off; there wasn't a night porter, labour was still scarce, and after ten-thirty the tenants looked after themselves.

"Hell of a night, Meadows," he observed, drawing a long breath. "I was beginning to wonder if I'd be brought in feet first."

The porter, a lugubrious creature, nodded with a sort of morbid zest.

"There'll be a lot of men meeting the Recording Angel in the morning that never thought of such a thing when they went out tonight," he said.

His companion preserved a poker face. "I suppose a fog always means deaths. Still, one man's meat. It means work for doctors and undertakers and ambulance men. . . ." He didn't say anything about Arthur Crook. He wasn't thinking of Arthur Crook. Still under the man's eye he went upstairs, unlocked the door of his flat, slammed it, and, having heard the man depart, came stealing down again, still meeting no one, and gained the street. So far everything had gone according to plan.

It took longer to get to Westminster than he had anticipated, because in the fog he lost his way once, and began to panic, which wasted still more time. His idea was to establish Smyth alive and talking on his own telephone at, say, ten-thirty P.M. Then, if questions should be asked, Meadows could testify to his own return at ten-thirty. On his way back, he would return the key to the dead man's pocket, replace the handkerchief, slip home under cover of darkness. . . . He had it worked out like a BBC exercise.

Luck seemed to be with him. As he entered the flats the hall was in comparative darkness. It was one of those houses where you pushed a button as you came in and the light lasted long enough for you to get up two floors; then you pushed another button and that took you up to the top. There wasn't any lift. As he unlocked the door of the flat the telephone was ringing, and when he unshipped the receiver there was Arthur Crook, of all the men on earth, calling up the dead man. He shivered to think how nearly he'd missed that call. He didn't stay very long; there was still plenty to do and the sooner he got back to his own flat the more comfortable he'd feel. And how was he to guess that he would never walk inside that flat again?

He congratulated himself on his foresight in tying the handkerchief to the arm of the bench; in this weather he might have gone blundering about for an hour before he found the spot where Smyth lay in the gutter, his feet scuffing up the drenched fallen leaves. As it was he saw his landmark, by torchlight, without any trouble. It was then that things started to go wrong. He was level with the seat when he heard the voice of an invisible man exclaim, "Hey there!" and he jumped back, automatically switching off his torch, and muttering, "Who the devil are you?"

"Sorry if I startled you," said the same voice, "but there's a chap here seems to have come to grief. I wish you'd take a look at him."

This was the one contingency for which he had not prepared himself, but he knew he dared not refuse. He couldn't afford at this stage to arouse suspicion. Besides, he could offer to call the police, make for the call-box, and just melt into the fog. Come what might, he had to return the dead man's key. He approached the curb and dropped down beside the body. Crook watched him like a lynx. This was the trickiest time of all; if they weren't careful he might give them the slip yet.

"Have you called the police?" enquired the newcomer, getting to his feet. "If not, I . . ." But at that moment both men heard the familiar sound of a door slamming, and an inspector with two men hovering in the background came forward saying, "Now then, what's going on here."

"Chap's got himself killed," said Crook.

X thought like lightning. He made a slight staggering movement, and as Crook put out his hand to hold him he said, "Silly—slipped on something—don't know what it was." He snapped on his torch again, and stooping, picked up a key. "Must have dropped out of his pocket," he suggested. "Unless," he turned politely to Crook, "unless it's yours."

Crook shook his head.

"Which of you was it called us up?" the inspector went on.

"I did," said Crook. "And then this gentleman came along and . . ." he paused deliberately and looked at the newcomer. It was a bizarre scene, the men looking like silhouettes against the grey blanket of fog, with no light but the torches of the civilians and the bull's-eyes of the force. "Seeing this gentleman's a doctor . . ." As he had anticipated there was an interruption.

"What's that you said?"

"Penalty of fame," said Crook. "Saw your picture in the papers at the time of the Baldry case. Dr. Noel Dunn, isn't it? And p'raps I should introduce myself. I'm Arthur Crook, one of the three men living who *know* Tom Merling didn't kill Miss Baldry, the others bein' Tom himself and, of course, the murderer."

"Isn't that a coincidence?" said Dr. Dunn.

"There's a bigger one coming," Crook warned him. "While I was waitin' I had a look-see at that little chap's identity card, and who do you think he is? Mr. Alfred Smyth, also interested in the Baldry case."

The doctor swung down his torch. "So that's where I'd seen him before? I had a feeling the face was familiar in a way, only . . ."

"He is a bit knocked about, isn't he?" said Crook. "What should you say did that?"

"I shouldn't care to hazard a guess without a closer examination. At first I took it for granted he'd been bowled over by a car. . . ."

"In that case we ought to be able to trace the car. He can't have gotten all that damage and not left any of his blood on the hood."

There was more noise and a police ambulance drove up and spewed men all over the road. Crook lifted his head and felt a breath of wind on his face. That meant the fog would soon start to lift. Long before morning it would have gone. The inspector turned to the two men.

"I'll want you to come with me," he said. "There's a few things I want to know."

"I can't help you," said Dunn sharply, but the inspector told him, "We'll need someone to identify the body."

"Mr. Crook can do that. He knows him."

"Always glad to learn," said Crook.

"But you . . ." He stopped.

"You don't know the police the way I do," Crook assured him. "Just because a chap carries an identity card marked Alfred Smyth—that ain't proof. I never set eyes on him before."

"Mr. Crook's right," said the inspector. "We want someone who saw him when he was alive."

They all piled into the car, Crook and Dunn jammed together, and no one talked. Dunn was thinking hard. Sold for a sucker, he thought. If I hadn't tried so hard for an alibi—perhaps, though, they won't touch Meadows. Meadows will remember, all the same. He'll think it's fishy. And the car. Of course there was blood on the car. If they examine it they'll notice it's washed clean in one place. They'll want to know why. No sense saying I was coming back from the pictures. Meadows can wreck that. Besides, Baron, the man who looks after the cars, may remember mine hadn't come in when he went off duty. Round and round like a squirrel in its cage went his tormented mind. There must be some way out, he was thinking, as thousands have thought before him. They've no proof, no actual proof at all. Outwardly he was calm enough, maintaining the attitude that he couldn't imagine why they wanted him. But inside he was panicking. He didn't like the station surroundings, he didn't like the look on the inspector's face, most of all he feared Crook. The police had to keep the rules; Crook had never heard of Queensberry. To him a fair fight was gouging, shoving, and kicking in the pit of the stomach. A terrible man. But he stuck to it, they hadn't got anything on him that added up to murder. He'd had the forethought to get rid of the spanner, dropped it in one of those disused pig buckets that still disfigured London's streets; but he'd had to use the one near his own flats, because in the dark he couldn't find any others. He thought now the river might have been safer.

He tried to seem perfectly at ease, pulled off his Burberry and threw it over the back of a chair, produced his cigarette case.

"Of course, our own doctor will go over the man," the inspector said, "but how long should you say he'd been dead, Dr. Dunn?"

He hesitated. "Not so easy. He was a little chap and it's a bitter cold night. But not long."

"But more than twenty minutes?" the inspector suggested.

"Yes, more than that, of course."

"That's screwy," said the inspector. "I mean, Mr. Crook was talking to him on the telephone in his flat twenty minutes before you happened along."

He couldn't think how he'd forgotten that telephone conversation. That, intended for his prime alibi, was going to ball up everything.

"I don't see how he could," he protested. "Not unless the chap's got someone doubling for him."

"You know all the answers," agreed Crook. "Matter of fact, the same chap seems to be making quite a habit of it. He rang me a bit earlier from Fragonard 1511 to tell me Smyth couldn't keep an appointment tonight. Well, nobody knew about that but Smyth and me, so how did X know he wasn't coming, if he hadn't made sure of it himself?"

"Don't ask me," said Dunn.

"We are asking you," said the inspector deliberately.

The doctor stared. "Look here, you're on the wrong tack if you think I know anything. It was just chance. Why don't you send a man round to Smyth's flat and see who's there?"

"We did think of that," the inspector told him. "But there wasn't anyone . . ."

"Then—perhaps this is Mr. Crook's idea of a joke."

"Oh no," said Crook, looking shocked. "I never think murder's a joke. A living, perhaps, but not a joke."

Dunn made a movement as though to rise. "I'm sorry I can't help you . . ."

"I wouldn't be too sure about that," drawled Crook.

"What does that mean?"

"There's just one point the inspector hasn't mentioned. When I found that poor little devil tonight he'd got a bit of paper in his hand. All right, inspector. I'll explain in a minute. Just now, let it ride." He turned back to Dr. Noel Dunn. "It was a bit of a treasury note, and it seemed to me that if we could find the rest of that note, why then we might be able to lay hands on the murderer."

"You might. And you think you know where the note is?"

"I could make a guess."

"If you think I've got it . . ." Dunn pulled out his wallet and threw it contemptuously on the table. "You can look for yourself."

"Oh, I don't expect it would be there," replied Crook, paying no attention to the wallet. "But—every murderer makes one mistake, Dunn. If he didn't, God help the police. And help innocent men, too. And a man with murder on his hands is like a chap trying to look four ways at once. Now that note suggested something to me. You don't go round carrying notes in a fog, as if they were torches. You'd only get a note out if you were going to pay somebody, and who's the only person you're likely to want to pay in such circumstances? I'm talking like a damned politician," he added disgustedly. "But you do see what I'm drivin' at?"

"I'm only a doctor," said Dunn. "Not a professional thought-reader."

"You'd pay a man who drove you to your destination—or tried to. There was some reason why Smyth had a note in his hand, and my guess is he was tryin' to pay some chap off. That would explain his bein' at Temple Station. On his own feet he wouldn't have passed Charing Cross, not a chap as frightened of the dark as he was. While he was offerin' the note, X knocked him out, and realizin' that funny questions might be asked if the note was found with him, he'd remove it. You agree so far?"

"I don't know as much about murder as you do, Mr. Crook," said Dunn.

"That's your trouble," Mr. Crook agreed. "That's always the trouble of amateurs setting up against pros. They're bound to lose. Let's go on. X removes the note. So far, so good. But he's got a lot to remember and not much time. He can't be blamed if he don't remember it's trifles that hang a man. If I was asked, I'd say X shoved that note into his pocket, meanin' to get rid of it later, and I'd say it was there still."

"You're welcome to search my pockets," Dunn assured him. "But I warn you, Crook, you're making a big mistake. Your reputation's not going to be worth even the bit of a note you found in Smyth's hand when this story breaks."

"I'll chance it," said Crook.

At a nod from the inspector the police took up Dunn's Burberry and began to go through the pockets. During the next thirty seconds you could have heard a pin drop. Then the man brought out a fist like a ham, and in it was a crumpled ten-shilling note with one corner missing!

"Anything to say to that?" enquired Crook.

Dunn put back his head and let out a roar of laughter. "You think you're smart, don't you? You planted that on me, I suppose, when we were coming. But, as it happens, Smyth's note was for a pound, not ten shillings. You didn't know that, did you?"

"Oh, yes," said Crook, "I did—because I have the odd bit of the note in my wallet. One of the old green ones it was. What I'm wondering is—*How did you?*"

"That was highly irregular, Mr. Crook," observed the inspector, drawing down the corners of his mouth, after the doctor had been taken away.

"It beats me how the police even catch as many criminals as they do," returned Crook frankly. "Stands to reason if you're after a weasel you got to play like a weasel. And a gentleman—and all the police force are gentlemen—don't know a thing about weasels."

"Funny the little things that catch 'em," suggested the inspector, wisely letting that ride.

"I reckoned that if he saw the wrong note suddenly shoved under his nose he wouldn't be able to stop himself. It's what I've always said. Murderers get caught because they're yellow. If they just did their job and left it at that, they might die in their beds at ninety-nine. But the minute they've socked their man they start feverishly buildin' a little tent to hide in, and presently some chap comes along, who might never have noticed them, but gets curious about the little tent. When you start checking up his story I bet you'll find he's been buildin' alibis like a beaver buildin' a dam. And it's his alibis are goin' to hang him in the end."

His last word in this case was to Tom Merlin and the girl Tom was still going to marry.

"Justice is the screwiest thing there is," he told them. "You're not out of chokey because Noel Dunn killed the Baldry dame, though he's admitted that, too. Well, why not? We know he got Smyth, and you can't hang twice. But it was his killing Smyth that put you back on your feet. If he hadn't done that, we might have had quite a job straightenin' things out. Y'know the wisest fellow ever lived? And don't tell me Solomon."

"Who, Mr. Crook?" asked Tom Merlin's girl, hanging on Tom's arm.

"Brer Rabbit. And why? Becos he lay low and said nuffin. And then they tell you animals are a lower order of creation!"

A POSTERIORI

Helen Simpson

Had she not been killed in the Nazi blitz of London, Helen Simpson might have become one of England's leading crime writers. The tale we've chosen to represent her work is a tongue-in-cheek spy piece that shows to advantage her ever so English sense of the absurd.

At about one o'clock on the last night of her stay in Pontdidier-les-Dames, Miss Agatha Charters was awakened by indeterminate noises sounding almost in her room, and a medley of feet and voices in the street. It was not the first time this had happened. Pontdidier had belied the promise, made by an archdeacon, that she would find it a harbour of calm. The fact was, the town was too near a frontier, and too unsophisticated. When politicians in Paris began to roar of treason, Pontdidier believed them, and the Town Council set up a hue and cry for spies. Miss Charters had not failed to observe this nervousness, and to despise it a little, without ill humour; but to be roused at one in the morning was a little too much, and she said so, in her firm French, to the landlady as she paid her bill the next day before leaving.

"Je ne suis pas sure *que je puis vous recommander à mes amis. Votre ville n'est pas tranquille du tout."*

The landlady sank her head between her shoulders, then raised and swung it deplorably to and fro.

"Las' naight," said the landlady, practising English, which reckoned as a commercial asset, "it is a man escape from the police. A spy that makes photographies. They attrape him, but the photographies—gone! Nobody know."

"Un espion!" repeated Miss Charters coldly, as one who had heard that tale before. *"Espérons qu'il n'échapper à pas."*

With that she walked upstairs to her room for a final inspection. Her hot-water bottle, as usual, had been forgotten in the deeps of the bed, and this she rescued thankfully. Going to the washstand to empty it, she set her foot on some round object and came to the floor with no inconsiderable bump. The object, obeying the impetus she had given it, rolled to rest against a chair leg, and Miss Charters, turning to eye it with the natural resentment of one tricked by the inanimate, instantly recognized it as a spool of film.

Her mind, with a gibbonlike agility, leaped from the spool to the noises in the night; linked these with her own wide-open window, probably the only one in the entire façade of the hotel; and came to the conclusion that this spool had reached her floor by the hand of the suspected spy now in custody—flung as he fled. But there had been, her subconscious seemed to think, *two* noises in the room. She looked for another possible missile, and perceived, under the bed, a flat wallet of some kind. It was quite inaccessible, the bed's frame hung low, she had no umbrella to rake for it, and some vague memory of criminal procedure insisted that the police must always have first cut at a clue. It was her duty to go downstairs, display to the landlady the spool, which she had picked up instinctively, and ask that the authorities should be informed.

She set foot on the stairs, and even as she did so, halted. It became apparent that she would have to give her evidence in person, swear to the noise in the night and to the morning's discovery. This would involve missing her train, and its subsequent connection, with the expense of warning domestics and relatives by telegram. More sinister considerations succeeded these. The French were hysterical. They were spy-conscious. They would refuse to believe that she and the fleeing man were strangers. As an excuse for open windows, a plea of fresh air would not satisfy.

Halting on the stairs, she rehearsed these reasons for holding her tongue, and came to the conclusion that silence, with a subsequent letter from England, would meet the case. To roll the spool under the bed until it lay near the wallet, and so depart, would be the dignified and comparatively honest course of action. But the turmoil of the morning had let loose in Miss Charters's mind hordes of revolutionary desires, which now found a rallying ground in the fact that she had not, in her forty-odd years, had one single unusual experience. She had never held unquestioned sway as chief talker at any party; she had never come within hail of being the heroine of any incident more lively than the spoiling of a Guide picnic by rain. The spool of film, now safe in her bag, tempted her; to take it home as proof of the adventure, to hand it over in the end, perhaps, to somebody from the Foreign Office or Scotland Yard! She hesitated, and the revolutionaries in that instant had her conscience down. No word of any discovery found its way into her farewells.

At the station she became aware of two things. First, that she had twenty minutes to wait for her train; second, that amid the excitements of the morning she had omitted a visit to that retreat which old-fashioned foreign hotels leave innominate, indicating it only by two zeros on the door. She cast a prudish but searching eye about her. The word *Dames* beckoned; Miss Charters bought a newspaper and, apparently purposeless, drifted towards it.

The usual uncleanness greeted her, and to protect herself from unspeakable contacts, Miss Charters sacrificed a whole sheet of her newspaper. It was newly printed, the ink had a bloom to it. Miss Charters, accustomed at home to entrust to newspapers the defense of musquash against moth, vaguely supposed that it might prove, on this analogy, deterrent to germs. She emerged without delay, glanced to see that her baggage was safe, and paced up and down reading what remained of *Le Petit Journal*. There were fifteen minutes still to wait.

Seven or eight of these had passed in the atmosphere of unhurried makeshift that pervades all minor French stations when a commotion was heard outside, chattering of motorcycles, and shouting. Through the door marked *Sortie* three policemen in khaki and képis made a spectacular entrance, followed by a miraculous crowd apparently started up from the paving stones. The three advanced upon Miss Charters, innocently staring, and required her, none too civilly, to accompany them.

"Pourquoi?" she inquired without heat. *"Je vais manquer mon* train."

They insisted, not politely; and their explanations, half inarticulate, contained a repetition of the word *portefeuille*. At once Miss Charters understood; the wallet had been found. (Who would have thought the French swept so promptly under beds?) She must give her account of the whole matter, miss her connection, telegraph her relations. Bells and signals announced the train to be nearly due; with a brief click of the tongue she summoned resolution for a last attempt at escape.

"Je suis anglaise," she announced. *"Mon passeport est en ordre. Voulez-vouz voir?"*

She opened her bag, and immediately, with a swift fatal motion, made to shut it. On top, surmounting the handkerchief, the eau de cologne, the passport, lay the damning red spool, so hurriedly, so madly crammed in. The foremost policeman saw it as soon as she did. He gave a "Ha!" of triumph, and snatched the bag away from her. His two companions fell in at her side, the crowd murmured and eddied like a stream swollen by flood. As she was marched from the station, out of the corner of an eye she saw the train come in; and as they entered the Grande Rue she heard the chuff and chug of its departure. Hope gone, she could give undivided attention to her plight.

It became evident, from the manner of the policemen, and from the fact that she was taken to the Hôtel de Ville, that matters were serious. She made one attempt to get her bag; certain necessary words were lacking in the formula of defense she was composing, and the bag contained a pocket dictionary. Her request was denied. A cynical-looking man at a large desk—mayor? magistrate?—fanned away her protests with both hands and listened to the policeman. So did Miss Charters, and was able to gather from his evidence that the wallet found in her room contained papers and calculations to do with the aerodrome nearby. Could anything be more unlucky? The one genuine spy who had ever frequented Pontdidier-les-Dames must needs throw his ill-gotten information into her bedroom!

The functionary asked at last what she had to say. She replied with the truth; and despite a vocabulary eked out with *"vous savez"* told her story well. The functionary noted her explanation without comment, and having done so, asked the inevitable, the unanswerable questions.

"You found these objects at ten forty-five this morning. Why did you not immediately inform the police? You insist that they have nothing to do with you. Yet you were actually attempting to carry out of this country one of the objects. How do you account for these facts?"

Miss Charters accounted for them by a recital, perfectly true, of her desire to shine at tea parties. It sounded odd as she told it, but she had some notion that the French were a nation of psychologists; also that, being foreign, they were gullible, and sympathetic to women in distress. The cynical man listened, and when her last appeal went down in a welter of failing syntax, considered awhile, then spoke:

"I regret, mademoiselle. All this is not quite satisfactory. You must be searched."

The French she had learned at her governess's knee had not included the word he employed, and it was without any real understanding of his intention that she accompanied a woman in black, who suddenly appeared at her side, looking scimitars. They progressed together, a policeman at the other elbow, to a small room smelling of mice. The policeman shut the door on them; the woman in black ejaculated a brief command; and Miss Charters, horrified, found that she was expected to strip.

In her early youth Miss Charters's most favoured daydream had included a full-dress martyrdom, painful but effective, with subsequent conversions. She now learned that it is easier to endure pain than indignity, and amid all the throbbing which apprehension and shame had set up in her temples, one thought lorded it: the recollection that she had not, in view of the dirty train journey, put on clean underclothes that morning.

The woman in black lifted her hands from her hips as if to help with the disrobing; there was a shuffle outside the door as though the policeman might be turning to come in. With a slight scream, Miss Charters began to unbutton, unhook, unlace her various garments; as they dropped, the woman in black explored them knowingly, with fingers as active as those of a *tricoteuse.* At last Miss Charters stood revealed, conscious of innocence, but finding it a poor defense, and ready to exchange the lightest of consciences for the lightest of summer vests.

The woman in black was thorough. She held stockings up to the light, pinched corsets; at last, satisfied, she cast an eye over the shrinking person of Miss Charters, twirling her slowly about. Now the words of dismissal should have come. Instead, at her back Miss Charters heard a gasp. There was an instant's silence; then the one word, ominous: *"Enfin!"*

The woman in black ran to the door and shouted through it. Miss Charters heard excitement in the policeman's answering voice, and his boots clattered off down the corridor, running. Her imagination strove, and was bested. Why? What? The woman in black, with a grin lineally descended from '93, informed her.

"And now, my beauty, we'll see what the pretty message is that's written on mademoiselle's sit-upon!"

The next few moments were nightmare at its height, when the sleeper knows his dream for what it is, knows he must escape from it, and still must abide the capricious hour of waking. An assistant in blue was vouchsafed to the woman in black. One deciphered such letters as were visible, the other took them down, ranting against the artfulness of spies who printed their messages backwards. In deference to Miss Charters's age and passport some decency was observed. Policemen waited outside the half-open door; there was much noise, but no threatening. The women heard her explanation (conjectural) of their discovery without conviction and did not even trouble to write it down.

At last the message was transcribed. The woman in blue compassionately gave Miss Charters back her clothes, a gesture countered by the woman in black, who refused to allow her to sit down lest the precious impression be blurred. With a policeman at her elbow and the two searchers at her back, her cheekbones pink, and beset by a feeling that this pinkness ran through to her skeleton, Miss Charters once more faced the functionary across his table. The transcription was handed to him. He considered it, first through a magnifying glass, then with the aid of a mirror. The policeman, the two searchers, craned forward to know the fate of France, thus by a freak of Fortune thrust into their hands.

"Et maintenant," they read in capital letters, *"j'ai du cœur au travail, grace aux PILULES PINK."*

The functionary's eyes appeared to project. He stared at Miss Charters, at the searchers; with a start, at his own daily paper lying folded, with his gloves upon it. He tore it open, seeking. Page seven rewarded him. *Maladies des Femmes,* said the headline; underneath, the very words that had been deciphered with such pains, accompanying an illustration of a cheerful young woman, whose outline appeared in transfer not unlike the map of a town. Silently he compared; his glass was busy. At last he looked up, and Miss Charters, meeting his eye, perceived something like comprehension in his glance, a kind of gloating, a difficult withholding of laughter—"Rabelaisian" was the word which shot across her mind like a falling star. It was a hard glance to face, but all

Englishness and spunk had not been slain in Miss Charters by the indignities chance had obliged her to suffer. She had one magnificent last word:

"Je rapporterai le W.C. *de la gare aux autorités sanitaires!"*

It was the best she could do. The larger threat which at first inflamed her mind, of complaints to the Ambassador in Paris, of redress and public apologies, would not do; both she and the Rabelaisian knew why. She could never, to any person, at any time, confide the truth of an experience so appalling. So far as vicarage conversation went, the thing was out of the question. Hateful irony! Something, after forty-odd years, had happened to her, and it had happened in such a manner that mere decency must strike her mute. In the words of a ceremony she had often in younger days read over fondly, she must, however difficult, hereafter forever hold her peace.

Miss Agatha Charters held it. The relations who welcomed her a day later were of the opinion that her holiday in France had not done her much good. They found her quiet, and discovered that what she wanted was to be taken out of herself. So they arranged little gaieties, at which Miss Charters listened silently, now and then pinching in her lips, to travellers' tales of those who had been seeing life in London and by the sea.

"But then," as a relative remarked, "poor Aggie never did have much to say for herself."

FEAR AND TREMBLING'S

Michael Gilbert

The spy story, like other forms of the mystery, has flourished in some periods more than in others. The first spy novel was written by Erskine Childers at a time of mounting tension between Britain and Germany in the years leading up to World War I. Childers later took part in the Irish Rebellion, and by an irony of fate ended his days in front of a British firing squad, though in his book he had been sympathetic to Britain. The genre enjoyed a second heyday in the decade prior to World War II, when tensions were again mounting in Europe and writers such as Graham Greene and Eric Ambler produced some of their best work. Michael Gilbert is a grandmaster of the Mystery Writers of America and an author widely acclaimed in England. His early spy stories chronicle the Cold War.

"You can book straight through to Heidelberg," said Mr. Leonard Caversham, "but it's a long and tiring journey, and I'd suggest that you break it at Cologne. You can go on next morning."

"I've never been to Germany before," said the man. "Matter of fact, I dropped quite a few bombs on it during the war."

"It might perhaps be wiser not to mention that when you get there," said Mr. Caversham, with a smile.

"Could you book me a room in a hotel at Cologne?"

"Certainly. It will take a couple of days to arrange. If you come back at the end of the week, I should have the tickets and reservations all ready for you."

"And if I am going to stop the night at Cologne, I suppose I ought to notify the hotel in Heidelberg that I shall be a day late."

"We could do that for you, too," said Mr. Caversham.

Before he had come to work at Trembling's Tours, Mr. Caversham sometimes wondered why anyone should employ someone else to do a simple job like booking a ticket or making a reservation. Now he was beginning to understand that such a simple assignment could be stretched to include quite a number of other services. He had spent the previous afternoon telephoning four different hotels in Amsterdam, in one of which a lady was certain she had left her jewel case. (It was found later in the bottom of her husband's suitcase.)

As the ex-bomber pilot departed, Roger Roche came through from the back office. He looked dusty, disorganized, and depressed. In the last two respects, as Mr. Caversham knew, appearances were deceptive. Roger had shown himself, in the short time he had been with Trembling's Tours, a competent and irrepressibly cheerful courier.

"What a crowd," he said, running his stubby fingers through his mop of light hair. "What a bleeding marvellous collection."

"Were they worse than the last lot, Roger?"

"Compared with this crowd, the last lot were a school treat. We had a dipsomaniac, a kleptomaniac, five ordinary maniacs, and two old women who never stopped quarrelling. What bothered 'em most was who sat next to the window. 'On my right,' I said, 'you will hobserve the magnificent Tyrolean panner-rammer of the Salzkammergut.' 'I *told* you it was going to be extra-special today, Gertrude. I can't think why I let you have the window. We'll change at lunchtime.' 'You had it all yesterday.' '*Yesterday* was just forests.' "

Mr. Caversham laughed. He noticed that when Roger was reporting his own remarks he lapsed into exaggerated Cockney, while the observations of his passengers were reproduced in accurate suburbanese.

"You get well tipped for your pains," he said. "The last lot were mad about you."

"Ah! There was a girl on the last lot—and when I say a girl, I mean—a girl. Nothing in this bunch under ninety."

The bell sounded behind the counter.

"I'm wanted," said Mr. Caversham. "You'll have to hold the fort."

"I was going to have lunch."

"It'll only be five minutes."

Mr. Caversham went through the door behind the counter and along the passage. He was of average height, thick, and he moved with deliberation.

The room at the end of the passage was still known as the Founder's Room, having belonged to Mr. Walcott Trembling, who had organized and accompanied tours at a time when a visit to the Continent was an adventure, when a tourist expected to be swindled from the moment he arrived at Calais, and a careful family carried its drinking water with it.

Arthur Trembling, his great-grandson, rarely found time to visit the Continent himself, being, as he told his friends, "snowed under" with the work of the agency, the largest in Southampton, and still one of the best known in the country.

Mr. Caversham looked at him inquiringly.

Mr. Trembling said, "I believe you've got a car here, haven't you?"

"Yes," said Mr. Caversham. He drove into Southampton every day, from the furnished cottage he had rented on the fringes of the New Forest.

"I wouldn't bother you, but my car's tied up at the garage. I wondered if you could run a parcel round to my brother Henry's shop."

"No trouble at all," said Mr. Caversham. "The only thing is that it'll leave the front office empty. Mr. Snow is away this week, and Mr. Belton's having lunch."

"Who's there now?"

"I left Roger holding the fort."

"He can go on holding it. It won't take you more than ten minutes."

"Right," said Mr. Caversham. "Where's the parcel?"

Mr. Trembling had the grace to look embarrassed.

"I'm afraid I assumed you'd say yes. The parcel's in the boot of your car already. It's quite a big one."

"That's all right," said Mr. Caversham. He was placid and obliging—qualities which, in the few weeks he had been there, had already endeared him to his employer.

His ancient Standard was in the corner of the yard, outside the garage (in which, when they were not speeding down the motorways of Europe, the Trembling forty-seater touring coaches were housed). Mr. Caversham glanced into the trunk compartment of his car. In it was a large square parcel, wrapped in brown paper and well corded. It would, he guessed, be books. Henry Trembling, Arthur's brother, was a second hand bookseller.

Mr. Caversham drove slowly and carefully. He was not sorry to be out of the office. His course took him along the quays, outside the ramparts of the old town, and into the modern area of shops clustered round the railway station. Henry, a stouter, whiter, more paunchy version of his brother, helped him take out the parcel. It was surprisingly heavy—but books always weigh a lot. Henry pressed a pound note into Mr. Caversham's hand.

"For your trouble and your petrol," he said. It seemed generous payment for a quarter-mile run, but Mr. Caversham said nothing. As he drove back to the office he whistled softly between his teeth.

Strangely enough, he was thinking of Lucilla.

Lucilla was something of a mystery in the office. She was Arthur Trembling's secretary. She had been there longer than any other member of the staff—which was not saying a great deal, for Trembling's paid their employees badly, and parted with them rapidly. But it made Lucilla all the more inexplicable, for she was not only competent, she was positively beautiful.

The only theory which made sense to the other employees of Trembling's was that she was Arthur's mistress. "Though what she can see in him," as Roger said to Mr. Caversham, "beats me. I should have said he had as much sex in him as a flat soda-water bottle." Mr. Caversham had agreed. He agreed with almost everybody.

When he got back, he found Lucilla in the front office, dealing with a lady who wished to take four children and a Labrador to Ireland. He thought she looked worried and, for a girl of her remarkable poise, a little off-balance.

When she had dealt with the customer, she came across to him.

"I suppose Roger wouldn't wait any longer for his lunch," said Mr. Caversham.

"The poor boy, yes. He was hungry. Where have you been?"

"Running errands for the boss," said Mr. Caversham. He was an observant man, and now that Lucilla was close to him he could read the signs quite clearly—the tightening round the mouth, the strained look in her eyes; he could even see the tiny beads of perspiration on her attractive, outward-curving upper lip.

"What's up?" he said.

"I can't talk now," she said. "I've got to go back—to him. Can you get out for half an hour at teatime?"

"Should be all right," said Mr. Caversham. "Four o'clock. Belton can carry things for half an hour. We'll go to the Orange Room."

Lucilla nodded, and disappeared. Mr. Caversham reflected that it was girls who were cool and collected most of the time who really went to pieces when trouble came. And trouble was coming. Of that he had been certain since the previous day, when he had heard Lucilla screaming at Arthur Trembling in his office.

The Orange Room was one of those tea shops which shut out the sunlight with heavy curtains, and only partially dispel the gloom with economy-size electric bulbs. A table in the far corner was as safe a place for the confessional as could have been devised.

Lucilla said, "He's a beast—a vile beast. And speaking for myself, I've stood it long enough. For over a year he's been stringing me along, promising to marry me. First he was ill. Then his mother was ill. His mother! I ask you. What's she got to do with whether he gets married or not?"

Mr. Caversham grunted sympathetically. It was all he felt that was expected of him.

"If he thinks he's going to get off scot-free, he can think again," said Lucilla. "He's up to something, something criminal, and I'm going to put the police onto him."

Mr. Caversham leaned forward, with heightened interest, and said, "Now what makes you think that?"

"It's something to do with the tours. Every time a tour comes back, there's a big parcel in his office. It's something he pays the tour drivers to bring back for him."

"All of them?"

"I don't expect all of them. Maybe there're some he can't bribe. But Roger's one of them. There's a secret compartment in each of the coaches."

"Did Roger tell you that?"

"No. Basil told me."

Mr. Caversham remembered Basil—a black-haired boy, with buckteeth, who had been very fond of Lucilla.

"What is it? Watches? Drugs? Perfume?"

"Basil doesn't know. It was just a big, heavy parcel. But I'm going to find out this evening. He's leaving early—there's a Rotarian meeting."

"The parcel isn't in his office now. I took it down to his brother's bookshop."

"Yes, but he took something out of it first. I came in when he was packing it up again. And if it's something valuable, it'll be in his private safe."

"To which," said Mr. Caversham, with a ghost of a smile, "you have, no doubt, a duplicate key."

"No, I haven't. But I know where he keeps his key. It's in a stupid little so-called secret drawer in the desk. I found out about it months ago."

"Few things remain hidden from an observant woman," said Mr. Caversham. "Are you asking me to help you?"

"That's just what I am asking."

"I agree. Two heads are better than one. What I suggest is this. I'll go down this evening and keep an eye on the bookshop. You have a look in the safe. I shouldn't take anything—just look. We'll meet later and add up what we've got. If it's enough to put old Trembling away, we'll let the police have it."

"Could we talk out at your place?"

"It's a bit off the beaten track."

"All the better. I've got a car."

"Eight o'clock, then," said Mr. Caversham. "Nip back now. We don't want to be seen together."

He gave her two minutes' start, paid the bill, and walked back thoughtfully. Possibly he was wondering how Lucilla knew where he lived. He could not recollect that he had ever told her.

At twenty past five Arthur Trembling walked through the front office, scattering a general "Good night" as he went. Mr. Caversham thought that he, too, looked preoccupied. Evidently his Rotarian speech was weighing on his mind.

Mr. Caversham helped Mr. Belton to close down the front office, got out his car, and drove it toward the station, parking it in the yard. The last bit, he thought, would be better done on foot. He had noticed a sidewalk café nearly opposite the bookshop. He took a seat in the bow window, ordered plaice and chips, opened an evening paper, and settled down to watch.

In the first half-hour one old lady and one schoolboy entered the bookshop. Neither stayed more than three minutes. Shortly after six

Henry Trembling emerged, put the shutters up, padlocked an iron arm into place across the door, and departed.

"And that," said Mr. Caversham, "would appear to be that." Nevertheless, he remained where he was. His interest had shifted to the office building next to the bookshop. This was a building with an entrance opening on the street, inside which he could see a board, with names on it, and a staircase which no doubt served the several offices in the building.

Mr. Caversham noted a number of men and women coming out. He also noted quite a few middle-aged and elderly men going in—a fact which seemed a little odd at that time of night. But what was odder still—none of them seemed to reappear.

Mr. Caversham scribbled a rough tally on the edge of his paper. "White hair, horn-rims, 6:18." "Fat, red carnation, 6:35." "Tall, thin, checked ulster, 6:50." By half-past seven he had a list of eleven people, and had exhausted the patience of his waitress. He paid his bill and left. As he came out of the café, a twelfth man was disappearing into the office building.

Farther down the street, on the other side, a red-faced man was sitting at the wheel of an old gray Buick. There was nothing odd about him except that Mr. Caversham, who missed little, had noticed him there when he went into the café, nearly two hours earlier.

He walked back to his car and drove home.

The furnished cottage he had rented lay at the end of a short straight lane, rutted and dusty in summer, barely passable in winter. Some people might have found it lonely, but Mr. Caversham was fond of solitude. Now, in late spring, the trees were in full leaf, and the approach to the cottage was a tunnel of shadow.

He touched on his headlights as he swung in off the main road, and braked just in time. The smart two-seater Fiat was parked in the middle of the drive, and not more than two yards in.

"Women!" said Mr. Caversham. He got out and approached the car cautiously. Lucilla was in the passenger seat. She did not turn her head as he came up. Mr. Caversham opened the door on the driver's side. The opening of the door operated the interior light, which came on and showed him Lucilla more clearly.

She was dead, and had been dead, he guessed, for some time. Her face was already livid. She had been strangled, and the cord which had strangled her was still round her neck, cut so deep into the flesh that only the ends could be seen, dangling at the front, like a parody of a necktie.

Mr. Caversham got out of the car and closed the door softly. He stood in the drive, balanced squarely on his legs, his thick body bent forward, his arms hanging loosely. His head turned slowly, left and right. He looked like a Western gunfighter at the moment of the draw.

Abruptly he swung round, returned to his own car, jumped in, backed it out into the road, and drove it a couple of hundred yards before turning through an open field gate and running in under the trees. He had switched off all the lights before he started. Now he locked the car, and ambled back, at a gentle trot, by the way he had come. At the corner of the lane he stopped again, to look and listen. Dusk was giving way to dark. Nothing disturbed the stillness of the evening.

Mr. Caversham allowed a slow minute to elapse. Then he walked up to the car, opened the door, and climbed in without a second glance at the dead girl. The ignition key, as he had noted, was still in the lock. The engine, which was still warm, started at first touch. He backed the car out into the road. From the direction of Southampton a car was coming, fast. He could see the headlights as it roared over the humpback bridge beside Shotton.

Mr. Caversham grinned to himself unpleasantly, swung the little car away from Southampton, and drove off.

Half a mile down the road he turned into a drive and got out. It took him five minutes to shift the body into the backseat and then cover it with a rug. After that he switched on his sidelights and took to the road again. He drove quickly and surely, handling the strange car as though he had been driving it for months. A fast circuit of Southampton's sprawling suburbs brought him into the town again from the west. A few minutes later he was examining the road signs in a large development which seemed to have been laid out by a naval architect.

Beyond Hawke Road and Frobisher Drive he found Howe Crescent. Number 17 was a pleasant, detached house, with a neat garden and a separate entrance to a fair-sized garage. Mr. Caversham drove straight in. The owners were, as he well knew, in Venice. He had himself sold them their tickets a fortnight before, and had helped them make arrangements for the boarding out of their cat.

A bus ride and a few minutes' walk brought Mr. Caversham back to the place where he had left his own car. He climbed in and drove it sedately toward Southampton. As he entered the car park of the cinema he looked at his watch. It was just over three-quarters of an hour since he had found Lucilla. He seemed to have covered a lot of ground.

It was a cowboy film, and Mr. Caversham settled back to enjoy it.

The film finished at eleven o'clock and ten minutes later he was turning into the lane which led to his cottage. A police car was parked in front of his gate.

"Can I help you?" said Mr. Caversham. "Perhaps you have lost your way."

"Is your name Caversham? We'd like a word with you."

"Come in," said Mr. Caversham. He opened the front door, which was not locked, turned on the lights, and led the way in. The last time he had seen the red-faced man he had been seated behind the wheel of an old gray Buick, on the opposite side of the road to Henry Trembling's bookshop.

The man said, "I'm Detective-Sergeant Lowther of the Southampton Police. This is Detective-Sergeant Pratt."

"Good evening," said Mr. Caversham. He managed to add a question mark at the end of it.

"We've come out here because we had a message that a girl's body had been found in a car."

"And had it?"

Sergeant Lowther looked at Mr. Caversham. It was not exactly a look of hostility, nor was it friendly. It was the sort of look that a boxer might give an opponent as he stepped into the ring.

He said, "Neither the body nor the car was here when we arrived."

"And had it been here?"

"According to a boy who came past the end of the road at half-past seven, there was a car here. A Fiat. He happened to notice the number, too."

"Boys often do notice these things. I expect you'll be able to trace it."

"We have traced it. It belongs to a Miss Lucilla Davies." The sergeant paused. Mr. Caversham said nothing. "We contacted her lodging. She hasn't been home."

"The night," said Mr. Caversham, "is still young."

"Look—" said the sergeant, "I said—Lucilla Davies. Do you mean to say you don't know her?"

"Of course I know her. She works in the same place that I do. On a rather superior level. She is Mr. Trembling's secretary."

"Then why didn't you say so before?"

"Why should I?"

"Look," said the sergeant, "do you mind telling us where you've been?"

"I've been to the cinema. The Rialto. The film was called *Two-finger Knave.* And just in case you think I'm not being entirely truthful, I should mention that the film broke down after the third reel, and we had to wait five minutes while it was being mended. The manager came on the stage and apologized."

"Look—" said the sergeant.

"And now, would you very much mind going away, and letting me get to bed. If you will, I'll consider forgiving you for entering my house, without a warrant, in my absence."

"Entering—?"

"Well," said Mr. Caversham. "I'm quite certain I didn't make that muddy mark on the linoleum there. You can see it quite clearly. It looks to me like a boot, not a shoe."

"Look—" said the sergeant.

"However, you did at least have the delicacy not to search my bedroom."

Sergeant Lowther's face got a shade redder than before. "Assuming," he said, "for the sake of argument, but not admitting it—assuming that we had a look in here, just to see if you were at home, how would you know that we didn't go upstairs as well?"

"I don't think you could have." Mr. Caversham whistled softly, and the great dog rose from the pool of shadow at the top of the stairs and came padding down, his tail acock, his amber eyes gleaming.

"Well, I'm damned," said Sergeant Lowther. "Has he been lying there all the time?"

"All the time," said Mr. Caversham. "And when you're gone, I expect he'll tell me all about you. I understand a lot of what he says—and he understands everything that I say."

The dog's mouth half opened in a derisory smile, revealing white teeth.

"He's our man, all right," said Sergeant Lowther to Inspector Hamish next morning. "I didn't like his attitude—not one little bit."

"That dog of his," said Sergeant Pratt. "Fair gives me the creeps to think he was lying there all the time, watching us, and never made a sound."

Inspector Hamish was tall, bald, and cynical, with the tired, empty cynicism of a life devoted to police duties.

"Have you checked at the cinema?"

"Yes, and there was a break in the film—just like he said."

"Then what makes you think he didn't go to the cinema?"

"He was too damned cool. Too ready with all the answers."

"You ask me," said Sergeant Pratt, "I wouldn't be surprised if you found he'd got a record."

"Do you think he's mixed up with Trembling's little game?"

"Could easily be. He was hanging round watching the bookshop last night, like I told you."

The telephone rang. Inspector Hamish answered it. His expression changed not at all. At the end he said, "All right, thank you." And to Sergeant Lowther, "We're going out to Seventeen Howe Crescent. The car's there. The girl's in the back."

At about this time Mr. Caversham and Roger were opening up the front office at Trembling's. Roger seemed to be suffering from a hangover. Mr. Caversham appeared to be normal.

"It was some party," said Roger. "One of the old duffers who was on the first tour organized it. A reunion—can you imagine it?"

"I can," said Mr. Caversham, with a slight shudder.

"The idea was, we had a bottle of booze from each of the countries we'd visited. All nine of them. We finished them, too. And that girl I was telling you about—the one on the first tour—"

The bell behind Mr. Caversham's desk rang.

"What does *he* want," said Roger. "He's never been in before ten o'clock since I've been here."

The bell rang again. Mr. Caversham sighed, put down the three-colour triptych advertising an economy tour in the Costa Brava, and made his way along the passage.

Mr. Trembling was sitting behind his desk. His face was half hidden by his hand. When he spoke his voice was under careful control.

"Have you any idea where Miss Davies is?"

"Hasn't she got here yet?"

"No," said Mr. Trembling. "I telephoned her house. The lady there was most upset. Lucilla hadn't been back all night. They've just telephoned the police."

"How *very* worrying," said Mr. Caversham. "But I expect she'll turn up. Mr. Foster was saying how sorry the Rotarians were to miss your speech last night."

For a moment it seemed that Mr. Trembling hadn't heard. Then he raised his head slowly, and Mr. Caversham saw his face. If he had not known what he did, he might have felt sorry for him.

"Yes," said Mr. Trembling. "I was sorry to disappoint them. I felt unwell at the last moment. A touch of gastric trouble."

"You ought to have gone straight home. Not come back to the office," said Mr. Caversham severely. "There's only one place when your stomach's upset. In bed, with a hot-water bottle."

What was left of the colour in it had drained out of Mr. Trembling's face. The pouches under his eyes were livid. Mr. Caversham thought, for a moment, that he might be going to faint, and took half a step forward.

"What do you mean?" It was a croak, barely audible.

In his most reasonable voice Mr. Caversham said, "I left my wallet in my desk and had to come back for it. I happened to see your car in the yard and a light on in the office. Are you sure you're all right?"

"Yes," said Mr. Trembling, with an effort. "I'm all right. That'll be all."

It won't be all, Mr. Caversham thought to himself, as he walked back. Not by a long chalk, it won't. You set a trap for her, didn't you? Let her see where you kept the key. Let her see you take something out of that parcel and put it in the safe. Let her know you were going to be away at a Rotarian meeting. Came back and caught her. She must have told you she was meeting me. Perhaps she did it in an attempt to save her own life. So when you'd finished, when she was no longer your secretary, no longer anything but a lump of dead flesh, you put her in her own car and drove her out to my place. Not very friendly. Then, I suppose, you rang up the police. Lucky you didn't do it ten minutes earlier. *I* should have been in trouble.

By this time Mr. Caversham was back in the shop. Mr. Belton was talking to a girl with a ponytail about day trips to Boulogne, and a sour old man was waiting in front of Mr. Caversham's desk with a complaint about British Railways. Mr. Caversham dealt with him dexterously enough, but his mind was not entirely on his work.

Most of it was on the clock.

The police, he knew, worked to a fairly rigid pattern. Fingerprinting and photography came first, then the pathologist. Then the immediate inquiries. These would be at Lucilla's lodgings. How long would all that take? A couple of hours perhaps. Then they would come to the place where she worked. Then things would really start to happen. No doubt about that.

"Where's that Roger?" said Belton.

"He was here earlier this morning," said Mr. Caversham. "I expect he's somewhere about."

"He's not meant to be gadding about. He's meant to be helping me," said Mr. Belton. "I don't know what's come over this place lately. No organization."

It was nearly twelve o'clock before Roger reappeared. He was apologetic, but impertinent. Nor did he explain where he had been. Mr. Caversham said, "Now that you are here, I'll go out and get lunch, if no one has any objections."

No one had any objections. Mr. Caversham hurried into the public house down the street and ordered sandwiches. He was back within twenty-five minutes, and found a worried Mr. Belton alone.

"I'm glad you've got back so quickly," he said.

"What's up?"

"I wish I knew. Mr. Trembling isn't answering his telephone. And Roger seems to have disappeared."

A prickle of apprehension touched the back of Mr. Caversham's neck.

"Which way?"

"What are you talking about?"

"I asked you," said Mr. Caversham, in a new and very urgent voice, "which way Roger went. Did he go out of the front door into the street?"

"No. He went out down the passage. Into the backyard, I should guess. What's happening? What is it all about, Mr. Caversham? What's going on, for God's sake?"

People had sometimes accused Mr. Caversham of being hard to the point of insensitivity. He did, however, appreciate that he was dealing with a badly frightened man, and at that moment, when there was so much to be done, he paused to comfort him.

"There's nothing here which need bother you," he said. "I promise you that. Indeed, I should say that right now you were the only person in this whole outfit who had nothing to worry about. Just keep the customers happy."

He disappeared through the door behind the counter, leaving Mr. Belton staring after him.

The door of the Founder's Room was closed, but not locked. Mr. Caversham opened it, without knocking, and looked inside. Arthur Trembling was seated in his tall chair behind his desk. He looked quite natural until you went close and saw the small neat hole which the bullet had made under the left ear, and the rather larger, jagged hole which it had made coming out of the righthand side of the head.

Mr. Caversham sat on the corner of the desk and dialled a number. A gruff voice answered at once.

"Southampton Police," said Mr. Caversham calmly. "I'm speaking from the offices of Trembling's Tours. Yes, Trembling's. In Fawcet Street. Mr. Trembling has been shot. About ten minutes ago."

The voice at the other end tried to say something, but Mr. Caversham overrode it.

"The man responsible for the killing is using the name of Roger Roche. He's thirty, looks much younger, has untidy, light hair, and is lodging at Forty-five Alma Crescent. Have you got that?"

"Who's that speaking?"

"Never mind me. Have you got that information? Because you'll have to act on it at once. Send someone to his lodgings, have the trains watched and the roads blocked."

"What did you say your name was?"

"I didn't," said Mr. Caversham, "but I told you what to do to catch this murderer, and if you don't do it quickly, you're going to be sorry."

He rang off and cast an eye round the office. There was no sign of any disturbance. A neat, cold, professional killing. If Mr. Belton had heard nothing, the gun must have been a silenced automatic.

The key was in the safe. Using a pencil, Mr. Caversham turned it, then carefully swung the safe door open. On the bottom shelf was a quarto-sized volume, in a plain gray binding, with no title.

He carried it to the desk and opened it. There was a blatant Teutonic crudity about the photographs inside which made even such an unimpressionable man as Mr. Caversham wrinkle his nose. He was still examining the book when a police car drew up in the yard, and Sergeant Lowther burst into the room.

"Ah," he said. "I might have known you'd be in on this one too. What's that you've got there? Yes, I see. *Very* pretty. Now, Mr. Caversham, perhaps you'll do some explaining."

"Not to you," said Mr. Caversham. He had heard another car draw up in the yard. A few seconds later Inspector Hamish came through the door. He looked coldly at Mr. Caversham.

"Have you picked him up yet?" asked Mr. Caversham.

"I got some garbled message," said the inspector, "about a man called Roger Roche. I thought I'd come and find out what it was all about before sounding a general alarm."

Mr. Caversham got to his feet. "Do you mean to say," he said, and there was a cold ferocity in his voice which made even the inspector stare, "that you have wasted ten whole minutes? If that's right, you're going to have something to answer for."

"Look here—"

"Would you ask the sergeant to leave the room, please."

Inspector Hamish hesitated, then said, "One minute, Sergeant—"

By the time he turned back, Mr. Caversham had taken something from his pocket. The inspector looked at it and said in quite a different tone of voice, "Well, Mr. Calder, if I'd only known—"

"That'll be the epitaph of the British Empire," said Mr. Calder. "Will you please, please get the wheels turning."

"Yes, of course. I'd better use the telephone."

An hour later Mr. Calder and Inspector Hamish were sitting in the Founder's Room. The photographers and fingerprint men had come and gone. The pathologist had taken charge of the body; and a police cordon, thrown round Southampton a good deal too late, had failed to catch Roger Roche.

"We'll pick him up," said the inspector.

"I doubt it," said Mr. Calder. "People like that aren't picked up easily. He'll be in France by this evening and God knows where by tomorrow."

"If someone had only told me—"

"There were faults on both sides," Mr. Calder admitted. "I expect I should have told you last night. There didn't seem any hurry at the time and I didn't know about Roger then."

"If you wouldn't mind explaining," said the inspector, "in words of one syllable. I am only a simple policeman, you know."

"Let's begin at the beginning then," said Mr. Calder. "You knew that Trembling was smuggling in pornographic books for his brother to sell?"

"Yes. We're onto that now. There's a side entrance into his shop, from the ground-floor office next door. The cash customers used to go in that way after the shop was shut, and out by a back entrance into the mews. You'd be surprised if I told you the names of some of his customers."

"I doubt it," said Mr. Calder. "However, it wasn't an easy secret to keep. Too many couriers were involved. Soviet Intelligence got onto it. They put in an agent—Lucilla Davies—to nurse it along. She blackmailed Trembling. He could go on bringing in his dirty books, as long as he agreed to take out letters—and other things as well—for them. Trembling's became the main South Coast post office for the Russians."

"Neat," said the inspector.

"Then our side got to hear about it, too. And sent me down. What happened was that Trembling got tired of being blackmailed into treason, and decided to remove Lucilla. I don't blame him for that, but I do blame him for leaving her in my front drive. I thought that was unnecessary. And very cramping for me. So I shifted her. However, I did ring up and tell you where to find her next morning."

"That was you, too, was it?"

"That was me. I thought if we played it properly, we'd be bound to provoke a countermove from the other side. They don't like their agents being bumped off. I guessed they'd send one of their best men down here—what I didn't realize was that he was *already* here. Roger fooled me completely."

"There's a moral to it somewhere, no doubt," said the inspector.

"The moral," said Mr. Calder, "is that if the various Intelligence Departments and MI5 and the Special Branch and ninety-six different police forces didn't all try to work independently of each other, but cooperated for a change, we might get better results."

"You'd better put that in your report," said Inspector Hamish. "Not that anyone'll take any notice."

"I'll put it in," said Mr. Calder. "But it won't do a blind bit of good."

BURNING END

Ruth Rendell

In the 1960s a star appeared on the mystery scene. Though she has been compared in stature to predecessors like Agatha Christie, Ruth Rendell could not be more different in style and substance from Dame Agatha and other Golden Age puzzle-spinners. Even in the Wexford police novels, her interest is primarily in characterization rather than plot. Ruth Rendell will always have a special place in the hearts of editors and readers of Ellery Queen's Mystery Magazine, *for her first mystery short stories were written at the suggestion of the magazine's previous editor, Eleanor Sullivan. The author of thirty-nine novels, Ruth Rendell recently celebrated her thirtieth anniversary as a mystery writer.*

After she had been doing it for a year, it occurred to Linda that looking after Betty fell to her lot because she was a woman. Betty was Brian's mother, not hers, and Betty had two other children, both sons, both unmarried men. No one had ever suggested that either of them should take a hand in looking after their mother. Betty had never much liked Linda, had sometimes hinted that Brian had married beneath him, and once, in the heat of temper, said that Linda was "not good enough" for her son, but still it was Linda who cared for her now. Linda felt a fool for not having thought of it in these terms before.

But she knew she would not get very far talking about it to Brian. Brian would say—and did say—that this was women's work. A man couldn't perform intimate tasks for an old woman, it wasn't fitting. When Linda asked why not, he told her not to be silly, everyone knew why not.

"Suppose it had been your dad that was left, suppose he'd been bedridden, would I have looked after him?"

Brian looked over the top of his evening paper. He was holding the remote in his hand but he didn't turn down the sound. "He wasn't left, was he?"

"No, but if he had been?"

"I reckon you would have. There isn't anyone else, is there? It's not as if the boys were married."

Every morning after Brian had gone out into the farmyard and before she left for work, Linda drove down the road, turned left at the church into the lane, and after a mile came to the very small cottage on the very large piece of land where Betty had lived since the death of her husband twelve years before. Betty slept downstairs in the room at the back. She was always awake when Linda got there, although that was invariably before seven-thirty, and she always said she had been awake since five.

Linda got her up and changed the incontinence pad. Most mornings she had to change the sheets as well. She washed Betty, put her into a clean nightgown and clean bedjacket, socks, and slippers, and while Betty shouted and moaned, lifted and shoved her as best she could into the armchair she would remain in all day. Then it was breakfast. Sweet milky tea and bread and butter and jam. Betty wouldn't use the feeding cup with the spout. What did Linda think she was, a baby? She drank from a cup, and unless Linda had remembered to cover her up with the muslin squares that had indeed once had their use for babies, the tea would go all down the clean nightgown and Betty would have to be changed again.

After Linda had left her and gone off to work, the district nurse would come, though not every day, not for certain. The Meals-on-Wheels lady would come and give Betty her midday dinner, bits and pieces in foil containers, all labelled with the names of their contents. At some point Brian would come. Brian would "look in." Not to *do* anything, not to clear anything away or give his mother something to eat or make her a cup of tea or run the vacuum cleaner around—Linda did that on Saturdays—but to sit in Betty's bedroom for ten minutes smoking a cigarette and watching whatever was on television. Very occasionally, perhaps once a month, the brother who lived two miles away would come for ten minutes and watch television with Brian. The other brother, the one who lived ten miles away, never came at all except at Christmas.

Linda always knew if Brian had been there by the smell of smoke and the cigarette end stubbed out in the ashtray. But even if there had been no smell and no stub she would have known because Betty always told her. Betty thought Brian was a saint and an angel to spare a moment away from the farm to visit his old mother. She could no longer speak distinctly, but she was positively articulate on the subject of Brian, the most perfect son any woman ever had.

It was about five when Linda got back there. Usually the incontinence pad needed changing again and often the nightdress too. Considering how ill she was, and partially paralysed, Betty ate a great deal. Linda made her scrambled egg or sardines on toast. She brought pastries with her from the cakeshop or, in the summer, strawberries and cream. She made more tea for Betty, and when the meal was over, somehow heaved Betty back into that bed.

The bedroom window was never opened. Betty wouldn't have it. The room smelt of urine and lavender, camphor and Meals-on-Wheels, so every day on her way to work Linda opened the window in the front room and left the doors open. It didn't make much difference but she went on doing it. When she had got Betty to bed she washed up the day's teacups, emptied the ashtray and washed it, and put all the soiled linen into a plastic bag to take home. The question she asked Betty before she left had become meaningless because Betty always said no, and she hadn't asked it once since having that conversation with Brian about whose job it was to look after his mother, but she asked it now.

"Wouldn't it be better if we moved you in with us, Mum?"

Betty's hearing was erratic. This was one of her deaf days.

"What?"

"Wouldn't you be better off coming to live with us?"

"I'm not leaving my home till they carry me out feet first. How many times do I have to tell you?"

Linda said all right and she was off now and she would see her in the morning. Looking rather pleased at the prospect, Betty said she would be dead by the morning.

"Not you," said Linda, which was what she always said, and so far she had always been right.

She went into the front room and closed the window. The room was furnished in a way which must have been old-fashioned even when Betty was young. In the center of it was a square dining table, around which stood six chairs with seats of faded green silk. There was a large, elaborately carved sideboard but no armchairs, no small tables, no books, and no lamps but the central light which, enveloped in a shade of parchment panels stitched together with leather thongs, was suspended directly over the glass vase that stood on a lace mat in the absolute center of the table.

For some reason, ever since the second stroke had incapacitated Betty two years before, all the post, all the junk mail, and every freebie news-sheet that was delivered to the cottage ended up on this table. Every few months it was cleared away, but this hadn't been done for some time, and Linda noticed that only about four inches of the glass vase now showed above the sea of paper. The lace mat was not visible at all. She noticed something else as well.

It had been a warm sunny day, very warm for April. The cottage faced south and all afternoon the sunshine had poured through the window, was still pouring through the window, striking at the neck of the vase so that the glass was too bright to look at. Where the sun-struck glass touched a sheet of paper a burning had begun. The burning glass was making a dark charred channel through the sheet of thin printed paper.

Linda screwed up her eyes. They had not deceived her. That was smoke she could see. And now she could smell burning paper. For a moment she stood there, fascinated, marvelling at this phenomenon which she had heard of but had never believed in. A magnifying glass to make boy scout's fires, she thought, and somewhere she had read of a forest burnt down through a piece of broken glass left in a sunlit glade.

There was nowhere to put the piles of paper, so she found another plastic bag and filled that. Betty called out something but it was only to know why she was still there. Linda dusted the table, replaced the lace mat and the glass vase, and, with a bag of washing in one hand and a bag of wastepaper in the other, went home to do the washing and get an evening meal for Brian and herself and the children.

The incident of the glass vase, the sun, and the burning paper had been so interesting that Linda meant to tell Brian and Andrew and Gemma all about it while they were eating. But they were also watching the finals of a quiz game on television and hushed her when she started to speak. The opportunity went by and somehow there was no other until the next day. But by that time the sun and the glass setting the paper on fire no longer seemed so remarkable and Linda decided not to mention it.

Several times in the weeks that followed Brian asked his mother if it wasn't time she came to live with them at the farm. He always told Linda of these attempts, as if in issuing this invitation he had been particularly magnanimous and self-denying. Perhaps this was because Betty responded very differently from when Linda asked her. Brian and his children, Betty said, shouldn't have to have a useless old woman under their roof, age and youth were not meant to live together, though nobody appreciated her son's generosity in asking her more than she did. Meanwhile Linda went on going to the cottage and looking after Betty for an hour every morning and an hour and a half every evening and cleaning the place on Saturdays and doing Betty's washing.

One afternoon while Brian was sitting with his mother smoking a cigarette and watching television, the doctor dropped in to pay his twice-yearly visit. He beamed at Betty, said how nice it was for her to have her devoted family around her, and on his way out told Brian it was best for the old folks to end their days at home whenever possible. If he said anything about the cigarette, Brian didn't mention it when he recounted this to Linda.

He must have picked up a pile of junk mail from the doormat and the new phone book from outside the door, for all this was lying on the table in the front room when Linda arrived at ten to five. The paper had accumulated during the past weeks, but when Linda went to look for a plastic bag she saw that the entire stock had been used up. She made a mental note to buy some more and in the meantime had to put the soiled sheets and Betty's two wet nightdresses into a pillowcase to take them home. The sun wasn't shining; it had been a dull day and the forecast was for rain, so there was no danger from the conjunction of glass vase with the piles of paper. It could safely remain where it was.

On her way home it occurred to Linda that the simplest solution was to remove not the paper but the vase. Yet, when she went back next day, she didn't remove the vase. It was a strange feeling she had, that if she moved the vase to the mantelpiece, say, or the top of the sideboard, she would somehow have closed a door or missed a chance. Once she had moved it she would never be able to move it back again, for though she could easily have explained to anyone why she had moved it from the table, she would never be able to say why she had put it back. These thoughts frightened her and she put them from her mind.

Linda bought a pack of fifty black plastic sacks. Betty said it was a wicked waste of money. When she was up and about she had been in the habit of burning all paper waste. All leftover food and cans and bottles got mixed up together and went out for the dustman. Betty had never heard of the environment. When Linda insisted, one hot day in July, on opening the bedroom windows, Betty said she was freezing, Linda was trying to kill her, and she would tell her son his wife was an evil woman. Linda took the curtains home and washed them but she didn't open the bedroom window again, it wasn't worth it, it caused too much trouble.

But when Brian's brother Michael got engaged, she did ask if Suzanne would take her turn looking after Betty once they were back from their honeymoon.

"You couldn't expect it of a young girl like her," Brian said.

"She's twenty-eight," said Linda.

"She doesn't look it." Brian switched on the television. "Did I tell you Geoff's been made redundant?"

"Then maybe he could help out with Betty if he hasn't got a job to go to."

Brian looked at her and shook his head gently. "He's feeling low enough as it is. It's a blow to a man's pride, that is, going on the dole. I couldn't ask him."

Why does he have to be asked, Linda thought. It's his mother. The sun was already high in the sky when she got to the cottage at seven-thirty next morning, already edging round the house to penetrate the front-room window by ten. Linda put the junk mail on the table and took the letter and the postcard into the bedroom. Betty wouldn't look at them. She was wet through and the bed was wet. Linda got her up and stripped off the wet clothes, wrapping Betty in a clean blanket because she said she was freezing. When she was washed and in her clean nightdress, she wanted to talk about Michael's fiancée. It was one of her articulate days.

"Dirty little trollop," said Betty. "I remember her when she was fifteen. Go with anyone, she would. There's no knowing how many abortions she's had, messed all her insides up, I shouldn't wonder."

"She's very pretty, in my opinion," said Linda, "and a nice nature."

"Handsome is as handsome does. It's all that makeup and hair dye as has entrapped my poor boy. One thing, she won't set foot in this house while I'm alive."

Linda opened the window in the front room. It was going to be a hot day, but breezy. The house could do with a good draught of air blowing through to freshen it. She thought: I wonder why no one ever put flowers in that vase, there's no point in a vase without flowers. The letters and envelopes and newsprint surrounded it so that it no longer looked like a vase but like a glass tube inexplicably poking out between a stack of paper and a telephone directory.

Brian didn't visit that day. He had started harvesting. When Linda came back at five, Betty told her Michael had been in. She showed Linda the box of chocolates that was his gift, his way of "soft-soaping" her, Betty said. Not that a few violet creams had stopped her speaking her mind on the subject of that trollop.

The chocolates had gone soft and sticky in the heat. Linda said she would put them in the fridge but Betty clutched the box to her chest, saying she knew Linda, she knew her sweet tooth, if she let that box out of her sight she'd never see it again. Linda washed Betty and changed her. While she was doing Betty's feet, rubbing cream round her toes and powdering them, Betty struck her on the head with the bedside clock, the only weapon she had to hand.

"You hurt me," said Betty. "You hurt me on purpose."

"No, I didn't, Mum. I think you've broken that clock."

"You hurt me on purpose because I wouldn't give you my chocolates my son brought me."

Brian said he was going to cut the field behind the cottage next day. Fifty acres of barley, and he'd be done by midafternoon if the heat didn't kill him. He could have seen to his mother's needs, he'd be practically on the spot, but he didn't offer. Linda wouldn't have believed her ears if she'd heard him offer.

It was hotter than ever. It was even hot at seven-thirty. Linda washed Betty and changed the sheets. She gave her cereal for breakfast and a boiled egg and toast. From her bed Betty could see Brian going round the barley field on the combine, and this seemed to bring her enormous pleasure, though her enjoyment was tempered with pity.

"He knows what hard work is," Betty said, "he doesn't spare himself when there's a job to be done," as if Brian were cutting the fifty acres with a scythe instead of sitting up there in a cabin with twenty kingsize and a can of Coke and the Walkman on his head playing Beatles songs from his youth.

Linda opened the window in the front room very wide. The sun would be round in a couple of hours to stream through that window. She adjusted an envelope on the top of the pile, moving the torn edge of its flap to brush against the glass vase. Then she moved it away again. She stood, looking at the table and the papers and the vase. A brisk draught of air made the thinner sheets of paper flutter a little. From the bedroom she heard Betty call out, through closed windows, to a man on a combine a quarter of a mile away, "Hallo, Brian, you all right then, are you? You keep at it, son, that's right, you got the weather on your side."

One finger stretched out, Linda lightly poked at the torn edge of the envelope flap. She didn't really move it at all. She turned her back quickly. She marched out of the room, out of the house, to the car.

The fire must have started somewhere around four in the afternoon, the hottest part of that hot day. Brian had been in to see his mother when he had finished cutting the field at two. He had watched television with her and then she said she wanted to have a sleep. Those who know about these things said she had very likely died from suffocation without ever waking. That was why she hadn't phoned for help, though the phone was by her bed.

A builder driving down the lane, on his way to a barn conversion his firm was working on, called the fire brigade. They were volunteers whose headquarters was five miles away, and they took twenty minutes to get to the fire. By then Betty was dead and half the cottage destroyed. Nobody told Linda, there was hardly time, and when she got to Betty's at five it was all over. Brian and the firemen were standing about, poking at the wet black ashes with sticks, and Andrew and Gemma were in Brian's estate car outside the gate, eating potato crisps.

The will was a surprise. Betty had lived in that cottage for twelve years without a washing machine or a freezer and her television set was rented by Brian. The bed she slept in was her marriage bed, new in 1939, the cottage hadn't been painted since she moved there, and the kitchen had last been refitted just after the war. But she left what seemed an enormous sum of money. Linda could hardly believe it. A third was for Geoff, a third for Michael, and the remaining third as well as the cottage, or what was left of it, for Brian.

The insurance company paid up. It was impossible to discover the cause of the fire. Something to do with the great heat, no doubt, and the thatched roof, and the ancient electrical wiring which hadn't been renewed for sixty or seventy years. Linda, of course, knew better, but she said nothing. She kept what she knew and let it fester inside her, giving her sleepless nights and taking away her appetite.

Brian cried noisily at the funeral. All the brothers showed excessive grief, and no one told Brian to pull himself together or be a man, but put their arms round his shoulders and told him what a marvellous son he'd been and how he'd nothing to reproach himself with. Linda didn't cry but soon after went into a black depression from which nothing could rouse her, not the doctor's tranquillizers, nor Brian's promise of a slap-up holiday somewhere, even abroad if she liked, nor people telling her Betty hadn't felt any pain but had just slipped away in her smoky sleep.

An application to build a new house on the site of the cottage was favourably received by the planning authority, and permission was granted. Why shouldn't they live in it, Brian said, he and Linda and the children? The farmhouse was ancient and awkward, difficult to keep clean, just the sort of place Londoners would like for a second home. How about moving, he said, how about a modern house, with everything you want, two bathrooms, say, and a laundry room, and a sun lounge? Design it yourself and don't worry about the cost, he said, for he was concerned for his wife, who had always been so practical and efficient as well as easygoing and tractable, but was now a miserable, silent woman.

Linda refused to move. She didn't want a new house, especially a new house on the site of that cottage. She didn't want a holiday or money to buy clothes. She refused to touch Betty's money. Depression had forced her to give up her job but, although she was at home all day and there was no old woman to look after every morning and every evening, she did nothing in the house and Brian was obliged to get a woman in to clean. Brian could build his house and sell it, if that was what he wanted, but she wouldn't touch the money and no one could make her.

"She must have been a lot fonder of Mum than I thought," Brian said to his brother Michael. "She's always been one to keep her feelings all bottled up, but that's the only explanation. Mum must have meant a lot more to her than I ever knew."

"Or else it's guilt," said Michael, whose fiancée's sister was married to a man whose brother was a psychotherapist.

"Guilt? You have to be joking. What's she got to be guilty about? She couldn't have done more if she'd been Mum's own daughter."

"Yeah, but folks feel guilt over nothing when someone dies, it's a well-known fact."

"It is, is it? Is that what it is, doctor? Well, let me tell you something. If anyone ought to feel guilt, it's me. I've never said a word about this to a soul. Well, I couldn't, could I? Not if I wanted to collect the insurance; but the fact is it was me set that place on fire."

"You what?" said Michael.

"It was an accident. I don't mean on purpose. Come on, what do you take me for, my own brother? And I don't feel guilty, I can tell you, I don't feel a scrap of guilt, accidents will happen and there's not a thing you can do about it. But when I went in to see Mum that afternoon, I left my cigarette burning on the side of the chest of drawers. You know how you put them down, with the burning end stuck out. Linda'd taken away the damned ashtray and washed it or something. When I saw Mum was asleep, I just crept out. Just crept out and left that fag end burning. Without a backward glance."

Awed, Michael asked in a small voice, "When did you realise?"

"Soon as I saw the smoke, soon as I saw the fire brigade. Too late then, wasn't it? I'd crept out of there without a backward glance."

MY FIRST MURDER

H. R. F. Keating

Early British mysteries often contained themes and characters drawn from India and other reaches of the British Empire. An independent India has proved a magnet for the imaginations of several current-day British writers, including H. R. F. Keating, creator of India's premiere series police detective, Inspector Ghote. "My First Murder" is not an Inspector Ghote story, but it evokes equally well Keating's Bombay. In it the author takes a wry look at a very special Brit and his experiences on the subcontinent.

I hadn't gone very far from my hotel, walking slowly in the fizzling Bombay heat, when someone came sidling up beside me.

"It is the notable British author?" he said, half a question, half a statement.

He'd got it right. Or, at least, he'd identified me as the person the paper I'd been interviewed in the day before, with picture, had headlined with that typically Indian English phrase.

"Yes?" I answered cautiously.

More than a little cautiously, in fact. There was something about this fellow that set doubts hopping in my mind. More than doubts. Plain distrust. No sooner had he put his question than his glance had flicked away, as if he preferred no one to look at him too closely. Nor was his whole appearance any more reassuring. Check shirt, faintly greasy at neck and cuffs. Cotton khaki trousers with a long dark smear down one thigh. Shoes, rather than sandals, on his sockless feet, their black leather cracked and dry from lack of polish. The only sign of respectability about him, apart from his reasonably good English, was the briefcase he carried. And that was suspiciously thin and empty looking.

But now he turned to me again, two enormous pointy ears poking forward, and flashed me a wide, white-toothed smile.

Too quick a smile?

"You will be very much wanting to know what I am able to tell," he said.

"Oh yes?"

Was money hopefully going to change hands? That what this was all about?

"Yes, yes. You see, I am private eye itself. Junior Investigator. Star of Hind Detective Agency. Soon-soon becoming Senior. Hike of salary also. Star of Hind Agency is full member A.I.S.O.I."

He slid one of a pack of large business cards out of his shirt pocket, thrust it out to me. I took it unwillingly, oily all round the edges as it was with sweaty handling. But before I put it into my own pocket—I could hardly get rid of it at once—I saw at least that it looked like the genuine article.

"But what is this A.I.S.—whatever?" I asked, before realising I had given this unsavoury fellow a new toehold.

"It is Association of Investigators and Security Organisation of India. Sahib, I am very much surprised you are not knowing a name of such all-India fame."

Another inch gained in keeping my acquaintance. Hadn't I been put in the position now of having to explain myself? Even apologise?

"Well, you know, I haven't been in India very long. And, writing about my Inspector Ghote, I'm really more interested in the police than—er—private investigators."

I should have left it at that. But, stupidly, I tried for a final brushoff.

"Readers of my books expect rather more than catching out naughty husbands."

"Then, sahib, I must be telling you about time I was committing my first murder."

I gulped.

A murderer? And—And didn't a first imply a second? Even a third? Maybe not a serial killer but, private eye though he might be, someone ready to end a life in the course of robbery? Had he got it into his head that an author from the affluent West was bound to have some huge amount on his person? Under that dirty shirt there could well be a knife. The work of an instant to slip it out, strike, snatch a wallet, melt into the crowd.

I thought fast. Even furiously.

"Er—Yes. Yes, I'd be very interested to hear about— About that. Very. But I imagine you'll want to be paid for such information. Such good information. And, as it so happens, I've left my wallet—Yes, in my hotel."

I began to turn back.

"Oh, sahib, no, no, no. What I am wishing to tell is out of respect only. Respect for one notable author visiting India."

Was that likely?

Well, the fellow's face seemed now to be shining with sincerity. Perhaps I had misjudged him. And it wouldn't be easy to get away without being brutally impolite.

"That's very kind of you. Most kind."

"Oh, very good, sahib. Very good. Here is one damn fine cold-drinks place. We should go in."

I allowed myself to be led into the place—it was called the Edward VIII Juice Nook—and we sat down on either side of one of the narrow tables.

But as my new acquaintance leant forward to lower himself onto his plastic-covered bench, his grease-edged shirt flopped open a little and I saw what could only be the top of a sheath for a knife.

Was I after all going to be one in the series that had begun with that first murder?

No, surely not. A sudden stabbing and a quick grab out in the street was a possibility, but surely not inside here. Surely?

And he might really have a story to tell. Good material.

Once we had been brought our drinks, a Mangola for me, something long, brightly coloured, and sticky-looking called a falooda for my friend, he began his tale. Innocently enough. If you could be innocent telling how, apparently, you had committed a murder. Your first.

"Sahib," he said, bringing those huge pointy ears of his to focus directly at me, "before I am recounting whole damn thing I will make one matter very-very clear. I am altogether good at my job. First class only. Let me give you example."

Could I stop that? Say, *Get on to this first murder of yours, that's what I want to hear about.* But no, I couldn't. He had me trapped.

"Sahib, I was once given task by our boss of tracing one girl who had been working for five-six years in prostitution line. She had auntie who had married a foreigner, and that fellow had died, leaving said auntie in possession of one lakh rupees. That is a big sum for us, you know."

"Yes, yes."

"Auntie was wishing to make her one and only living relative as heir to all her wealths. But one condition only. She was to give up prostitution racket, even if it was high-class itself."

"Okay, I understand, I understand. So what happened?"

"I was finding and locating that prostitute. Not too hard to do. Ask and ask and before too long you are learning. But question was: Would this prostitute be scared to be found out by hundred-percent-respectable auntie? So what was I doing? Oh, sahib, very-very clever. Under disguise of customer I was booking this girl for night at five-star hotel. I tell you also, sahib, I was very much wishing to do some side-business with her, isn't it?"

Eyes in the ratty face opposite rolled and rolled.

"But I was not at all attempting same. Payment in advance was company money. What would I be able to say in my report? So duty was calling and I was just only chitchatting that girl. I gave out I was one damn-good fortuneteller. Then straightaway she was asking me to read her palm. And I was telling her her own history, which I was all the time damn well knowing from what Auntie had told. You have just only one female relative not seen for many-many years, I told. Correct, correct, she was answering. Next I was saying her palm told this auntie was rich, rich lady. Good, good, she was replying. So at last I was asking what would feelings be if fate brought her to meet this lady. Very fine, very fine, was her answer."

My friend leant back and burst into loud brays of laughter. I looked round in embarrassment. But no one in the little place seemed to be taking much notice.

"You know what was happening when Auntie was saying she would give and bequeath to this prostitute one lakh rupees?" my acquaintance plunged on when at last he had brought himself to stop laughing. "No? You are not at all able to guess. But I will tell. Prostitute was saying: In one night I am making rupees fifteen-hundred, half to my boss, but still more in one year than you are offering as total, Auntie. So goodbye and back to foreign."

More brays of raucous laughter.

"But you were going to tell me about a murder," I broke in exasperatedly. "Your first murder."

He leant across the narrow table towards me. A strong whiff of mingled falooda sweetness and sheer bad breath.

"Yes, yes. Well, I had thought that day was going to be a good day for me itself. When I was reporting for duty I was finding I had not been assigned some hard-work, no-fun job. What we are calling market survey. Number Two product being sold under false tiptop trademark. Keeping one close watch on shop until you are seeing supplier come, and then follow-following until you are able to track down entire organisation. No, no. That day it was erring-wife job."

Across the table I was given an appalling leer.

"Such I am always liking best. When it is matter of seeing with own eyes moment of hanky-panky itself. So I was setting off with what we are calling keyhole camera in briefcase. No bugging apparatus, you understand, because such is illegal under Indian Wireless and Telegraphic Act, nineteen thirty-three."

"Very commendable, but—"

"Yes, yes. So I was watching until lady in question would come out of husband's posh flat, Malabar Hill. After some time I saw their driver take car from garage and sit waiting for memsahib. At once I was securing taxi to be hundred percent ready to follow. In five-ten minutes Madam was coming. Then I in my taxi was trailing-trailing until we were reaching building at Marine Lines. There, as previously ascertained by my co-colleague, was staying Madam's good friend known by the name of Laxmi. But what colleague had not at all considered was the block was having side exit also. But I in my taxi went, quick-quick, round corner, and in one minute, yes, please, Madam was coming out and waving-waving for taxi herself."

Hands rubbed vigorously together in delight.

I began to think I had wasted the price of a Mangola and a falooda.

"To Colaba, Madam was going, just only where we are now. Myself following, promise-promising money to my taxiwalla. Here in Colaba, Madam was hurry-scurrying down some lane and into one Class-Two hotel. Five-ten minutes I was giving her, and then I was going in there also. Rupees five to fellow at Reception, and he was telling which room she had gone to and that also Mister was there in advance. Very good, very good."

He tapped his tall glass sharply on the table. I was already aware it had been drained to the last dreg. The prolonged sucking sound had not been very agreeable.

Ah, well, I thought, might as well hear the end of the story. One more falooda won't break the bank.

A long sticky swallow of the new tall glass and he was off again.

"Oh, you would have liked to see what I was seeing, sahib, when I was putting eye to keyhole. By twisting-twisting I was able to see bed itself. Lady's sari hanging down from end. Madam one hundred percent invisible. Underneath big-big gentleman. Big-big bottom up and down, up and down. Like pile driver only. By God, I was so damn interested I was nearly forgetting my bounden duty."

Yes, yes, you squitty little horror. Get on with it. Your sordid details are never going to form part of an Inspector Ghote investigation. But this murder . . . your first.

"You are liking-liking this story, yes? Then I am telling Part Two. At last, you understand, I was remembering keyhole camera. You know, what you must be getting in my line always is photographic evidence. Damn fool husbands never willing to believe naughty-naughty lady's doings without evidence of own blasted eyes."

"I dare say."

"But then— Oh, sahib, sahib, damn-damn shame."

"No film in your camera?"

Not a very nice thing to say, but I felt I was owed it.

"No, no, sahib. Not at all, not at all. I was telling, isn't it, I am damn good operator. Always check-checking."

"I'm sure you are. It was just that you said something was a shame."

"Yes, yes. Two hundred percent shame. You must be knowing keyhole camera is able to take shot just only directly in front. And that bed with the up-down bottom going and going was not in exact straight line with door. I myself was able to see funny goings-on. Yes, yes. But I was able somewhat to wriggle round. Camera, no."

He took a long swallow at his second falooda. Perhaps for consolation.

"But this murder . . ." I prompted.

Once more I could not help glancing at the tip of the leather sheath under my friend's shirt.

"Yes, yes, I am coming to murder only. But it is important-important you should first be acquainted with each and every detail of beforehand. Or you would not be understanding whole damn affair."

"No? Well, go on then."

"So after looking and looking through what they are calling viewfinder— You are knowing viewfinder?"

"Yes, yes."

"Well, at last I was having very-very quietly, you understand, to open door two-three inches and try for shot from changed angle. Perhaps better. Face of Madam now visible. One expression, utmost delight."

"Yes, yes. But what happened?"

"Oh, sahib, bloody disaster. You see, at that moment Mister Big-Behind was turning face in that direction also. And, even if Madam was so enjoying she was having no eyes for door opening just only one crack, Mister was different kettle-fish to one hundred percent."

I began to hope my peeping friend had got the thumping he deserved. But when was this first murder of his coming in?

"Yes, I can see you were in big trouble," I said, by way of urging him on.

"Oh, sahib, you are not at all knowing how much of troubles I was in."

"No?"

"No, no, sahib. You see, when I was observing whole of that man, just only as he was jumping off the bed, off lady also, I was at once seeing who it was. And, sahib, then I was knowing real-real disaster was there."

"Why was that?"

"Sahib, perhaps, coming from foreign, you are not even knowing name of Bombay Number One top smuggler. Sahib, it is Munna Thakur. Thakur Dada, we are calling him. Famous-famous. Name in papers each and every day. Police very much respecting. And bad also. Bad-bad-bad."

"And he had seen you? Is that it?"

"Oh yes, sahib. He had damn well seen all right. And I also had seen, I had seen he was not once ever going to forget this face."

Well, I thought, as a face it's not exactly prepossessing. But with those two great big pointy ears, you're right, my friend, it's certainly memorable.

"Yes, I suppose you must have felt you were in a pretty tight corner.

Did you manage to do anything about it? Or are you still trying to dodge—what did you call him?—Thakur Dada?"

"Oh no, sahib. Altogether okay now. I was telling, it is my first murder."

"You mean you murdered him? This top smuggler? Feared by the police even? But didn't he have a gang? Bodyguards? What do you call them? *Goondas.*"

"Yes, yes. He was having many-many tough-tough *goondas.* That was why I was needing to act damn quick. I was just only lucky the gentleman was in state of undress itself."

"Yes, I suppose he could hardly chase you out into the street."

"Correct, correct. But I tell you, he was into a trouser and out of that hotel room even before I had run down each and every stair."

"He chased you then? Was he armed at all?"

"Oh yes, sahib. A gentleman like Thakur Dada is always carrying a gun. He was waving and waving same as he ran after me along lane going towards Colaba Causeway."

"But I suppose he couldn't fire at you? Not in a lane crowded with people?"

"Oh, sahib, such would not have stopped Thakur Dada. If he had been able, he would have put bullets three-four into myself, and walk off laughing only."

"But wouldn't the passersby have set on him? Held him until the police came?"

"Sahib, it was Thakur Dada there."

"Really? He has that much power, does he?"

I was beginning to wonder if, after all, I might be learning something to put into some future book. To show your hero in a really good light you need a villain of real stature.

"Oh, sahib. Thakur Dada cannot be touched."

"Cannot? So he's still there? After you?"

"No, no, sahib. I should have been saying *He could not be touched.*"

"Then it was him that you— Who was the— The victim of your first murder?"

"*Ji haan,* sahib."

It was clear only his own language would do to make that claim. *Ji haan:* Yes, indeed.

"But how? How did you manage to—to murder a man like that?"

"Sahib, I will tell you. But you only. Because I have such respect for notable British author."

"That—That's very kind. Well, thank you. Thank you."

"Sahib, this is what was happening. Truly. There I was, running and running, and thinking with each and every step Thakur Dada is there. He would wipe me out just only like I would slap one mosquito. And he is big-big and I am small-small itself. In two-three minutes I will be feeling his big-big hands round my throat. What to do? What to do?"

"What did you do?"

My heart had begun to pound almost as thumpingly as my friend's must have done.

"Oh, sahib, at that moment, just as I was coming into Colaba Causeway itself. Sahib, just outside here, going straight-straight from Prince of Wales Museum to utmost tip of Bombay."

"Yes, yes. I've been here before. Very crowded. Traffic hooting and honking everywhere."

"Very good, sahib. Well, just as I reached, I was seeing a fellow with a handcart selling mangoes. Hundred percent rotten fruit. Cheap, cheap. And idea was coming to me that if I was taking one of those baskets and tipping same on ground, perhaps Thakur Dada would be slipping and sliding and falling down to his very face."

"Good thinking. And it came off? You got away?"

Could I use that trick in a Ghote story? There were times when I had him chased by *goondas* and outnumbered. But this seemed a little too good to be true.

As it turned out to be.

"Sahib, I was not so clever as that. And also, if I had got away that time, how long would it be before one dark night I was meeting four-five *goondas* and coming to my very end?"

"So, what happened?"

"What was happening was that this mangowalla was not at all liking some passing individual seizing his basket, however much of rotten were his fruits."

"So . . . ?"

"And colliding also with Thakur Dada."

"So that put an end to the chase, I suppose. But surely it can't have been what saved you?"

"No, no, sahib. But, you see, this mangowalla was coming out fast, impact was sending Thakur Dada, who was dancing here and there so as not to slide on those fruits, falling-sprawling right into roadway."

"Yes?"

"And, sahib, bus was passing. Number One Limited, very much of nonstop."

I admit I felt a tumbling sense of anticlimax. So this first murder was no murder at all. I suppose I should have been glad to find I was not sitting opposite a killer—he had just drained his second falooda, every bit as noisily—but somehow at that moment I felt distinctly cheated.

"And then you ran off?" I said.

"Sahib, no, no, no. What good would be there? If the fellows of Thakur Dada's gang were finding out who had caused death of their hero, then once more I would be in big-big soup."

"I suppose you would be. So you didn't run off? Is that it?"

My big-eared friend sat up straighter and gave me a look of terribly greasy cockiness.

"No problem, sahib, no problem."

"I would have thought—"

"Sahib, I was seeing out of corner of eye what had happened. So at once, quick-quick, I was running back. I was taking out this knife I have." He flicked open his shirt, and I saw to my surprise that his long leather sheath actually contained nothing. "Sahib, you must be knowing that private eye is sometimes needing one weapon only. And, sahib, I was at once kneeling down and plunging same deep-deep into body of Thakur Dada and leaving there."

"But why did you do that? Wasn't he dead? Or what?"

"Oh, sahib, yes. Dead-dead. But that knife was having on it my name. So in not much of time entire Bombay was knowing who had disposed of Thakur Dada. Who had the daring to do it. So now no one will do anything against me. They are damn well knowing, if so, they are facing Murder Number Two."

I looked at my friend.

No, I thought, no. I don't really believe Inspector Ghote is ever going to have to solve the case of the serial-killer private eye.

THE PASSING OF MR. TOAD

Jeffry Scott

Times have changed since Agatha Christie introduced readers to St. Mary Mead, the place that will forever be for mystery buffs the true English village. The local folk of Jeffry Scott's Drawbel Valley have many similarities to the inhabitants of St. Mary Mead, but into their midst, true to the times, the author has thrown urbanites, advertising execs, and others who don't belong. Jeffry Scott is the pseudonym for an editor at Britain's Daily Mail, *who is also a prolific short story writer.*

The day was idyllic, almost uncannily perfect. That made what followed seem so much worse.

I remember standing with one foot up on the log, morning woodland scents blending with the aroma from a mug of coffee in my hand, and feeling a rare sense of awe and gratitude, my nearest approach to a religious response. Appropriate, since it was Sunday.

If you have no patience for ain't-nature-grand and This-sceptred-isle stuff, skip the next bit. But be assured that it's relevant . . .

My cottage being set among trees, a formal garden (any garden apart from spring bulbs in concrete tubs, replaced by bedding plants come summer) is a waste of time. There's a patio, a ledge I hacked out of the hillside, with a tree trunk set at the edge to stop me strolling over the brink after the second or third sundowner. The ground falls away so steeply that standing out there is like riding in the basket of a hot-air balloon.

St. Mary's is a ten-minute walk away but the little church's steeple is only yards off in a straight line, and almost directly below my place;

one looks *down* on the gilded weathercock instead of up at it. As for the surroundings . . . What do they boast about in Ireland, a hundred shades of green, a thousand? We have a mere fifty along the Drawbel Valley, but that's enough. Trees and bushes, mainly rhododendrons run wild since the heyday of a landscaped and manicured Victorian estate. Some laurels, many pines, and at a widened turn of the zigzag track, a veteran cedar to shade the horses when carriages brought ladies to the house to execute anaemic watercolours on clement days, last century.

Admiring all that, I was half asleep, caused by being very late to bed, and up early. To, as the old joke goes, get home again. An ignoble part of my mind—men really are the limit, some of us, that is—was gloating. Nothing adds spice to an affair like conducting it in secrecy. My partner was unmarried, but she had an image to protect. As a bachelor with no image to speak of, I cared less about keeping village gossips in the dark. But she was the boss.

Out there on the patio, another side of me was enquiring what had happened to my scorn for no-future flings, and warned that any amount of issue-confronting and assessment of emotions lay ahead. Conscience nagged that I wasn't a teenager. Nor, for that matter, was the lady.

But all that faded as I took another look across the valley. My end of the Drawbel is deep and narrow, the wound left by a titanic axe—how *that* simile made me wince in hindsight! As mist burned off, the landscape emerged like a photograph defining in developer fluid. Trees, the steeple, houses amid greenery on the far slopes were all fresh-minted, in that overture to a glorious summer day. Intellect insisted that Bristol, no small city, was only ten miles away, but it might as well have been a million.

"Dear God, it's pretty," I mumbled inadequately, and smacked my lips over the coffee, which had no chance of keeping me sleepless. Aching to get to bed yet too idle to move, I compromised by sitting on the fallen tree.

Right after the event I kept telling myself, "Nobody ought to die on a day like this." It showed how shaken I was. Not the hardened man of semi-action (witnessed a lot, partaken of little) that vanity had suggested. Before lucking out with the novels, I was a trained observer—sounds better than reporter, don't you think?—and had seen a fair amount of violence and carnage. Was shot at, arrested by the breed of police imposing force rather than upholding laws, survived an air raid:

standard been-there-done-that experiences of most foreign correspondents.

None of that prepared me for what befell poor Ben Basgate. . . .

Living on the edge of Petticoat Wood ought to have accustomed me to lethal violence. Stoats and weasels kill rabbits, foxes kill hens (and rabbits), magpies kill songbirds even before they hatch. The rabbits don't get much of a look-in, but are known to kill their own young, not to mention endless vegetation, and so it goes, day and night on my doorstep. However, human beings count more in the scheme of things. Or so they believe.

But given the context of that cathedral hush and almost daunting beauty, death was unthinkable. When it struck, the impact was all the greater.

I must have dozed, surfacing with a stiff neck and clutching a mug of cold coffee, some of its spilt contents soaking my jeans. It was about nine o'clock, birds sang and there was the faintest whisper of traffic on distant, invisible roads, sounds giving the amphitheater added texture, somehow.

And gradually I became aware of another instrument in the orchestra, suggesting the rattle of a busy woodpecker, but slowed down and oddly close, though it could not be. *Tock . . . tock . . . tock.* Certain noises do float across the valley in still weather, possibly echoing off the slate tiles of St. Mary's steeple to reach me so clearly.

The measured knocking aroused my curiosity. I knuckled my eyes and gazed around for the source.

A flash of pillar-box red drew my attention. Monks Farm was better than a quarter-mile away on the opposite side of the valley, its chimneys puncturing the froth of trees like masts poking from green clouds. The red fleck was a lot lower down, about the level of the farmhouse's front lawn. My vision is less than hawklike, but I gathered that Ben Basgate was up and about.

The majority of local folk had no time for Ben, regarding him as a traitor of sorts. Village small-mindedness and envy shaped that opinion. It's the classic can't-win syndrome of country communities anywhere in the world—I have recognised the phenomenon from Australia to America, Vietnam to, well, England. Anyone leaving a village to better himself is scorned as a loser if he fails, a show-off if he comes back. . . .

Ben Basgate was no loser. He quit school at fifteen, ran away to London, made money in advertising, and amassed more by selling out and going into the restaurant business. After his widowed father died, Ben came home to the valley to take over the farm.

His idea of agriculture disgusted Drawbel's opinion makers. In their eyes he let the holding go to rack and ruin, compounding the sin by getting paid for it because Common Market regulations encourage farmers to leave their fields fallow. Set-aside subsidies was the name of the game, and didn't it put local noses out of joint when Ben Basgate cashed in.

He ran a pop festival on his derelict acres—the village loved that three-day ordeal and the mess left in its wake—to turn a supposedly tax-free profit. Ben opened a "farm shop" stocked with stuff bought at city cash-and-carry outlets, passing it off as organically raised on the premises . . . until county council snoops closed it down.

There was no harm in him, but then I didn't live near Monks Farm, except as the crow flies. Half his larks were dreamed up to annoy the natives, simple as that. We got on fine; my secret nickname for Ben Basgate was Mr. Toad, he had that *Wind in the Willows* air of self-importance and innocent glee at being himself. A hairless head, bulging eyes, and wide mouth endorsed my label.

The one I felt sorry for was his nephew, Tom Oates. Tom had always wanted to be a farmer. So when Ben went off to seek his fortune and his dad got doddery, there was Tom Oates to act as proxy son and work the place for him. In an ideal world he would have inherited Monks Farm. As it was, Ben kept him on as manager, though precious little remained to manage. All credit to him, Tom stood up for his uncle, though privately he must have agonised over Ben's misuse of prime land.

Anyway, I lounged on my log, emulating the proverbial bump, watching a speck of red and wondering what the man wearing it might be doing. Ben never went outdoors without that baseball cap. All I could make out was the spot of colour, but it seemed to be bobbing to and fro. Every now and then came a silver flash . . . And that *tock* would stammer across the valley.

It took minutes for the message to sink in. Then I jumped up and, ludicrously, shouted, "Oi, stop it! Ben, stop that!" My voice sounded hoarse and feeble, as well it might.

The cheek, the nerve, the . . . sheer Mr. Toadness going on over there, appalled me.

Of course the vandal had got up early. Of course the red cap was moving in an arc with the rest of Ben Basgate. Of course steel caught the sun from time to time.

To explain: Monks Farm was rather grand, in its mid-Victorian, box-of-nursery-bricks way. Three floors, a pillared porch, gravel drive—and in the centre of the lawn, soaring thirty feet or so, one of the finest monkey-puzzle trees in the county. Ben Basgate claimed that it was an eyesore, darkening his lounge. He had threatened to cut it down (largely to annoy his neighbours, whom he taunted as stick-in-the-muds). They, as inimical neighbours will, whispered in councillors' ears, and as councils will, ours slapped a preservation order on the monkey puzzle. An Englishman's home is his castle, but only while council planners aren't looking.

Now Mr. Toad was having the last word by chopping the thing down. The worst that could occur was a fine of a few hundred pounds. Knowing Ben Basgate, he'd consider it money well spent. The subsequent row, daunting to most people, would strike him as a bonus. . . .

The axe swung, and an instant later the sound of steel on timber bounced off the spire below me. *Tock,* pause, *tock.* Evidently he was tiring. Ben was no lumberjack, but a bald, podgy amateur.

Dithering, first I made for the cottage, meaning to phone him. Then I changed direction to the garage. He might ignore the phone, always supposing he heard it out there, but a visitor couldn't be overlooked. Only it would take me a quarter-hour to drive down the zigzag track—very slowly if I wanted the muffler in place on reaching the road—and get to Monks Farm. So maybe the phone was a better idea after all, though the chances were that the monkey puzzle was past saving, either way.

Confirming my pessimism, a creaking, tearing noise rippled through still air, followed by a faint crash from over there. A scribble of birds defaced the sky over Monks Farm, danced briefly, and erased itself. I stood still, caught between cursing and laughter.

Mr. Toad had been and gone and done it, my word he had.

If it's not labouring the point, we had plenty more trees around Drawbel. And I have never been fond of monkey puzzles with their multiple "tails" of branches; for my money they're grotesquely ornate, unless it's ornately grotesque, like so many ugly examples of Victoriana.

All the same, I got the car out and set off to see Ben. The man was a fool to himself, and needed to be reminded of it before the lynch mob arrived. Not a real necktie party, but Peter Stuckey and his shrewish wife were probably phoning round the village by now, stirring up trouble for Ben. The Stuckeys were "proper farmers," Ben Basgate's nearest neighbours, and they detested him. He was quite likely to jeer when they turned up to protest, and that might well increase the amount of his fine when the inevitable case came to court and they gave evidence. Ben could spare whatever the magistrates decreed—on the other hand, I was the nearest thing he had to a friend, and owed him advice. The fact that Mr. Toad would ignore it was another matter. . . .

"Idiot!" I said out loud.

It didn't take long to reach Monks Farm, once out of Petticoat Wood. You go half a mile in the opposite direction, then up the dog-leg of lane to Ben Basgate's home, the Stuckeys' place, and a few other dwellings.

Gravel sputtered under my tires and suddenly the car was skidding across Ben's drive because I'd tramped on the brakes. I jerked forward and stalled with a nasty, expensive sound which I forgot about until the following day.

The monkey puzzle was down all right, its tip spearing across the lawn. About halfway along the trunk, a foot and a hand were visible under the tangle of bottle-brush tails of foliage. I got out, mouth dry, fighting that underwater-walking sensation of nightmares.

Gross, heartless humour is a blessing at such times. It's a form of anaesthetic. Going down on one knee, I pawed among the leafy monkey tails, telling myself that if Ben Basgate wasn't dead, then he had found a way of surviving with his head and chest smashed flat. As a matter of form I tried for a pulse in his wrist, and of course there was none.

"What the hell are you playing at?"

The angry shout made me gasp and topple sideways, heart hammering. Tom Oates barged past, only to recoil, a hand clamped over his mouth. "God . . . it's Uncle Ben."

"Come away," I gabbled, "we can't do anything." Tom looked terrible, as well he might—pallor startling in contrast to all that blue-black hair, shiny with grease.

"We've got to get him out," Tom whimpered. He was thirty-five, a stolid, sturdy, thoroughly capable man, but shock had reduced him to a faltering youngster. He started wrenching at the nearest branches, teeth bared, a vein rising on his forehead; I had to wrestle him back.

"Tom! He's past help. Use your head, they'll need lifting gear to shift this thing." I cleared my throat. "I think we're supposed to leave everything as it is. For the police."

Not appearing to take that in, he demanded, "What's been going on here?"

"What does it look like? You must have heard the tree come down." Tom lived in a bungalow a few hundred yards along the lane.

He blinked at me, working things out. "Yes . . . it would have made a right racket. I was cleaning house, it's my day for it. Had the music on." He was wearing jeans and T-shirt, and now I noticed the Walkman clipped to his belt with the earphones slung round his neck, stethoscope fashion. "Saw you drive past like a madman, thought there might be a fire here or something," Tom explained.

"You'd better ring for . . . well, an ambulance, I guess. And the police."

Tom didn't move. Face twisting, he muttered, "Uncle, Uncle, what *did* you think you were doing?" Gently I drew him away. In the end I had to make the calls. Doglike, Tom simply refused to leave the body.

I sat on the doorstep, wishing I hadn't given up smoking. The next twenty minutes were interminable. After ten of them, I badgered him into going indoors and making us a cup of tea. He needed distraction.

Swept off his head by a flying branch, Ben's baseball cap caught my eye. Automatically I picked it up and set the thing on a window ledge, wiping my fingers afterwards. Dismiss it as squeamishness, but while I can handle blood, literally or metaphorically, there was something uncommonly disturbing about the momentary touch of a dead man's sweat. . . .

Stan Ethrington beat the ambulance to the scene. We don't have a village bobby anymore, but PC Ethrington lives in the area, so we see more of him than his colleagues. He was in gardening togs, grass-stained flannels and green rubber boots. "The coroner's office will be along soon, but County HQ gave me a bell, seeing as I'm nearest."

Then Stan, repeating Tom Oates, asked, "What're you doing here, Billy?"

"I saw it happen. Sort of. Heard him chopping away at that damned tree, you know how sound carries on a day like this. Heard it come down. Dashed over to act as umpire in case Pete Stuckey and his she-devil were giving Ben a hard time. And I found . . . this. Him."

"Ah. Then you had better wait for PC Dennis, he's the coroner's officer." Stan Ethrington gave the monkey puzzle and its victim a cursory examination. He sighed and shook his head. "Typical, eh? Mr. Basgate was a bit childish, for all his smart business ways. See-and-must-have kind of style, no foresight. Did you think he meant it about doing away with the old monkey puzzler? 'Course not. But the fancy took him, and that was it. . . . My kids are just the same, but the oldest is six, so there's some excuse."

He wasn't being snide, just expressing oblique regret for Ben. "Wouldn't care to fell anything that was taller than me," he continued. "Seems simple, but there's more to it than you'd bargain for. Downright dangerous—shame he wasn't much for stopping and thinking."

"The trunk looks quite slim," I agreed, "it must have seemed easy to deal with." And then everybody arrived at once: the ambulance, the police surgeon in tennis whites and a brand-new Volvo, and the coroner's officer, a kid looking hardly old enough to shave, aboard a motorbike.

The ambulance men could do nothing for Ben Basgate, but Tom Oates was in a pitiable state, shaking uncontrollably, so they bore him away to Barford General "just to be on the safe side."

Cherubic PC Dennis took my statement, and he and Stan measured the tree and charted its position in relation to the body and the front of the house, with Dennis photographing everything for good measure.

Once I told them what little I could, there was—for me, at least—an awkward pause. PC Dennis and Stan Ethrington had to wait for County HQ to send a mobile crane, unlikely to appear swiftly on a Sunday. "If I don't get some sleep soon," I yawned, "I shall fall over. If you don't need me anymore . . ."

"Off you go, sir," said PC Dennis. But I didn't, for a minute. Illogically, it seemed wrong to slope off and leave Ben Basgate, tragic Mr. Toad, pinned there waiting to be tidied away. "That's his cap, it's how I spotted him," I said. "I'm afraid I moved it, picked it up, don't know why."

"Not to worry," said Stan. "Get home, Billy, you've done all you can."

And so I had. Though not the way that either of us meant, let alone understood.

The inquest did not last long. Tom Oates, stilted and uneasy in his Sunday-best suit, gave evidence of identity, a pathologist stated that Benjamin Harold Basgate, a fifty-eight-year-old male, had died of multiple injuries. I gave my two-pennyworth about hearing the chopping noises and becoming aware of what Ben was doing.

PC Dennis was surprisingly authoritative, though even younger-looking in the courtroom. He produced photographs of the monkey puzzle's severed trunk, and a chart showing the tree upright, with a large V-shaped notch a couple of feet from the ground and another smaller one on the opposite side. "Deceased obviously intended to throw the tree, make it fall, that is, away from the house. Apparently he misjudged the amount of wood to leave in place, stepped back to judge the direction the tree would topple, and was crushed when it fell the wrong way."

Verdict: misadventure. Mr. Foster, the coroner, added a warning, "which I hope the press will promulgate," about the danger illustrated by the accident. It was a tragic reminder that tree felling was a task for professionals. The press, a girl trainee from the *Drawbel Weekly News,* blushed and nodded and scribbled away; some of us exchanged wry smiles. Charlie Foster's son-in-law happens to run a landscape gardening business, timber felling a speciality. Still, the coroner's point was valid. . . .

The funeral at St. Mary's was better attended than I expected, a cynical view being that certain Drawbel citizens were pleased to see the back of Ben. Talking of which, Peter Stuckey was there with Iris—nothing like a service for the dead to bring British hypocrisy to life. Waiting to enter, I fell into conversation with Stuckey, a big, grizzled fellow with a face like a turnip lantern.

Probably he guessed my thoughts about humbug, for he began defensively, "Never liked the chap, but nobody would have wished that on him. Bloody fool." As with Stan Ethrington's similar remark, Stuckey's voice held more compassion than contempt.

"Ben would be alive today if me and the missus had been home," he asserted. "Blimey, if you could hear him all the way over to Petticoat Wood, we wouldn't have missed it. I'd have been round in two shakes to stop him. He was breaking the law, right? But our Jenny's just had her baby, the missus was on fire to see the first grandson. We set off before it was light, to get back in time for evening milking."

He'd solved a minor puzzle: why the busybody Stuckeys hadn't intervened that morning. Then the roof of the hearse came into sight over the churchyard hedge, and we all trooped in.

My attention wandered during the service. I spent much of it admiring Selina Grace. Her designer suit might be a little too much for a country funeral, but then Selina ran a boutique in Bristol and always dressed to the nines.

The coffin stayed on trestles in the chancel when the service ended. Ben was to be cremated. Tom Oates and a trio of elderly strangers whom I took to be distant relatives left together. I fell into step beside Selina.

"Poor Tom," she murmured, "he looks dreadful."

"He'll get over it." He looked a damned sight better than he had last Sunday. But then so did I, no doubt.

"That's you all over, offhand, shrugging everything off. Tom loved that man. It's hard to think of Ben as fatherly, more of a big kid himself, but he *was* Tom's uncle—and Tom lost his own parents when he was young."

"True," I agreed soothingly. And more quietly, "I must be responsible for every second message on your answering machine. We've got to talk."

Frowning, Selina whispered, "You do pick your moments. I'll phone when I'm ready. Not today, I've got to help Tom, those doddery third cousins or whatever expect a funeral tea." She hurried after them, disclosing rather a lot of elegant thigh while getting into the funeral director's boxy limo.

Trudging up the zigzag path through the trees, I loosened my black tie and undid the shirt collar. Tom Oates had invited me back to Monks Farm, too, but I'd lied about having to take a timed call from overseas. Funerals are bad enough, let alone the old-fashioned aftermath of tea and sandwiches and guarded jubilation over the mourners' survival.

Selfishly, I consigned Mr. Toad to the past, concentrating on Selina Grace and the fact that despite appearances, we were more than casual friends. Was it a simple reflex—until recently I had been celibate for a long while—or something deeper? And what did she want or expect or dread from me?

Not for the first time, I decided that platonic relationships had a lot going for them. The drawback being that they are less fun. . . . Half the trouble was that knowing myself best, I was deeply suspicious of my motives.

Selina was gorgeous, and "spoken for," as this part of the world says when a couple aren't officially engaged yet might marry some day. That made her doubly interesting, God forgive me. I can resist anything save temptation, and the lure of the forbidden runs it a close second. I liked her a lot, it could be love, but initially at least, Selina had represented a challenge.

I hadn't chased her. We knew each other, that was all—for a time. Then the Arts Council sponsored a Year of Wessex Culture or some such nonsense. Selina and I found ourselves on a dim subcommittee charged with choosing a logo. I was Mr. Local Literature and she Ms. Fashion and Design. There's nothing like shared dislike to foster intimacy, and the committee chairman was a pain's pain. We got into the habit of adjourning to an Italian restaurant after suffering him, to slander the old fool.

Committee meetings were held in Bristol. One evening I forgot about having to drive home and drank too much. Selina whisked me to her boutique in Park Street to sober me up with black coffee. The upshot being that neither of us got back to Drawbel that night.

Since then there had been four or five discreet meetings at a motel on the far side of Bristol. We'd have a hell of a good time, then ruefully agree it was silly and pointless, and from Selina's standpoint, a menace to her stable future. All very immature for thirty-mumble year olds. On the other hand, there was the chemistry. . . . Both of us kept saying it couldn't go on like this; but it and we did.

The most frustrating feeling in the world is to worry about something indefinable.

Days passed and Selina didn't ring back. I fretted: an obvious diagnosis was bruised ego. However, I've lost count of attractive women who have tired of and dropped me; such treatment is not a male monopoly. So it wasn't hurt feelings, sprained pride, or not only that. My malaise might have nothing to do with her.

Imagine trying to grasp soap when your hands are wet. I kept getting flashes of that horrible Sunday morning, a mad montage of images: Mr. Toad partially visible under the tree, Tom Oates's damaged hands after he strove to shift several times his own weight, and Ben's pathetic cap resting on the windowsill. Somewhere in there was a message I could not get straight.

The tragedy had got to me. Belatedly it registered that if I had been one of Mr. Toad's few friends, the reverse was true. Acquaintances far outnumber my friends, and none of them spends much time around Drawbel.

Clearly what I needed was a holiday. My agent pestered me to go sailing in the Grenadines, a berth was going begging on the schooner he'd chartered, all it would cost was the fare to Barbados and a few pounds a day towards food and drink. . . . I was all set until a producer friend offered an obscene amount of money to script-doctor a pilot show, so the vacation fell through. I'm still unsure whether I am glad or sorry about that. Because if the trip had been made, then Solly might never have confided in me. . . .

Three weeks after Ben Basgate's funeral, I was still up there on my hillside, and the camping-gas ran out. The cottage has mains water and drainage, but wood fires provide the heating and my cooking stove runs on butane gas.

I keep running out because—this makes weird sense, if only to me—Solly Purchis keeps nagging me about always running out. He has a vulturine air, most appropriately. Solly urged me to keep a reserve cylinder, a spare. When the stove's flame dwindled, I could hook up the reserve and get the empty one refilled.

However, that involved buying a second cylinder. From Solly. He loves money so much that malicious pleasure is gained from refusing to listen to him. Local lore proclaims that he ran one and a half miles after a tourist in a sports car, having given him one penny too much in change for a road map. Solly sputters, "People round here will say anything—that feller went off with *ten pence* of mine." (In Britain a ten-penny coin will not buy the cheapest postage stamp.) "And I only went to the crossroads, never no one and a half miles."

That afternoon I hefted the empty gas cylinder and pushed through the door of the lean-to beside the filling station, gritting my teeth at the prospect of Solly's invariable sermon. He wrong-footed me by accepting the cylinder in silence, before rolling a fresh one out from behind the counter. It's not a store, or doesn't look it, that lean-to. More of a barn and workshop where he repairs garden tools and sharpens mowers.

I was thankful for the truce. Solly Purchis broke it by grumbling, "I suppose you're another as doesn't want a chain saw." He sounded bitterly resigned. One had to smile: such a novel pitch that I filed it away for a possible sketch about an anti-salesman desperate to be turned down.

"That's right," I agreed, poker-faced. "Top marks, Solly."

"Daft, living in a wood and buying logs by the half-ton." His voice trailed away. My logs are bought from Solly Purchis. He decided to plunge for a profit in the hand rather than several, come winter. "Top-of-the-line saw, Japanese, can't say fairer nor that. Cut your own logs, eh? Let you have it at discount, fi—um, two and a half percent off."

For obvious reasons, not many customers chat to Solly. They get out in a hurry while their wallets are still in one piece. But I find him good value. . . . "Not like you, keeping inventory on spec," I teased. He is notorious for selling from catalogues before ordering the goods, sooner than have costly merchandise on his shelves.

"Customer let me down. Speak no ill of the dead, but Mr. Basgate let me down good and proper. Ordered that saw, he did. My own fault, showing a bit of initiative, see. When there was all that fuss about his ruddy tree, him wanting it down, ol' Pete Stuckey swearing he'd take him to court if he touched it . . . I sort of mentioned a chain saw was what he needed.

"Should have kept my trap shut. He wasted hours of my good time, fiddle-faddling over which one to get. Wanted it light. Great paunch on him and arms like wet string, 'course it had to be light. Had to be powerful, though, to get the job done quick. I never asked for a deposit, more fool me. Trusting, I am. Never again."

"You should have been quicker off the mark. In fact, you probably got the poor devil killed," I accused, half seriously. "He got sick of waiting and took an axe to the thing. Might be alive today if you hadn't kept him waiting."

Solly's face darkened. "There wasn't no wait! Chap who delivers my paraffin, his brother works at a wholesale place down Yeovil, he could get me what Basgate wanted. I give him the cash the same day Mr. Basgate made his mind up. My driver brought it two days later. I phoned right away, that was the Saturday. 'I'm busy now,' he says, 'and you don't open Sundays. Tell you what, I shall be in first thing Monday.' Fat chance, with what happened! Now I'm stuck with the ruddy thing."

Follow the impulse to tell Solly Purchis he was the most selfish, quietly despicable character to be found in a long day's march, and he would be indignant. So I confirmed that I could get by without a chain saw and went home.

You will think me remarkably dense, but hours passed before I asked myself why Ben Basgate had gone to all the trouble of chopping down the hated monkey puzzle when by waiting a day he could have let a machine do the work for him. A machine, moreover, that he had ordered for that purpose.

All right, he was Mr. Toad, impatient, volatile, capricious. Yet as Solly Purchis had pointed out, he wasn't a strong man. It had taken time to hack those notches into the trunk, and knowing Ben, his enthusiasm would have wilted after a few strokes and vanished once he began sweating.

I had a drink, and another. Between one sip and the next, all those flashbacks assumed significance as never before.

It was like staring at an overtly senseless pattern, nagged by a hunch that it is nothing of the kind—and then somebody turns the sheet of paper forty-five degrees and you marvel at not having recognised the picture of a faucet or a sleeping cat.

The chat with Solly did that for me.

Doubt over Ben wanting or even needing to take an axe to the monkey puzzle brought a replay of what I had seen. Okay, memory is treacherous, and I tend to embroider and adjust as time passes. It's part of being a writer. But those pictures were branded into my mind by mental and emotional trauma.

Start with Ben's baseball cap, Mr. Toad's headgear. Something made me grimace and wipe my fingers after picking it up off the ground. Now I fancied that I could feel the texture on my skin again: the strip of fabric inside the cap, where the brim met the rest of it, had been faintly greasy. Not sweat, since it wasn't damp, exactly. I had touched hair oil.

Ben was totally bald, so he didn't use anything of that kind. Tom Oates, by contrast, soaked his hair in the stuff.

Another snapshot from that Sunday morning: Tom's hands after he had struggled with the tree and I dragged him away. They were scratched, bleeding, one knuckle raw. Unwarranted damage, I realised, for a few seconds' exposure to abrasive bark and leaves.

Hands . . . I tried to remember what Ben's right hand looked like when I had made that futile check for a pulse. But I was looking away, eyes shut while my fingers rested on his wrist. Ben had been cremated, so there was no way of proving my new certainty that his palm would have been soft, unmarked, free of dirt or blisters.

It was such a weird feeling to see Tom as a killer. As if he had suddenly sprouted an extra head while we played darts at the Huntsman. I *knew* he had killed Ben Basgate and yet part of me couldn't believe that.

He had, though.

He'd killed his uncle and seen the trouble he was in and thought fast, improvised feverishly. Ben's bluster about felling that tree had provided Tom with the seed of his plan.

Just as I and every other local was aware, he knew that in the country, somebody is always watching. Only in cities can you count on being unseen. He had to work outdoors, and though Monks Farm is remote and secluded, there was always the chance of an early-morning poacher or hiker, a sharp-eyed shepherd or wandering child witnessing what he was up to. At the time they might think nothing of it, but once news of the "accident" got out, they would remember. . . .

So he'd jammed the trademark red baseball cap on his head. Anyone sighting him from a distance would assume they were watching the master of the house. If they came right up to the house while he toiled to stage the accident, then he was finished anyway, so a perfunctory disguise had been sufficient. . . .

Tom had felled the tree on top of a newly dead man, tossing the axe in beside him at the last moment. Then he'd thrown Ben's cap down and slipped back to his bungalow. It need not have taken more than a quarter of an hour, start to finish—Tom Oates was strong and adept, unlike poor Mr. Toad.

And he'd had an unwitting accomplice in me.

That was not the nastiest insight while I swirled scotch in the glass, unable to drink because I felt so sick. The worst part was that I couldn't prove a thing.

Toward dawn the following day, sleep out of the question, I crammed a few things into an overnight bag and fled to London.

I must have been operating on automatic pilot along the M4 motorway, since I rolled past Hyde Park some hours later with no recollection of events since bumping down the track into Drawbel Valley.

Tom? Tom Oates? He couldn't have. But he did, and you know it. Round and round went the arguments.

Tom had been distraught, that wasn't acting. Or not wholly. And ever since, he had behaved like a man in shell shock. Selina Grace had been right, at the funeral, saying that he loved Ben Basgate. Old farmer Basgate, Ben's dad, had taken orphan Tom in, but Ben was older brother and father figure rolled into one.

The killer had lied and deceived, yet his grief was sincere: because he hadn't planned to do away with Ben and had not wanted to. Somewhere on the Avon-Wiltshire border, zombie-driving over those undulating, ocean-roller hills, it came to me that not being able to make a case against Tom might be a good thing.

Instinct told me that he was a killer but not a murderer. He did not belong in jail and he would punish himself harder than any court could decree.

The only sane explanation was that for some reason he had snapped, lashing out at Ben—hence the skinned knuckle. Lost his temper in a flash (now I retrieved hazy memories of Tom having a hell of a temper as a kid) and been aghast at the result. They'd been out in the garden, Ben had been more than usually exasperating. . . .

I could even divine why Tom had covered up for himself. It wasn't fear of prison, but a killer cannot benefit by his crime, and Tom Oates could not bear the prospect of Monks Farm being sold to strangers and barred to him forever.

Ironically, he had not killed for gain—it wasn't in him—but that was the outcome.

In London I crashed with friends and must have proved poor company, constantly preoccupied. Still half incredulous over my conclusions, wanting them to be wrong. I even played devil's advocate, seeking to disprove what I'd worked out.

Was I mistaken about the grease inside Ben's cap? No, the slippery touch on my fingers had revolted me, making me wipe them on my trousers, though I was too shaken at the time to identify what upset me. Not perspiration, but oil or hair cream.

There had been an autopsy on Ben Basgate. Surely the pathologist must have discovered that Ben's death occurred before massive injuries were inflicted, if only by a few minutes? Had he checked Ben's hands for confirmation that a sedentary man had been swinging an axe for a long while? Obviously not. There was no suggestion of foul play—partly due to my input. The pathologist was presented with the victim of a typical country accident, and he had accepted that version.

Very well, what about Solly Purchis? Could I be the only villager told about Ben's purchase of the chain saw? Others might have added two and two, shared doubts with the police, and had them dispelled. A hopeful line—I so wanted to be wrong—but it did not last. I may not have friends in Drawbel (Selina didn't count, she was more than that, and a secret besides), but people do tend to confide in me. It was likely that Solly had tried to get rid of the saw without going into details; probable, indeed, since admitting that he was stuck with the item rather than just having it in stock would invite them to haggle. . . .

Turn and twist as I might, it all came back to a certainty impossible to prove.

One . . . accepts things. Ridiculous to exile myself on the strength of intuition and clues perceptible only to me—the material ones no longer available. To my hosts' barely disguised jubilation, I went home to Drawbel.

Naturally the great bugbear was encountering Tom Oates. Naturally he was just about the first man I met; he came into the post office shop for cigarettes while I was stocking up on groceries. I looked away, mumbling for him to go ahead, I had a stack of stuff to pay for. Tom grunted thanks and was on his way again within a minute.

"Poor chap," sighed Betty Higgs, misunderstanding my flinching from him. "Ghost of hisself, these days. Those shadows round his eyes. . . . Gives my hubby the creeps, puts him in mind of them Nazi prison camps, he says."

I couldn't follow that. Betty said, "Well, the weight Tom's lost, clothes hanging off him like a starving man. Never known a fellow grieve so. Tisn't as if his precious uncle did him many favours, but he thought the world of him. What Tom needs is to get married." She regards matrimony as Jewish mothers regard chicken soup.

Gradually I eased back into the village rut. Staying out of Tom's way was easy enough, neither of us being overly gregarious. After a month or so I was having supper in the Huntsman when he appeared. We nodded to each other. I shut my brain down and still contrived to talk soccer to Albert behind the bar.

Studying his reflection in a copper warming pan on the wall, I saw that Mrs. Higgs and her hubby had been exaggerating, but not much. Tom was less trim than stringy, gaunt, and that oily black hair was frosted with grey. When he spoke to me, some casual remark, I answered quite naturally.

There, that wasn't so bad, I thought, walking up to the cottage through twilight trees. Crazily, I felt . . . not obligation or guilt, though there were cobweb-fine tendrils similar to them, but an ambivalent sense of reluctance to let Tom Oates know that I knew. Extraordinarily, embarrassment and self-consciousness outweighed human aversion to a taker of life.

Later that night I heard a car labour up the track, headlights swept across my sitting-room window, and for no good reason, I expected the caller to be Tom.

It was Selina. "I won't come in," she called when I opened the front door. She leaned out of the car window. "What happened to you? I rang here for weeks, then gave up on you."

"Must be your turn, now you know how it feels."

"Touché." She hesitated, then blurted, "I'm getting married."

"Nothing more to be said, then," I replied woodenly.

"You don't seem broken up."

"Do you want me to be?"

"I think I do, isn't that awful." She smiled sheepishly. "You might at least look shattered."

I reached in and touched her hand. "I'm not making much sense to myself these days, not tracking properly. We had lovely times, Sel', and I'll never forget them. Best wishes, goes without saying."

"Thanks. Come to the wedding, promise." The sheepish look returned. She didn't want to add that having known the bridegroom since he was in short pants, and being a casual friend of hers, I would start tongues wagging if I stayed away.

"If I'm in-country, I'll throw rice and toast the pair of you," I replied, thankful for darkness to blur a smile produced by willpower.

That ought to have been the end of it, but these things never end.

When Selina walked up the aisle of St. Mary's, I was better than four thousand miles away, appearing on a TV chat show in New York. The host got my name nearly right and mentioned the latest book twice. In Chicago the name came out right during radio interviews, but one muttonhead forgot to ask about the book and another left listeners with the firm impression that I was peddling a whodunit while I was hyping a historical novel. In New Orleans, final stop, a charming guy got all the facts straight, allowing me to quit while ahead.

Tom Oates has gone fully grey now, his face drawn and furrowed, but the weight is back on and he's a healthier colour. Predictably, Ben left Monks Farm to him. Tom has gone in for organic farming. There's a good market for naturally grown vegetables and Ben's neglect left the fields fallow long enough for chemical fertilizers to leech out. Tom breaks even, which is all he need do, thanks to money inherited along with the estate.

Not long ago I stumbled on the last pointer to his guilt: the motive. I was lecturing at a weekend creative writing school—love hearing myself talk, even without a fee. Over dinner, one student explained that he ran a property development company ("You've heard of Sunday painters, I'm a Sunday scribbler, ha-ha-ha"). Oddly enough, his work, right down to its dense thickets of syntax, read eerily like a less genteel Henry James who knew far too much about bribery over zoning matters.

When I mentioned living at Drawbel, Don Maxwell went into a boisterous pantomime, holding his index fingers towards me in a cross, vampire-defying fashion. Steadying our bottle of excellent wine, I said mildly, "It's a nice part of the world and they gave up burning witches and eating babies . . . oh, ages ago, hasn't happened since nineteen fifty-five."

Maxwell chuckled inordinately, he was pretty high by then. "Drawbel Valley is written on my heart like Calais on Queen Mary's. Lost a fortune there. Could have made one, leastways, and didn't. Pal o' mine retired there, asked me down. You know how it is, 'If you're ever in the area,' and I stuck his address in the Filofax. Lo and behold, not a month later I went to an auction in Bath; Ben's place was an hour down the road by Jag', so I took him up on the invite.

"Well, he had this farm he didn't know what to do with and the minute I set eyes on it—golf course, I go. Golf course. Knock the house down or extend it, whichever keeps the planners happy, and there you are, clubhouse and pro shop. We shook hands on the deal, and no sooner have I set up legal meetings than the silly beggar snuffs it. Left the place to a man who carried on alarming when I said the king was dead, long live the king, let's make a cartload of money. No sale, no dice, no golf course and trimmings."

So that was the long-ago trigger. Ben had broken the news to Tom one fine Sunday morning, and died in the subsequent explosion.

Maxwell frowned concernedly. "You all right, mate? Look like you had a bad oyster."

But even that, more's the pity, was not the finish.

Not long after dinner with my rich friend I was strolling up Park Street towards Bristol University to collect some research material. And I started assessing, in a chauvinist pig's window-shopping manner, a very short skirt and long legs.

Then she glanced back and it was Selina. Fortunately my face is naturally impassive. I hadn't seen her close-to in several years. It was not that she had aged, but there were elements of hardness and dryness, an aura as much as a look. Makeup more emphatic than before, a discontented pucker to her mouth. "Billy! Are you following me?" Big smile, wet kiss.

Like a fool, effusive through guilt at being disappointed in her, I asked Selina to lunch. "Lovely! I'll just tell my manageress. . . ." Truly, it had slipped my mind that her boutique was in Park Street.

Once we had ordered, Selina burbled that she only looked in at the shop twice a week now and as for me, I was a recluse, what were the odds against the two of us, et cetera and so forth. Pleased to a borderline nerve-wracking extent.

I don't like the sound of this, whined the base, self-serving swine at the back of my mind. Married women have always been off-limits to me, less from concern over adultery than simple prudence. Affairs of that brand generally end in tears before bedtime; afterwards, actually, and because of.

Cue for tepid, neutral small talk, how was the boutique faring, what were her holiday plans . . . er, this Turner exhibition due to open at Bristol art gallery next month, wouldn't that be a treat.

The smoked salmon couldn't be ignored any longer. As soon as I paused for the first mouthful, Selina jumped in with, "I made a terrible mistake, you know." And it all poured out: husband a morose workaholic, jealous, possessive, yet unwilling to spend much time with her. "Any attention he spares is the wrong kind, checking on me. I have to keep an eye on the business, but every time I come here, there's a scene. He's probably ringing the shop right now; I told Mandy to say I'm out looking at fabrics."

"No need for that," I said firmly. "We're just having lunch, probably won't happen again for years."

"You've always been a friend," said Selina, deaf to that warning shot. "Let's not lose touch again, Billy." Which was rich, considering she had kept me uncertain and distanced in the past, dates refused, calls unanswered as often as returned, and our liaison ended without discussion.

The pattern was depressingly familiar: damned if I did, damned if I didn't, a rat either way. I could snub Selina right now, reminding her that then was then, and she was married now. Or I could stand by her, leading to meetings on the sly. I'd make a pass, it's the way I am, and the overwhelming probability was that Selina would respond, that being the way she was.

Tucking my feet under the chair to avoid knee contact, unplanned or otherwise, I thought about a friend of mine in the Metropolitan Police, a murder investigator.

He says there are two tribes of killers, and there is no point in punishing one sort, because having taken a life, they would kill themselves sooner than do it again. The downside, according to this expert, is that for some of the other tribe, murder gets easier with practice.

"I'm not talking serial killers," he explains, "just your outwardly normal citizen, driven to violence. A few degenerate into being capable of knifing the bloke who beats 'em to a parking space or compliments their girlfriend on her hairdo."

Tom Oates belonged to the never-again tribe. Ben Basgate told him that the place to which Tom had devoted all his adult life was doomed to become a golf course, and—detonation. A freak event, an unrepeatable anomaly. I was utterly sure of that . . . but not utterly enough to bet my life.

And Selina, as you will have guessed by now, wasn't just any old wife. She was Mrs. Tom Oates.

Even if I didn't make a pass (Tom represented an inhibiting factor powerful enough to discourage that), the danger was that sooner or later I would be tempted to tell Selina why her husband was morose. Then . . . who knows? The best possible prediction was one hell of a mess.

Say I kept my mouth shut and my hands to myself. Selina wanted a male admirer to share her woes and provide implicit assurance that her company was valued. Jealous husbands resent such males. Somebody was bound to see us together, or merely intercept and interpret a look between us, generating gossip until . . .

Until, for the sake of argument, I had an accident.

So—I reflected as duckling in orange sauce was served and she said what a pretty restaurant this was, I'd always known places she would like—the only solution was polite but firm rejection.

"Selina," I began, and she asked, "Yes?" on a rising note. The light was flattering in there, but I noticed the lipstick on her wineglass and the way her hands looked older than the rest of her. And, heart twisting, I chickened out.

"Just Selina," I lied. "Good to see you again."

From the way she tucked in, the cuisine was good. I couldn't taste the food.

Before the year was out my phone would ring and a familiar voice would ask if I was alone in the cottage because she needed a friendly ear. Or she'd be walking her dog—well after dark, of course—and just happen to drop in. For the first time in my fairly disgraceful life, the prospect was deeply repugnant.

Again I opened my mouth. Again I could not bring myself to tell Selina to grow up and get lost, in whichever order she preferred.

Painted into a corner, I did what any upright country gentleman would have done.

Two or three times a year I go to London for a council of war with my agent, Hal Maitland. Needless get-togethers in this era of phone, fax, and computer, but we eat and drink tax-deductibly, spinning yarns about the good old days (good because they're behind us) when he was a publisher's PR man and I a persecuted hack on the *Daily Excess.* We invariably pronounce a solemn curse on that dreadful rag; and still read the thing every day.

Hal and I were in the Groucho Club a few days after that distressing reunion with Selina. He'd outlined sundry interesting possibilities, then guffawed. "Nearly forgot. . . . There's this idealist at a tiny little West Coast college who thinks you're a loss to academe and wants to do something about it."

"Whereabouts on the West Coast—Dorset, Devon, Cornwall?"

"California, you dolt. Head of English department at this place has gone overboard about *Wails and Whispers.* According to the professor, and she should know, it's a—" Hal squinted in an effort of memory, and recited " 'an allegory of Britain's vanishing class structure, at once elegiac and profoundly pessimistic.' "

We looked at each other. *Wails* began as an entry for a BBC-TV drama anthology of social comedy. The Beeb said they didn't want vulgar farce, thanks all the same. Waste not, want not: I turned it into prose, cut the custard pies, added copious French quotations and Latin tags, and Hal found a publisher who believed what agents told him. It sold all of two hundred and fifty copies—fifty of those bought at special rates and entombed in a carton at the back of my garage.

When he'd wiped his eyes, not to mention evidence of Caesar salad off his tie, I asked Hal for more details.

He snorted dismissively. "Left the letter at the office, nearly put it in the round file, my wastebasket. One of those writer-in-residence deals. Nothing there for you, chum. They'll spring for a round-trip air ticket and provide an apartment on campus, but the place is at the back end of nowhere and they wanted you there by the end of next week when whatsit, semester, starts. Far too short notice."

"Wrong," I said. "I'm on my way."

A LITTLE DOSE OF FRIENDSHIP

Margaret Yorke

One of the finest English writers of our day, if not one of the best known, is Margaret Yorke. By the time her first mystery novel appeared in 1970, the former librarian already had eleven mainstream novels in print, so it is no surprise that her mystery novels and stories have tended to turn less on the art of deceptive plotting than on detailed character development. A resident of Aylesbury, England, the author knows how to create a sinister sense of foreboding out of subtle revelations about her characters.

Mrs. Wilberforce sat knitting by a window. Outside, the Atlantic Ocean spread before her, dark and mysterious, huge rollers billowing but with scarcely a whitecap to be seen. The ship rode with the sea's movement like a hobbyhorse at a fair. Mrs. Wilberforce had sailed, by way of Bermuda, to the United States of America and the Canadian eastern seaboard, and now the vessel in which she was a passenger was heading home.

She cruised annually, often, as this year, for a full month. In the past, she had flown to far-off areas and traversed distant seas. Expense was not a problem. At ports, she took sightseeing tours, clambering into coaches to be driven around strange cities, staring out at skyscrapers and scenic wonders, a goldfish in a bowl, seeing but not experiencing the local life. Sometimes the motion of the coach sent her to sleep, though she slept well on board, lulled like a baby in its cradle by the movements of the great white ship which carried her.

On this cruise, she shared a table in the restaurant with two couples travelling together, and Amelia. There was usually an Amelia of one kind or another on her voyages—another solitary soul. Cruises attracted solitary ladies, even solitary gentlemen, but Mrs. Wilberforce sought no partner for her remaining years. What she looked for was only a little dose of friendship.

"I'm all alone," she had told the pretty woman in the bright blue slacks and spotless white sweatshirt who had paused beside her in the Fiesta bar, out of whose large windows she enjoyed looking at the ocean. She had spoken brightly, accepting her situation in the world. The pretty woman—Isobel—had asked her if she had been ashore, had described the energetic walk she and her husband had taken round the city of Quebec in brilliant, chilly autumn sunshine. She'd spoken of Montcalm and Wolfe, of artists' studios and cobbled streets, alighting like a butterfly beside Dorothy Wilberforce to point out locations on a map.

Mrs. Wilberforce had dropped her statement into their talk, irrelevantly.

"You mean cruising alone?" Isobel, fortunately partnered, knew that many of the passengers were not accompanied.

"Yes—that, of course, but in every way," said Mrs. Wilberforce in a cheerful tone, picking up a stitch she had dropped, through inattention while window-gazing, in the square she was knitting to form part of a blanket for the needy. Who would sew together all those different squares, Isobel, no knitter, wondered; the crafts organizer, whose job seemed to be a sort of occupational therapy for the passengers? "I'm a widow," Dorothy was adding.

"No children?" asked Isobel, wishing now that she had not stopped to chat.

"No. I had a sister, but she died last year," said Dorothy. "She had no children either."

"Oh, dear. I'm sorry," said Isobel. She stood up, irresolute, not wanting to offend but not ready to listen to the story of the older woman's lonely life. "That's sad," she said, comforted in the knowledge that she had two sons and a daughter and the probability ahead of her, when the time was right, of grandchildren.

"It doesn't matter," said Dorothy. "I'm used to it."

Why had she said that, she wondered, as Isobel, declaring she must write some postcards, moved away. This pleasant woman would not talk to her again. Meanwhile, however, Mrs. Wilberforce's new and faithful friend Amelia would be there at lunch, her thin pointed nose alert as if to sniff the details of Dorothy's quiet morning spent on board.

This afternoon they were setting out together on a trip to view the autumn leaves; "Fall Foliage," as the tour was attractively described. The itinerary was not demanding and included tea at a mountain vantage point.

Amelia, a keen walker and a lot younger than Dorothy Wilberforce, had been ashore that morning, but Dorothy had not felt up to walking round the ramparts of the city, even though there was a funicular to take one to the top. Amelia would describe it all and would have bought some postcards. She'd be writing to her nephew, as she did from every port. He lived in Purley and Amelia often stayed with him and his wife Theresa, who was expecting a baby. Dorothy had liked hearing about the hardworking young couple devoted to their aunt, and she'd helped Amelia choose a soft cuddly bear for the baby.

When Amelia returned to the ship, her nose was pink from the cold outside, her eyes bright. For a disloyal instant, Dorothy was reminded of a ferret, nostrils quivering, scenting prey, then banished the reflection. Amelia was a plain woman who had missed the joys of marriage—something Dorothy had enjoyed for twenty years—and the grief of loss. Dorothy's husband had been well insured; she was, if not rich, very comfortably off, living in a large bungalow near Bournemouth. They had retired there, and two years later Jack had died, dropping dead one day while planting a new rosebush, a weeping standard, Alberic Barbier, which now thrived. Dorothy had scattered Jack's ashes round it, forking them in a little, not wanting the fragments to disperse. She had loved Jack gently and sincerely and he'd loved her too. There had been that brief escapade with his secretary when he was in his forties; she'd watched and waited, aware of the danger, doing nothing to precipitate a crisis, and gradually things had settled down. Maura had left, he'd told her, the information imparted in a throwaway manner one Friday evening just before friends invited to dinner had arrived.

"Oh," Dorothy had answered calmly. "That's sudden."

"Yes," he'd agreed, drawing the cork from a bottle of burgundy which he then set to breathe on the sideboard. "Some family trouble. Her sister's ill."

Dorothy had never known that Maura had a sister. She hoped the trouble was not of a more personal nature, but there were some things it was better not to know.

"I see," she said. "You'll miss her."

"I'm promoting Hazel," he had replied. Hazel worked in the typing pool. She was a plump, jolly girl in her first job; she'd lasted four years with Jack before marrying and having several babies, and she had been followed by Karen, a divorced mother of two teenagers who had remained with Jack until he retired.

Dorothy wrenched her thoughts back from the past, wherein they often strayed, and directed them to the fall foliage as she accompanied Amelia to the ship's restaurant for lunch. She consumed soup, sole, and apple crumble, then set off for the coach.

Their tour was pleasant, though Dorothy, after her good meal, dozed off once or twice and missed some of the fine vistas of golden leaves interspersed with bright splashes of scarlet from the maples. They stopped in a small village and entered a little church, whitewashed within and spare.

"How modern," said Amelia.

"Not at all," said Dorothy. "It's three hundred years old." Her response sounded tart to her own ears and she softened it by adding, "Though I suppose that is modern, by our standards, when our churches are so much older."

"That's what I meant," said Amelia, apparently unruffled.

That night she went to the cabaret while Dorothy took herself off to the concert given by the professional pianist who was one of the entertainers. He played various Chopin pieces and then requests suggested by the audience. During his performance the ship began to roll and that night the seas grew rough.

Dorothy did not mind the gale, but she found walking round the passages a problem as the vessel lurched and rocked. Her own cabin was amidships, so her discomfort was minimised by being at the centre of the axis, but she knew that Amelia's, on a lower deck, was in the bow, and feared that she would suffer. Each day, Dorothy went up on deck to get some air, but she did not walk about. Amelia had disappeared, absent for meals, so Dorothy telephoned her cabin to learn that she was most unwell. She did not wish to be visited; the steward was taking care of her and she would ring the doctor if she felt no better.

When she surfaced, Amelia's nose had a pale tip and her cheeks were gaunt. Dorothy advised soup and cream crackers, suggesting food might help to settle the sufferer's stomach. The seas abated to a degree and Amelia began to eat again. She went to Bingo, while Dorothy continued knitting squares, a pink one and a yellow. The blankets would be gaudy when they were assembled; perhaps they would cheer up the recipients, the children or the elderly, thought Dorothy. She was elderly herself, and ahead lay the long winter with the garden cold and uninviting. Mr. Forster, who ran the local taxi service, would take her shopping once a week—she could no longer drive. He would meet her when they docked.

She went to a film about San Francisco and dozed off at a crucial moment, missing the point of the story. Then the last night came.

By now the ship was in calmer waters and land was visible, to everyone's relief. Farewells were exchanged, addresses written down. Dorothy thought it was rather like the end of term. Some of the crew, including several of the entertainers, were going home; they were excited and happy.

"Goodbye, Amelia. We'll keep in touch," said Dorothy, who did not mean to do so. Shipboard acquaintances were better kept as such, with perhaps a Christmas card the first year and then silence.

She thought she might not cruise again. All those white heads and walking sticks depressed her, and she worried about the stewards and crew, most of them from India or other countries where poverty was endemic: What did they feel about the extravagance and waste, the endless courses on the menu, the heaped-up plates of those using the buffet on the deck? Greedy passengers ate in a day enough to keep an impoverished family for a week. But their fares paid the crew's wages.

Donating the sum she had spent on this holiday to a charity could have been a better use for the money, Dorothy reflected, closing up the holdall which contained her toilet things and nightdress. On the other hand, she had been looked after and had company, surely worthwhile ends in themselves. But what use was she to anyone?

Such thoughts were negative. She turned her mind towards home, to the prospect of Mr. Forster carrying in her luggage and Linda Cherry, her cleaning lady, brewing coffee—really good, fresh coffee. She'd bought a soapstone polar bear and a bottle of duty-free scent for Linda, and whisky for Mr. Forster, who liked a nip. Perhaps, next year, she'd spend a week in Cornwall, in a good hotel.

The passengers disembarked in sections, upper decks first. Dorothy looked for Mr. Forster, who would have had to park his black Granada in the pound and claim her on foot before being allowed to drive in and collect her.

She could not see him. Cars and taxis were coming and going; happy reunions were achieved; and people got into cars which had been left with a local garage that returned them to the dockside for this moment. None of those looking about for passengers was Mr. Forster. Then she saw a man holding a large card bearing the name MRS. DOROTHY WILBERFORCE.

She wasn't Mrs. Dorothy Wilberforce. She was still Mrs. Jack Wilberforce. Dorothy had been proud of that position, the status it had granted her. Before she married Jack she had been a bank clerk, and had not considered herself high in the pecking order. However, for practical purposes, these days, such niceties were of no account, and, tentatively, she approached.

The man, who was about thirty, thickset, with sandy hair clipped very short, wore a chauffeur's cap and dark jacket. He stepped forward as she approached and said, "Mrs. Wilberforce of Poplar Lodge?"

"Yes," said Dorothy. "Where's Mr. Forster?"

"He's broken his leg," said the man. "I'm helping him out. Ron Baldwin's the name."

"Oh," said Dorothy. "I see. Poor Mr. Forster."

"These your bags?" asked Ron, and he picked up her two cases, one of which ran on wheels. Despite the rules, his car was parked nearby.

"Yes," said Dorothy. "Thank you."

Ron stowed them in the boot of the car—a grey Sierra—helping Mrs. Wilberforce into the rear seat and aiding her as she secured the seat belt, then slid behind the wheel.

"How did Mr. Forster break his leg?" she asked as Ron drove swiftly out of the dock area.

"It was a road accident," said Ron. "He stepped in front of a car which didn't stop."

"Oh dear! Where was this?" asked Mrs. Wilberforce.

"At his garage. It was very dark—a moonless night. The car reversed away from one of the pumps instead of going forward."

As well as running a taxi service, Mr. Forster did repairs and sold petrol, employing one lad to help him.

"How dreadful. Is he in hospital?"

"He is, and he'll be there awhile yet, all tied up to ropes and pulleys," Ron informed her.

"Traction. It must be bad," said Mrs. Wilberforce.

Ron did not reply, concentrating on accelerating as they passed the city limits and reached the open countryside. Sunlight slanted amongst the trees, oaks and beeches and a few surviving elms. The fall foliage here was just as lovely as the spectacle she had seen across the Atlantic, thought Mrs. Wilberforce; it was simply on a smaller scale. She sat silent; already her homecoming was not as she expected, but Linda Cherry would be waiting for her when she reached home. She clung to that thought until Ron spoke again.

"Mrs. Cherry has had to leave you," he said. "She's ever so sorry, but there it is. She's been offered a full-time job elsewhere and she couldn't afford to turn it down, but she's made arrangements for you. My auntie will be helping out. I'll be bringing her to see you this afternoon."

Helping out, he'd said, just as he was helping out Mr. Forster.

"I see," said Mrs. Wilberforce, who didn't see at all. Linda Cherry had been with her for years, coming twice a week to clean the house and polish the silver. She went also to another house nearby, and professed herself content with these two jobs. She simply liked to earn enough to feel independent and provide a treat or two for herself and Fred, who was a bus driver. They had one daughter, still in school, the apple of their eye.

As if to match Mrs. Wilberforce's change of mood, the sky grew dark and it began to rain. To and fro went the Sierra's wipers as her spirits sank. No Mr. Forster, and now no Linda, but instead of them, Ron and his unknown auntie. She sat quietly, trying to adjust as they drove along. After a while, Ron removed his chauffeur's cap and laid it beside him on the passenger's seat. Then he turned on the radio, and pop music was relayed to Mrs. Wilberforce's unwilling ears, but she did not like to protest. Anyway, the noise prevented conversation; she did not want to hear news of other changes.

After past cruises, she had regaled Mr. Forster with tales of her travels, descriptions of ports visited and the people she had met. Now there was nothing to say. She stared at the back of Ron's head, where the fair hair sprang strongly from his thick red neck. His ears were large, with big pendant lobes. She had never liked large ears. Looking away from this alien sight, she caught his eye in the driving mirror and glanced quickly away; his expression was almost sly, she thought, annoyed that he had noticed her interest.

After today, they need not meet again. Mr. Forster would recover. There was the weekly shopping, though: Would Ron expect to take her? She need not employ him; there were several taxi firms in the area. But would Mr. Forster lose income if she hired someone else? And there was the aunt. Well, she need not decide about either of them now. She closed her eyes and briefly dozed, waking when Ron braked suddenly as he cut in past a cruising Rover Montego on the dual carriageway. After that she sat tensely, aware that he was not as careful a driver as Mr. Forster.

At Poplar Lodge, he waited while she found her key and unlocked the front door, then took her bags in, just as Mr. Forster always did. She wrote him a cheque, and he asked her to make it out to him, which seemed reasonable as he had done the journey in what was, presumably, his own car. It was only after he left, and Dorothy was starting to unpack, that she realised he had taken her luggage to her bedroom without being told which door to open. How had he known where to go?

Tired and depressed, she dismissed the question as foolish and went into the kitchen to make coffee. This was the moment when Linda Cherry should have been there, hiding her expectancy, waiting for the present her employer would certainly have bought for her. Mrs. Wilberforce settled for instant coffee and, because breakfast on the ship had been early, nibbled a digestive biscuit which she did not finish. Somehow, it had no flavour. She returned to finish her unpacking, a task Linda had always helped her with before, folding tissue paper and hanging up the black evening skirt and array of blouses which were the answers to problems of attire for nights of varying formality.

There was mail waiting, some bills and circulars, but no personal letters; so many of Mrs. Wilberforce's contemporaries had died that nowadays she received few letters that were not to do with business—her stocks and shares, her pension, her statements from the bank. She sat at her desk and wrote cheques, addressed envelopes, and stamped them; she would take them to the letter box on the corner in the morning, if the postman did not call. He would always take them for her when he visited the house.

After this she felt tired and decided to lie down. She'd had no lunch, but she wanted none. She might thaw out a frozen meal this evening and watch television; that would pass the time. In bed, under the quilt, her skirt off and her shoes placed neatly on the floor, she fell asleep, forgetting about Ron and his aunt, due that afternoon.

A sound woke her. Her legs were no longer strong and she needed spectacles, but her hearing was still acute. What she had heard was the front door opening. Who could it be? Only Linda Cherry had a key. Perhaps she had come to explain her abrupt departure. Mrs. Wilberforce sat up, clutching the quilt to her thin chest, and she heard the sound of voices from the hall, first a man's and then a woman's.

With a pang of dismay, she remembered Ron's promise to bring round his aunt, but they would ring the bell. These were burglars, imagining that she was still away. She was stretching out her hand to lift the telephone when the bedroom door was opened.

"Well, dear, isn't this nice?" said Amelia from the ship, her thin nose pinker than ever as she entered the room, smiling what Dorothy Wilberforce now saw as a Judas smile. "Ron said you'd be needing some help, and here I am. I'm sure you'd appreciate a nice cup of tea. Ron's just putting the kettle on." She advanced and stood looking down at Dorothy. "Just rest, my dear," she instructed. "Your worries are all over. We'll take care of everything. Ron's my nephew," she added superfluously.

When Linda Cherry received a letter from Mrs. Wilberforce, written from the ship, saying that her services would no longer be required, she was most upset. The letter stated that on the cruise Mrs. Wilberforce had met a very pleasant lady who, when they returned, would be moving into Poplar Lodge as a companion-helper. There was not even a cheque in lieu of notice, which was unlike Mrs. Wilberforce, who had always been most generous. Linda was bitterly hurt. So was Mr. Forster, who also received a letter. His told him not to meet her at the port as a friend would give her a lift home. He and Linda Cherry did not compare notes with one another as, whilst Linda lived one mile from Poplar Lodge, Mr. Forster's garage was two miles in the other direction. Eventually they met when Linda stopped to fill her car with petrol at Mr. Forster's pump, and by then they had both decided that if this was the way Mrs. Wilberforce wanted things, so be it. Linda found another job and Mr. Forster, his legs undamaged, carried on as normal.

Mrs. Wilberforce's bills were paid, her dividends were received, and a letter authorising Amelia Dixon to cash cheques on her account was accepted by the bank. Mrs. Wilberforce's signature was witnessed by Ron Baldwin. A grey Sierra car went, unremarked, in and out of Poplar Lodge. It was succeeded by a blue Mercedes. The bungalow was screened from the road by banks of trees and shrubs; comings and goings were not observed by neighbours, although a blond woman in a white Porsche was sometimes seen and occasionally there seemed to be late parties.

A letter stating that Mrs. Wilberforce's account was overdrawn came from the bank, with a request that she make an appointment to see the manager. Amelia telephoned, speaking on behalf of Dorothy Wilberforce and saying that matters would be attended to as soon as she had recovered from an attack of influenza. After this, boards went up outside the house, advertising it for sale.

Isobel saw them when, a year after meeting Mrs. Wilberforce on the cruise, she drove that way after a visit to friends in the neighbourhood. She had suddenly remembered the pleasant, lonely old woman she had seen standing on a verandah, a little forlorn, staring at the autumn leaves from the viewpoint at the foot of the Laurentian mountains. Isobel had felt guilty at abandoning the woman earlier that day in the ship's lounge and had sought to make amends. They had had tea together in the timbered clubhouse at the golf course, which was the spot from which they gazed upon the foliage. Golf carts bearing happy players trundled past the window as they drank tea and ate shortcake. Isobel's husband was not there; he had met a business friend in Quebec, leaving her to take the excursion without him. Later, before the ship docked, she had obtained Mrs. Wilberforce's address and had sent her a Christmas card, though she had not received one in return, but you shouldn't expect too much from the old. She remembered that Dorothy had said she was alone in the world, without even, it seemed, a cousin.

She decided to pay her a call. It wouldn't take up much time.

The bungalow could not be seen from the road. Isobel recalled Mrs. Wilberforce mentioning the garden; she had been fond of it, and her roses. Hadn't she mentioned a weeping Alberic Barbier? Isobel, a woman who kept her word, had not ignored Mrs. Wilberforce during the remainder of the cruise; they had had brief chats in the Fiesta Lounge, and on deck, braving the Atlantic gale. Now, Isobel saw the For Sale boards by the gates, then the neglected state of the place, the long grass on either side of the drive, the overgrown rosebushes. There was a straggling Iceber, loaded with withered blooms. From the car, she could not see the Alberic Barbier. Wasn't it yellow? It might have ceased blooming now; most of the roses were over.

Had Mrs. Wilberforce died? Was that why the house was for sale? It was possible: She must have been about eighty.

Filled with foreboding, Isobel parked the car and got out. The curtains hung flat at the blank windows which were, she saw, rather dirty. On the ship, Mrs. Wilberforce had always been well dressed. She was, though old, elegant, and not the type of person to tolerate an untidy garden and grubby windows.

Increasingly uneasy, Isobel rang the bell, and after some delay the door was opened by a young woman in leopardlike leggings and a gold-spangled knitted tunic. She wore high-heeled shoes, and several flashy bracelets jangled on both wrists as she took a cigarette from her mouth in order to speak.

"Yes?" she said. "Have you come to see the house? Appointments have to be made through the agent."

"Mrs. Wilberforce is dead, then," said Isobel flatly. "Who are you?" She couldn't be a niece or a granddaughter; there were none.

"Who's Mrs. Wilberforce?" asked the young woman.

"This is her house," said Isobel firmly. "Or it was a year ago."

She knew she had come to the right place; the name, Poplar Lodge, had been visible on a board by the gate.

"Oh, you mean Ron's old gran, do you? Yes, she's dead, poor old thing," said the woman.

But there had been no grandson Ron. What could the woman mean?

"When did she die?" asked Isobel. "What of?"

"I don't know. You'll have to ask Ron. She left him the house and everything, but we're selling up. It's too quiet here," said the woman.

"You're Ron's wife?" Isobel uttered the question carefully. Something was very wrong here, or else Mrs. Wilberforce had been playing for sympathy, professing an isolation that did not exist.

"Not exactly," said the woman, and laughed. "It's only a bit of paper, isn't it? Common law, it's called. Ron's out now. I'll tell him you came." But she did not ask Isobel's name.

"It doesn't matter," said Isobel, now anxious to get away. "Where does Mrs. Cherry live?" she asked as she turned to go.

"Never heard of her," said the woman.

There were such things as telephone directories. Isobel got back into her VW Golf and drove carefully down the drive to the gates. As she went, she saw the umbrella shape of the weeping rose in the unkempt grass at the side of what had once been the lawn. Five minutes after she left, Ron, in his Mercedes, returned.

Isobel traced Linda Cherry. There were several Cherrys in the directory and she tried three before finding the one who had worked for Mrs.

Wilberforce for so many years. Dorothy Wilberforce had mentioned her when Isobel, waiting to disembark from the ship, had enquired if there would be someone to help her when she reached home. Thank goodness she had remembered the name; it was a pretty one; she had said so when she heard it and Dorothy had said that Linda was a pretty woman.

"Well, pleasant-looking, really," she amended. "I'm fond of her."

Tracked down, Linda suggested that Isobel should come straight round to Number Six, Parson's Way, where she lived, and she gave directions. Soon, Isobel was sitting in Linda's lounge with a cup of tea and a piece of gingerbread while Linda described how upset she had been at her sudden dismissal and how, using Christmas as her excuse, she had gone to Poplar Lodge with a card and a home-baked sponge cake such as Mrs. Wilberforce so enjoyed. The door had been opened by a thin-faced woman with a pointed nose, the new companion, who had said that Mrs. Wilberforce was resting and could see no one that day. She had accepted the cake and the card, but there had been no acknowledgement, no note of thanks nor a telephone call. Linda had not repeated her visit.

"She had no relations," Isobel said.

"That's right," said Linda. "No one at all, and her friends had died. It gets ever so lonely when you're old."

"Yes," agreed Isobel, and shivered suddenly. "But that woman who answered the door said that Mrs. Wilberforce was her partner's grandmother. She's dead," she added. "Dorothy Wilberforce, I mean. She left everything to Ron, this woman said, and they're selling up because it's so quiet."

"But that's not right," said Linda. "We'd have known if she'd died, surely? Or Mr. Forster would. He often helps out the undertaker."

"Who's Mr. Forster?"

"The taxi. He drove her such a lot, but he was told not to meet her off the boat," Linda said. "A friend was giving her a lift, she said, in a note."

But Isobel remembered mention of a taxi.

"What friend?" she wanted to know, and Linda could not tell her.

Isobel had to return home that night, but she came back two days later and visited Mr. Forster. She called, also, at the office of the estate agent who was handling the sale of Poplar Lodge. Linda Cherry knew which doctor looked after Mrs. Wilberforce, and Isobel went to the surgery, but she received a dusty answer there because patients' affairs were sacrosanct. A nurse, however, admitted that Mrs. Wilberforce had not been seen for more than a year, which was surprising, as she often got bad colds in the winter and usually needed a little attention.

"I'm going to call the police," said Isobel. "If there's nothing wrong, they'll tell us, and if there is, the sooner it's discovered the better."

Since Isobel was not a relative, the police took some convincing that there was cause for concern, but Linda knew where Mrs. Wilberforce kept her bank account, and a detective was able to discover that cheques had been cashed for more than a year by an authorised person, Amelia Dixon, and later by a Ronald Baldwin. Signatures had seemed to be authentic; such arrangements were quite customary for the elderly, and there had been no occasion to question the practice. However, Mrs. Wilberforce had been spending more freely than in years past, it was true, the bank conceded, not revealing that she was in debt.

An inspector and a woman officer went round to Poplar Lodge where a man opened the door to them and told them that Mrs. Wilberforce was away on her annual cruise. Meanwhile, he was looking after the place, which was up for sale. She was moving into a sheltered accommodation, he declared. The inspector asked for the name of the ship, and when told, made contact with the cruise line, to learn that no passenger of that name was registered at present. The vessel was now in the South Pacific.

By the time the inspector and his colleague, with two uniformed officers, returned to Poplar Lodge, Ron had gone; so had the woman whom Isobel had met, and they had stripped the place of every bit of furniture. It was quite empty; curtains and carpets had gone: Everything that had marked a life had vanished.

The bodies were found in the garden. Mrs. Wilberforce's was close to the rose tree that had thrived on her husband's ashes; it was naked, and ringless, in an advanced state of decomposition and identified by her dentist. Amelia's was near the lily pond and it had been disposed of more recently. A large quantity of barbiturate was found in the remains, and there were signs of suffocation, possibly by means of a plastic bag. The cause of Mrs. Wilberforce's death was more difficult to establish, but because of the method of disposal, foul play was a near certainty. Traces of barbiturate were later found, and fragments of wool, proved to come from a sweater which was on the corpse of Amelia, were found around the hands, as if Mrs. Wilberforce had dragged at the wearer's garment as she lost consciousness, perhaps as she was held down by Amelia.

It took patience and many interviews to piece the story together. Amelia—whom Isobel identified from a photograph taken aboard the ship—had befriended Dorothy Wilberforce and learned of her solitary state. She had taken Dorothy's door key at some point—perhaps offering to mind her handbag while Dorothy visited the library—and had had another cut in Quebec, then sent this back to Ron Baldwin, who was genuinely her nephew, in a letter innocently carried by a dancer from the ship's entertainment troupe who flew back to England from Montreal. Amelia had also written to Linda Cherry and to Mr. Forster, and enclosed the letters with the key so that Ron posted them all in England. She had had ample opportunity to practice Dorothy Wilberforce's signature, which she had copied from the charge card carried on board. This had been enough, too, to secure the arrangements at the bank and to effect other business deals, for Ron had been able to witness his aunt's forgeries. Amelia saw no reason why they should not live out the rest of their lives at Poplar Lodge, but Ron had broken up with his wife, the blonde with the Porsche, who had never, in fact, been pregnant but was seen occasionally at first at Poplar Lodge. There had been payments to her to keep her quiet; then his new girlfriend had been extravagant and greedy. She had known nothing about Amelia.

If he'd managed to sell the house before Isobel's visit, he might have got away with it.

"Or if you'd never called," said Linda Cherry, who was wishing she had been more persistent, though it was clear that Mrs. Wilberforce had been murdered almost at once after her return from the fatal cruise.

"Or if you'd done nothing about it," said Mr. Forster. This was after Dorothy's belated funeral at the local church.

"They'd have been found out in the end," said Isobel. "The bank would have become suspicious eventually, or some business transaction would have needed investigating."

But they didn't catch Ron until his estranged wife realised, from the newspaper reports about the bodies in the garden, that he had killed his own aunt, and she shopped him.

A GOOD THING

Simon Brett

Simon Brett is one of the mystery genre's few successful humorists. He wrote his first crime fiction after serving for ten years as a producer for BBC Radio, and later took a position as a producer for London Weekend Television. His background in the entertainment business has served him well, for when he writes about the theater, as in his Charles Paris mystery series, it is with real assurance. Through his short stories, the author tries to explore other areas of the crime field, but even when his theme is serious, there is usually a wicked touch of irony to his work.

Generally speaking, it has to be said I'm quite good with money. I mean, I think about it, I don't just rush out and do daft things; I'm careful about whose advice I listen to. I can always spot a good thing.

Obviously, having been born to it helps. I mean, I have got this kind of genetic aptitude. You know, some ancestor of mine back in the seventeenth century or whenever caught on to the idea that there was money to be made in this new slave-trade business, and he went for it. Then subsequent generations chose their moment to go into coffee, or rubber, or railways, or armaments, or whatever it happened to be and, generally speaking, they got it right. Money breeds money, as the saying goes, though my view is more that breeding breeds money.

And it has to be said, we Foulkeses have got the breeding. Obviously we didn't have it when we started, but then who did? Mind you, once one of my distant ancestors had saved up enough to buy a peerage from James I of England—and VI of Scotland, don't let us forget—well, we were up and away.

And haven't really looked back since. Entrepreneurial we've always been—that's the word—entrepreneurial. We haven't just let our money sit and vegetate—good heavens, no—we've been out there watching it work for us. I mean, I've got a lot of chums who caught nasty colds over the Lloyds insurance debacle, and though I feel sorry as hell for the poor buggers—and particularly for their wives—I have to say they had it coming to them.

I'd never get involved in something like that—just salting the money away and sitting quietly at home, waiting for the divvies to come in. No, I invest in things I can see. And let me tell you, I'm pretty damned sharp about recognising the kind of guy who's going to point me in the direction of the right sort of investments. I'm an extremely good judge of character. I know a good thing when I see it.

Which is why I was so delighted when I first met Roland Puissant.

It was in my club, actually. Blake's. The Foulkeses have been members there virtually since the place started, back in the—what?—1830s, some time 'round then. Roland himself isn't a member—he'd come as the guest of a friend. He told me frankly when we met at the bar that Blake's wasn't really his scene. Didn't like the idea of being anywhere where he had to wear a suit and tie. Wasn't that he hadn't got suits and ties—he was wearing a very nice pinstriped number and the old Harrovian colours that day, actually—but he didn't like being *forced* to conform by club regulations. Said he thought it was an infringement of the rights of the individual.

And I respected him for that. Respected him for coming out with his opinion right there, at the bar in Blake's, surrounded by all those crusty old members. As I discovered later, there's never any pretence about Roland. If he thinks something, he says it. Would rather run the risk of offending someone than compromise his opinions and values.

Good thing, so far as I'm concerned. There are so many bullshitters around these days, who'll contort themselves into knots agreeing with everything you say to them, that a direct approach like Roland's is very refreshing.

Anyway, we got talking at the bar. His friend had nipped off to make a phone call—though Roland secretly suspected that the phone call would quickly lead to a nearby hotel where the friend had set up an assignation with a rather dishy little thing from a public relations company. Roland had a nasty feeling that he was being used simply as an alibi for the chap's wife.

Well, the bloke I was meant to be meeting hadn't shown, either. Can't say I was too disappointed. Some fellow I'd apparently known from Eton, though the name didn't ring a bell. Phoned up saying he'd been out of the country for some years and was dead keen to meet up with old chums like Nicky Foulkes. This already made me a bit leery; so many times that sort of introduction leads to someone trying to sell you insurance. Even been known for people in that world to lie about having been at school with you. Buy a tie and invent some rigmarole about having been three years below you in a different house and always looking up to you, soften you up a bit then wham, in with the "I don't know if you'd ever stopped to consider what your family would stand to receive if—and heaven forbid—what *if* something were to happen to you . . ."

So, basically, I was standing at the bar wondering why the hell I'd agreed to meet this bloke, and getting chirpier with every passing minute that he didn't show up. I was beginning to feel confident that the danger had passed, reconciling myself quite cheerfully to an evening's drinking, assuming I could find someone congenial to drink with . . . when—lo and behold—Roland Puissant turned up.

Answer to a maiden's prayer, eh? The other members I was surrounded with in the bar were of the crotchety nothings-been-the-same-since-we-lost-the-Empire persuasion, so it was a relief simply to see someone round my own age, apart from anything else.

And, once we got talking, it pretty soon became clear that Roland hadn't just got age going for him. Oh no, he was very definitely an all-round good bloke.

Could put back the sauce too. I'm no mean performer in the tincture stakes, but he was more than matching me glass for glass. We were on the malt. Lagavulin from Islay's my favourite. Turned out Roland loved the stuff too. Clearly a man of taste.

Well, after an hour or so on the blessed nectar, I suggested eating something by way of blotting paper. And since the food at Blake's is indistinguishable from blotting paper, I said we should eat in the club dining room. Roland said fine, so long as it was his treat—he insisted on that. I said, your treat next time, old lad. Nonmembers aren't allowed to pay at Blake's.

At first he wasn't keen on being in my debt, but he came round graciously enough. So we got stuck into the club claret. Long experience has taught me that the only way to deal with Blake's food is to anaesthetise the old tastebuds with alcohol. Always works for me—I can never remember what I've ordered and don't notice what it is while I'm eating the stuff. Perfect.

We were into the second bottle before we got talking about money. Roland just let something slip by mistake. He tried to cover it up, but I'm pretty Lagavulin- and claret-resistant, so I leapt on it straight away.

All he actually said was ". . . and you know that wonderful feeling of confidence when you're on to an absolute copper-bottomed cert of a good thing."

He could have been talking in purely general terms, but the way he hastily moved the conversation on told me he was dealing with specifics. I'm pretty sharp about that kind of stuff. Something of an amateur psychologist, actually. Well, you need to be in the kind of circles I move in. Stuffed full of shysters trying to put one over on you—particularly if you happen to have a bit of the old inherited.

So I pounced. " 'Good thing,' Roland?" I said. "And what particular 'good thing' are you talking about at the moment?"

"Oh, nothing."

But I stuck at it. "Horse?"

"No, not a horse in this instance."

I was rather pleased with myself. My line of questioning had made him admit that he was talking about something specific rather than general.

"Investment opportunity?" I pressed on.

He was embarrassed that I'd seen through him so quickly, but nodded.

"Tell me more," I said. "Always like to hear the details of any investment opportunity. We Foulkeses have traditionally had a nose for this kind of thing."

Still Roland prevaricated. "Oh, I don't think it'd interest you."

"Let me be the judge of that. Go on, tell me—unless of course you've got the whole thing sewn up yourself and don't want to let anyone else in on it."

"No, for heaven's sake," he protested. "I wouldn't do that. It's just I do hate giving tips to friends. It's like selling them a car—hellish embarrassing if the thing breaks down."

"Listen," I said. "I'm a grownup. I'm quite capable of making my own decisions. I don't get taken in by anything iffy. Don't forget, my surname's Foulkes, and we Foulkeses have had quite a reputation over the years for making some pretty damned good business decisions. Come on, Roland, you bloody well better tell me what this is all about!"

That little barrage broke down his resistance. He sighed, shrugged, and told me what it was all about.

Basically, like most financial projects, it was buying and selling. Buying cheap and selling expensive—the principle on which the British Empire was built. And the principle by which the Foulkeses had done so well out of the British Empire.

Like the slave trade on which the family's fortunes had been built, Roland's investment scheme was not illegal. Some people might perhaps go a bit wobbly about its ethics, but it was undoubtedly within the law. Sounded just the sort of "good thing" a member of the Foulkes family should get involved in.

In fact the project's parallels with the slave trade didn't stop at its legality. The commodities being bought and sold were domestic servants. Men and women from the Caribbean were offered a complete service—flight to London, job found, work permit sorted out. The investment required was to pay for these services. The profit came from the fee the clients paid to the agency which handled their cases.

When Roland mentioned this, I shrewdly asked whether the word "fee" was appropriate. Wasn't "bribe" nearer the mark? He just gave me a charming grin and said we didn't want to get bogged down in semantics.

But wasn't it hellish difficult to arrange work permits for foreigners? was my next question. Roland agreed it was. "This is the beauty of the scheme, though," he went on. "My contact has an 'in' with the Home Office."

It was the first time he'd mentioned a "contact." Felicia Rushworth, she was called. She had had the idea for the business and needed capitalization. Roland Puissant had backed her to the tune of fifty grand six months before. The return on his stake had quadrupled since then. People from the Caribbean definitely did want to get jobs in England.

I didn't ask how much the "fee" they paid for this privilege was. Nor did I ask the rates they were paid once they started working in London. When you're investing in something, there are some details you just don't need to know about.

By the end of the evening—rather late, as it happened, because we'd moved on to a little drinking club I know round the back of Bond Street—Roland had agreed that the next week he'd introduce me to Felicia Rushworth.

It has to be said—she was bloody stunning. I mean, I've known a lot of girls, but Felicia Rushworth definitely took the Best of Show rosette. Generally speaking, I keep girls at arm's length. Of course I go around with a good few—everyone needs sex—but I don't let them get close. Always have to be on the lookout if you've come into a bit—lots of voracious females out there with their beady eyes fixed solely on the old inherited. So I've never even got near marriage. Never wanted to. Mind you, the sight of a creature like Felicia Rushworth could go a long way towards making a chap change his mind about that kind of thing.

She had this long blond hair that looked natural. I don't know much about that stuff, but if it wasn't natural it was damned cleverly done. Come to that, if it *was* natural, it was damned cleverly done.

Shrewd blue eyes. Intelligent. Normally, I don't look for that in a girl, but then what I'm looking for in most of them isn't a business partnership. Anyway, in Felicia's case, the intelligence in the eyes wasn't so overpowering they stopped being pretty.

And a beautifully tanned skin. I suppose that's one of the perks of doing business with the Caribbean. Slender brown arms and endless brown legs, of whose unseen presence beneath the table I was aware right through that lunch at Nico at Ninety.

I'd suggested the venue. One of my regular bread-and-watering-holes. Sort of place that can impress clients when they need impressing. Mind you, Felicia Rushworth looked cool enough to take anything in her stride.

Roland was kind of formal with her. Don't know why I thought that odd. I'd probably assumed he knew her better than he did. After all, she was just someone he was doing business with. He was done up to the nines again, old Harrovian tie neatly in place. I think he was probably trying to impress her.

Felicia had a no-nonsense approach to the reason for our meeting. "Let's get the serious bit out of the way first," she said firmly. "Then we can enjoy the rest of our lunch."

And she spelled it all out to me. The more she said, the better I felt about the whole picture. That old Foulkes nose for a "good thing" was twitching like a ruddy dowsing rod. Felicia's long-term plan was to run the business completely on her own with her own savings, but in the short term she needed startup capital. The experimental six months with Roland's fifty grand had worked so well that now she wanted to expand the operation—set up offices in London and Kingston, Jamaica, take on staff, put the whole affair on a more permanent footing.

"One thing I should ask at this point . . ." I said, "is about the legality of what's going on. Roland's told me it's kosher, and obviously I believe him, but in my experience you don't get the kind of profits we're talking about here without the odd rule being ever so slightly bent."

Felicia turned the full beam of those shrewd blue eyes on me. "You're not stupid, are you, Mr. Foulkes?"

I gave her a lazy grin back. "No. And please call me Nicky. Everybody does."

"All right, Nicky. Well, you've probably worked out that the area where the rules are being bent a little is round the work permits." I nodded, confirming her assumption that I was way ahead of her. "And, yes, people involved in that area of the business are running risks. They're being well paid to run risks, but I suppose in a worst-case scenario they might get found out. In that eventuality no blame could possibly be attached to the investors in the company . . . although of course trouble of that sort could cut down the kind of returns they'd get." Once again she fixed those unnerving blue eyes on mine. "But I'm looking for the kind of investor who likes risks."

"I like risks." Then I added, "In all areas of my life."

She didn't give me anything so rude as a wink, but I could see she'd salted the message away. There was now a kind of private bond between us, something that excluded Roland.

I moved briskly on. "So what size of investment are you looking for at the moment?"

"Over the next year I need a quarter of a million," she replied coolly. "Immediately a hundred thousand. Roland's supplying most of that, so I'm just looking for top-up funds at the moment."

"Top-up to the tune of how much?"

"Ten grand."

"What, Roland, you're already committed for the ninety?"

He nodded. "Seeing the return I got on my fifty, can you blame me?"

"No." I was silent for a moment. "Pity I came in so late on the deal, isn't it?"

"What do you mean?"

"Well, ten grand's not much of a stake for a real *risk-taker,* is it?" As I said the word, I fixed Felicia with my eye. She gave an almost imperceptible acknowledgment of the secret between us.

"There'll be more opportunities," she said soothingly. "Better for you to start small. See how it goes. I mean, the next six months may not go as well as the first. I don't want you to be out of pocket."

"Not much danger of that, is there?"

She shook her head firmly and, with a little smile, said, "No."

"So are you going in for the ten grand, Nicky?" asked Roland.

"You try and stop me." I took a sip of wine. "You sure I can't go in for more, Felicia?"

"Absolutely positive."

"But look, if you're after a quarter of a million over the next year, surely I could—"

The blue eyes turned to steel. "Mr. Foulkes, I am offering you a stake of ten thousand pounds in my business. That is the offer. Ten grand—no more. Take it or leave it."

Felicia Rushworth was quite daunting in that mode. I left it there for the rest of the lunch. But I was a bit miffed. She'd opened up this glowing prospect to me, and then severely limited my access to it. Ten grand's nothing to an entrepreneur like me. I knew this was a really good thing, and I wanted to be into it a lot deeper than that.

Still, we didn't talk about it further, just enjoyed Nico Ladenis's cooking. Bloody good. Makes you realise just how bad the garbage is you get dished up at places like Blake's. We got through a couple of rather decent bottles of Pouilly-Fumé too.

Which inevitably led to Roland and me needing an excursion to the Gents. It was there that I moved on to the next stage of the plan I'd been forming during the lunch.

"Any chance of my getting in for more, do you reckon?" I asked casually.

"Mm?" Roland was preoccupied with his zip.

"More than ten grand . . . in Felicia's little scheme. . . . I mean, ten grand's nothing. . . . I want to be a serious player."

Roland grimaced. "Hm . . . Felicia's a strong-willed lady. She says she'd let you in for ten grand, that's what she means. Probably just protecting herself. I mean, she doesn't know much about you—only what I've told her. I know you're the genuine article, but you can't blame her for being cautious. There're a lot of villains about, you know."

"You don't need to tell me that. Do you think it's worth my having another go—asking Felicia straight out if I can invest more?"

He jutted out a dubious lower lip. "Like I say, when she's decided something. . . ." He turned thoughtfully to wash his hands in the basin. "Tell you what," he said after a moment, ". . . I could cut you in on a bit of mine."

"How do you mean?"

"Well, so long as I give Felicia the ninety grand, she's not going to know where it comes from. If you give me another ten, your stake goes up to twenty, doesn't it?"

"Yes, but that's cutting down your profits, isn't it?"

Roland Puissant shrugged. "I did all right first time round. Got a few other good things I could divert the spare into."

"What are they?"

"Hm?" He shook the water off his hands and reached for a towel.

"The other good things?"

He grinned at me and shook his head. "Have to keep some secrets, you know, Nicky."

"Okay. Point taken." I straightened my old Etonian tie in the mirror. "You wouldn't consider letting me in for more than another ten . . . ?"

We haggled a bit, but basically I got what I was after. I'd pay ten grand to Felicia and forty to Roland. She'd get the promised ninety from him, and not know that I'd contributed nearly half of it. Then Roland would account the profits back to me.

I felt pretty pleased with my day's work. Though I say it myself, I'm a bloody good negotiator. And I had achieved a fifty-grand stake in one of the most lucrative little projects I'd ever heard of. Lunch for three at Nico at Ninety was a small price to pay.

Struck me as I was walking down Park Lane from the restaurant that in fact I was almost going into the family business. The Foulkes fortune had been built up by ferrying Africans across the Atlantic. What I was now involved in was ferrying them back the other way. Rather neat, I thought.

"I just feel so dreadful about this."

Roland Puissant looked pretty dreadful too. We were at dell'Ugo, noisy as ever but smashing nosh.

"Tell me about it," I said.

"I'm almost embarrassed to."

"Come on, you don't have to be embarrassed with me. I'm unembarrassable. Anyway, I'm a mate, aren't I? Not to mention a business partner. You, me, and Felicia, eh?"

"That's it. Felicia," he said glumly.

"Come on, me old kipper. Pour it all out."

And he did. It was bad.

Basically, we'd been had. Felicia Rushworth had calmly taken our money and gone off to Jamaica with it. Whether there actually was any employment agency business seemed doubtful. Whether there was some useful contact at the Home Office who could fix work permits for Caribbean visitors seemed even more doubtful. Roland and I had fallen for the oldest ploy in the book—a pretty girl with a convincing line of patter.

"And I just feel so guilty towards you," Roland concluded. "I should never have mentioned the project to you."

"Oh, now come on. I have to take my share of the blame too. You never volunteered anything. You never wanted to talk about it. Every detail I got out of you was like drawing a tooth."

"Yes, but I shouldn't have got you involved. Or I should have seen to it that your stake stayed at ten grand."

"Well, you didn't. You were bloody generous to me about that, Roland. At the time you were taking a considerable potential loss just to give me a chance."

"A chance I bet you wish now you hadn't taken?"

"Look, it's done. I did it. Maybe I was bloody stupid but I did it. If you take risks, some of them are going to pay off and some aren't. Anyway we're in the same boat—both of us fifty grand to the bad . . ." My words trailed off at the sight of his face. "You mean more than fifty . . . ?"

Roland Puissant nodded wretchedly. "Practically cleaned me out, I'm afraid."

"But I thought you said you'd got a lot of other good things going?"

"Yes, I did. Trouble is, all of those were recommended by Felicia. She generously took care of those investments too."

"Oh. So she's walked off with the whole caboodle?"

"About one point two million in all," he confessed.

I whistled. "Bloody hell. That is a lot."

"Yes. God, I'm stupid. I suppose . . . someone who looks like that . . .

someone who's as intelligent as that . . . it just never occurs to you that they'd . . . I was putty in her hands. Is there anything more ridiculous than a man of my age playing the fool because of a pretty face? Some of us just never learn, eh?"

I didn't tell him how closely I identified with what he was saying. Instead, I moved the conversation on. "Question is . . . what're we going to do about it?"

"Bloody well get revenge!" Roland spat the words out. I'd never seen him so angry.

"How?"

"I don't know." He shook his head hopelessly. "No idea. Mind you, if I was out in Jamaica, I could do something. . . ."

"Like what?"

"I know people out there. People who could put pressure on Felicia. Reckon they could persuade her to return our money."

"Are you talking about criminals?"

He shrugged. "Often hard to say where legitimate business practice stops and criminality starts, wouldn't you say? But, yes, this lot's means of persuasion are perhaps more direct than traditional negotiations."

"Would she get hurt?" The words came out instinctively. Whatever Felicia might have done to us, the idea of injury to that fragile beauty was appalling.

"She's a shrewd cookie. I think she'd assess the options and come across with the goods before they started hurting her."

"So you think we'd get the money back?"

"Oh, yes. I mean, obviously we'd have to pay something for the . . . er, hired help . . . so we wouldn't get everything back . . . but we wouldn't be that much out of pocket."

"Well, then, for God's sake, let's do it."

Roland Puissant gave me a lacklustre look. "Yeah, great. How? I told you, she's cleaned me out."

"Couldn't I go to Jamaica and organise it?"

"Wish you could." He shook his head slowly. "Unfortunately, the people whose help we need are a bit wary of strangers. They know me, they've dealt with me before. But the last unfamiliar bloke who tried to make contact with them . . . ended up with his throat cut."

"Ah."

"No, I'm sorry. It'd have to be me or no one. But . . ." He spread his hands despairingly wide. ". . . I don't currently have the means to fly to Jamaica—let alone bribe the local villains. At the moment I'd be pushed to raise the bus fare to Piccadilly Circus."

"Well, look, let me sub you, Roland."

"Now don't be ridiculous, Nicky. You're already down fifty grand. I absolutely refuse to let you lose any more."

"Look, it's an investment for me. It's my only chance of getting my fifty grand back."

He still looked dubious. "I don't like the idea of you . . ."

"Roland," I said, "I insist."

It was nearly a month later when Roland next rang me. He was calling from Heathrow. "I wanted to get through to you as soon as possible. I've had one hell of a time over in Jamaica, I'm afraid."

"Any success?"

"Not immediately, no. I was just beginning to get somewhere, but then the money ran out and—"

"You got through the whole ten grand I subbed you?"

"Yes. As I said, the kind of help I was enlisting doesn't come cheap."

"But why didn't they come up with the goods? I thought you said they'd just put the frighteners on Felicia and she'd stump up the cash."

"That's how it should have worked, yes. But I'm afraid she was a step ahead of us."

"In what way?"

"She'd hired some muscle of her own. I'm afraid what I got into was like full-scale gang warfare. Bloody nasty at times, let me tell you. This time last week I didn't reckon I'd ever see Heathrow again."

"Really? What, you mean your life was at—"

"You don't want to hear all this, Nicky. It's not very interesting. Main point is I've let you down. I said I'd go over there and get your money back and I haven't. And I've spent your extra ten grand. In fact, you're now sixty grand down, thanks to me."

"Listen, Roland, I walked into it quite knowingly. If you want to blame anyone, blame me. Blame my judgment."

"That's very sporting of you to put it like that, but I can't buy it, I'm afraid. You're out of pocket and it's my fault. But don't worry, I'll see you get your money back."

"How? You've lost one point two million."

"I know, but there's stuff I can do. There's something I'm trying to set up right now, actually. And if that doesn't work out, I'll take another mortgage on the house. Anything to stop this awful guilt. I can't stand going round with the permanent feeling that I've let an old chum down."

"Roland, you're getting things out of proportion. I won't hear of you mortgaging your house just for my sake. We can sort this thing out. Best thing you can do is get a good night's sleep and we'll meet up in the morning. See where we stand then, eh?"

"Well, if you . . ."

"I insist."

"Where're we going to meet?"

"Roland, you don't by any chance play Real Tennis, do you?"

Don't know if you know the Harbour Club. Chelsea, right on the river. Converted old power station, actually, but they've done it bloody well. Very high spec. Pricey, of course, but then you have to pay for class. And the clientele is, it has to be said, pretty damn classy.

Anyway, I try to play Real Tennis down there at least once a week. Enjoy the game, and it stops the body seizing up totally. Good way of sweating out a hangover too, so I tend to go for a morning court.

I thought it'd be just the thing to sort out old Roland. He'd sounded frankly a bit stressed on the phone, but I reckoned a quick canter round the court might be just the thing to sort him out. I was glad to hear he knew the game—not many people do—but surprised when he said he'd played it for the school. I didn't know Harrow had a Real Tennis court. Still, Roland was at the place and I wasn't, so I guess he knew what he was talking about.

I said we should play the game first, to kind of flush out the old system and then talk over a drink. Roland wasn't so keen on this—his guilt hadn't gone away and he wanted to get straight down to the schemes he had for replacing my money—but I insisted and won the day. I can be quite forceful when I need to be.

I must say his game was pretty rusty. He said he hadn't played since school, but in the interim he seemed to have forgotten most of the rules. I mean, granted they are pretty complicated—if you don't know them, I haven't got time to explain all about penthouses and galleries and tambours and grilles and things now—but I thought for anyone who had played a bit, they'd come back pretty quickly. Not to poor old Roland Puissant, though. Acted like he'd never been on a Real Tennis court in his life.

Still, I suppose he was preoccupied with money worries. Though, bless his heart, he seemed to be much more concerned about my sixty grand than his own one point two million. I think he was just an old-fashioned gentleman, who hated the idea of being in debt to anyone—particularly a friend of long-standing. The idea really gnawed away at him.

The game seemed to come back to him a bit more by the end of the booking and, when our time was up, we'd got into quite a decent knock-up. Enough to work up a good sweat, anyway, and dictate that we had showers before we got stuck into the sauce.

It was when Roland was stripped off that I noticed how tanned he was. Except for the dead white strip where his swimming shorts had been, he was a deep, even brown all over.

"I say," I joked as he moved into the shower, "you been spending all my money laying about sunbathing, have you, Roland?"

He turned on me a look of surprising intensity. "Damn, I didn't want you to see that," he hissed.

"Why? My suggestion true then, is it?" I still maintained the joshing tone, but for the first time a little trickle of suspicion seeped into my mind.

"No, of course not," Roland replied impatiently. "This happened when I got captured."

"You got captured? You didn't tell me."

"No, well, I. . . . No point in your knowing, really—nothing you could do about it now. And I . . . well, I'd rather not think about it." He looked genuinely upset now. I'd stirred up some deeply unpleasant memories.

"What did they do to you, Roland?" I asked gently.

"Oh, they. . . . Well, they stripped me off down to my boxer shorts and left me strapped out in the sun for three days."

"Good God."

He gave me a brave, wry grin. "One way to get a suntan, eh? Though there are more comfortable ones."

"But if you were strapped down . . ." I began logically ". . . wouldn't you just be tanned on your front *or* your back . . . ? Unless of course your captors came and turned you over every few hours." I chuckled.

Roland's eyes glowed painfully with the memory as he hissed, "Yes, they did. That's exactly what they did. So that I'd have to have the pressure of my body bearing down on my sunburnt skin."

"Good heavens! And those scratches on your back—were they part of the torture too?"

"Scratches?"

I pointed to a few scrapes that looked as if they might have been made by clutching fingernails.

"Oh yes," said Roland. "Yes, that was when they . . ." He coloured and shook his head. "I'm sorry, I'd really rather not talk about it."

"I fully understand, old man." I patted him on the shoulder. "Still, you escaped with your life."

"Yes." He gritted his teeth. "Touch and go on a few occasions, but I escaped with my life. . . ." He sighed mournfully. "Though sadly not with your money."

"Don't worry. We'll have another go. We'll get our revenge on Felicia Rushworth one way or the other."

"Hope so," said Roland ruefully as he ducked in under the spray of his shower.

At that moment his mobile phone rang. It was in the clothes locker he had just opened. "Shall I get it?" I asked.

"Well, perhaps I should—"

I pressed the button to establish contact. The caller spoke immediately. It was a voice I recognised.

I held the receiver across to Roland, who had emerged from the shower rubbing his eyes with a towel. "Felicia Rushworth," I said.

He looked shocked as he took the phone. He held his hand over the receiver. "Probably better if I handle this privately," he said, and moved swiftly from the changing room area to the corridor outside.

I sat down on the wooden bench, deep in thought. The words Felicia Rushworth spoke before she realised the wrong person had answered had been: "Roland, is the idiot still buying the story?"

Now I'm a pretty shrewd guy, and I smelled a rat. For a start, Felicia's tone of voice had sounded intimate, like she and Roland were on the same side rather than ferocious adversaries. Also, if one was looking round for someone to cast in the role of the "idiot" who was hopefully "buying the story" . . . well, there weren't that many candidates.

Roland's wallet was in the back pocket of his trousers, hanging in the locker. Normally I wouldn't pry into a chap's private possessions, but, if the ugly scenario slowly taking shape in my brain was true, then these weren't normal circumstances.

Nothing in the wallet had the name "Roland Puissant" on it. All the credit cards were imprinted with "R.J.D. Rushworth." In the jacket pocket I found a book of matches from the Sunshine Strand Luxury Hotel, Montego Bay, Jamaica.

I heard the door to the changing room clatter closed and looked up. "Roland" was holding the phone, and had a towel wrapped round his waist.

"God, she's got a nerve, that woman—bloody ringing me up to taunt me about what she's done."

"Oh, yes?"

He must've caught something in my tone, because he looked at me sharply. "What's up, old man?"

"The game, I would say, 'Roland Puissant.' "

He looked genuinely puzzled. "Look, I'm sorry. I told you I haven't played for a while, bit rusty on the old—"

"Not that game. You know exactly what I mean."

"Do I?"

I hadn't moved from the bench. I'd curbed my anger, not even raised my voice while I assessed how I was going to play the scene.

I still didn't raise my voice, as I said, "I've just looked in your wallet. All your credit cards are in the name of R.J.D. Rushworth."

"Yes," he replied in a matter-of-fact way. "I only got back last night. I haven't got round to changing them yet."

"What do you mean? Aren't you R.J.D. Rushworth?"

He looked at me incredulously. "Of course I'm not, Nicky. For God's sake—you know I'm Roland Puissant, don't you? But you surely never thought I was going to travel to Jamaica under my own name, did you? I didn't want to advertise to Felicia what I was up to."

For a second I was almost convinced, until another discordant detail struck me. "But why, of all the names in the world, did you choose her name—'Rushworth'?"

"Well, I had to get to see her, didn't I? Felicia's got her security pretty well sorted out. I had to pretend to be her husband, so that they'd let me through to her."

"But the minute she saw you, your cover'd be blown."

"That was a risk I was prepared to take." He winced. "An ill-advised one, as it turned out."

"What do you mean?"

"I'd been hoping that I'd get to see her on her own, but a couple of her heavies took me in. Well, I had no chance then, had I?"

"That's when the torturing started?"

He nodded, then shook his head. "I'd rather not talk about it, if you don't mind."

My heart went out to him. Poor bugger, not only had he lost all his money and been tortured by Caribbean thugs, now one of his best friends was suspecting him of . . .

Just a minute. Just a minute, I said to myself, hold your horses there, old man. The way he'd accounted for the credit cards was maybe feasible, but it didn't explain the words with which Felicia had opened her telephone call.

"When I answered your phone," I began coolly, "Felicia, presumably thinking she'd got through to you, said: 'Roland, is the idiot still buying the story . . . ?' "

"Yes," he agreed, totally unfazed.

"Well, would you like to explain to me what she meant by that, because I'm not much enjoying the only explanation my mind's offering."

Roland looked torn. At last he sighed and said, "Well, all right. I suppose I'll have to tell you. I wanted to keep it a secret, but . . ." He sighed again. "Nicky, you've heard of Jeffrey Archer?"

"Hm? Yes, of course I have, but what the hell's he got to do with what we're talking about?"

"Well, you may know that he lost a lot of money in an investment that went wrong . . ."

"Yes. I've heard the story."

". . . and then he fixed the situation by writing his way out of it."

"Mm."

"He sold books and ideas for books and made another huge fortune from that."

"Yes, I still don't see—"

"That's what I've been trying to do, Nicky. I've felt so absolutely lousy about the way you've lost money over this—and all because of me—that I've been trying to sell a book idea so that I can pay you back."

"Really?"

"Yes. I've worked out a synopsis. A story about a con man and—touch wood—it's looking good. There's a publisher who's expressing interest—strong interest. Trouble is, I was stupid enough to mention this to Felicia when I was in Jamaica, and now of course she'll never let me hear the end of it. She's tickled to death that she's driven me to try and make money as a writer."

"So what she said . . . ?"

"Exactly. She was talking about this publisher . . . for whom she doesn't have a lot of respect. That's why she said, 'Roland, is the idiot still buying the story?' "

I couldn't think of anything to say.

"And the answer," Roland went on, "is—please God—yes. Because if the idiot *does* buy the story, then I have a chance of paying back at least some of the money that my foolish advice has cost one of my best mates—Nicky Foulkes."

I felt very humbled, you know, by the way Roland was taking my troubles on himself in this way. And to think of the suspicions I'd been within an ace of voicing about him. Well, thank God some instinct stopped me from putting them into words.

Even a nature as generous and loyal as Roland Puissant's might have found that kind of accusation a bit hard to take. Sort of thing that could ruin a really good friendship.

Roland's back in the country again. Called me a couple of days ago. He's been having a dreadful time. Well, we'd both agreed after Felicia managed to escape him in Jamaica he should have another go to try and retrieve our money. He went on again about mortgaging his house, but I said, don't be daft, we're in this together, and stumped up a bit of ante for his expenses.

Trouble was, when he got to Jamaica, he found Felicia'd moved on. To Acapulco. So he's had to spend the last month down there trying to find her and put the pressure on. Poor bugger, rather him than me, I must say. But one can't but admire his dedication. I'm lucky to have someone like him out there rooting away on my behalf.

Anyway, we've fixed to get together next week. Roland's a bit busy at the moment. But he's making time to meet up with me. Letting me take him out for dinner at Bibendum. Expensive I know, but it'll be a small price to pay. Roland never stops, you know. Always grafting away on some new scheme or other. He's got a whole lot of new investment opportunities he's going to put my way. If I play my cards right, you know, I think I could be on to another good thing.

THE PUSHOVER

Peter Lovesey

Peter Lovesey began his career with a submission to a first-novel contest run in conjunction with Macmillan/Panther, in 1970. A schoolteacher at the time, he won the contest with a tale set in Victorian England and has gone on to write many more books about the period. His first-place finish in the Mystery Writers of America's Fiftieth Anniversary Short Story Contest in 1994 forms another bookend to his career to date. His ability to combine successfully the demands of good plotting with true characterizations and insightful prose led to his taking the MWA's top honors with the following story.

During the singing of the Twenty-third Psalm, the man next to me gave me a nudge and said, "What do you think of the wooden overcoat?"

Uncertain what he meant, I lifted an eyebrow.

"The coffin," he said.

I swayed to my left for a view along the aisle. I could see nothing worth interrupting the service for. Danny Fox's coffin stood on trestles in front of the altar looking no different from others I had seen. On the top was the wreath from his widow, Merle, in the shape of a large heart of red roses with Danny's name picked out in white. Not to my taste, but I wasn't so churlish as to mention this to anyone else.

"No handles," my informant explained.

So what? I thought. Who needs handles? Coffins are hardly ever carried by the handles. I gave a nod and continued singing.

"That isn't oak," the man persisted. "That's a veneer. Underneath, it's chipboard."

I pretended not to have heard, and joined in the singing of the third verse—the one beginning "Perverse and foolish oft I strayed"—with such commitment that I drew shocked glances from the people in front.

"She's going to bury Danny in the cheapest box she could buy."

This baboon was ruining the service. I sat for the sermon in a twisted position, presenting most of my back to him.

But the damage had been done. My response to what was said was blighted. If John Wesley in his prime had been giving the Address, I would still have found concentration difficult. Actually it was spoken by a callow curate with a nervous grin who revealed a lamentable ignorance about the Danny I had known. "A decent man" was a questionable epithet in Danny's case; "a loyal husband" extremely doubtful; "generous to a fault" a gross misrepresentation. I couldn't remember a time when the departed one had bought a round of drinks. If the curate felt obliged to say something positive, he might reasonably have told us that the man in the coffin had been funny and a charmer capable of selling sand to a sheik. I cared a lot about Danny, or I wouldn't be here, but just because he was dead we didn't have to award him a halo.

My contacts with the old rogue went back thirty years. Danny and I first met back in the sixties, the days of National Service, in the air force, at a desolate camp on Salisbury Plain called Netheravon, and even so early in his career, Danny had got life running the way he wanted. He'd formed a poker school with a scale of duties as the stakes and, so far as I know, served his two years without ever polishing a floor, raking out a stove, or doing a guard duty. No one ever caught him cheating, but his silky handling of the cards should have taught anyone not to play with him. He seduced (an old-fashioned word that gives a flavour of the time) the only WRAF officer on the roll and had the use of her pale blue Morris Minor on Saturdays to support his favourite football team, Bristol Rovers. Weekend passes were no problem. You had to smile at Danny.

I came across him again twelve years later, in 1973, on the sea front at Brighton dressed in a striped blazer, white flannels, and a straw hat and doing a soft-shoe dance to an old Fred Astaire number on an ancient windup Gramophone with a huge brass horn. I had no idea Danny was such a beautiful mover. So many people had stopped to watch that you couldn't get past without walking on the shingle. It was a deeply serious performance that refused to be serious at all. At a tempo so slow that any awkwardness would have been obvious, he shuffled and glided and turned about, tossing in casual gull turns and toe taps, dipping, swaying, and twisting with the beat, his arms windmilling one second, seesawing the next, and never suggesting strain. After he'd passed the hat around, we went for a drink and talked about old times and former comrades. I paid, of course. After that we promised to stay in touch. We met a few times. I went to his second wedding in 1988—a big affair, because Merle had a sister and five brothers, all with families. They were a crazy bunch. The reception, on a river steamer, was a riot. I've never laughed so much.

Danny was fifty-seven when he died.

We sang another hymn and the curate said a prayer and led us out for the committal. The pallbearers hoisted the coffin and brought it along the aisle. I didn't need the nudge I got from my companion as they passed. I could see for myself that the wood was a cheap veneer. I wasn't judgmental. Quite possibly Danny had left Merle with nothing except his antique Gramophone and some debts.

"She had him insured for a hundred and fifty K," Mean-mouth insisted on telling me as we followed the coffin along a path between the graves. "She could have given him a decent send-off."

I told him curtly that I wasn't interested. God knows, I was trying not to be. At the graveside, I stepped away from him and took a position opposite. Let him bend someone else's ear with his malice.

Young sheep were bleating in the field beside the churchyard as the coffin was lowered. The clouds parted and we felt warmth on our skins. I remembered Danny dancing on the front that summer evening at Brighton. *Bon voyage,* old buccaneer, I thought. You robbed all of us of something, sometime, but we came in numbers to see you off. You left us glittering memories, and that wasn't a bad exchange.

A few tears were shed around that grave.

As the Grace was spoken I became conscious of those joyless eyes sizing me up for another approach, so I gave him one back, raised my chin to the required level, and stared like one of those stone figures on Easter Island. My twenty years of teaching fifteen-year-olds haven't been totally wasted. Then I turned away, said "Amen," and smiled benignly at the curate.

Mean-mouth walked directly through the lych gate, got into his car, and drove off. Why do people like that bother to come to funerals?

Most of us converged on the Red Lion across the street. A pub lunch. A corrective to nostalgia. It fitted my picture of Danny that his mourners should be forced to dip into their pockets to buy their own drinks. The only food on offer was microwaved meat pies with soggy crusts. Mean-mouth must have known. He would have told me that Merle was the skinflint, and on sober reflection it is difficult to believe otherwise. It seemed Danny had ended up with a tightwad wife. A nice irony.

And the family weren't partying at the house. They joined us, Merle leading them in while "Happy Days Are Here Again" came over the music system. Her choice of clothes left no one in any doubt that she was the principal lady in the party—a black cashmere coat and a matching hat with a vast brim like a manta that flapped as she moved. She was a good ten years younger than Danny, a tall, triumphantly slim, talkative woman who chain-smoked. I'd heard that she knew a lot about antiques; at their wedding, Danny had got in first with the obvious joke about his antiquity, and frankly the way Merle had eyed him all through the reception, you'd have thought he was a piece of Wedgwood. Yet we all knew he was out of the reject basket. Slightly chipped. Well, extensively, to be truthful. He'd lived the kind of free-ranging life he'd wanted, busking, bartending, running a stall at a fairground, a bit of chauffeuring, leading guided walks around the East End, and for a time acting as a croupier. Enjoyable, undemanding jobs on the fringe of the entertainment industry, but never likely to earn much of a bank balance. With his innocent-looking eyes and deep-etched laughter lines, he had a well-known attraction for women that must have played a part in the romance, but Merle didn't look the sort to go starry-eyed into marriage.

Someone bought her a cocktail in a tall glass and she began the rounds of the funeral party, cigarette in one hand, drink in the other, giving and receiving kisses. The mood of forced bonhomie that gets people through funerals was well established. I overheard one formidably fat woman telling Merle, "Never mind, love, you're not bad-looking. Keep your 'air nice and you'll be all right. Won't 'appen at once, mind. I 'ad to wait four years. But you'll be all right."

Merle's hat quivered.

She moved towards me and I gave her the obligatory kiss and muttered sympathetic words. She said, "Good of you to come. We never really got to know each other, did we? You and Danny go back a long way."

"To his air force days," I said.

"Oh, he used to tell wonderful tales of the RAF," she said, calling it the "raff" and clasping my hand so firmly that I could feel every one of her rings. "I don't know if half of them are true. The night exercises."

"Night exercises at Netheravon?" said I, not remembering any.

She took hold of my hand and squeezed it. "Come on, you know Danny. That was his name for that pilot officer whose car he used."

"Oh, her."

"Night exercises. Wicked man." She chuckled. "I couldn't be jealous when he put it like that. To Danny, she was just an easy lay. I envy you, knowing him when he was young. He must have been a right tearaway. Anyway, sweetie, I'd better not gossip. So many old mates to see." She moved on, leaving me in a cloud of cigarette smoke.

Another woman holding a gin and tonic sidled close and said, "What's she on, do you think? She's frisky for a widow."

"I've no idea."

"Danny's brother Ben must have given her some pills."

"Which one is Ben?"

"In the blue suit and black polo neck. Handy having a doctor for your brother-in-law."

"Yes." I glanced across at brother-in-law Ben, a taller, slimmer version of Danny. "He looks young."

"Fourteen years younger than Danny. They were stepbrothers, I think."

On an impulse I asked, "Was he Danny's doctor also?"

She nodded. "They never paid a bean for medicines."

Malice must be infectious. This wasn't Mean-mouth speaking. This was a short, chunky woman in a grey suit. She introduced herself as their neighbour. Not for much longer, it seemed. "Merle told me she'll be off to warmer climes now. She was always complaining about the winters here, was Merle."

"To live, you mean?"

She nodded. "Spain, I expect."

I remembered the life insurance payout. Merle's antique had, after all, turned out to be worth something if she was emigrating. Watching the newlyweds at their wedding reception, only four years ago, it hadn't crossed my mind to rate Danny as an insurance claim. Had it occurred to Merle?

What a sour thought to have at a funeral! I banished it. Instead I talked to the neighbour about the weather until she got bored and wandered off.

I did some circulating of my own and joined a crowd at a table in the main bar I recognised as more of Danny's close family. They all had large teeth and lopsided grins like his. A man who looked like another younger brother was saying what a shock his death had been. "Fifty-seven. It's no age, is it? He was always so fit. I never knew Dan had a dicky heart."

"He didn't look after himself," a woman said.

"What do you mean—didn't look after himself?" the brother retorted. "He wasn't overweight."

"He didn't exercise. He avoided all forms of sport. Never learned to swim, hold a tennis racket, swing a golf club. He thought jogging was insane."

"He danced like a dream."

"Call that exercise? He never worked up a sweat. I tell you, he didn't look after himself."

"He had two wives," one of the men chipped in.

"Not at the same time," another woman said, giggling.

"What are you saying—that two wives strained his vital powers?"

There was some amusement at this. "No," said the man. "*You* said he didn't look after himself and I was pointing out that he had two women to do the job."

"That's what marriage is for, is it, Charlie?" the woman came back at him. "So that the man's got someone to look after him?"

"Hello, hello. Have you turned into one of those feminists?" retorted Charlie.

"I'm sure being looked after wasn't in Danny's mind when he married Merle," said the giggly woman.

"We all know what was in Danny's mind when he married Merle," said the feminist.

Resisting the temptation to widen the debate by asking what had been in Merle's mind, I went back to the bar for a white wine. When I picked it up, my hand shook. A disturbing possibility had crept into *my* mind. The law allows a doctor considerable discretion in dealing with the death of a patient in his care. Provided that he has seen the patient in the two weeks prior to the death, and the cause of death is known to him and was not the result of an accident, or suspicious circumstances, he may sign the death certificate without reporting the matter to the coroner. Merle's brother-in-law Ben had treated Danny.

Across the bar, Ben was talking affably to some people who hadn't attended the funeral. This was his village, his local. Most of the family lived around here. He was at ease. Yet there was something more about his manner, a sense of relief; or perhaps it was triumph.

As for Merle, she was remarkably animated for a woman who had only just buried her husband. It must be an act, a brave attempt to get through the day without weeping, I tried telling myself. Watching her, I wasn't convinced. Her eyes shone like a bride's.

Another curious thing I noticed was that Merle spent time with everyone in that bar except her doctor brother-in-law, Ben. She kept away from him as if he were radioactive. Yet they were keenly aware of each other. Each time Merle moved, Ben would look across and check her position. Occasionally their eyes locked briefly. I was increasingly convinced that they had agreed not to be seen talking together. They weren't being hostile; they shared a secret.

When I left about six, the party was still going on. I didn't blame anyone for turning it into a wake. I was sure Danny would have approved. He would have been in the thick of the junketing, well pickled by this time, full of good humour, just as long as he didn't have to buy a round.

My unease about the circumstances of Danny's death dispersed within a week. I had more urgent things going on in my life that don't play any part in these events except that by February, six months after the funeral, I was tired and depressed. Then someone made things worse by breaking into my car and stealing my credit cards. The police were useless. The only positive thing they suggested was that I inform the people who issued the cards. When my shiny and pristine replacement cards arrived, I had an impulse to use them right away to give myself a boost. I walked into a travel agent's and booked two weeks in the sun. Immediately.

In Florida, I spotted Merle Fox. By pure chance, or fate, I walked into the Guild Hall Gallery on Duval Street in Key West and there she was, looking at stained-glass pictures of fish. She'd bleached her hair and cut it short and she was deeply tanned and wearing a skimpy top and white trousers that fitted like a second skin. Something new in widow's weeds, I thought unkindly—for I recognised her straightaway. Of course, she hadn't altered her features, but her stance was the giveaway, the suggestion of swagger in the shoulders. It was no different from the way she'd swanned around the bar of the Red Lion after Danny's funeral.

I didn't speak to Merle. In fact, I moved out of range, hidden from her view by a rotating card stand. But when she came out of the shop I followed, intrigued, you may say, if you don't call me nosy. I was pretty inconspicuous in T-shirt and shorts, like most of the tourists strolling along the street.

Halfway along Duval Street she turned up a side road that was mainly residential and lined with two-story Bahamian-style wood-frame buildings shaded by palms and wild purple orchid trees and fronted by white picket fences. She walked two blocks (with me in discreet attendance) and let herself into an elegant three-bay house with a porch and—more irony here—a widow's walk. Had I really seen Merle? The moment she'd stepped out of my view I became doubtful. It isn't the custom in Key West to have one's name on the mailbox, so it was difficult to make certain without speaking to the woman. I wasn't sure I wanted a face-to-face.

I crossed the street for a longer view of the house. The shutters were open, but the louvred windows effectively screened the interior.

You wouldn't believe that a leafy street bathed in sunlight could make you feel uneasy. After the crowds on Duval Street, this was eerie in its quietness.

A cat leaned against my shin and made a plaintive sound. I stooped to stroke it.

A voice startled me. "We call him Rocky, after the boxer. He has the most formidable front paws."

I looked behind me. This elderly woman had been sitting unnoticed in her porch swing in front of a small white house.

"He's a champion," I remarked, wondering if my luck was still running. "I was looking for a friend of mine who came to live in Key West. Mrs. Fox. Do you know her?"

She paused some seconds before answering, "I can't say I do."

"She must have arrived sometime in the last three months," I ventured. "She's a widow."

"The only lady who came to Southard Street since the summer is Mrs. Finch in the house across the street, and she's no widow," she informed me.

My confidence ebbed. "Mrs. Finch, you said?"

"Mrs. Merle Finch, from England. They're both from England."

"Ah. That wouldn't be the lady I know," I said, mentally turning a back-flip of triumph. "But thank you for your help, ma'am. Rocky is a cat in a million." I walked away, reflecting that Merle must have kept her hair extra nice to have charmed Mr. Finch, whoever he was, into such a quick marriage. A little over six months since she had buried Danny, she was remarried, settled in her new home. If her tan was any guide, she had already been in Florida some time.

The big insurance payout, the death certificate provided by her brother-in-law, the quick marriage, and the escape to Florida. Had they all been planned? Was it any wonder I felt suspicious?

My holiday routine altered. Next morning I made sure of passing the house on my way to the shops. I lingered across the street for ten minutes or so. Wherever I went in Key West I was hawk-eyed for another sighting.

It came the next evening. Merle stepped out of Fausto's Food Palace on Fleming Street, crossed my path to a moped, and put her bag on the pannier. My heart rate stepped up. The hours of watching out for her, passing the house and so on, had made me feel furtive. Now I was ready to panic. Ridiculous.

I don't like being sneaky. That isn't my nature. I like to be straight with people. Confrontation is the honest way. So I steeled my nerves, stepped towards her, and said, "Hi, Merle."

She stopped and stared.

"Remember me?" I said. "Danny's oppo from his air force days. Isn't this amazing? I must buy you a drink."

She couldn't deny her identity. Recovering her poise, she said in her very British accent that she would have been delighted, but she had to get back to the apartment. She had something cooking.

I almost laughed out loud at the phrase. Instead I insisted we must meet and suggested a nightcap later at one of the quieter open-air bars. She had a hunted look, but she agreed to see me there at ten.

"You got your wish, then," I said when we shared a table in a dark corner of the bar drinking Margaritas.

"What do you mean?" She was tense.

"A warm place to live. I presume you live here."

"Yes, I do."

"And not alone. You're Mrs. Finch now."

She frowned. "How did you know that?"

"I was told. Is he British, your husband?"

She gave a nod.

"Anyone I know?"

She said, "Why are you asking me these things?"

I said, "What's the matter? Don't you want to talk about them?"

She said, "I left all that behind. It's painful. I don't want to be reminded."

"I wasn't reminding you about the past, Merle. I was enquiring about the present. Your present husband. What's his name?"

She took a long sip of her drink. "Have you seen him?"

"No. But I'd love to meet him—if you let him out."

She pushed aside the drink. "I'll pay for these. I'm leaving."

I put a hand on her arm. "I'm sorry. That was insensitive. Don't take offence."

She brushed my hand away and got up. I didn't follow. I knew it would be no use. I *had* been insensitive. But she had fuelled my suspicions. She had behaved like a guilty woman. Meeting me had been an unpleasant shock. The geography of the Florida Keys—the long drive south from Miami over bridges that span the sea—fosters a feeling of escape, of reaching a haven in Key West bathed in sun and goodwill. You don't expect sharp questions about your conduct.

I believed Merle and her brother-in-law Ben had conspired to murder Danny. A lethal injection seemed the most likely means. Ben had written something innocuous on the death certificate and Merle had claimed the insurance, paid Ben for his services, and escaped to Florida to marry her lover, the fascinating Mr. Finch.

I believed this, yes. But it was only belief so far. The evidence I had was circumstantial. A cheap funeral, an alleged insurance payout, some sly glances, and a quick marriage. None of this was sufficient to justify fingering Merle for murder.

Unable to sleep that night, I asked myself why I wanted to pursue the matter, for it was taking over my holiday. Was it anything as high-minded as a concern for justice? Or was it morbid curiosity?

No.

It was more personal. Danny had been important in my life. The link between us was stronger than I'd admit to anyone. I was angry, deeply angry, at what I believed had happened. Our lives had touched only intermittently since 1961, and I regretted that. Face it, I thought. His murder killed a part of you.

Yet I knew if I pursued this, I was putting myself at risk. If I threatened Merle with exposure, I would give her a reason for killing me. Or having me killed.

These were the thoughts I grappled with the next day. They made me sick with self-disgust because I had discovered I was a coward. I was scared to do any more about my suspicions. I despised myself.

So I became a tourist again, instead of a snoop. I lounged by the hotel pool in the morning and later took a trip to the coral reef in a glass-bottomed boat. I spent an hour in the cemetery. Morbid, you may think, but the gravestones are on the tourist trail. I found the famous epitaph *"I told you I was sick."* It didn't seem funny when I saw it.

Late in the afternoon, I had a quiet drink in one of the smaller bars on Duval Street, watching the movement of people towards Mallory Square. There's a tradition in Key West that people converge on the dock to celebrate the sunset. When I'd finished my drink, I joined them.

I didn't expect to meet Merle there. As a resident, she'd regard the sunset spectacle as a sideshow for tourists. Even so, as I sidled through the good-natured crowd I caught myself looking more than once at women who resembled her and the men they were with. I still wanted keenly to catch a glimpse of Mr. Finch, the new husband.

The sky became pastel blue and the sun dipped towards the sea, becoming ever more red. The heads of some of the crowd were in silhouette. At one end a tightrope was slung between tripod posts and the performer was teasing his audience, keeping *them* in suspense with patter and juggling. I ambled on, past a guitarist and a dog trainer. Ahead, someone else had drawn a fair crowd. A fire-eater, I guessed. There's something hypnotic about the sight of a flame, particularly in the fading light. But I decided the aerialist would be better value and I turned back. I was actually retracing my steps when I heard a scratchy sound that froze my blood, an old 78 record of a band playing some song from way back. It was coming from behind the crowd at the end.

I returned, fast.

I couldn't see for the tightly packed people. I circled the crowd in frustration while that infernal tune blared out. Unable to contain my feelings, I scythed through the crowd saying, "I'm sorry, I have to get through"—until I had a view.

Danny was wowing them in his straw hat, blazer, and flannels, hoofing it just as smoothly as he had in the old days. Far from dead, he had a better colour than most of his audience. The old Gramophone was behind him on the ledge, grinding out "Let's Face the Music and Dance."

He saw me and winked.

I stared back, stunned. Maybe I should have rejoiced, but I'd grieved for this fraudster. I was more angry than relieved. It was a kind of betrayal.

Coward that I am, afterwards, when the sun had set and the crowds had dispersed, I sat tamely with Danny on a ledge of the sea wall at the south end of the dock, our backs to the sea. He had a six-pack of Coors that he systematically emptied. Dancing, he explained, was thirsty work. He offered me some, and I declined.

"Merle told me she met you," he admitted. "She didn't want me to come out tonight, but I'm a performer, damnit. The show goes on. She doesn't understand that you and I go back a long way. You wouldn't blow the whistle on your old RAF buddy."

I didn't rise to that. "You've played some cool poker hands in your time, Danny, but this beats everything. I don't know how you managed it."

He grinned. "No problem. My stepbrother Ben is my doctor. He signed the death certificate. Merle picked up the life insurance and here we are—Mr. and Mrs. Finch. The fake passports cost us a packet, but we could afford them. Isn't this a great place to retire?"

"But there was a funeral."

"That didn't cost much."

"Too true."

"A lot of them were in on this," he confessed. "My cousin Jerry runs an undertaking business in the next village. He supplied the coffin."

"And a corpse?" I said, appalled.

"A couple of sandbags."

"You're a prize bastard, Danny Fox."

He chuckled at that. "Aren't I just? And the prize is in the bank."

"What you did is sick."

"Oh, come on," he said. "Who loses out? Only the insurance company. I had to pay huge premiums."

"There were people in that church who genuinely grieved for you."

"Horseshit."

That hurt. "I grieved."

"Jesus—what for?" His eyebrows jutted in genuine puzzlement.

I started to say, "If you don't remember—"

Danny cut me off with, "All that was thirty years ago. And then it was only—"

"Night exercises," I completed the statement for him.

"What?"

"Night exercises. That's what you thought of me, didn't you?" I stood up and faced him. "Admit it. Say it to my face, you skunk."

There was a pause. The night had virtually closed in. Danny upended his last can of beer. "All right, if that's what you heard from Merle, it must be true." He laughed. "Let's face it, Susan—that's what you were. P.O. didn't stand for Pilot Officer in your case, it stood for pushover."

I said, "That's unbelievably cruel."

Unmoved, Danny told me, "If you really want to know, I couldn't even remember your name that day we met in Brighton. I remembered your car, though."

That was one injury too many—even for a coward like me. The precious flame I'd guarded for thirty years was out. Our relationship had been the one experience in my life that I thought I could call truly romantic. Nothing since had compared to it. Danny had made me feel beautiful, desired, a woman fulfilled.

He knew the pain he had just inflicted. He *must* have known.

"Danny."

"Yes?" He looked up.

By that time Mallory Dock was deserted except for us. The water there is deep enough to moor a cruise liner.

The body of the middle-aged male washed up on Key West Bight a week or so later was identified as that of the man who sometimes danced on the dock at sunset. Nobody knew his name and nobody claimed the body for burial.

DEATH OF A DEAD MAN

Gillian Linscott

Without a tale of Oxbridge, our collection would not be complete. Gillian Linscott's story, set in Saint Dubricius' College, Oxford, is peppered with erudition, as, of course, were Dorothy Sayers's Oxford mysteries. In mood and tone, however, Gillian Linscott's story is a completely different kettle of fish, more somber, reflecting the disaffection of the sixties. The author is a parliamentary reporter for the BBC who has also written a series of historical mysteries featuring a British suffragette.

It might help you to know, Inspector, that Andreas Tithe died at exactly five minutes past eleven on the morning of June first, nineteen sixty-six."

The Master of Saint Dubricius' College let the words float towards the bookcases opposite, over the head of the plainclothes inspector in the leather armchair. His voice was weary, his hair thin and silver in the October sunshine. The inspector, in his late forties, had the air of a man long past being surprised, but he raised his eyebrows, looked at his digital watch. "Andreas Tithe was stabbed to death at some time between seven-oh-three and seven forty-two yesterday evening, October twenty-four, nineteen ninety-four. It's notoriously difficult to establish an exact time of death, but that apparently gives us a discrepancy of some twenty-nine years and five months."

Silence, apart from the Master's sigh. Inspector Caswold flexed a leg, adjusted a trouser crease, stared critically at his sleek black sock. It took him some moments to realise that the Master's sigh contained a word—a word he'd used himself a few seconds earlier. Now it came wafting back like a shuttlecock returned, but so slowly that it seemed to hover in the air above him. "Apparently."

"Apparently," said Andreas Tithe, "I've kept you waiting." Immediate laughter from his audience. Six minutes past eleven on the first morning in June with plenty of distractions outside, and yet this echoing room in Oxford Examination Schools was so crowded that there were still people looking for seats. Only two other lecturers achieved full houses and both of those were a generation older than Andreas Tithe. From a distance he looked much the same age as the students, who were trying to lounge on hard seats, men in denims, girls in skirts that were no more than friezes for pale thighs, academic gowns twisted into near invisibility. Tithe had a way of wearing his own long gown that seemed to transform it into ironic fancy dress. Today he was wearing it over black corduroy trousers, black shirt, black knitted tie. His brown hair curled down past his collar. He brushed a quiff of it back from his forehead as he paused for the laugh he'd known would come on the word "apparently." A private joke between him and several hundred philosophy students. They'd been exploring it all term. What did it mean if you said that something was apparently the case? Did that imply the possibility that it might not be what it appeared to be? If so, could you make any statement about the appearance of something that did not carry with it its own negation?

"I say apparently I've kept you waiting. We shall, for once, slide over the enticingly thin ice of 'apparently' to 'I've,' or rather to 'I.' I have kept you waiting. But how can you decide if this assemblage of sense impressions apparently standing in front of you and calling itself 'I' is connected with the apparently similar assemblage that went under the same label for my previous lectures?"

Some students began taking notes, but the trio in the front row, just under the lecturer's podium, had no notebooks. The central figure was a girl with a pale, intense face and long dark hair, wearing a brief blue shift under her scholar's gown. She stared at Tithe as if unconscious of the men on either side of her. The one on her right was good-looking and had a self-assured air. He wore white cotton trousers and a cowboy belt of embossed leather. He kept glancing at the girl, but she wouldn't look at him. The man on her left seemed deathly tired, leaning back in his seat, legs stretched out, dark circles around his closed eyes. He was almost skeletally thin, with bare ankles and long dusty feet in leather sandals sticking out from faded jeans. Farther back, near the door, a man of about Tithe's own age watched with a look of contempt on his face.

When Tithe noticed the man he smiled. He took a step forward, placed his left hand on his chest.

"A label to which we must now add RIP." He crossed his right hand over his left and closed his eyes, a tombstone effigy made vertical. "Andreas Tithe died one minute ago, as he was about to walk in to give this lecture."

Some uneasy laughter. The thin student, without opening his eyes, mouthed one word: "Clown." The man on the girl's right glanced across at him warningly, but she took no notice.

"Fortunately, I happened to be here to take his place. I am Andreas Tithe's identical twin brother, also, through lack of inspiration on the part of our parents, named Andreas. I share my ideas with Andreas. I have a mole on my left buttock in exactly the same place as Andreas. . . ."

Laughter, more assured now they knew where this was heading. The thin student opened his eyes and looked sideways at the girl.

". . . and yet I stand here and assure you that I am not Andreas Tithe, although I am in every respect identical with Andreas Tithe. Now the first question this might raise . . ."

The man who'd been watching from the back slid out so quietly that only the lecturer noticed.

"It was, of course, an extremely facile point he was making."

Even twenty-nine years later the contempt was still there in the Master's voice.

"Do I take it that it was some kind of joke?"

"I assume you have no interest in philosophy, Inspector."

"I could never quite grasp what it was. Was there a twin brother?"

"Of course there wasn't. Nor did Andreas Tithe drop dead on his way into the lecture hall. It was the same man."

"The same man who had a kitchen knife stuck into his heart yesterday evening?"

"Yes."

"So you think when he made his call to the station at seven-oh-three yesterday it had something to do with what he said at a lecture all that time ago?"

There was a cassette tape recorder on the table by the inspector's chair. He pressed a button.

"Good evening. This is Andreas Tithe, fellow of St. Dubricius' College. I wish to report that I'm dead. That's all."

There was the sound of a receiver being put down, quite gently, over the policewoman's voice asking him please to repeat the message.

"As you hear, he'd rung off."

"Yes, that would be quite normal."

"Normal to ring up the police station and report yourself dead?"

Coffee arrived. The Master poured.

"I'm surprised your colleagues didn't tell you. Have you been working in Oxford long?"

"Three weeks. I'm a long way from my usual patch. Half the officers from your force have been sent off to investigate allegations of corruption in three other forces, so they've had to fill in from wherever's not being investigated at the moment."

The Master blinked, drank.

"That explains why you didn't know about poor Tithe. These outbreaks of his happened only every few months or so."

"He made a habit of this?"

"In recent years, yes. The summer we've been talking about, nineteen sixty-six, represented the high point of Tithe's career. He'd already made something of a name for himself among the students and in the popular press protesting about the war in Vietnam. The students were always organizing demonstrations and occupations, and Tithe appointed himself their apologist. So some of the less responsible tabloids decided to join in the joke about his death—if you could consider it a joke. He achieved what you might call his apotheosis on a television programme discussing the nature of reality with the manageress of a striptease club and a geriatric Trotskyist guerrilla from one of the Latin American countries. It was broadcast very late at night."

"So in his dotage he was harking back to his past successes."

"I'd hardly use the word dotage, Inspector. Tithe and I were almost exactly the same age."

"I'm sorry. But apart from that . . ."

"Yes. Tithe had taken to ringing up the police, writing to the obituary editors, and so on to announce his own death. The call you've just played to me was probably one of a dozen or so he made over the past few years."

"Yes, but last night there was a difference, wasn't there? Within thirty-nine minutes of making that call Andreas Tithe was dead. Really dead."

The Master winced. He said, almost humbly, "I wonder if you'd mind telling me exactly what happened. There was so much to think about last night that I . . . well, I'm not sure that I took it all in." He grimaced, either from the taste of the homely phrase in his mouth or the hot coffee.

"You've heard our duty officer taking the phone call. She immediately reported it to me. Not knowing what you've just told me, I took it seriously and drove straight to St. Dubricius'. I established from your porter that there was a fellow of the college by the name of Andreas Tithe and asked for directions to his room. The door was unlocked."

"And you found him?"

"Yes. It looks as if he was stabbed in the armchair where he was sitting. The knife was driven in with considerable force. It's quite difficult, you know, to push a knife into somebody's heart. Physically difficult."

The Master closed his eyes.

"Yes. I recall reading somewhere that they almost invariably get it wrong . . . in productions of *Tosca.*" It was a brave effort, but came out as a series of gasps.

"The murderer probably had the chair back to push against. He or she could have put a knee in Mr. Tithe's lap and driven the knife home. A preliminary report from the pathologist suggests that's how it might have been done. No fingerprints on the knife, unfortunately."

"Gloves?"

"Almost certainly. I checked my watch when I knew he was dead. It was seven forty-two. What happened after that, you know."

A night of disbelief giving way to numb shock, of shaken undergraduates and dons made uneasy by being powerless.

"As far as we've been able to establish, he was last seen alive at about two o'clock yesterday afternoon. Nobody in the college admits to visiting him after seven-oh-three when he made the phone call to us. The porter is convinced that nobody who was not a member of college came in between seven-oh-three and my arrival."

"I hope you're not implying that the murderer must have been a member of this college. This is not a high-security establishment. Anybody might have come in earlier, stayed in . . ."

"We've checked your own alibi. The bursar confirms that you were with him from just before seven o'clock until the porter came and found you at about ten to eight."

The Master didn't respond to that. He sat there with the inspector's eyes on him and it was some time before he said anything.

"One might call it an odd coincidence. If you had not taken that telephone call seriously, the murder might not have been discovered until this morning."

"Do you attach any particular significance to that?"

A defeated shake of the head. The inspector stood up.

"The bursar's kindly allowing us to use his room to go on questioning the staff and students. It will take most of the day, I'm afraid."

On his way to the door he said as an afterthought, "So this death business attracted a lot of attention at the time."

"I'm afraid so. Some of the students even held a mock funeral."

The plywood coffin, black-painted in hasty streaks, lurched down the ramp at the punt station beside Folly Bridge on the shoulders of four men in evening dress and academic gowns. A less formal procession followed them, about thirty students in jeans and sweaters with bottles, torches, and carrier bags. A few tourists watched from the bridge, silhouetted against the last light of a June evening.

On the ramp, in the shadow of the bridge, it was dusk already. The bearers paused on the landing stage and somebody came forward with a makeshift wreath of ivy and syringa, plundered from the gardens of north Oxford lodgings. As the coffin was loaded into a punt the lid slipped off, revealing emptiness, and had to be lodged on again. Once it was safely aboard, one of the bearers took a punt pole and the others formed an impromptu guard of honour, paddles raised in salute. Somebody began humming a dead march, and as the party took it up it spread over the darkening water.

"Who's travelling with the coffin? Chief mourner. Come on, Cherry."

The dark-haired girl was urged to the front of the group and took her place neatly in the punt, wedged on the seat alongside the coffin. Without invitation, the two men who'd been sitting next to her in the lecture hall followed. The thin man folded himself on the seat facing her, the other stepped over him to get to the bow. The painter was untied and the punt pushed off into the current. The dead march trailed away raggedly as the rest of the party scrambled for places in other punts. By the time they turned out of the Isis and into the smaller, tree-darkened River Cherwell there were five punts on the water, the one carrying the coffin well in front. The man in evening dress punted impassively, as if he really were a funeral mute, while the three round the coffin talked in low tones. The thin man, Hal, was the angry one.

"I wish we were burying the bastard. I wish we really were burying the bastard." He slapped his hand on the coffin.

Cherry, looking ahead into the gathering darkness, said, "You really can't blame Andreas." She was drawing slowly on an untidy cigarette. She offered it to Hal but he waved it aside and the man in the bow reached over to take it. He took a long drag before echoing what she'd said.

"You can't blame him. You'd do the same in his place. Besides, he didn't put them there."

"Who did then? Do you think I'd keep two thousand tabs of LSD under my bed? In a shoe box, for Christ's sake."

"Does that make it worse?"

"Somebody must have put them there."

The other man laughed. "Not necessarily. Andreas would tell you that the presence of an object in a place implies nothing about its past—or anything else."

Hal grunted. "He could try telling that to the police tomorrow."

"You can't expect him to go to the police."

Cherry reclaimed the cigarette from the other man and offered it again to Hal. He took one long, angry drag then threw the butt in a high arc into the river. "Why not? At the very least he could go to the police and proctors and tell them I was a model student, wouldn't have anything to do with drugs."

"They wouldn't believe him. It would only damage his career for nothing."

"His bloody career. What about my career?"

The other man said, "But you hate it here, you're always saying so. Last term you were supposed to be going to Hanoi to fight for the Viet Cong."

"Perhaps I shall. It's a big world out there."

"Well then."

"So why don't you come with me, all three of us? And Andreas bloody Tithe as well if he likes. Do something besides talk, talk, talk for a change."

Silence.

"You won't, will you? Too wrapped up in your cosy little worlds. Andreas will get his professorship, you two will get your bloody firsts. Cherry will go on screwing Andreas when he's got the time and you when he's too busy. Roses and CND signs round the door and bourgeois complacency flowering all pink and white in the front garden."

He picked up the wreath from the coffin and sent it skittering over the dark river, white flowers breaking away from it like sparks from a Catherine wheel. The punt went on under Magdalen Bridge, nosed its way to the point where the channel divided. The other punts were some way behind, more heavily loaded, but they could hear the occasional shout or laugh coming from them. Hal said, "I've had enough of this."

"It's a long way to walk back. You might as well stay for the wake."

Hal muttered something but later, as the punt came alongside the island, he was still with them, feet resting on the coffin, staring at Cherry like somebody making an accusation.

Cherry Delmer, philosophy tutor from another college, was standing at the window of the Master's study looking out. The sun shone on her glossy dark hair, expensively cut with only a few strands of grey in it. She wore a dark-green trouser suit and soft leather boots.

The Master said, "There was something I didn't tell the police inspector. Not that it was relevant."

"What was that?"

"That at one time I hated Andreas Tithe quite enough to want to stop his heart with a kitchen knife."

"That was a long time ago."

"Twenty-nine years ago. The feeling was usually at its worst just after you'd come to me for a tutorial."

He waited to hear if she'd say anything. She went on staring out of the window.

"You'd read me your essay, regurgitating his half-baked arguments.

And you'd cross your legs and look at me, making sure I knew you'd just got out of his bed to come to my tutorial."

She turned, smiling.

"I don't think I was doing that. Not consciously."

"At one time I'd have asked you what you meant by 'consciously.' "

"At one time I shouldn't have used the word without writing an essay about it. I didn't know you knew."

"That would be another essay. Oh yes, I knew. I seriously considered telling the principal of your college that you were having an affair with a senior member of the university, a man twenty years older than you."

"Of course, if you had, everybody would have assumed you'd done it because you were envious of him—academically, I mean."

"They'd have been right."

"Not that you needed to be."

"No. I got the professorship and ended up as Master of the college of which poor Tithe had become such an undistinguished fellow."

"The whirligig of time."

She turned back to the window. They were near equals now, had attended too many university occasions, sat on too many committees together to have kept a tutor and pupil relationship. The gap between forty-nine and seventy was narrower than the gulf between twenty and forty-one.

"It was good of you to take so much trouble to let me know."

A touch of irony in her voice. As he'd passed on to her in detail all the inspector had told him, the knee in the lap, the thrust against the back of the armchair, it had come to her that he was taking a kind of revenge, a revenge by proxy for something almost half a lifetime away.

"I should have telephoned you earlier, only I was talking to the inspector."

"Has the inspector any hypotheses?"

"Not that I could discover. The police are questioning all of us, senior members, students, staff."

"Is that the inspector out there with your porter?"

Two men were standing on the opposite side of the quad, looking up at something.

"Yes. That will be poor Tithe's window they're looking at. I suppose somebody might have climbed in but . . ."

"I must go. You'll have so much to do."

"Something I meant to ask you. Did you ever know of any relations?"

She stared at him, not understanding, then, "Oh, you mean Andreas Tithe's relations? No, we never discussed them."

"No, I don't suppose you did. There's the question, you see, of the funeral. . . ."

The soil of the island was soft but heavy. They dug, taking it in turns with the two spades they'd brought with them, by the light of a bonfire that illuminated the scrub of elder and pussy willow like the green walls of a marquee. Inside that space, with darkness all around them and the sound of the river just a few dozen yards away on either side, they laughed and talked and drank. Somebody had brought a guitar, somebody else a mouth organ. They sang the songs they usually kept for the coach journeys to Grosvenor Square for demos. "No More Napalm" and "I'm the Man that Waters the Workers' Beer." Cherry sang with the rest. Hal wandered off sulkily by himself with a bottle of beer and a cigarette and sat on the very tip of the island under a big willow, as if on the prow of a boat thrusting against the current into the darkness upriver. The smell of bonfire, of baking sausages, of pot, warmed the air, with the tang of wet river earth under it as the hole grew deeper. People kept tripping over the empty coffin. Some couples had already taken themselves off into the bushes and the occasional giggle or whisper drifted back in lulls between the singing.

"It must be deep enough by now."

The bearers picked up the coffin.

"Listen."

There was a sound of splashing from upstream, then a call from Hal, surly and alarmed.

"Who's there?"

They ran to join Hal by the willow tree, carrying sticks from the bonfire for light. A figure was bending over beside Hal, tying a painter to a bush. When it straightened up and more light fell on it they saw it was Andreas Tithe, holding a dripping kayak paddle.

"I could hardly miss my own funeral, could I?"

The laughter was a little uneasy. He was, for all his popularity with them, a senior member of the university, out of place at a party that was breaking several dozen sets of regulations. But they took him to the bonfire, pressed a paper cup of red wine into his hand. When the other hand found its way round Cherry's waist there was a general relaxation. For the night, at least, he was sharing their outlawry.

"Want to pronounce your own funeral oration, Andreas?"

"I thought I'd done that already. It's somebody else's turn."

One of the coffin bearers took over, his evening trousers blotched with damp earth.

"Dearly beloved brethren and sisters, we are apparently gathered here, assuming that the concept of place has any validity . . ."

Cries of "Get on with it!"

". . . we therefore commit his notional body to the earth, in the unsure and entirely unsustainable hypothesis that he once existed, now exists—assuming he ever did—no longer, and will rise again on the third day . . ."

A shout from the back. "Why wait?"

The bearers took it literally, picked up the light coffin and knelt to ease it down into the hole, which was more than deep enough. They rained a few spadefuls of earth on it, enough to cover the lid but no more, then went back to the party. The singing grew wilder, hiding entirely the rustlings of the couples in the bushes. Then the bonfire began to die down and the darkness changed to the clear white sky of predawn. The wine ran out, the singing ended, and the party sorted itself dazedly into punt-loads and drifted back down the river with the current. The partly filled grave was a dark pit in the half-light.

"I'm certain that it was never properly filled in that night."

Cherry Delmer was quite at ease in the superintendent's office. When the superintendent had introduced her to Inspector Caswold he'd mentioned that she was deputy chairperson of the liaison committee between police and university authorities, a clear warning to the new officer on the block to mind his manners. He added that Miss Delmer had known the deceased, Andreas Tithe, for some thirty years and had come to him with information that might have some bearing on the murder.

Inspector Caswold had made no comment. He'd looked at her in an appraising way when they shook hands, but with no obvious hostility. While she'd talked about the undergraduate party twenty-nine summers ago, he'd glanced sometimes at her face, sometimes at her slim legs in their sheer grey-tinted tights. Now he asked his first question.

"Even if it wasn't filled in, why do you think that was connected with Mr. Tithe's murder last night?"

She met his eyes, calm and confident.

"Because I think there's a body in the grave."

He glanced at the superintendent but got no help, beyond a stony expression that told him Miss Delmer must not be mocked.

"Why do you think that?"

"I went back to the island about five months after the party. I hadn't intended to, but there was a particularly fine day that October and a woman friend and myself took a punt out. I'd been telling her about the party, so we tied up and landed there. We found the grave easily enough, but it was filled up, right to the top. There were even weeds and grass growing on it as if it had been filled in months before, soon after the party."

"Perhaps somebody who was at the party went back and filled it in properly."

"But why? It was only an empty plywood box. And mostly nobody set foot on the island from one summer term to the next."

He said, with a sharpness he hadn't shown in talking to the Master, "Isn't that what you'd call a logical hiatus? A mock grave is filled in, so you assume there must be a real body in it?"

She didn't seem offended. "As you say, a logical hiatus. A belief, though capable of being empirically tested."

The superintendent translated, "Miss Delmer thinks we should dig it up."

"Yes sir, but I ask again what bearing it could have on Mr. Tithe's death."

"Are you making much progress in other directions?"

"Certain lines of inquiry are being followed."

The superintendent knew what that meant.

"In that case, you might as well try it, mightn't you? At least we don't have to get Home Office permission to dig up an empty box."

He seemed to think that should be an end to the matter, but Caswold said, "May we ask why Miss Delmer didn't think of reporting her suspicions to the police at the time?"

She gave him a straight look. "You may remember that relations between students and police were not particularly cordial in nineteen sixty-six, Inspector."

Caswold shrugged, his only sign of impatience so far. He seemed to prefer to put his questions to her through the superintendent.

"Twenty-nine years ago Miss Delmer thought there might be somebody in the grave. Did she have any more theories? Who it was, for instance?"

Accepting his methods with good grace, she directed her reply at the superintendent.

"There was a man named Hal Brown, a second-year student like most of the rest of us. We never saw him again after the party. Nobody remembered leaving the island with him."

"Surely inquiries were made."

"Yes. The day before the party the police had searched his lodgings and found a large quantity of LSD tablets under his bed. He denied putting them there or knowing anything about them, but he'd been charged with possession and let out on bail."

"Had he put them there?"

"I don't know. A lot of students had digs in the same house, including me as it happens. People were in and out of each other's rooms all the time."

"So you all assumed he'd run off?"

He put the question directly to her this time.

"Yes, we thought he'd gone abroad. He'd talked about going to North Vietnam. A lot of people did at the time."

"Went to Vietnam?"

"No, talked about it."

The superintendent began shuffling papers.

"All this should be in the records for nineteen sixty-six, Inspector. You can get somebody to look it up for you while you take Miss Delmer to her island."

Caswold made no comment as he held open the door for her.

There were a few tourists watching as they loaded themselves into a punt at Folly Bridge. Cherry Delmer had changed back into her trouser suit and boots. They were accompanied by two constables in overalls with spades and gardening gauntlets. A battery-powered strimmer and some secateurs had been added at the last minute when she reminded them that the island would be overgrown. Apart from that there hadn't been much conversation since the meeting in the superintendent's office. With one of the constables poling inexpertly they traced a zigzag course along the Isis and grounded under a tree almost as soon as they'd turned into the Cherwell. After watching his struggles for a few minutes, Cherry Delmer said, "I could take over it if you like. I'm quite good at punting."

"No."

They untangled themselves from the tree and pushed on against the current.

"I suppose your career hasn't brought you into much contact with punts, Inspector."

"No."

The constable was sweating and red-faced before she pointed to a tangle of trees ahead. "That's the island."

"Sure?"

"Quite sure. If we go to the left we can tie up where we used to tie up for the parties."

When they stepped onto the wet soil, between twisted roots, they were facing a head-high screen of nettles and pussy willows. She went first, her slim body breaking a path for them. After fifty yards or so the nettles cleared, giving way to browning stalks of willow herb with seed fluff clinging to them.

"It was about here."

This time he didn't ask if she were sure, but she explained. "I'm going by the big willow tree on the end. Hal was sulking there for most of the party."

"Was that where you said Andreas Tithe landed in his kayak?"

"Yes, he'd come down from Bardwell Road, the opposite direction to the way we went."

"Did he leave with the rest of you?"

"I don't know. I suppose he'd have been going back in the opposite direction as well."

"So you didn't see him leave and you didn't see Hal Brown leave?"

"No."

She dug the toe of her boot into layers of dead leaves. He saw she was scuffing leaf mould away from a charred branch.

"Bonfire."

"Not from twenty-nine years ago."

"People tend to make them in the same place. Hadn't you noticed?"

She turned back towards the big willow tree.

"The grave was towards the willow but not far from the bonfire, because we were digging by the light of it."

She took a couple of paces, moved sideways, stopped.

"Somewhere here. Not more than ten yards from here, left or right."

The constables moved in with strimmer and spade. While the machine buzzed and tattered weeds fell in swathes, she watched as if she were paying somebody to do the gardening. The digging began in earnest, first leaf mould, then yellowish brown soil.

At two feet or so she said, "It wouldn't have been any deeper than that. Try to the right."

The constables looked to Caswold for instructions, expressions asking how long this game was supposed to continue.

"If Miss Delmer says so."

She didn't react to the sarcasm in his voice. Eighteen inches or so down, with the men tiring and every jab of their spades a comment, she darted forward and picked up something from the last spadeful of earth thrown clear.

"Plywood." A piece no wider than a hand, slimy grey on one side, fresh yellow on the other where layers had been gashed apart by the spade. The inspector took it from her.

"Right, carefully from now on, just in case."

They dug shallow spadefuls, gradually exposing a sheet of plywood, almost horizontal but tilted a little.

"See if you can get your spades under it."

"It wouldn't have been nailed," she said.

The spades prised it away from the earth, threw it back onto strimmed willow herb.

"Christ!"

Just one word from a constable. The inspector stepped forward. Cherry Delmer stayed where she was.

"Bell, I suppose you left your radio in the punt. Get on to it and call the scene-of-crime team. Tell them to come down by motorboat from Bardwell Road if they can. Tedder, you'd better go with him. See if you can find a tarpaulin or something in the punt and bring it here."

With the constables gone, the two of them stood looking down. The sides of the makeshift coffin had collapsed outwards, letting in earth, but the bones were there. The jaw had fallen away from the skull. The bones of one hand had settled in formation, as orderly as the stones of a necklace.

"They'll be able to identify him from dental records," she said.

The inspector dropped the piece of plywood she'd given him carefully onto a pile of fresh soil.

"Your people will be checking the records by now. Students missing in the summer of nineteen sixty-six. They'll have found that there were two of them at the same time, Hal and another man. Both friends of mine."

He said nothing.

"I don't suppose the police looked for them long. Students were always going off—Kabul or California or Katmandu. They might have been anywhere in the world."

"I suppose so."

"They might even enroll at an American university, get a degree after all, come back in ten years or so as respectable citizens."

"As respectable as a tutor of philosophy, for instance?"

His voice was different. She looked at him.

"Yes. As respectable as that, or even more so. Only Hal didn't, did he?"

"If it is Hal."

"Oh yes, it's Hal. I'm quite sure of that."

He didn't respond. From beyond the bushes and nettles they heard the raised voice of the constable speaking into a radio, but couldn't make out the words.

She said, "Hal would have been sent down in any case. He wasn't a particularly good student and a court would never have believed he didn't know about the LSD tabs, even if he told the police about the others."

"Others?"

"My other friend, the other missing man. And Andreas Tithe. Andreas and the other man were distributing LSD. I know that."

"You're telling me that you have certain knowledge that Andreas Tithe dealt in drugs?"

"We wouldn't have used a heavy word like deal. It was more a case of doing it for your friends. But that's the way the police would have seen it, yes."

"Did he go on doing it?"

She laughed. "You mean, did he go on pushing drugs into his seventies? Of course not. When the police charged Hal, that scared him off for good. He was scared off quite a lot of things that summer."

He glanced sideways at her.

They heard somebody pushing heavily through the undergrowth, something being dropped and retrieved. The second constable was on his way back.

"That October when you found the grave filled in, you knew what had happened?"

"I didn't know which of them it was. But I suppose I guessed it was more likely to be Hal."

"But you didn't say anything until today."

"Two things happened in the last twenty-four hours. One was that Andreas Tithe was murdered."

"And the other?"

"The other was a direct consequence. The Master of Dubricius used to be my tutor. He knew Andreas and I had been lovers a long time ago. He called me round to break the news. I'm still not sure whether it was kindness or revenge."

"After all these years?"

"After all these years. While I was in his study he pointed out the inspector hard at work investigating Tithe's murder. I had a closer look at you on my way out. You were busy with the porter so you didn't see me."

"No."

"I was certain then, as I hadn't been certain twenty-nine years ago, that it was Hal in the grave."

He said nothing. The nettles were swaying wildly.

"Two friends of mine disappeared on the night of the party. One of them's down there."

Silence.

"And you came back in the end, with your degree from America or wherever. I wonder why you decided to join the police? At one time we'd have thought it was worse than going into a leper colony. Was that why?"

He said, almost under his breath, "What are you going to do?"

"Do? I'm a philosopher, remember."

The top of a hurrying head was in sight above the nettles.

He said, softly and quickly, "Andreas must have killed him, very early that morning after the rest of us went. Killed him to stop him talking about the LSD."

"And now somebody's killed Andreas. It must have been a shock when the duty officer told you about that phone call. You probably saw it as a threat to you, though it wasn't."

He insisted, voice scarcely under control, "It must have been Andreas. He kept him talking here on the island, they argued, then he killed him. Don't you see, it was Andreas?"

The constable arrived, arms loaded with bright blue punt cushions.

"No tarpaulin or anything, sir. We thought these might do to cover it over with."

Caswold looked at her, his face begging for a response.

"Apparently," she said.

THE GENTLEMAN IN THE LAKE

Robert Barnard

A visit to England's beautiful Lake District, an inspiration to numerous other writers and poets, gave Leeds resident Robert Barnard the idea for "The Gentleman in the Lake," which received nominations for three awards in 1994: the Edgar Allan Poe Award, the Agatha Award, and the Anthony Award. Robert Barnard was a professor at the University of Tromsö, Norway, before retiring to Yorkshire to write fiction. Although he considers himself a writer in the classic tradition, his daring in terms of subject matter and his sometimes outrageous wit have earned him a reputation as an innovator amongst contemporary crime writers.

There had been violent storms that night, but the body did not come to the surface until they had died down and a watery summer sun sent ripples of lemon and silver across the still-disturbed surface of Derwent Water. It was first seen by a little girl, clutching a plastic beaker of orange juice, who had strayed down from the small car park, over the pebbles, to the edge of the lake.

"What's that, Mummy?"

"What's what, dear?"

Her mother was wandering round, drinking in the calm, the silence, the magisterial beauty, the more potent for the absence of other tourists. She was a businesswoman, and holidays by the Lakes made her question uncomfortably what she was doing with her life. She strolled down to where the water lapped onto the stones.

"There, Mummy. *That."*

She looked towards the lake. A sort of bundle bobbed on the surface a hundred yards or so away. She screwed up her eyes. A sort of *tweedy* bundle. Greeny-brown, like an old-fashioned gentleman's suit. As she watched she realised that she could make out, stretching out from the bundle, two lines . . . *Legs.* She put her hand firmly on her daughter's shoulder.

"Oh, it's just an old bundle of clothes, darling. Look, there's Patch wanting to play. He has to stretch his legs too, you know."

Patch barked obligingly, and the little girl trotted off to throw his ball for him. Without hurrying the woman made her way back to the car, picked up the car phone, and dialed 999.

It was late on in the previous summer that Marcia Catchpole had sat beside Sir James Harrington at a dinner party in St. John's Wood. "Something immensely distinguished in Law," her hostess Serena Fisk had told her vaguely. "Not a judge, but a rather famous defending counsel, or prosecuting counsel, or *something* of that sort."

He had been rather quiet as they all sat down: urbane, courteous in a dated sort of way, but quiet. It was as if he was far away, reviewing the finer points of a case long ago.

"So nice to have *soup,*" said Marcia, famous for "drawing people out," especially men. "Soup seems almost to have gone out these days."

"Really?" said Sir James, as if they were discussing the habits of Eskimos or Trobriand Islanders. "Yes, I suppose you don't often . . . *get it.*"

"No, it's all melons and ham, and pâté, and seafood cocktails."

"Is it? *Is* it?"

His concentration wavering, he returned to his soup, which he was consuming a good deal more expertly than Marcia, who, truth to tell, was more used to melons and suchlike.

"You don't eat out a great deal?"

"No. Not now. Once, when I was practising. . . . But not now. And not since my wife died."

"Of course you're right: People don't like singles, do they?"

"Singles?"

"People on their own. For dinner parties. They have to find another one—like me tonight."

"Yes . . . Yes," he said, as if only half-understanding what she said.

"And it's no fun eating in a restaurant on your own, is it?"

"No . . . None at all. . . . I have a woman come in," he added, as if trying to make a contribution of his own.

"To cook and clean for you?"

"Yes . . . Perfectly capable woman. . . . It's not the same, though."

"No. Nothing is, is it, when you find yourself on your own?"

"No, it's not. . . ." He thought, as if thought was difficult. "You can't *do* so many things you used to do."

"Ah, you find that too, do you? What do you miss most?"

There was a moment's silence, as if he had forgotten what they were talking about. Then he said: "Travel. I'd like to go to the Lakes again."

"Oh, the Lakes! One of my favourite places. Don't you drive?"

"No. I've never had any need before."

"Do you have children?"

"Oh yes. Two sons. One in medicine, one in politics. Busy chaps with families of their own. Can't expect them to take me places. . . . Don't see much of them. . . ." His moment of animation seemed to fade, and he picked away at his entrée. "What *is* this fish, Molly?"

When, the next day, she phoned to thank her hostess, Marcia commented that Sir James was "such a sweetie."

"You and he seemed to get on like a house on fire, anyway."

"Oh, we did."

"Other people said he was awfully vague."

"Oh, it's the legal mind. Wrapped in grand generalities. His wife been dead long?"

"About two years. I believe he misses her frightfully. Molly used to arrange all the practicalities for him."

"I can believe that. I was supposed to ring him about a book I have that he wanted, but he forgot to give me his number."

"Oh, it's two-seven-one-eight-seven-six. A rather grand place in Chelsea."

But Marcia had already guessed the number after going through the telephone directory. She had also guessed at the name of Sir James's late wife.

"We can't do much till we have the pathologist's report," said Superintendent Southern, fingering the still-damp material of a tweed suit. "Except perhaps about *this.*"

Sergeant Potter looked down at it.

"I don't know a lot about such things," he said, "but I'd have said that suit was dear."

"So would I. A gentleman's suit, made to measure and beautifully sewn. I've had one of the secretaries in who knows about these things. A gentleman's suit for country wear. Made for a man who doesn't know the meaning of the word 'casual.' With a nametag sewn in by the tailor and crudely removed . . . with a razor blade probably."

"You don't *get* razor blades much these days."

"Perhaps he's also someone who doesn't know the meaning of the word 'throwaway.' A picture seems to be emerging."

"And the removal of the nametag almost inevitably means—"

"Murder. Yes, I'd say so."

Marcia decided against ringing Sir James up. She felt sure he would not remember who she was. Instead, she would call round with the book, which had indeed come up in conversation—because she had made sure it did. Marcia was very good at fostering acquaintanceships with men, and had had two moderately lucrative divorces to prove it.

She timed her visit for late afternoon, when she calculated that the lady who cooked and "did" for him would have gone home. When he opened the door he blinked, and his hand strayed towards his lips.

"I'm afraid I—"

"Marcia Catchpole. We met at Serena Fisk's. I brought the book on Wordsworth we were talking about."

She proffered Stephen Gill on Wordsworth, in paperback. She had thought as she bought it that Sir James was probably not used to paperbacks, but she decided that, as an investment, Sir James was not yet worth the price of a hardback.

"Oh, I don't . . . er . . . Won't you come in?"

"Lovely!"

She was taken into a rather grim sitting room, lined with legal books and Victorian first editions. Sir James began to make uncertain remarks about how he thought he could manage tea.

"Why don't you let me make it? You'll not be used to fending for yourself, let alone for visitors. It was different in your generation, wasn't it? Is that the kitchen?"

And she immediately showed an uncanny instinct for finding things and doing the necessary. Sir James watched her, bemused, for a minute or two, then shuffled back to the sitting room. When she came in with a tray, with tea things on it and a plate of biscuits, he looked as if he had forgotten who she was, and how she came to be there.

"There, that's nice, isn't it? Do you like it strong? Not too strong, right? I think you'll enjoy the Wordsworth book. Wordsworth really *is* the Lakes, don't you agree?"

She had formed the notion, when talking to him at Serena Fisk's dinner party, that his reading was remaining with him longer than his grip on real life. This was confirmed by the conversation on this visit. As long as the talk stayed with Wordsworth and his Lakeland circle it approached a normal chat; he would forget the names of poems, but he would sometimes quote several lines of the better-known ones verbatim. Marcia had been educated at a moderately good state school, and she managed to keep her end up.

Marcia got up to go just at the right time, when Sir James had got used to her being there and before he began wanting her to go. At the door she said: "I'm expecting to have to go to the Lakes on business in a couple of weeks. I'd be happy if you'd come along."

"Oh, I couldn't possibly—"

"No obligations either way: we pay for ourselves, separate rooms *of course,* quite independent of each other. I've got business in Cockermouth, and I thought of staying by Buttermere or Crummock Water."

A glint came into his eyes.

"It would be wonderful to see them again. But I really couldn't—"

"Of course you could. It would be my pleasure. It's always better in congenial company, isn't it? I'll be in touch about the arrangements."

Marcia was in no doubt she would have to make all the arrangements, down to doing his packing and contacting his cleaning woman. But she was confident she would bring it off.

"Killed by a blow to the head," said Superintendent Southern, when he had skimmed through the pathologist's report. "Some kind of accident, for example a boating accident, can't entirely be ruled out, but there was some time between his being killed and his going into the water."

"In which case, what happened to the boat? And why didn't whoever was with him simply go back to base and report it, rather than heaving him in?"

"Exactly. . . . From what remains, the pathologist suggests a smooth liver—a townee not a countryman, even of the upper-crust kind."

"I think you suspected that from the suit, didn't you, sir?"

"I did. Where do you go for a first-rate suit for country holidays if you're a townee?"

"Same as for business suits? Savile Row, sir?"

"If you're a well-heeled Londoner that's exactly where you go. We'll start there."

Marcia went round to Sir James's two days before she had decided to set off North. Sir James remembered little or nothing about the proposed trip, still less whether he had agreed to go. Marcia got them a cup of tea, put maps on his lap, then began his packing for him. Before she went she cooked him his light supper (wondering how he had ever managed to cook it for himself) and got out of him the name of his daily. Later on she rang her and told her she was taking Sir James to the Lakes, and he'd be away for at most a week. The woman sounded sceptical but uncertain whether it was her place to say anything. Marcia, in any case, didn't give her the opportunity.

She also rang Serena Fisk to tell her. She had an ulterior motive for doing so. In the course of the conversation she casually asked: "How did he get to your dinner party?"

"Oh, I drove him. Homecooks were doing the food, so there was no problem. Those sons of his wouldn't lift a finger to help him. Then Bill drove him home later. Said he couldn't get a coherent word out of him."

"I expect he was tired. If you talk to him about literature you can see there's still a mind there."

"Literature was never my strong point, Marcia."

"Anyway, I'm taking him to the Lakes for a week on Friday."

"*Really?* Well, you are getting on well with him. Rather you than me."

"Oh, all he needs is a bit of stimulus," said Marcia. She felt confident now that she had little to fear from old friends or sons.

This first visit to the Lakes went off extremely well from Marcia's point of view. When she collected him, the idea that he was going somewhere seemed actually to have got through to him. She finished the packing with last-minute things, got him and his cases into the car, and in no time they were on the M1. During a pub lunch he called her "Molly" again, and when they at last reached the Lakes she saw that glint in his eyes, heard little grunts of pleasure.

She had booked them into Crummock Lodge, an unpretentious but spacious hotel which seemed to her just the sort of place Sir James would have been used to on his holidays in the Lakes. They had separate rooms, as she had promised. "He's an old friend who's been very ill," she told the manager. They ate well, went on drives and gentle walks. If anyone stopped and talked, Sir James managed a sort of distant benignity which carried them through. As before, he was best if he talked about literature. Once, after Marcia had had a conversation with a farmer over a dry stone wall, he said:

"Wordsworth always believed in the wisdom of simple country people."

It sounded like something a schoolmaster had once drummed into him. Marcia would have liked to say, "But when his brother married a servant he said it was an outrage." But she herself had risen by marriage, or marriages, and the point seemed to strike too close to home.

On the afternoon when she had her private business in Cockermouth she walked Sir James hard in the morning and left him tucked up in bed after lunch. Then she visited a friend who had retired to a small cottage on the outskirts of the town. He had been a private detective, and had been useful to her in her first divorce. The dicey method he had used to get dirt on her husband had convinced her that in his case private detection was very close to crime itself, and she had maintained the connection. She told him the outline of what she had in mind, and told him she might need him in the future.

When, after a week, they returned to London, Marcia was completely satisfied. She now had a secure place in Sir James's life. He no longer looked bewildered when she came round, even looked pleased, and often called her "Molly." She went to the Chelsea house often in the evenings, cooked his meal for him, and together they watched television like an old couple.

It would soon be time to make arrangements at a Registry Office.

In the process of walking from establishment to establishment in Savile Row, Southern came to feel he had had as much as he could stand of stiffness, professional discretion, and awed hush. They were only high-class tailors, he thought to himself, not the Church of bloody England. Still, when they heard that one of their clients could have ended up as an anonymous corpse in Derwent Water, they were willing to cooperate. The three establishments which offered that particular tweed handed him silently a list of those customers who had had suits made from it in the last ten years.

"Would you know if any of these are dead?" he asked one shop manager.

"Of course, sir. We make a note in our records when their obituary appears in the *Times.*"

The man took the paper back and put a little crucifix sign against two of the four names. The two remaining were a well-known television newsreader and Sir James Harrington.

"Is Sir James still alive?"

"Oh certainly. There's been no obituary for him. But he's very old: We have had no order from him for some time."

It was Sir James that Southern decided to start with. Scotland Yard knew all about him, and provided a picture, a review of the major trials in which he had featured, and his address. When Southern failed to get an answer from phone calls to the house, he went round to try the personal touch. There was a For Sale notice on it that looked to have been there for some time.

The arrangements for the Registry Office wedding went without a hitch. A month after their trip, Marcia went to book it in a suburb where neither Sir James nor she was known. Then she began foreshadowing it to Sir James, to accustom him to the idea.

"Best make it legal," she said, in her slightly vulgar way.

"Legal?" he enquired, from a great distance.

"You and me. But we'll just go on as we are."

She thought about witnesses, foresaw various dangers, and decided to pay for her detective friend to come down. He was the one person who knew of her intentions, and he could study Sir James's manner.

"Got a lady friend you could bring with you?" she asked when she rang him.

" 'Course I have. Though nobody as desirable as you, Marcia love."

"Keep your desires to yourself, Ben Brackett. This is business."

Sir James went through the ceremony with that generalized dignity which had characterised him in all his dealings with Marcia. He behaved to Ben Brackett and his lady friend as if they were somewhat dodgy witnesses who happened to be on his side in this particular trial. He spoke his words clearly, and almost seemed to mean them. Marcia told herself that in marrying her he was doing what he actually wanted to do. She didn't risk any celebration after the ceremony. She paid off Ben Brackett, drove Sir James home to change and pack again, then set off for the Lake District.

This time she had rented a cottage, as being more private. It was just outside Grange—a two-bedroom stone cottage, very comfortable and rather expensive. She had taken it for six weeks in the name of Sir James and Lady Harrington. Once there and settled in, Sir James seemed, in his way, vaguely happy; he would potter off on his own down to the lakeside, or up the narrow abutting fields. He would raise his hat to villagers and tourists, and swap remarks about the weather.

He also signed, in a wavering hand, anything put in front of him.

Marcia wrote first to his sons, similar but not identical letters, telling them of his marriage and of his happiness with his dear wife. The letters also touched on business matters: "I wonder if you would object if I put the house on the market? After living up here I cannot imagine living in London again. Of course the money would come to you after my wife's death." At the foot of Marcia's typed script Sir James wrote at her direction: "Your loving Dad."

The letters brought two furious responses, as Marcia had known they would. Both were addressed to her, and both threatened legal action. Both said they knew their father was mentally incapable of deciding to marry again, and accused her of taking advantage of his senility.

"My dear boys," typed Marcia gleefully. "I am surprised that you apparently consider me senile, and wonder how you could have allowed me to live alone without proper care if you believed that to be the case."

Back and forth the letters flew. Gradually Marcia discerned a subtle difference between the two sets of letters. Those from the MP were slightly less shrill, slightly more accommodating. He fears a scandal, she thought. Nothing worse than a messy court case for an MP's reputation. It was to Sir Evelyn Harrington, MP for Finchingford, that she made her proposal.

Southern found the estate agents quite obliging. Their dealings, they said, had been with Sir James himself. He had signed all the letters from Cumbria. They showed Southern the file, and he noted the shaky signature. Once they had spoken to Lady Harrington, they said: A low offer had been received, which demanded a quick decision. They had not recommended acceptance, since, though the property market was more dead than alive, a good house in Chelsea was bound to make a very handsome sum once it picked up. Lady Harrington had said that Sir James had a slight cold, but that he agreed with them that the offer was derisory and should be refused.

Southern's brow creased: Wasn't Lady Harrington dead?

There was clearly enough of interest about Sir James Harrington to stay with him for a bit. Southern consulted the file at Scotland Yard and set up a meeting with the man's son at the House of Commons.

Sir Evelyn was a man in his late forties, tall and well set-up. He had been knighted, Southern had discovered, in the last mass knighting of Tory backbenchers who had always voted at their party's call. The impression Sir Evelyn made was not of a stupid man, but of an unoriginal one.

"My father? Oh yes, he's alive. Living up in the Lake District somewhere."

"You're sure of this?"

"Sure as one can be when there's no contact." Southern left a silence, so the man was forced to elaborate. "Never was much. He's a remote bugger . . . a remote sort of chap, my father. Stiff, always working, never had the sort of common touch you need with children. Too keen on being the world's greatest prosecuting counsel. . . . He sent us away to school when we were seven."

Suddenly there was anger, pain, and real humanity in the voice.

"You resented that?"

"*Yes.* My brother had gone the year before and told me what that prep school was like. I pleaded with him. But he sent me just the same."

"Did your mother want you to go?"

"My mother did as she was told. Or else."

"That's not the present Lady Harrington?"

"Oh no. The present Lady Harrington is, I like to think, what my father deserves. . . . We'd been warned he was failing by his daily. Dinner burst in the oven, forgetting to change his clothes, that kind of thing. We didn't take too much notice. The difficulties of getting a stiff-necked old . . . man into residential care seemed insuperable. Then the next we heard he's married again and gone to live in the Lake District."

"Didn't you protest?"

"Of course we did. It was obvious she was after his money. And the letters he wrote, or she wrote for him, were all wrong. He would *never* have signed himself 'Dad,' let alone 'Your loving Dad.' But the kind of action that would have been necessary to annul the marriage can look ugly—for *both* sides of the case. So when she proposed an independent examination by a local doctor and psychiatrist, I persuaded my brother to agree."

"And what did they say?"

"Said he was vague, a little forgetful, but perfectly capable of understanding what he'd done when he married her, and apparently very happy. That was the end of the matter for us. The end of *him.*"

Marcia had decided from the beginning that in the early months of her life as Lady Harrington she and Sir James would have to move round a lot. As long as he was merely an elderly gentleman pottering around the Lakes and exchanging meteorological banalities with the locals there was little to fear. But as they became used to him there was a danger that they would try to engage him in conversation of more substance. If that happened, his mental state might very quickly become apparent.

As negotiations with the two sons developed, Marcia began to see her way clear. Their six weeks at Grange were nearing an end, so she arranged to rent a cottage between Crummock Water and Cockermouth. When the sons agreed to an independent assessment of their father's mental condition and nominated a doctor and a psychiatrist from Keswick to undertake it, Marcia phoned them and arranged their visit for one of their first days in the new cottage. Then she booked Sir James and herself into Crummock Lodge for the relevant days. "I'll be busy getting the cottage ready," she told the manager. She felt distinctly pleased with herself. No danger of the independent team talking to locals.

"I don't see why we have to move," complained Sir James when she told him. "I like it here."

"Oh, we need to see a few places before we decide where we really want to settle," said Marcia soothingly. "I've booked us into Crummock Lodge, so I'll be able to get the new cottage looking nice before we move in."

"This is nice. I want to stay here."

There was no problem with money. On a drive to Cockermouth

Marcia had arranged to have Sir James's bank account transferred there. He had signed the form without a qualm, together with one making the account a joint one. Everything in the London house was put into store, and the estate agents forwarded Sir James's mail, including his dividend cheques and his pension, regularly. There was no hurry about selling the house, but when it did finally go Marcia foresaw herself in clover. With Sir James, of course, and he was a bit of a bore. But very much worth putting up with.

As Marcia began discreetly packing for the move Sir James's agitation grew, his complaints became more insistent.

"I don't want to move. Why should we move, Molly? We're happy here. If we can't have this cottage we can buy a place. There are houses for sale."

To take his mind off it, Marcia borrowed their neighbour's rowing boat and took him for a little trip on the lake. It didn't take his mind off it. "This is lovely," he kept saying. "Derwent Water has always been my favourite. Why should we move on? I'm not moving, Molly."

He was beginning to get on her nerves. She had to tell herself that a few frazzled nerves were a small price to pay.

The night before they were due to move, the packing had to be done openly. Marcia brought all the suitcases into the living room and began methodically distributing to each one the belongings they had brought with them. Sir James had been dozing when she began, as he often did in the evening. She was halfway through her task when she realised he was awake and struggling to his feet.

"You haven't been listening to what I've been saying, have you, Molly? Well, have you, woman? I'm not moving!"

Marcia got to her feet.

"I know it's upsetting, dear—"

"It's not upsetting because we're staying here."

"Perhaps it will only be for a time. I've got it all organised, and you'll be quite comfy—"

"Don't treat me like a child, Molly!" Suddenly she realised with a shock that he had raised his arm. "Don't treat me like a child!" His hand came down with a feeble slap across her cheek. "Listen to what I say, woman!" Slap again. "I am not moving!" This time he punched her, and it hurt. "You'll do what I say, or it'll be the worse for you!" And he punched her again.

Marcia exploded with rage.

"You *bloody* old bully!" she screamed. "You brute! That's how you treated your wife, is it? Well, it's not how you're treating me!"

She brought up her stronger hands and gave him an almighty shove away from her even as he raised his fist for another punch. He lurched back, tried to regain his balance, then fell against the fireplace, hitting his head hard against the corner of the mantelpiece. Then he crumpled to the floor and lay still.

For a moment Marcia did nothing. Then she sat down and sobbed. She wasn't a sobbing woman, but she felt she had had a sudden revelation of what this man's—this old monster's—relations had been with his dead wife. She had never for a moment suspected it. She no longer felt pity for him, if she ever had. She felt contempt.

She dragged herself wearily to her feet. She'd put him to bed, and by morning he'd have forgotten. She bent down over him. Then, panic-stricken, she put her hand to his mouth, felt his chest, felt for his heart. It didn't take long to tell that he was dead. She sat down on the sofa and contemplated the wreck of her plans.

Southern and Potter found the woman in the general-store-cum-newsagent's at Grange chatty and informative.

"Oh, Sir James. Yes, they were here for several weeks. Nice enough couple, though I think he'd married beneath him."

"Was he in full possession of his faculties, do you think?"

The woman hesitated.

"Well, you'd have thought so. Always said, 'Nice day,' or 'Hope the rain keeps off,' if he came in for a tin of tobacco or a bottle of wine. But no more than that. Then one day I said, 'Shame about the Waleses, isn't it?'—you know, at the time of the split-up. He seemed bewildered, so I said, 'The Prince and Princess of Wales separating.' Even then it was obvious he didn't understand. It was embarrassing. I turned away and served somebody else. But there's others had the same experience."

After some minutes Marcia found it intolerable to be in the same room as the body. Trying to look the other way, she dragged it through to the dining room. Even as she did so she realised that she had made a decision: She was not going to the police, and her plans were not at an end.

Because after all, she had her "Sir James" all lined up. In the operation planned for the next few days, the existence of the real one was anyway something of an embarrassment. Now that stumbling block had been removed. She rang Ben Blackett and told him there had been a slight change of plan, but it needn't affect his part in it. She rang Crummock Lodge and told them that Sir James had changed his mind and wanted to settle straight into the new cottage. While there was still some dim light, she went into the garden and out into the lonely land behind, collecting as many large stones as she could find. Then she slipped down and put them into the rowing boat she had borrowed from her neighbour the day before.

She had no illusions about the size—or more specifically the weight—of the problem she had in disposing of the body. She gave herself a stiff brandy, but no more than one. She found a razor blade and, shaking, removed the name from Sir James's suit. Then she finished her packing, so that everything was ready for departure. The farming people of the area were early to bed as a rule, but there were too many tourists staying there, she calculated, for it to be really safe before the early hours. At precisely one o'clock she began the long haul down to the shore. Sir James had been nearly six foot, so though his form was wasted, he was both heavy and difficult to lift. Marcia found, though, that carrying was easier than dragging, and quieter too. In three arduous stages she got him to the boat, then into it. The worst was over. She rowed out to the dark centre of the lake—the crescent moon was blessedly obscured by clouds—filled his pockets with stones, then carefully, gradually, eased the body out of the boat and into the water. She watched it sink, then made for the shore. Two large brandies later, she piled the cases into the car, locked up the cottage, and drove off in the direction of Cockermouth.

After the horror and difficulty of the night before, everything went beautifully. Marcia had barely settled into the new cottage when Ben Brackett arrived. He already had some of Sir James's characteristics off pat: his distant, condescending affability, for example. Marcia coached him in others, and they tried to marry them to qualities the real Sir James had no longer had: lucidity and purpose.

When the team of two arrived, the fake Sir James was working in the garden. "Got to get it in some sort of order," he explained, in his upper-class voice. "Haven't the strength I once had, though." When they were all inside, and over a splendid afternoon tea, he paid eloquent tribute to his new wife.

"She's made a new man of me," he explained. "I was letting myself go after Molly died. Marçia pulled me up in my tracks and brought me round. Oh, I know the boys are angry. I don't blame them. In fact, I blame myself. I was never a good father to them—too busy to be one. Got my priorities wrong. But it won't hurt them to wait a few years for the money."

The team was clearly impressed. They steered the talk round to politics, the international situation, changes in the law. "Sir James" kept his end up, all in that rather grand voice and distant manner. When the two men left, Marcia knew that her problems were over. She and Ben Brackett waited for the sound of the car leaving to go back to Keswick, then she poured very large whiskies for them. Over their third she told him what had happened to the real Sir James.

"You did superbly," said Ben Brackett when she had finished.

"It was bloody difficult."

"I bet it was. But it was worth it. Look how it went today. A piece of cake. We had them in the palms of our hands. We won, Marcia! Let's have another drink on that. We won!"

Even as she poured, Marcia registered disquiet at that "we."

Sitting in his poky office in Kendal, Southern, with Potter, surveyed the reports and other pieces of evidence they had set out on the desk.

"It's becoming quite clear," said Southern thoughtfully. "In Grange we have an old man who hardly seems to know who the Prince and Princess of Wales are. In the cottage near Cockermouth we have an old man who can talk confidently about politics and the law. In Grange we have a feeble man, and a corpse which is that of a soft liver. In the other cottage we have a man who gardens—perhaps to justify the fact that his hands are *not* those of a soft-living lawyer. At some time between taking her husband on the lake—was that a rehearsal, I wonder?—and the departure in the night, she killed him. She must already have had someone lined up to take his place for the visit of the medical team."

"And they're there still," said Potter, pointing to the letter from the estate agents in London. "That's where all communications still go."

"And that's where we're going to go," said Southern, getting up.

They had got good information on the cottage from the Cockermouth police. They left their car in the car park of a roadside pub, and took the lane through fields and down towards the northern shore of Crummock Water. They soon saw the cottage, overlooking the lake, lonely. . . .

But the cottage was not as quiet as its surroundings. As they walked towards the place they heard shouting. A minute or two later they heard two thick voices arguing. When they could distinguish words, it was in a voice far from upper crust:

"Will you get that drink, you cow? . . . How can I when I can hardly stand? . . . Get me that drink or it'll be the worse for you tomorrow. . . . You'd better remember who stands between you and a long jail sentence, Marcia. You'd do well to think about that *all the time.* . . . Now get me that scotch or you'll feel my fist!"

When Southern banged on the door there was silence. The woman who opened the door was haggard-looking, with bleary eyes and a bruise on the side of her face. In the room behind her, slumped back in a chair, they saw a man whose expensive clothes were in disarray, whose face was red and puffy, and who most resembled a music hall comic's version of a gentleman.

"Lady Harrington? I'm Superintendent Southern and this is Sergeant Potter. I wonder if we could come in? We have to talk to you."

He raised his ID towards her clouded eyes. She looked down at it slowly. When she looked up again, Southern could have sworn that the expression on her face was one of relief.

THE MAN WHO HATED TELEVISION

Julian Symons

In November of 1994, Julian Symons, his generation's leading critic and historian of the mystery, and a crime writer of the first rank, died in Kent, England. "The Man Who Hated Television" is Julian Symons's last published short story, a work that shows his willingness to experiment and stretch the limits of the genre, even in the latter part of his long and distinguished career. Julian Symons's last novel is awaiting publication. As the curtain closes on his career as a mystery novelist and short-story writer, we salute him and all the other great British writers past and present whose work has played so important a role in the development and popularity of the mystery.

You say it may help if I tell the story of my father's tragedy as I saw it, and I will try to do that. The origin of it was that my father, Jacob Pryde, hated television.

There was a reason for this. His own father was an insurance salesman who cheated his employers by claiming commission on nonexistent sales which he justified by forged orders and invoices. When this could not be covered up any longer, he took his wife out in their car, stopped in a quiet country road, and shot first her and then himself.

My father was small, I believe five years old. He was taken away from home by an aunt and told his parents had gone on holiday. He learned of their deaths because he was watching the TV news when an item was shown with pictures of the car and their bodies. I'm told that for some time after that he screamed whenever the television was switched on. So it is not surprising that he refused to have a set in our home.

Television was not the only thing father hated. I think he also hated his wife Susan, and perhaps he hated the people to whom he sold the rare books in which he dealt, books he sometimes said he would sooner have kept on his own shelves in the extension added to our little house in Wandsworth, which is a district in southwest London. The extension was called the library, but really it was just a brick addition to the house, joined to it by a covered passageway.

So did my father hate everybody? Not quite. He loved one person, his daughter Elvira. Me.

These were the characters in the tragedy, one that seems to me in retrospect inevitable. There was also Doctor Finale, but of course he did not exist. Let me tell the story.

There was a time—the pictures in my mind flicker uncertainly like those in an old film—when father was a lover, not a hater. I remember, or *think* I remember, for it is hard to be sure about such scenes from early years, a time when father was happy, and loving not only to me but also to Susan. I see him bending over my cot, lifting me out, his moustache tickling my neck so that I scream with laughter, and he laughs too. I see him holding my mother, they are performing a kind of dance across the room, then they collapse onto a bed. I am standing up in my cot watching; she shrieks something, he cries out, and I cry out too because I think he is hurting her. Later they hold me, pass me from one to the other, make cooing, encouraging sounds.

There are other pictures, similarly fuzzy, particularly of Susan in the kitchen. She loved the kitchen, and was a great cook. I see her busy with a fruitcake, making pancakes on Shrove Tuesday and throwing them up and catching them in the pan, putting a joint of beef in the oven. She is always cheerful, often laughing. Sometimes she sang, out of tune, a snatch of a popular song. Father was in the extension or library, cataloguing his old dark books, cleaning them, perhaps even reading them. She would send me in to tell him when a meal was ready.

I remember the day when her laughter stopped. I was very young, four or five, but I remember it.

She was cooking something, I don't know what, something in a pan with hot fat. I was playing beside the kitchen table near her, perhaps putting a doll to bed, I can't remember. She was singing. Then suddenly her song changed to a scream. I saw there were flames in the pan, bright yellow, and some fat had splashed onto her hand. My father ran in from the extension. His first thought was for me, that I might be splashed by the burning fat. He picked me up, and as he did so he or I must have knocked against the pan. The fat in it went straight into my mother's face. Then there were screams and screams.

When she came out of hospital after the skin grafts, one side of her face was stiff and unreal, as if it was made of wood or hard wax, and the left side of her mouth was fixed in what looked like a sneering grin. When I first saw her I cried, ran away, and hid.

From that time our life changed. My father could not bear ugly things. Susan was ugly now, and I think he blamed her for it. He spoke to her as little as possible, and would sometimes ask if she couldn't look at him without that grin on her face. She had changed too. She was very silent now, never sang, looked after the house as before, and cooked, but took no pleasure in it. She rarely left the house, never with him. I don't think he offered to take her.

His attention now was focussed almost exclusively on me. We spent hours together in the library where he told me about the books, which were valuable and why, showed me how to distinguish between typefaces and tell which was appropriate for a particular kind of book or size of page, the way in which he described books when he sent out lists to attract the interest of possible clients.

The whole of his business was carried on through these lists or catalogues, which he prepared with immense care. When he received an order he would be both pleased and upset, upset because he hated to part with any of the books. Orders would be packed first in tissue paper, then plastic wrapping, cardboard, and finally thick brown paper. He tried vainly to teach me what he called the art of packing. In part this was because my fingers seemed all thumbs when I tried to put the wrapping round, but also I felt that to take such care about packing a book was ridiculous. Not until I was thirteen or fourteen did I realise that all those evenings and weekends spent in the library were preparation for the time when he expected me to carry on the business. One day he showed me a sheet of the writing paper headed *Jacob Pryde, Fine Books,* and said: "The time will come when this will be *Jacob and Elvira Pryde,* and then just *Elvira.*"

I knew then that this would not be so. I had little interest in books, none in bookselling. Those hours spent in the library or extension were time wasted for me, hours of boredom. Why did I not say so? Because I both admired and feared my father. He was a handsome man, rather above the ordinary height, slim, hair and moustache iron grey, face lean, nose aquiline, expression generally stern.

He had only two recreations in life apart from his books. One was his car, an old Mercedes which he cared for as if it were a child, washing, leathering, and polishing it weekly. The other was a local club for those who, like him, had been in the Territorial army. He had somehow managed to retain the revolver used by his own father, and he used it to practice in the club's little shooting gallery. He took me to the club once, but I did not care for the beer-drinking, back-slapping atmosphere, and perhaps he realised this. Certainly he never suggested I should pay another visit.

And my mother, she who had laughed and sung? She was like a lamed bird, trying always to hide the damaged part of her face with its unintended sneer. Are you thinking I should have pitied her, loved her? No doubt I ought to have done, but in truth her appearance repelled me and I took no pains to conceal the fact. Of course she noticed my behaviour, and it must have pained her.

This may sound like a miserable household, yet when young one becomes accustomed to any way of life. What I missed most was the lack of a television set. At school all the girls talked about the programmes, the sexy women and the hunky men ("hunky" was a great word at the time among my friends—"He's really hunky" meant more than sexy, rather like "macho," but intelligent and understanding as well). I hadn't seen the hunky men on TV, couldn't talk about them. I felt deprived, and illogically blamed my mother, and not my father.

At fourteen I began smoking pot and using amphetamines. I also had my first sexual coupling, with a boy who acted with me in the school play. These were experiments. I found them pleasant and continued experimenting. The boys were callow, not hunky, the drugs soothing rather than exciting. I know psychiatrists attribute what they call the early resort to sex and drugs to the nature of my home life. Personally I put it down to being deprived of TV. If I'd seen hunky men on the screen I don't think I'd have started experimenting with a schoolboy.

One day, under the soothing influence of speed (I know it's supposed to excite, but can only say I *felt* perfectly calm), I told Jacob my name would never be on the writing paper. For a moment he seemed not to have heard, then he asked what I meant. He was in the midst of a tedious exposition about the qualities of some rare editions he had recently bought. I picked up the book—though it was not really a book but a pamphlet, something to do with Swinburne or Rossetti or one of that lot—and said I wasn't interested, everything to do with his business bored me. As I spoke the pamphlet drifted away and sank slowly to the floor, yet some of it remained in my hand. I had torn it in two, an act performed quite unconsciously and at the time causing me no alarm. I repeat that speed *felt* soothing.

Jacob—it was at this moment he changed in my perception from *Father* to *Jacob*—at first looked unbelievingly from what remained in my hand to the papers on the floor. Then I saw his hand raised, heard the sound as it struck my cheek (the sound, though, faint and fading like an echo). The paper I held was removed from my grasp, and then he was on the floor picking up the rest of the pamphlet, saying something I failed to hear or understand. But I could not mistake the look in his dark eyes as we stood close together, the pages still in his trembling hand. It was a look of hatred.

I ran out of the library, my feet seeming to bounce lightly on the ground, and spent the rest of the evening in my room. It had been my custom to kiss Jacob's cheek, and that of my mother—the good side of course—when I came down to breakfast, but on the next morning my lips brushed only her cheek. Then I sat down. Jacob stared at me. I stared back. Then he spoke, not to me nor to Susan, simply a ruler laying down the law in his kingdom.

"Elvira has been stupidly disobedient. She has destroyed a valuable first edition. She says also that she does not wish to do the work for which I have trained her, as my assistant and eventual partner. She must be taught obedience. Elvira will receive no allowance for a month, nor leave this house in the evening without my permission. Her evenings will be spent with me in the library, learning more about her future occupation."

But, you will say, how could anybody talk like that? This was the twentieth century, the place London and not some rural area where time had stood still. I was fifteen years old. I can only say that strange things happen in the heart of great cities, and that Jacob Pryde was an unusual, an extraordinary man. The fixity of his dark gaze was compelling, it excluded any possibility of doubt that he would be obeyed. He drove me to school that day in the Mercedes, sitting bolt upright, immovable as a statue. When we arrived he said he would be waiting for me in the afternoon. I saw the future stretching before me, as it seemed endlessly, long days in classrooms and longer evenings in the library, forced to learn more about the world of book dealing I had come to detest. That evening my mother, the wounded bird, said in a moment when we were alone that she was sorry, there was nothing she could do. I knew this was true. Jacob had bent her to his will, as he now meant to bend me.

Yet this *was* the twentieth century, I *was* fifteen years old and not literally a prisoner. There were people I knew through the drugs circuit, and through the school play I had met one or two students at RADA. On the third night spent under Jacob's Law, I took money from my mother's purse, left a note in my bedroom saying I was not coming back but would be in touch, and shinned down a drainpipe outside my bedroom window. I spent that night on the sofa of a girl at RADA.

I don't want to describe the next six years in detail. I slept around (contracting neither AIDS nor any venereal disease), worked in shops, got hooked on drugs, and then unhooked myself when I realised what they were doing to me—and I made a career in TV. I had hated those old smelly books Jacob caressed with such pleasure, and was bored by the theatre, yet I wanted some sort of career connected with the arts, modern arts, and what is more modern than TV? It's here today and forgotten next week, and I like that too. I hate the sort of stuff Jacob loved, that lingers on and on, stuff people like simply because it's old.

Anyway, I made a career on the box, first with the help of the RADA student, who introduced me to her agent. I'm supposed to have a wistful little-girl-lost look, and I played mostly what you might call victim parts in sitcoms and thrillers, never a lead player. I suppose I was typecast, but typecasting can have its advantages. If you're lucky it can keep you in steady work. And I was lucky. At twenty-one I had my own little flat, a bit of money in the bank, no steady boyfriend.

I used my own name, Elvira Pryde, why not? I talked quite often to Susan on the phone, but Jacob would never speak. Soon after I started appearing on the box I paid for a set and had it sent to her. Of course I knew Jacob would never buy her one, but I couldn't have imagined his reaction. When I rang to ask if she had enjoyed seeing me, she told me Jacob had been angry when he saw the set, and had been beside himself when he heard it came from me. He made her look while he smashed it up with a hammer, then threw it away. Perhaps I should have realised then that he was crazy.

Susan told me about this without apparent emotion. The accident had changed not only her face but also her voice, making it dry and thin. I asked why she didn't leave Jacob, come and live with me. She said she was his wife, what would he do without her? I was going to say what I thought of that when she added: "He's a good man, you know. He only wanted the best for you."

"The *best.*" I couldn't believe what I heard.

"He loves you. You know that."

"He's mad. He must be, to hate television the way he does."

"He wants you to come back. He would make you a partner at once. And I would be pleased."

She said it in that same dry voice. Suppose she had pleaded with me, would it have made a difference? I don't suppose so.

Then I got the job as Doctor Finale's assistant. That was a real boost for me, regular work in a thirteen-part series, and a bigger part than anything I'd had. After the tragedy, of course the show came off the air. It's never mentioned now, and I don't suppose anything like it will be done again. So I'd better describe it briefly.

It was called a horror soap, and that's about right. Doctor Finale, as his name suggests, was a kind of last resort. One man came to him because he was dying of AIDS and believed his heir had deliberately arranged his infection, a woman wanted revenge on the man who'd killed her young daughter in a car accident and been acquitted on trial, a man whose family had been wiped out by a terrorist bomb wanted Doctor Finale's help in turning himself into a living bomb that would blow up the terrorist state's embassy.

Mostly these were revenge stories, always they were violent. Doctor Finale, whose degree was in psychology and not medicine, had no regard for the law and was absolutely ruthless. Once he discovered a client had been trying to trick him, and arranged a trap that left him financially ruined and physically damaged. Doctor Finale respected only money and power. He was an emotional sadist who treated everybody, clients, opponents, and his own assistants, with contempt. Those who did not hate him worshipped him, and I was one of the worshippers. He was played by Lester Morton, a handsome actor in his forties made up to look suitably sinister. I was his secretary Jennifer, a prissy worshipper who was the subject of constant sneers at her accent, love life, and lack of clothes sense.

Lester was apologetic. "I've never played such an A-one bastard," he said. "I don't know why you stay with him."

He laughed, and I did too. "It's your psychic magnetism, Doctor. That and the viewing figures." Lester was undeniably an attractive man, everybody said so. And we all knew the show was a success. There had been a short series before I came into it, starting as a cult oddity admired by a few critics. Then it had shot up in the ratings, gaining more viewers every week. One producer, asked to explain its success, said: "Sadism and violence, how can it fail?" It's always nice to be associated with success, although something about my scenes with Lester made me faintly uneasy.

One day when I rang Susan her voice seemed duller and drier than usual. I asked her if something was wrong.

"This play you are in—"

"Not really a play, it's a series. About someone called Doctor Finale, and people who come to him with problems."

"This Doctor Finale, what is he like?"

"He's a monster."

"But what does he look like?" Before I could reply, she went on: "Does he look like your father?"

The question stunned me. Lester was balding a little and wore a grey wig, he was made up round the eyes and had a way of opening them wide and then half-closing them that was frightening, his complexion was dark and his nose aquiline—was it a likeness to Jacob that had made me feel uneasy when playing scenes with him? My mother went on to say that at one of the book sales Jacob attended, somebody had congratulated him on my success as a TV actress. That would have been sufficiently uncongenial to him, but the man went on to say the principal actor had been made up to look exactly like Jacob. He added that other dealers had noticed it and it had caused much amusement.

Susan was upset. She said Jacob thought I had arranged deliberately that the actor should look like him, that I was sneering at him by making an odious character recognisable as Jacob. I tried to make her understand how absurd it was to suppose an unimportant actress like me could have had any part in the casting.

"This actor who is playing Doctor Finale, how well do you know him?" I did not reply. How well I knew Lester was not her business. "Does he look like your father?"

I said I could see no resemblance, but when I put down the telephone I wondered. When I left home I had taken with me a photograph of Jacob, and now I compared it with one of Lester as Doctor Finale. At times it seemed to me there was no likeness, at others the two faces seemed to blend into each other and become one. I found Jennifer's scenes with Doctor Finale disturbing, especially those when the doctor touched her and, on one occasion when she had made a mistake, hit her so that she fell and lay whimpering in a corner of the room. The director was pleased with the scene but Lester was concerned, said he hoped he hadn't hurt me. I replied that he couldn't possibly have hurt *me,* he would have hurt Jennifer, and since she had recovered enough to be in a car chasing a pair of graverobbers a few minutes later, she had not been hurt. Lester laughed, but I'm not sure he understood what I meant, which was that Jennifer is one person, I am another.

When I rang Susan again three or four days later, she surprised me by saying Jacob had hired a television and a video recorder. He had taped the last two Doctor Finale programmes, including the one in which Jennifer was knocked across the room, and played them again and again. She said he was beside himself, at one moment raging against my betrayal of him by putting him on the screen, the next saying he must protect me against the way I was being treated. She wanted me to come home and talk to him. I asked how she thought that would help. I was very calm.

"He believes this Doctor Finale is made up to look like him, and it's your doing." I repeated that this was ridiculous. "The men at the club all think it's a great joke, they've started calling him Doctor Finale. If you could explain to him—"

"There's nothing to explain." But there was something I wanted to know. "You saw the programmes, did you think she was good, Jennifer? Did she convince you?"

"Good? Oh yes, I suppose so." She spoke in that strangled voice, as if she didn't mean it. "I wish you would talk to him. He's not himself. He hates the television, but he sits in front of it playing those scenes with you in them, sometimes shouting at you and at the man. I'm afraid of what he'll do."

I didn't take her seriously. I should have done. I said I had no intention of coming home or talking to Jacob. I repeated what I had said before: She should leave Jacob and come and live with me. That might have been awkward, because Lester had moved in with me, but I suppose I really knew she would never leave Jacob.

So I come to the last scene of the tragedy.

The episode in production was based on what was said to be an actual plot by the CIA to assassinate Castro by poisoning the wet suit he used. The intended victim here was a Middle East dictator who had already foiled several assassination attempts, the most recent being shown in a violent opening scene where two agents were caught trying to fix limpet bombs to the dictator's yacht and then tortured to death. Doctor Finale, approached by the government, produces the plan for the poisoned wet suit, then gains the dictator's confidence by revealing the plan to him. The doctor plans with the dictator to blow up the House of Commons and install a friendly prime minister. The dictator fancies Jennifer, and attempts to rape her. Doctor Finale, who has appeared to arrange the rape, breaks in before the dictator has his wicked way, shoots him with a poisoned dart from a cigarette lighter, and escapes with Jennifer in a submarine lurking off the coast, mission accomplished.

Tosh, with plenty of action, lots of nastiness, scenes with the dictator's other women, et cetera.

We were shooting a scene between the doctor and Jennifer, in which he tells her she must go to the dictator's bedroom and do whatever he asks. Jennifer at first refuses but finally agrees, compelled by the mesmeric power of Doctor Finale's malevolent gaze. At one moment she says he wouldn't care if she was given to the guards to be raped and brutalised. She waits for him to contradict her. "Would you care? Would you?" she asks, and he replies calmly: "Not in the least."

It was a difficult scene to do—not to mention the over-the-top dialogue—and Joe Frawley, the director, was on his fourth take when there was a lot of noise from the dark area at the back of the set. It sounded as if props were being knocked over, then there were voices. After that, silence. And then Jacob Pryde came out of the darkness onto the studio floor.

Joe said: "Who the hell are you?" Then he was silent as Jacob moved towards Lester. The revolver, that fatal revolver, was in his hand. Jacob said: "You are Doctor Finale. You have corrupted my daughter."

Lester muttered something about it being just a play, shrank away. Seeing the two together, I recognised the likeness discovered by Jacob's friends. It was not just that they were physically of a size. The shape of the lean head, the bell-like ring of the voice and its contemptuous tone, the look that pierced the personality of the person it was aimed at and punctured self-confidence and self-belief—that look to which I had been exposed daily during my most susceptible years—those were the similarities I recognised. There was this difference, that Lester was an actor assuming such qualities, while in Jacob they were real.

I knew what I had to do. "Jacob," I said. "Father."

He turned. That gaze of fire and ice was bent on me. "I have come to take you home," he said, and I replied that I would come home. I said he should give me the revolver. He came very close to me, held out the blue shining thing, and I took it. His arms were spread wide, wide as those of a fallen angel, as I moved into his embrace. But then, as he looked over my shoulder, he must have seen Lester again. He shouted something incoherent about corrupting and saving me and struggled to get the revolver. I knew why he wanted it, to kill Lester—I suppose that would have been in a way to kill himself—and I did my best to keep hold of it when I felt his hand on mine. The rest of them seemed to stay still, like figures in a tableau, as Jacob and I struggled. I heard a crack, another crack. I could not have said where it came from. Then Jacob sighed, and said something again about our going home together. And that was all. It seemed somehow right that he should have died in my arms—or was it in Jennifer's arms? Now that I think about it afterwards, I believe he really was Doctor Finale.

"Interesting, but I'm afraid not very satisfactory," Dr. Margetson said. Her eyes behind the large square glasses were gentle as a gazelle's. "The idea of suggesting to patients that they should write about the experiences in the outer world that have brought them here is to see how near they get to facing what actually happened."

"Does that really matter?" the visitor asked.

On Dr. Margetson's desk there was a telephone, a diary pad, a paperweight in the shape of a lion's head, and a jar of red and yellow roses. She paused for a moment as if giving the visitor's novel idea consideration before she answered. "Oh yes. Yes, I think it matters if they are unable to accept reality." Her voice was delicate, light, comforting, although the words were not. "Elvira is happy here at Fernley Park. She has made friends, I don't think she really wants to leave. It may even be possible to use her acting abilities in the Christmas play."

"Nobody can like being shut up."

"We try to make patients feel they are not shut up but cared for. But in any case—you've read this?" She indicated the exercise book written in a round, almost childish hand. "Or rather, you've read a typed copy of it. What did you think?"

"It's very vivid. And quite clear, quite coherent."

"But not accurate."

"Oh yes, I thought so. Leaving home, getting out of the window—"

"But not about the reason for leaving. Elvira didn't leave because her father smacked her face. Nor because she was bored with what she learned about the book trade. In our conversations, long friendly conversations in which Elvira spoke freely, with no constraint or inducement, she told me of the many occasions when her father sexually abused her in the extension or library, whichever you call it. And Elvira consented; when she was a girl she was in love with her father. He was a handsome man, and she liked handsome men. Then she fully realised what she was doing and felt revulsion from it—"

"There is no proof, no proof anything happened at all. It's only what she says now. She said nothing at the time."

Softly Dr. Margetson said: "And you never asked questions?"

"Why should I have done?" Susan Pryde's hands were clasped tightly. "If there had been any proof—"

"Positive proof is often lacking in such matters. But we know, you and I, that Elvira was capable of deceit. And that she could be vicious. What she says here about your own tragedy is not the truth."

Susan Pryde had been sitting, as she always tried to do, with the good side of her face turned towards Dr. Margetson, but now she turned to show the waxen half of her features with their curious smiling sneer. "It was an accident. I have always said so."

The doctor's voice was dulcet. "I don't mean to criticise you in any way. But Elvira is not telling the truth. She says she was four or five years old, and perhaps playing with a doll. In fact she was eight, and perhaps already being molested."

"It was a long time ago. I've tried to put it all out of my mind."

"Elvira says you tried to stop her going into the library one day, perhaps because you suspected what happened there. There was an argument, and she caught hold of the pan of fat and threw it in your face."

"Why should you believe her? It's her word against mine."

"I believe what she tells me, that she felt the need to atone for what she had done. That was partly why she telephoned so often. For that, and to have news of her father. He had never got over her departure, longed for her to come back. Isn't that so?"

"Perhaps."

Miriam Margetson's gaze was friendly through the square lenses. "But he wanted the girl he had known, not the woman who appeared on a television screen. So he destroyed the television." She waited for a comment, but none came. "He wanted to resume their relationship, something Elvira contemplated with horror at the same time that she desired it."

"All this is simply something you are inventing."

"Did you notice her hints about Lester? First that she knew him well, then the casual remark that he had moved in with her. He was a replacement for the father she loved and feared."

"She happened to mention him, that's all. You make too much of everything."

Dr. Margetson shook her head. "Such remarks are never accidental, they have meaning. And so does what she says about the final scene, blending fact with invention. It's true your husband went to the studio, with the idea that he could persuade or force Elvira to give up her work as an actress and return to him. And she agreed, so why should he want to fire the revolver?"

"To hurt the actor, Lester Morton, Doctor Finale."

"Why should he do that when he thought Elvira had agreed to go with him? Is it really likely that the shots that killed him were fired by accident? Elvira says that when his arms closed on her she tried to keep hold of the revolver. And she did keep hold, her prints were on it."

"It was the pressure of his hand that fired the shots." Now Susan looked steadily, full face, at the doctor. "I want my daughter home again. To live with me. Perhaps eventually to resume her career."

"I have to remind you that it was to avoid the trauma of appearing in court with all it would have entailed that Elvira became a voluntary patient here at Fernley Park."

"Until she might be ready for release. That was three years ago."

"She is not ready yet."

"Let me judge for myself. It's over a year since I have seen her. I want to see my daughter."

"As you wish." The doctor picked up the telephone, murmured words. Her gentle eyes looked at Susan sympathetically.

Any doubt Susan Pryde felt about her daughter's health was dispelled by the sight of her. She wore a bright print dress, her bare arms were brown, she was smiling. A uniformed nurse stood beside the door.

Elvira's voice was clear and high as she said, "Miriam, I didn't know I was going to see you this afternoon." She stopped. "Who's this?"

She shrank back as Susan came towards her and said: "It's me. Your mother."

"No." Elvira shook her head. "You're ugly. My mother isn't ugly. Ask my father, he knows my mother isn't ugly."

Dr. Margetson said: "Elvira, be quiet and listen. Your mother wants—"

Elvira shrieked, "No," again, picked up the paperweight, and threw it at Susan. There was a tinkle of broken glass as it hit a picture on the wall. Elvira moaned with distress, launched herself at Dr. Margetson. They grappled for a moment, then the nurse pinned Elvira's arms behind her back and took her away.

The doctor retrieved her glasses, which had been knocked off. "You see."

"Is she often like that?"

"She lives in the present, which is Fernley Park, some other patients, me. She has eliminated the past. But if she is to leave here she must come to terms with it, remember it as it was." She tapped the exercise book. "This was a trial run. It is disappointing, but we shall try again, perhaps in another form. One day she will be ready to come out. But not yet."

"She seems to like you."

"Affections are often transferred. One must be careful not to reject them. But also not to accept. If you understand me." The doctor permitted herself a small smile.

"You believe she did this to my face, killed her father. Those things are not true. I *know* it, I tell you." She turned the waxen side of her face to the doctor, the lip curled in its sneer.

"You are her mother. I respect your feelings."

Susan Pryde's voice rose. "You have institutionalised her, turned her into a zombie. You are the guilty one."

"Perhaps it helps you to think so. But I am glad you've seen Elvira." She picked up the lion's head paperweight, replaced it on the desk. "And whatever you think, no harm has been done. Except, of course, for a little broken glass."